Collins Cobuild 英語語法精要

Collins Cobuild Elementary English Grammar

Dave Willis, Jon Wright

商務印書館

Second Edition 2003

Latest Reprint 2005

©HarperCollins Publishers 1995, 2003

Collins®, COBUILD®, and Bank of English® are registered
trademarks of HarperCollins Publishers Limited.

www.collins.co.uk

Acknowledgements
We would like to thank those authors and publishers who
kindly gave permission for copyright material to be used in
the Collins Word Web. We would also like to thank Times
Newspapers Ltd. for providing valuable data.

The COBUILD Series

PUBLISHING DIRECTOR
Lorna Sinclair Knight

FOUNDING EDITOR-IN-CHIEF
John Sinclair

EDITORIAL DIRECTOR (1ST EDITION)
Gwyneth Fox

EDITORIAL DIRECTOR (2ND EDITION)
Michela Clari

MANAGING EDITOR
Maree Airlie

LEXICOGRAPHERS
Kerry Maxwell
Alison Macaulay

EDITOR
Maggie Seaton

CARTOONISTS
Ela Bullon
Ham Kahn
Duncan McCoshan

書　　名：Collins Cobuild 英語語法精要
編　　著：Dave Willis, Jon Wright
中文翻譯：周治淮
責任編輯：黃家麗
出　　版：商務印書館 (香港) 有限公司
　　　　　香港筲箕灣耀興道3號東滙廣場8樓
　　　　　http://www.commercialpress.com.hk
發　　行：香港聯合書刊物流有限公司
　　　　　香港新界荃灣德士古道220-248號
　　　　　荃灣工業中心16樓

印　　刷：中華商務彩色印刷有限公司
　　　　　香港新界大埔汀麗路36號中華商務印刷大廈
版　　次：2022年1月第10次印刷
　　　　　© 2006 商務印書館 (香港) 有限公司
　　　　　ISBN 978 962 07 1747 5
　　　　　Printed in Hong Kong

　　　　　版權所有　不得翻印

目錄 Contents

出版說明　1

前言　3

第 一 編 Cycle 1

第一單元　　Am, is, are　4

第二單元　　現在進行時 Present continuous　6

第三單元　　簡單現在時 Present simple　8

第四單元　　Do/does 和 have/has 用於疑問句和否定句　10
　　　　　　Do/does and have/has in questions and negatives

第五單元　　現在完成時（一）Present perfect (1)　12

第六單元　　現在完成時（二）Present perfect (2)　14

第七單元　　Was, were　16

第八單元　　簡單過去時 Past simple　18

第九單元　　過去進行時 Past continuous　20

第十單元　　過去完成時 Past perfect　22

第十一單元　現在時態表示將來 Present tenses used for the future　24

第十二單元　Will and going to　26

第十三單元　There　28

第十四單元　What...?　30

第十五單元　Wh- 疑問句 Wh-questions　32

第十六單元　具數名詞 Count nouns　34

第十七單元　單數名詞、複數名詞和集體名詞 Singular, plural and collective nouns　36

第十八單元　不具數名詞（一）Uncount nouns(1)　38

第十九單元　A, an, some　40

第二十單元　The　42

第二十一單元 The 的其他用法 Other uses of *the*　44

第二十二單元 物主詞 Possessives　46

第二十三單元 指示形容詞 Demonstrative adjectives　48

第二十四單元 人稱代詞 Personal pronouns　50

第二十五單元 This, that, these, those, one, ones　52

第二十六單元 物主代詞 Possessive pronouns　54

第二十七單元 時間狀語 Adverbials of time　56

第二十八單元 較大可能性狀語和程度狀語 Adverbials of probability and degree　58

目錄 **Contents**

第二十九單元　持續狀語 Adverbials of duration　60

第三十單元　　In、on 和 at（用於時間）In, on, at (time)　62

複習　第一編 1－30單元　64

第 二 編　Cycle 2

第三十一單元　May 和 might（用於表達可能性）May, might (possibility)　72

第三十二單元　Can、could 和 be able to（用於表達可能性和能力）74
　　　　　　　Can, could, be able to (possibility and ability)

第三十三單元　Can、could、will 和 would（用於表達主動幫助和提出請求）76
　　　　　　　Can, could, will, would (offers and requests)

第三十四單元　Would like 和 want（用於表達需要與願望）Would like, want (wants and wishes)　78

第三十五單元　Have to、have got to、must 和 mustn't（用於表達責任義務）80
　　　　　　　Have to, have got to, must, mustn't (obligation)

第三十六單元　Should、ought 和 had better（用於表達提建議）Should, ought, had better (advice)　82

第三十七單元　非人稱代詞 It　Impersonal *it*　84

第三十八單元　雙賓語動詞 Verbs with two objects　86

第三十九單元　Make and do　88

第四十單元　　不具數名詞（二）（有關不具數名詞的內容參見第十八單元）90
　　　　　　　Uncount nouns(2) (See Unit 18 for patterns with uncount nouns)

第四十一單元　量詞（一）與 of 連用的結構 Quantifiers (1) － patterns with *of*　92

第四十二單元　量詞（二）（複習第四十一單元的結構。該單元所有的例句都是與具數名詞連用的。）94
　　　　　　　Quantifiers (2) (Review the patterns in Unit 41. All the examples there are with count nouns.)

第四十三單元　量詞（三）few、a few 和 any Quantifiers (3)－few; a few; any　96

第四十四單元　名詞修飾其他名詞 Nouns to describe other nouns　98

第四十五單元　地點表達式 Expressions of place　100

第四十六單元　時間表達式 Expressions of time　102

第四十七單元　方式副詞 Adverbs of manner　104

第四十八單元　At 和 in（用於地點）At, in (place)　106

第四十九單元　與交通方式連用的介詞 Prepositions with forms of transport　108

複習　第二編 31－49單元　110

總複習 A：第一編和第二編　116

目錄 Contents

第 三 編 Cycle 3

第五十單元　Should、ought、must 和 can't（用於表達可能性）118
Should, ought, must, can't (probability)

第五十一單元　Can、could、may 和 need（用於提出要求和請求同意）120
Can, could, may, need (requests and permission)

第五十二單元　喜歡、不喜歡和邀請 Likes, dislikes, invitations　122

第五十三單元　説與想（＋賓語）＋ to-不定式 Saying and thinking (+ object) + to-infinitive　124

第五十四單元　Make、let、help ＋ 不帶 to 的不定式 Make, let, help + bare infinitive　126

第五十五單元　感知動詞 ＋ 賓語 ＋ 不定式或-ing Verbs of perception + object + infinitive/-ing　128

第五十六單元　乏詞義動詞（give、take、have、go）Delexical verbs (give, take, have, go)　130

第五十七單元　短語動詞（一）Phrasal verbs（1）132

第五十八單元　短語動詞（二）Phrasal verbs（2）134

第五十九單元　與介詞連用的動詞 Verbs with prepositions　136

第六十單元　　反身代詞 Reflexives　138

第六十一單元　-ing形容詞和-ed形容詞 -ing and -ed adjectives　140

第六十二單元　不定代詞 Indefinite pronouns　142

第六十三單元　比較級 Comparatives　144

第六十四單元　The -est；than；as...as...　146

第六十五單元　So, such　148

複習 第三編 50－65單元　150

總複習 B：第一編　158

總複習 C：第二編　161

總複習 D：第三編　164

第 四 編 Cycle 4

第六十六單元　不能用於進行時態的動詞 Verbs not used in continuous tenses　166

第六十七單元　被動語態 The passive　168

第六十八單元　轉述過去 Reporting the past　170

第六十九單元　省略回答 Short answers　172

第七十單元　　附加疑問 Question tags　174

第七十一單元　Too, either, so, neither　176

第七十二單元　限制性關係從句 Defining relative clauses　178

第七十三單元　與 to- 不定式小句連用的形容詞 Adjectives with to clauses　180

目錄 **Contents**

第七十四單元　Too, enough　182

第七十五單元　現在時態與 if 和 when 等連用 Present tenses with *if, when* etc.　184

第七十六單元　過去時與 wish 和 if 連用 Past tense with *wish* and *if*　186

第七十七單元　目的和理由 Purpose and reason　188

第七十八單元　結果 Result　190

第七十九單元　對比和比較 Contrast and comparison　192

第八十單元　　描述性從句 Describing clauses　194

複習 第四編 66－80 單元　196

總複習 E　207

拼寫 Spelling　211

讀音 Pronunciation　214

數詞 Numbers　220

數詞練習 Numbers Practice　221

字母 Letters　222

答案 Answer Key　223

附件 Appendices

規則動詞的時態 Regular Verb Tenses　244

名詞和可數性 Nouns and Countability　246

形容詞的位置與順序 Position and Order of Adjectives　248

介詞：in、on、at Prepositions: in, on, at　250

英式英語和美式英語 British and American English　251

前綴和後綴 Prefixes and Suffixes　253

英漢語法術語對照表 Glossary of Grammar Terms　257

索引 Index　267

出版説明

語法是英語學習中不可缺的重要範疇之一，也是初學者必須認真學好的基本功。

本書面向基礎至初級英語程度的讀者，提供一本可讀可練的語法書，幫助讀者掌握最必要，最根本的語法原則。

本書編排非常有特點，依類別的難易和讀者能夠接受的方式，分作四編，每編首先講述動詞詞組的語法，其次講述名詞詞組的語法，最後講述狀語詞組的語法。每編的內容，有的按不同範疇分類，如第二編裏，狀語詞組以地點、時間、方式劃分；有的按思想感情表達來分類，如第三編裏，動詞詞組以表達愛好、想法、感覺劃分。另外，為幫助不熟悉語法術語的初學者直接明白所學內容，部分主題不以語法術語分類，而以常見詞語如 am、is、are；so、such 引出相關的語法點。

本書着重溫故知新，邊學邊練，學習單元左頁的語法重點之後，完成單元右頁的練習題，可達到即時重溫的目的。在每編末的複習部分，完成複習題目，可檢查自己學過的內容。這種編排形式，有助讀者按部就班地學習，並且定期評估自己的學習進度。

本書配插圖，以提高學習趣味，並可透過插圖提供例句的語境，例如講解 There 句型時，用一幅打劫銀行的插圖，表達出 There's a lot of trouble... 究竟有多麻煩，又運用生動幽默的插圖，來強調某個語法特點，例如解釋 Present Perfect Continuous Tense 時，附圖畫出一個等巴士的男人，因等得太久，臉上長滿鬍鬚，且身後的巴士站也結滿蜘蛛網，非常形象化地説明此種時態用於強調漫長的過程。

學好語法並非一朝一夕的事，使用本書，可在比較短的時間內，掌握最精要的內容，是學習語法、通曉英語的有效方法。

商務印書館編輯出版部

前　言

　　編寫一本初級英語語法書是一件難事。難就難在界定英語的基本句型，並按照初學者能夠接受的方式組織這些句型並配備例句。難在要為教師和學生提供一種清晰而權威的闡述。不過更難的是讓闡述文字和各種例證真實地反映出英語的真實面貌。

　　誠然，語法本身不能成為一門課程。但它應該成為日常教學有價值的補充讀物，應該成為有價值的自學教材。為做到這一點，我們把本書內容分為四編。在每一編裏，我們首先講述動詞詞組的語法，其次講述名詞詞組的語法，最後講述狀語詞組的語法。

　　第一編的動詞部分，比如說，主要講述了基本時態的用法、疑問句的形式和先導詞 There 作主語的句型。而在第四編則論述帶有時間從句、目的從句、原因從句、條件從句等的複合句。在每一編的後面，我們都附有關於本編內容的詳細複習資料，以及上一編相關內容的複習資料。這種溫故知新的編排形式有助教師方便地將語法教學納入現有的教學計劃。為方便讀者自學，書中所有的練習都配有詳盡的答案。

　　在正文後面，我們還提供拼寫、數詞和讀音等附錄資料。這些參考材料對初學者來說都是至關重要的。我們從不同方面對動詞、名詞、形容詞和介詞進行了更加詳盡的論述，也論及了構詞最常用的前綴和後綴。此外，我們還提供詳盡的〈英漢語法術語對照表〉，對最重要的語法術語進行了簡明扼要的闡述，為初學者提供了學習英語應知的所有信息，有助他們在學習英語時充滿信心。

Dave Willis, Jon Wright

1 | Am, is, are

1 動詞 am 、 is 和 are 後面可以接：

a. 名詞詞組：Mr. Brown **is a teacher**. It **isn't my book**. **Are** you **a student**?

b. 形容詞：She**'s tall**. I**'m tired**. **Are** you **happy**? They**'re hungry**.

c. 地點或時間表達式：Mary**'s at home**. It**'s six o'clock**. It**'s on the table**.

d. 年齡表達式：I**'m sixteen**. She**'s fourteen years old**.

2 上述動詞的各種形式如下：

a.

肯定（positives）		
陳述句（statements）		疑問句（questions）
全寫形式（full form）	省略形式（short form）	
I am late.	**I'm** late.	**Am I** late?
You are next.	**You're** next.	**Are you** next?
My mother is here.	**My mother's** here.	**Is your mother** here?
She is at home.	**She's** at home.	**Is she** at home?
My brother is out.	**My brother's** out.	**Is your brother** out?
He is fifteen.	**He's** fifteen.	**Is your brother** fifteen?
It is on the table.	**It's** on the table.	**Is it** on the table?
We are right.	**We're** right.	**Are we** right?
They are my parents.	**They're** my parents.	**Are they** your parents?

b.

否定（negatives）			
陳述（statements）			疑問句（questions）
全寫形式 (full form)	省略形式 1 (short form 1)	省略形式 2 (short form 2)	
I am not late.	**I'm not** late.		**Aren't I** late?
You are not next.	**You're not** next.	**You aren't** next.	**Aren't you** next?
She is not in.	**She's not** in.	**She isn't** in.	**Isn't she** in?
He is not at home.	**He's not** at home.	**He isn't** at home.	**Isn't he** at home?
It is not here.	**It's not** here.	**It isn't** here.	**Isn't it** here?
We are not happy.	**We're not** happy.	**We aren't** happy.	**Aren't we** happy?
They are not ready.	**They're not** ready.	**They aren't** ready.	**Aren't they** ready?

1 練習 Practice

A 寫出以下問題的答案,答案要用完整句子及動詞的省略形式。

1 How old are you? _____

2 Are you a teacher? _____

3 Where are you now? _____

4 Is it morning, afternoon or evening? _____

5 What's the weather like — is it warm or cold? _____

6 What day is it? _____

B 請看圖,在正確的句子旁打上 ✓ ,並在不正確的句子旁打上 ✗:

1 The exercise book is on the table.

2 The ball is on the chair.

3 The big book is on the table.

4 The shoes aren't under the table.

5 The pen and pencil aren't on the chair.

6 The shoes are under the chair.

7 The ball and the big book are on the chair.

8 The pen and pencil aren't on the table.

C 改正以下句子:

1 The big book is on the table. _The big book isn't on the table. It's on the chair._

2 The shoes are on the chair. _____

3 The exercise book is on the chair. _____

4 The ruler and the pen are on the chair. _____

5 The pencil's next to the ruler. _____

6 The ball and the big book are on the floor. _____

D 按你的真實情況改正以下句子:

1 My name is Kim. _My name isn't Kim, it's_

2 I'm three years old. _____

3 I'm from Scotland. _____

4 I'm a pop singer. _____

5 I'm English. _____

用同樣的內容描述你的一個朋友:

6 _His / Her name isn't Kim, it's_

7 _____

8 _____

9 _____

10 _____

2 現在進行時 **Present continuous**

1 現在進行時的構成是：

am/is/are +'-ing'

a. 可在 am/is/are 後面加上 not 構成否定：
I **am not working** at the moment.

b. 可用縮略形式 aren't 和 isn't：
We **aren't going** by bus.

I'**m not playing** today.

It **isn't raining** now.

2 現在進行時用於：

a. 談及現在發生的行動或事情：
They'**re talking**; they'**re not eating**.

It'**s raining**, but it'**s not snowing**.

The kids **are playing** tennis; they'**re not working**.

b. 談及當前的情景：
I'**m living** with my friends at the moment.
We'**re staying** at a wonderful hotel.
I'**m not feeling** well today.
My sister'**s working** as a waitress for a month.

c. 談及將來的計劃：
Mike **is coming** home on Thursday.
They'**re having** a party next week.

d. 談及變化、發展和進展：
Life **is getting** easier thanks to technology.
Do you think your English **is improving**?
Inflation **is rising** and unemployment **is getting worse**.

e. 與 always 連用，批評或抱怨某人的行為：
You'**re always interrupting** me!
My father **is always losing** his car keys.

We're going to the theatre tomorrow.

You're always leaving your clothes on the floor!

2 練習 **Practice**

A 以下句子是"當前行為"（用PA標注），還是"未來計劃"（用FP標注）？：

1 Be quiet. I'm trying to relax. _____
2 We're having a party soon. Can you come? _____
3 Who is making that noise? It's terrible! _____
4 They're going to a restaurant tonight. _____
5 Are you working now? _____
6 What are you doing tomorrow? Do you want to come to a match? _____
7 They're learning English now. _____
8 I'm wearing my new jeans. _____
9 Is the sun shining? _____

B 你正在做甚麼呢？用 I am... + -ing 或 I'm not...+ -ing 寫出合符事實的陳述句：

1 wear jeans _____
2 study English _____
3 sit at home _____
4 watch TV _____
5 smoke a cigarette _____
6 talk with friends _____
7 relax _____
8 listen to music _____

C 請看下圖，用以下的動詞完成句子：

eat push shine buy walk read listen to wear

1 The boy _____ sweets.
2 The businessman _____ across the road.
3 It's a fine day. The sun _____ .
4 A jogger _____ music on a personal stereo.

5 The man at the bus stop _____ a newspaper.
6 The woman in the park _____ a pram.
7 No one in the picture _____ a hat.
8 Some customers _____ fruit.

D 選擇適當答案回答以下問題：

1 Where are you going on holiday this year?   To Malta probably.
2 What are you doing this evening?   We're going camping.
3 Why are you learning English?   I'm watching a video.
4 Are you doing anything this weekend?   Because it's useful.

3 簡單現在時 Present simple

1 簡單現在時用於：

a. 用來談論總是正確的事情：
   It **gets** cold in winter here. Water **boils** at 100 degrees.
   February **is** the shortest month.

b. 與 never、sometimes、often、always 連用，或與 every day、at the weekend 等時間表達式連用，談及有規律或重複的活動，或談及習慣：
   We **often go** to the cinema on Fridays.
   My parents **never eat** meat.
   I **get up** late **at the weekend**.

I **read** the newspaper every day.

c. 談及生活中的普遍事實：

We **live** in a small house in Bristol.

I **wear** a jacket and tie to work, and jeans when I am at home.

2 動詞的形式隨 he、she 和 it 而變化：

I **work** from 9 to 5.
You **work** very hard.
She **works** in the supermarket on Saturday.
He **works** for my father in our office.
We **work** for the new company in the centre of town.
They **work** in uniform.
She **enjoys** English classes. He**'s** a student, he **reads** a lot.

My father sometimes **smokes** a pipe.
It **smells** awful!

3 以 -o、-s、-ch 和 -sh 結尾的動詞，其簡單現在時的形式是 -es：

He **goes** out every weekend. She **watches** a lot of TV.
The film **finishes** at 9.30 tonight.
He **does** everything for his children.

4 以輔音 -y 結尾的動詞，用於 he、she、it 時，其簡單現在時的形式是 -ies

a. study — He **studies** languages at university.
   fly — The plane **flies** twice a week.

   但是：

   I play — he plays   I buy — she buys

b. 注意：have — has：
   They **have** everything you want in that shop.
   She **has** a house in St James' Square.

He **stops** and **has** a cup of coffee at eleven o'clock.

3 練習 Practice

A 用以下詞彙完成句子：

go goes do does have has like likes live lives

1 I _____ a lot of friends in London.

2 My son _____ in Los Angeles, so I _____ there every year to see him.

3 Most people _____ going on holiday.

4 The new BMW sports car _____ a top speed of 220 km per hour.

5 The sun _____ down in the west.

6 The Smiths are very kind. They _____ a lot of work for people in hospital.

7 He's so clever! He always _____ well in exams.

8 More than 11 million people _____ in Tokyo.

9 My neighbour _____ rock music, unfortunately.

B 用括號中動詞的正確形式完成句子：

1 Tony is a great reader. He _____ lots of books. (read)

2 Pat's favourite music is reggae. He _____ to it all the time. (listen)

3 My father is a businessman in an international company. He _____ all over the world. (travel)

4 The Strongs are farmers. They _____ in the country. (live)

5 I have a friend called Fabrice. He _____ from France. (come)

6 The hotels here are very expensive. The rooms _____ a lot! (cost)

7 My mother is good at languages. She _____ French, German, Russian and Arabic. (speak)

8 Andrea is a tourist guide. She _____ everything about the history of the city. (know)

C 回答以下問題：

1 I always get up before seven o'clock, but Steve normally gets up late.

   And you? _____

2 Steve goes to bed late. I normally go to bed before midnight.

   And you? _____

3 I play sports every day. Steve never plays sport.

   And you? _____

4 Steve visits his friends in the evening. I usually visit my friends at the weekend.

   And you? _____

5 I like classical music and blues. Steve likes rock and roll.

   And you? _____

6 Steve wears jeans every day.

   I wear smart clothes.

   And you? _____

4 Do/does 和 have/has 用於疑問句和否定句
Do/does and have/has in questions and negatives

1 do 和 don't 可構成簡單現在時態的疑問句和否定句：

A: **Do you know** Peter?
B: Yes. We are old friends.

A: **Do you like** this music?
B: Yes. It's great.

A: **Do they live** here?
B: No. They live next door.

A: What's that?
B: **I don't know**.

A: **Do they enjoy** the theatre?
B: No. **They don't go out** very often.

2 does 和 doesn't (或does not) 可與 he、she 或 it 構成疑問句或否定句：

A: Is Helen at home?
B: Helen? She **doesn't live** here.

A: **Does David go** to university?
B: No. He's still at school.

A: 'Oh dear. I'm sorry.'
B: 'Don't worry. It **doesn't matter**.'

He doesn't speak English.

3 have 的否定形式通常是 don't have 或 doesn't have，但也可用 haven't 或 hasn't：

I haven't any money. She's got some, but **he hasn't** any.

4 常見的疑問句形式是 Do you have...? 和 Does he have...？但也可用 Have I...?，
Have you...?、 Have they...? 和 Has he/she/it...?：

A: **Have you** any children?
B: Yes. Two girls and a boy.

A: **Has he** any brothers?
B: No. But he has two sisters.

5 在英國，人們一般用 have got 代替 have：

I haven't got any money.

She**'s got** some, but he **hasn't got** any.

A: **Have you got** any children?
B: Yes. Two girls and a boy.

A: **Has he got** any brothers?
B: No. But he's got two sisters.

Have you got any children?

What's the matter?

I've got a headache.

4 練習 Practice

A 按真實情況完成以下句子：

1 Study English _I study English._
2 Play cricket _I don't play cricket._
3 Speak French _____
4 Study Japanese _____

5 Go to England every year _____
6 Like jazz _____
7 Live in a flat _____
8 Live in a house _____

B 想一想你的一位好朋友，按他（她）真實的情況回答題目 A：

1 _She doesn't study English._	5 _____
2 _She plays cricket._	6 _____
3 _____	7 _____
4 _____	8 _____

C 用下面各項內容寫出疑問句：

1 Watching television every day _Do you watch television every day?_
2 Buying a newspaper every day _____
3 Going abroad on holiday every year _____
4 Working in an office _____
5 Living alone _____
6 Like rock music _____
7 Playing the piano _____
8 Living in a big city _____

按真實情況回答上述的疑問句：

9 _I don't watch TV every day._
10 _____
11 _____
12 _____

13 _____
14 _____
15 _____
16 _____

D 重寫上述的疑問句和否定句，不用 do 和 does：

1 I don't have any friends in England. _I haven't any friends in England._
2 Do they have a big house? _____
3 He doesn't have much money. _____
4 They don't have any pets. _____
5 Does she have any nice new clothes? _____

用 have got 把上述的習題再做一次：

6 _I haven't got any friends in England._
7 _____
8 _____

9 _____
10 _____

11

5 現在完成時（一）Present perfect (1)

1 現在完成時的構成形式是：

have/has + 過去分詞

2 某事在過去發生，但在當前仍有影響時，可用現在完成時：

A: 'Are you going to the film tonight?'
B: 'No. I**'ve** already **seen** it.'

A: 'Why isn't John at work?' (present)
B: 'Don't you know? He**'s had** a bad accident.'

3 現在完成時通常表示最近的過去：

Karen **has** just **passed** her exams. I**'ve** just **seen** your mother at the shops.

4 某事始於過去，但現在仍在繼續，可用現在完成時：

I know London very well. I**'ve lived** there for five years.
He's her closest friend. He **has known** her **since** they were children.

或就過去到現在的事情提問，可用現在完成時：

A: **Have** you **heard** of Boris Becker?
B: Yes. He plays tennis.

A: **Have** you **been** to America?
B: No. But I**'ve been** to Canada.

A: How many times **has** she **been** to England?
B: I think she**'s** only **been** once.

Have you ever seen a Yeti?

No. Have you?

或某事尚未發生但預期發生，可用現在完成時：

A: May I borrow your book?
B: I'm sorry. I **haven't finished** it yet.

A: Do you know Henry?
B: No. We **haven't met** yet.

注意 現在完成時不能與帶過去時間表達式的從句連用：

They've just finished work. They finished **ten minutes ago**.
I've read that book. I read it **last week**.

5 練習 Practice

A 根據以下疑問句找出相應答案：

1　Do you know Michael?
2　Where's Andreas?
3　Are you going out tonight?
4　Is James at home?
5　Is Maria at the University?
6　Do you want a sandwich?
7　Are Linda and Sam coming tonight?
8　Can I borrow your grammar book?

a　No. I haven't done my homework.
b　No thanks. I've just had lunch.
c　Yes. We've met many times.
d　No. He has gone on holiday.
e　No. We haven't invited them.
f　He's gone to the shops.
g　I'm sorry, but I've lost it.
h　No. She hasn't finished school yet.

B 你聽說過這些人，去過這些地方，看過這些電影或讀過這些書嗎？

1　Brazil　*I haven't been to Brazil.*
2　Don Quixote _____
3　Honolulu _____
4　Andre Agassi _____

5　Emilio Zapata　*I've heard of Emilio Zapata.*
6　Oliver Twist _____
7　Madrid _____
8　Charlie Chaplin _____

C 在圖的下面寫出這些人發生了甚麼事：

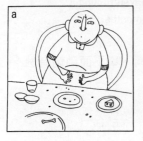

He's eaten too much.
_____

_____
_____

_____
_____

_____
_____

_____
_____

_____
_____

_____
_____

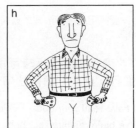

_____
_____

以下是參考提示： ... broken her arm; ... had an accident; ... lost all his money; ... fallen down; ... lost their way; ... eaten too much; ... won a prize; ... caught a fish.

6 現在完成時（二）Present perfect (2)

1 在 when、after、until 和 as soon as 等詞後面用現在完成時，說明將來會發生的事情：

Tell me **when** you **have finished**.　I'll write to you **as soon as I have heard** from Jenny.

[有關簡單現在時在句子中的類似用法，請看第十一單元]

2 說某人 has gone to 某地的含意，是指此人仍在那裏：

A: Where are the children?　B: They**'ve gone** to school.
Ken and Angela **have gone** to London for a holiday.

說某人 has been to 某地的含意，是指此人曾到過那裏，但現在已不在那裏了：

The children **have been** to school. They're back at home now.
I**'ve been** to Paris but I've never **been** to Rome.

[請看第五單元練習部分，習題 B]

3 翻閱第四單元的第三和第四節中與 have 連用的疑問句和否定句。

現在看下面使用現在完成時的疑問句和否定句：

A: **Have** you **found** your book yet?　　　B: No. I've looked everywhere, but I still **haven't found** it.
A: **Have** you **seen** Bill lately?　　　　　B: No. I **haven't seen** him for a couple of months.

4 有些動詞經常使用進行時形式，因為它們表示的動作要延續一段時間。舉下面動詞為例：

drive live make stand study travel watch wait walk work

這些動詞常與現在完成進行時形式連用，來強調某事到
現在已經持續了多久：

I've been waiting here for ages.

We**'ve been travelling** for three hours.
He**'s been working** very hard.
She's **been watching** TV all day.

[一般不用進行時形式的動詞，請看第六十六單元]

5 現在完成進行時可用來表示某事現在仍在
進行。比較下面兩個句子：

I **have read** your book. I enjoyed it very much.
I**'ve been reading** your book. I'm enjoying it very much.

6 現在完成進行時可用來表示某事在當前或過去是暫時性的：

I **have been working** as a ski instructor, but now I'm looking for a new job.

6 練習 Practice

A 在以下時間表達式中，簡單現在時表述的是將來的某一時間。將簡單現在時變成現在完成時：

1 When I finish Oliver Twist I will read Don Quixote.

When I have finished Oliver Twist I will read Don Quixote.

2 You can do the shopping after you make the beds. _____

3 Don't go out before you do your homework. _____

4 I'm going to stay in class until I finish my essay. _____

B 用動詞的現在完成時疑問形式和否定形式寫出以下對話：

1 A: (Your sister/pass her exams)?

   Has your sister passed her exams?

   B: I don't know. (She/not get/the results)

   I don't know. She hasn't got the results.

2 A: (Your brother/go/to America)? _____?

   B: No, (he/not go/yet) No, _____.

3 A: (Peter/start/school)? _____?

   B: No, (he/not start/yet) No, _____.

4 A: (You/read/the newspaper)? _____?

   B: No, (I/not read it/yet) No, _____.

C 在圖的下面寫出這些人正在幹甚麼：

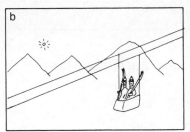

He's been waiting for a bus.

7 | Was, were

1 was 用作 am 和 is 的過去式（否定式是 was not 或 wasn't），後面可以接：

名詞詞組： He **was a good student**, now he**'s a teacher**.
My favourite book when **I was a child was** *Robinson Crusoe*.

形容詞： My grandfather **was** very **tall**.
I **wasn't happy**.

時間表達式或地點表達式： It **was three o'clock**.
He **was at school in 1999**.

年齡表達式： He **was twenty** in June.
She **was nineteen** when she married.

2 were 用作 are 的過去式（否定式是 were not 或 weren't），其用法與 was 一樣：

Dear Sue,

We're in Florida now.
We were in Miami
yesterday. The weather
was fantastic.
We were on the beach all
afternoon.

Love,

3 was、were、wasn't 和 weren't 可用來構成疑問句：

Were you here yesterday?
Who **was** that man?
You walked fifty kilometres — **weren't** you tired?
When did we arrive? **Wasn't** it on Friday?

4 練習：完成下表：

	現在時 **Present**	過去時 (肯定) **Past (positive)**	過去時 (否定) **Past (negative)**	過去時 (疑問) **Question**
I	am busy	was busy	wasn't busy	Was I busy?
He				Was he there?
She		was angry		
It	is cold			
We				Were we late?
You	are sad			
They			weren't at home	

16

A 根據以下疑問句找出相應答案：

I was in town.　　　　　　　No, I was fine, but my brother was ill.
　　　I was in bed, but I wasn't asleep.
It was really hot.　　　　　　No, I was with a friend.

1　A: Where were you yesterday at 3 p.m.?　　　　B: _____
2　A: Were you alone?　　　　　　　　　　　　　B: _____
3　A: What was the weather like yesterday?　　　　B: _____
4　A: Were you ill last week?　　　　　　　　　　B: _____
5　A: Were you in bed asleep at midnight?　　　　　B: _____

B 現在按真實情況寫出你對上述疑問句的答案。

1　_____
2　_____
3　_____
4　_____
5　_____

C 下圖是一間屋子被盜前後的情景。

根據以下物品，用 was 或 were 完成句子：

1　The vase _____ on the table
　　on the right.
2　The video recorder _____
　　under the television.
3　The paintings _____ on the
　　wall behind the desk.
4　The books _____ on the shelf
　　near the door.
5　The camera _____ on the desk.

被盜前：　　　　　　被盜後：

D 下面的陳述句是否屬實？改正不屬實的陳述句：

1　Winston Churchill is the Prime Minister of Britain. _____
2　Charlie Chaplin was a famous musician. _____
3　Cities are smaller now than in 1900. _____
4　The world record for the 100 metres sprint is 10 seconds. _____
5　Istanbul was the capital of Turkey before Ankara. _____
6　Latin is the most useful international language. _____

E 用 was、wasn't、were 或 weren't 完成以下句子：

1　'Where _____ you yesterday?' 'I _____ ill so I stayed at home.'
2　I left school when I _____ 17 and started university when I _____ 18.
3　The film we saw last week _____ terrible.
4　'What _____ the weather like yesterday?' 'Oh, it _____ terrible.'
5　'We've just finished the exercise.' ' _____ it difficult?'
6　I called my parents half an hour ago but they _____ in.

8 簡單過去時 Past simple

1 簡單過去時可用來談及過去發生的事情：

I **stayed** in that hotel last week.
He **worked** all night and finally **finished** the project when the secretaries **arrived** in the morning.

2 簡單過去時可用來泛指過去，也可用來談及過去的慣常性活動：

We **lived** in Rome for a year when I **was** a child.
Our friends often **visited** us there.

3 大多數動詞的簡單過去式都是以 -ed 結尾。

有些動詞的過去式是不規則的。你能將下面 20 個動詞不定式與它們的簡單過去式連起來嗎？

begin _____   give _____

break _____   go _____

buy _____   have _____

come _____   make _____

do _____   pay _____

drink _____   say _____

drive _____   see _____

eat _____   take _____

find _____   tell _____

get _____   write _____

did   found   went   told   drove   bought   got
    saw   came   had   paid
ate   broke   wrote   took   drank   said   made   gave
                      began

4 所有規則動詞和不規則動詞的過去式，在各種人稱中 I/you/he/she/it/we/you/they 都是一樣。(但 be 除外，請看第七單元)

5 did ... + 不定式可用來構成過去疑問句：

Did you **get** home all right?
Did he **go** out last night?
Did you **tell** them about the party?
Who **did** you **see**?
Where **did** you **buy** that hat?
When **did** she **arrive**?

6 did not (or didn't) + 不定式，可用來構成過去否定句：

I **didn't understand**, so I asked a question.
He **didn't give** me his address.

They **didn't buy** anything.

8 練習 Practice

A 用第八單元第三節中的動詞完成以下句子：

1 I _____ Mike in the street yesterday.
2 When I was in Spain, I _____ this sombrero as a souvenir.
3 After the concert we _____ home by taxi.
4 He opened the packet and _____ a chocolate biscuit.
5 Have you got that letter Bob _____ us last week?
6 My uncle _____ me a couple of interesting books for my birthday.
7 Ivor _____ his leg and was taken to hospital in an ambulance.

8 I _____ it all myself!

B 在簡單過去式的動詞下面加上底線：

The police are looking for a man who stole £25 and a jacket from a crowded fashion shop in Brighton last week. The man, who was between 20 and 25, with short brown hair, took the jacket from a staff changing-room. 'I'm not worried about the money, really,' said the victim, Sally Walker, 25, who works in the shop. 'But the jacket cost me £150. I got it when I was on holiday in Turkey.' The police do not think the man is dangerous, but warned the public to be careful.

C 根據右邊的答案完成以下疑問句：

1 When _____ the jacket?   When she was on holiday
2 Where _____ on holiday?   Turkey
3 What _____ steal?   A jacket and £25
4 Where _____ from?   From the staff changing room
5 How much _____ cost?   £150

D 弗朗西絲在一家業務繁忙的公司當經理，看看她昨天的工作日誌，然後寫出她昨天做了的事和沒有做的事：

例如：
She had a meeting with the bank manager.
She didn't have time to write a letter to Gerry.

8.30	Buy paper and magazine for mother ✓
9.00	Have meeting with bank manager ✓
10.00	Call Export International ✓
10.15	Write to Gerry ✗
10.30	Talk with Jan and John about new products ✓
11.30	fax ISB in Munich about training course ✗
12.00	write letter to Directors of XYZ to confirm meeting ✓
1.00	meet David for lunch ✗
2.00	take taxi home ✓
2.30	pack suitcase ✓
4.00	take train to London ✓

E 你又怎樣？下面這些事你昨天有沒有做？

watch TV have a shower cook a meal read a paper make a phone call write a letter play a sport speak English listen to music go out visit a museum

例如：
I didn't watch TV yesterday.
I wrote a letter to a friend yesterday.

9 過去進行時 **Past continuous**

（請複習第二單元有關現在進行時的內容）

1 過去進行時的構成形式是：

was/were + -ing

2 一個動作被另一個動作打斷時，可用過去進行時：

I **was reading** the newspaper when the doorbell rang.
They **were flying** from London to New York when the accident happened.

注意 如果兩件事發生有先後次序，這兩個動詞都要用簡單過去時態。

As soon as he **saw** me he **waved**.

I **woke up** when my alarm clock **rang**.

3 一個動作在過去特定的時間內仍在進行，可用過去進行時：

At **2.15** we **were** still **waiting** for the bus. It was just before midnight. We **were talking** quietly.

4 敘述一個故事或一連串事件可用過去進行時：

It was 1975. We **were living** in a small house in Liverpool.
On the day I had my accident, I **was preparing** for my examinations.

5 描述某事過去在變化、發展或進行時，可用過去進行時：

The children **were growing** up quickly.

We **were learning** quickly.

9 練習 Practice

A 完成以下句子。一個動詞用簡單過去時，另一個動詞用過去進行時：

1 I (meet) _____met_____ Peter while I (shop) _____was shopping_____ this morning.

2 We (walk) _____ home this evening when it suddenly (begin) _____ to rain.

3 I (hurt) _____ my back when I (work) _____ in the garden.

4 I (stay) _____ in Oxford, so I (go) _____ to see Tim.

5 Ken (do) _____ his homework last night and he (forget) _____ to telephone home.

6 We (live) _____ in Greece when our first daughter (be) _____ born.

7 She (work) _____ in the library when she (see) _____ Maria.

8 We (go) _____ to the opera when we (stay) _____ in Milan.

B 用簡單過去時或過去進行時完成以下句子：

1 When he (hurt) _____ his back he (go) _____went_____ to see the doctor.

2 When she (hear) _____ the news she (begin) _____ to cry.

3 We (listen) _____ to the radio when Fred (come) _____ home.

4 I (hear) _____ a strange noise and the dog (begin) _____ to bark.

5 Everyone (talk) _____ and suddenly the lights (go) _____ out.

6 I (have) _____ a nice hot shower when the doorbell (ring) _____.

7 I (have) _____ a nice hot shower when I (get) _____ home.

8 The children (play) _____ happily when their mother (arrive) _____ home.

10 過去完成時 Past perfect

（複習第五、第六單元有關現在完成時的內容）

1 過去完成時的構成形式是：

had + 過去分詞

2 過去完成時可用來談及過去的時間，如果某事發生的時間早於所談及的時間，而且它在談及的時間裏仍有影響，可用過去完成時：

I didn't go to the film with my wife because I **had** already seen it.
John wasn't at work because he **had had** a bad accident.

3 表示某事剛剛發生，通常用過去完成時：

It was July. Karen **had** just passed her exams. I told Rosa I **had** just seen her mother at the shops.
I was feeling very tired because I **had** just **finished** work.

4 某事較早發生，到所談及的時間仍在進行，可用過去完成時：

I **knew** London very well.
I **had lived** there for five years.

He was her closest friend. He **had known** her since they were children.

或談及的時間一直延續到所指時間，可用過去完成時：

A: In **1987 had** you **been** to America before? B: No, but I **had been** to Canada.
I didn't know anything about rock'n roll. I **had** never **heard** of Elton John.

或某事到談及時仍未發生，可用過去完成時：

She wanted to borrow my book but I **hadn't finished** it.
I didn't know Henry. I **had** never **met** him before.

5 談及某事在過去進行了一段時間，可用過去完成進行時：

We **had been travelling** for three hours.
She **had been watching** TV all day.

或談及某事過去正在進行或是暫時性的，可用過去完成進行時：

I **had been reading** her book.
I was enjoying it very much.

I **had been working** as a ski instructor, but I was looking for a new job.

10 練習 Practice

A 根據以下疑問句找出相應答案：

1 Did you know Michael?
2 Where was Luis?
3 Did you go to the cinema last night?
4 Did you see James and Leila?
5 Were you feeling hungry?
6 Were you locked out?
7 Did you have any money left?
8 Did you know Paris well?

a He had gone to the shops.
b Yes. We had met many times before.
c No. They had gone away for the day.
d Yes. I hadn't eaten since breakfast.
e Yes. I had forgotten my key.
f No. I had spent everything.
g Yes. I had been there twice before.
h No. I hadn't finished my homework.

B 將下面兩部分連成句子：

1 I couldn't understand very much
2 We didn't know where to go
3 I didn't enjoy the film very much
4 Everything was very wet
5 They knew they would be late
6 They were very brown
7 We were tired out
8 John couldn't open the door
9 I had to go to the bank
10 I couldn't see very well

a because I had seen it before.
b because they had been working in the sun.
c because he had lost his key.
d because I had spent all my money.
e because I hadn't been learning English very long.
f because I had forgotten my spectacles.
g because we had lost our map.
h because it had been raining all day.
i because they had missed the last train.
j because we had been working all day.

C 完成以下句子，一個動詞用簡單過去時，一個動詞用過去完成時：

1 I (go) _____*went*_____ home as soon as I (finish) _____*had finished*_____ work.
2 Everybody (go) _____ out for the day. There (be) _____ nobody at home.
3 Bill (live) _____ in Leeds ever since he (be) _____ a boy.

4 After I (eat) _____ I (order) _____ a cup of coffee.

5 He (feel) _____ awful.
   He (catch) _____ a bad cold.

6 He (take) _____ the book back after he (read) _____ it.

11 現在時態表示將來
Present tenses used for the future

1 談及安排在將來一確定時間內進行的事物時，要用簡單現在時。這些句子通常含時間表達式：

The next train **arrives** at 11.30. The meeting **starts** straight after lunch.
We **have** a holiday tomorrow. We **leave** at two o'clock tomorrow afternoon.

2 陳述將來已確定的日期時，通常要用簡單現在時：

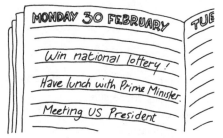

Tomorrow **is** Tuesday.

Monday **is** the thirtieth of February.

It**'s** my birthday next month.

Friday **is** my birthday.

3 談及人們將來的計劃或安排時，要用現在完成進行時：

I**'m seeing** Jill next week.

They**'re getting** married before Christmas.

We**'re having** a party next week. I**'m doing** my homework this evening.

4 談及將來尚未確定的安排時，要用現在時態的動詞，如 hope、expect、intend 和 want 等，並要與 to-不定式小句連用：

We **hope to see** you soon. He **wants to catch** the last bus home.
Henry **expects to be** at the station to meet us tomorrow.

5 動詞 hope 後面使用簡單現在時，常用來表述將來：

I **hope** you enjoy your holiday. June **hopes** she passes her exam all right.

6 在帶 if 的從句或帶 when、before 等時間詞的從句裏，現在時態常用來表述將來：

You won't get lost **if** you **have** a good map. Have a drink **before** you **go**.

* 本頁中有一個故意留下的錯誤，看看你能不能找到？

11 練習 Practice

A 閱讀下面的信。在所有現在式的動詞下面加上底線，再把表述將來的動詞用括號括起來：

> Dear Monica,
>
> Many thanks for your letter. I _am_ pleased you _are enjoying_ your holiday. When (_do you come_) home? It will be great to see you again.
>
> We are going to Greece this year - next Friday in fact. I am trying to get everything ready in time, but it is very difficult with three small children. Our plane leaves at six o'clock on Friday morning, so we are taking a taxi to the airport at four o'clock in the morning - I hope the children behave themselves and get ready quickly without too much trouble. Peter has three weeks holiday this year so when we get back from Greece we are staying with his mother in Brighton for a week. She has a big flat in a block right next to the sea. The children love it.
>
> Lydia is starting school this September. I hope she likes it. Jimmy hates going to school. He shouts and screams every morning. Perhaps he will be better when Lydia starts. Thank you for your news. I am very pleased to hear that Isabel has done so well at University. What is she doing next year? Has she decided yet? What about the twins? When do they leave school?
>
> Give my love to Norman. I am sorry about his accident. I hope he gets better soon.
>
> Much love,
>
> Teresa.

I hope he gets better soon.

We are taking a taxi to the airport at four o'clock.

B 用簡單現在時或現在進行時回答以下疑問句：

1 What day of the week is your birthday on? _My next birthday is on a Friday._

2 What time does this lesson finish? _____

3 What are you doing tomorrow morning? _____

4 How many English lessons do you have next week? _____

5 What day is it the day after tomorrow? _____

6 What is the date next Thursday? _____

7 What are you having for supper tonight? _____

8 What are you doing after your lesson? _____

9 When is the next exam? _____

10 How old are you on your next birthday? _____

12 Will and going to

1 已知某事會在將來發生時，要用簡單現在時或現在進行時：

The next train **arrives** at 11.30. We'**re having** a party next week.

2 預料某事將要發生時，要用 will 或 going to：

The weather tomorrow **will be** warm and sunny. I think it'**s going to rain**.

3 當前的事實或事件可能導致某事在將來發生時，通常要用 going to：

4 警告某人某事馬上會發生時，要用 going to：

'Watch out, **we're going to crash!**'

'Be careful, you'**re going to drop** those glasses.'

5 作承諾或提建議時，要用 will：

I'**ll ring** you later tonight. I'**ll come round** and help you later.

6 告知某人你所做的決定時，通常要用現在進行時或 going to：

I'**m staying** at home tonight. I'**m going to do** some work.

而談及他人所做的決定時，通常要用 going to：

She'**s going to write** you a letter. They'**re going to call** in and see us.

7 將剛做的決定告知某人時，通常要用 will：

Ken lives near here. I think I'**ll go** and see him.

A: Did you know it's Winnie's birthday? B: Really? Thanks. I'**ll send** her a card.

練習 **Practice**

A 把左欄與右欄相關的句子連起來：

1 It's very cold.
2 The children are really tired.
3 I feel awful.
4 She's bought a new dress.
5 Oh dear, I've missed my train.
6 There's a big queue.

a I think I'm going to be sick.
b I'm going to be late.
c We're going to have some snow.
d It's going to be very crowded.
e They're going to fall asleep.
f She's going to look very smart.

B 用 will 或 going to 完成以下對話：

1 A: Dad, (you/lend?) (1) _____*will you lend*_____ me the car next week? Annette and Andy (have) (2) _____ a party and they've invited me.

B: I'm sorry, your mother and I (see) (3) _____ that new film at the Odeon. We probably (not get back) (4) _____ until ten o'clock.

2 A: What (you/do?) (5) _____ this summer?

B: We haven't decided yet. Perhaps we (share) (6) _____ a house with my parents in the Lake District. They (borrow) (7) _____ a cottage from some friends for a few weeks.

A: (there/be?) (8) _____ enough room for you and the children?

B: Oh no. The children (not come) (9) _____ They (take) (10) _____ a trip to Singapore. They (stay with) (11) _____ Andrew's brother for a month.

A: That (be) (12) _____ exciting. I'm sure they (have) (13) _____ a wonderful time.

C 用 will 或 going to 完成以下句子：

'Wait a minute. (I/open) _____ the door for you.'

(I/write) _____ every day.'

'Help! (I/fall) _____ !'

'Oh dear (We/get) _____ wet.'

'You have a rest this evening. (I/cook) _____ the supper.'

'I think (I/get into trouble) _____ .'

第一編

13 There

1 there 可用來：

講述某物的存在：

Once upon a time **there** was a little girl called Red Riding Hood.
In the forest **there** was a wicked wolf.

談及一個活動或事件：

There was a party last week. **There**'s a football match tomorrow.

談及數量：

There was a lot of trouble
at work this morning.

In the kitchen **there** was a large table
and four chairs.

2 當 there 後面的名詞是單數時，要用 is 或 was：

There is a book on the table. **There was** an extra English class yesterday.

兩個名詞由 and 連接時，如果第一個名詞是單數，就要用單數動詞：
There was a man and two women. **There was** a table and some chairs in the room.

當 there 後面的名詞是複數時，要用 are 或 were：
There are three beds in the room. **There were** two big beds and a little bed.

3 要構成疑問句，可將 there 置於 is、was、were 之後：

Is there anyone at home? **Were there** many people at the meeting?
Are there some oranges left? **Isn't there** a good film on TV tonight?

或將 there 置於 be 或 been 之前：

Will **there be** enough time? Could **there be** anyone there?
Has **there been** anyone here? Will **there be** any children there?

4 與 there 連用的常見表達式：

There are a few ...	**There** are a lot of ...	**There** isn't/wasn't any ...	**There** aren't/weren't any ...
There's/are no ...	Is/are **there** any ...?	Was/were **there** any ...?	**There's** nothing to do.
There's plenty to eat.	**There's** nowhere to go.		

13 練習 Practice

A 用 there 回答以下疑問句：

1 How many people are there in your class? _____ *There* _____

2 How many people are there in the room? _____

3 Are there any pictures on the walls? _____

4 Is there anything on your desk? _____

5 How many people are there in your family? _____

6 How many small beds and how many big beds were there in the room? _____

B 把下面的句子改寫成以 there 開頭的句子：

1 We have an English class every day. _____ *There's an English class every day.* ___

2 A meeting will be held at three o'clock. _____

3 An accident happened this morning. _____

4 A lot of people came to the concert. _____

5 Three books lay on the desk. _____

6 Lots of children will be at the party. _____

7 We have nothing to eat or drink. _____

8 Three people waited in the shop. _____

C 用與 there 連用的表達式完成以下對話：

there was nobody at home   there's good film   Is there anything good
I don't think there'll be anything   There wasn't anything

A: _____
on TV tonight?

B: No, _____
very interesting.

A: Do you think _____
on at the cinema?

B: I don't know. _____
last week.

A: Shall we go round and see Joe and
Pamela?

B: Let's telephone first. Last time we went
_____ .

14 What...?

1 What...? 後面要用疑問句形式：

What does he want? **What** have you done? **What** will they say?

2 What...? 可用於：

定下計劃或詢問計劃：
What are you doing tomorrow? **What** are you going to do? **What** shall we do?

查問發生了何事：
What happened? **What** did you do? **What** did you say?

請某人重述或解釋某事：
What do you mean? **What** did she mean? **What** does it mean? **What** does 'repeat' mean?
I'm sorry, **what** did you say?

要弄明白某類問題：
What's the matter? **What**'s wrong? **What**'s up? **What** happened?

要弄清楚某動物或某人的樣子：

What sort of dog is it?

'**What** does he look like?'

What kind of ... is it? **What** sort of ... is it? **What**'s it like? **What** colour is it/are they?
What does he look like?

提出建議：
So Monday's no good. **What** about Tuesday? **What** about some lunch?

提出新想法或引出新話題：
I'm ready for lunch. **What** about you? So Tom's OK. **What** about Marie?

詢問時間：
What time is it? **What** time do you finish work?

3 What do you think...? 常用來進行提問。 What do you think...? 後面不能用疑問句形式：
What do you think they will say? **What** do you think it means?

14 練習 Practice

A 改寫以下疑問句，改寫時不要用 ...do you think... :

1 What do you think they are going to do?   *What are they going to do?*

2 What work do you think he does?   ?

3 What do you think it means?   ?

4 What time do you think they will arrive?   ?

5 What colour do you think she wants?   ?

B 根據以下疑問句找出相應答案：

1 What did it look like?
2 What's your new house like?
3 What's your new job like?
4 What was the wolf like?
5 What's it like learning English?

a It's very big. It has four bedrooms.
b He was very wicked.
c It's great! But it's hard work.
d It looked very nice.
e I don't know really. I've just started.

C 選用下面的名詞完成對話：

colour   kind   sort   language   size   work   time   day

1 A: What _____*sort*_____ of person is he?
   B: He's very quiet, but he's really nice.

2 A: What _____ does the next train leave?
   B: I'm not sure. I'll have to check the timetable.

3 A: What _____ shoes do you take?
   B: I don't know. Those look about right.

4 A: What _____ is it today?
   B: It's Monday.

5 A: What _____ is your car?
   B: It's sort of light blue.

6 A: What _____ do they speak in Austria?
   B: Mainly German I think.

7 A: What _____ of food do you like?
   B: I love Chinese and Indian food.

8 A: What _____ does your mother do?
   B: She's a doctor.

D 用以下短語寫出六句與插圖相符的簡短對話：

A: What's wrong?/What's the matter?
B: a It's my leg. I think it's broken.
    b I haven't any money. I've spent it.
    c I didn't sleep very well last night.

    d I think I've run out of petrol.
    e I've lost my key. I can't get in.
    f I feel awful. I've eaten too much.

15 Wh- 疑問句 Wh-questions

1 Wh- 詞後面要用疑問句形式，請看下面這些常用的表達式：

Where ...? （何處？）
Where is she now? **Where** are you going? **Where** shall I put this? **Where** do you live?

When ...? （何時？）
When can you start? **When** did she arrive? **When** does she leave?

Why ...? （為甚麼？）
Why do you want to know? **Why** don't you buy a new one? **Why** did you do that?

Who ...? （是誰？）
Hello, **who** is it? **Who** was that? **Who**'s been eating my porridge? **Who** did you see?

How ...? （如何？）
How do you know? **How** do I get to your grandmother's house? **How** much is it?
How many people are there? **How** long is it? **How** old is Peter now?

2 在對話時常使用省略疑問句：

A: We're going on holiday.
B: **Where** to?
A: Florida.

A: These shoes are cheap.
B: **How** much?
A: Only twenty-five pounds.

A: I have to go out tonight.
B: **What** time?
A: About half-past seven.

A: I'm very angry.
B: **Why?**
A: I've lost my passport.

A: It's a long way to walk.
B: **How** far?
A: Nearly ten miles.

A: I saw a friend of yours.
B: **Who?**
A: Antonia.

3 其他提問方式：

When Where What Who How Why	do you think ...?	I wonder	when ... where ... what ... who ... how ... why ...

當說話者不確定別人是否知道答案時，通常使用上表中的方式提問。請仔細看下面的例子，並注意詞序。

How old is Jack's brother?
I wonder **how** old Jack's brother is.
How old do you think Jack's brother is?

Where do Bill and Jenny live?
I wonder **where** Bill and Jenny live.
Where do you think Bill and Jenny live?

Why did she do that?
I wonder **why** she did that.
Why do you think she did that?

'I wonder **who** it is.'

15 練習 Practice

A 用下表的內容寫出對話：

A: Let's go and see Peter and Mary some time.	B: What?	A: Italy, I think.
A: They live in that big house on the corner.	B: Who?	A: Well, we could go this weekend.
A: We could probably get there quite quickly.	B: When?	A: You know – those friends of Michael's.
A: I'm afraid I've lost it.	B: Where?	A: Well, we could take a taxi.
A: I think they're away on holiday.	B: How?	A: My library book. I don't know where it is.
		A: I don't know. I think I've left it at school.

B 用 Wh _____ do you think ...? 或 I wonder ...? 改寫以下句子：

1 What's she like?   1 *I wonder what she's like.*

2 What did she mean?   2 _____

3 Who does this belong to?   3 _____

4 Why are they so late?   4 _____

5 What does he want?   5 _____

6 How old is he?   6 _____

7 Where have they gone?   7 _____

8 What will they say?   8 _____

C 你能在第十五單元中找出與以下這些答案有關的疑問句嗎？

1 Last month.   5 Next week.   9 On that table.

2 In Scotland.   6 By bus.   10 Turn left here.

3 £ 1.30.   7 In the office.   11 To the shop.

4 To Glasgow.   8 For a holiday.

'What do you think it means?'

D 把下面的句子改寫成一般 wh- 疑問句：

1 How long do you think it will take?   1 *How long will it take?*

2 I wonder how much it will cost.   2 _____

3 What do you think it means?   3 _____

4 I wonder where they come from.   4 _____

5 I wonder when they will arrive.   5 _____

6 I wonder where he's gone.   6 _____

16 具數名詞 Count nouns

1 英語中大多數名詞都是具數名詞。這就是説它們具有單數形式和複數形式。名詞的複數形式主要是詞尾加 -s 構成的：

singular 單數	plural 複數
I haven't read a **book** for ages.	**Books** are cheap here.
Where's the **bus stop**?	We need more **bus stops**.
I need a **holiday**.	We get three **holidays** a year.

2 以 -ss、-s、-ch、-sh 或 -x 結尾的名詞，構成複數時要加 -es：

I'm in **class** A.	I have two **classes** today.
Which **bus** do you take?	There are no **buses** on Sundays.
It's a Swiss **watch**.	He can repair **watches**.
That's my **dish**.	He washed the **dishes**.
Put the **box** down.	Where are the shoe **boxes**?

大多數以 -o 結尾的名詞構成複數時要加 -es：

Is that a **potato**?	I had some **potatoes** for lunch.
I want a **tomato**.	I don't like **tomatoes**.

（但在 photo、radio 和 piano 後面只加 -s。）

He washed the **dishes**.

3 以 "輔音＋y" 結尾的名詞要變成 "輔音＋-ies"：

Which **country** are you from?	We visited ten **countries**.
This is a photo of me as a **baby**.	I can hear **babies** crying.

（但 "元音＋y" 結尾時，只加-s，如：day－days；boy－boys。）

4 有些普通具數名詞是不規則的。你能在以下名詞的單數形式旁邊填上複數形式嗎？

women sheep feet men fish mice children teeth people

child _____   fish _____   sheep _____

foot _____   man _____   tooth _____

mouse _____   person _____   woman _____

5 談及人或事時通常要用複數名詞，而且不要與 this、that、the 和 a 這樣的限定詞連用：

My brother doesn't like **spiders**.   **Computer games** are expensive.

Children start school at the age of 6.

Cars cause pollution.

16 練習 Practice

A 填上以下名詞的複數：

baby _____	box _____	child _____
shoe _____	shop _____	day _____
church _____	foot _____	radio _____
sandwich _____	city _____	story _____

B 在圖的下方寫出以下名詞的複數：

photo fish mouse watch tooth bus box baby sheep

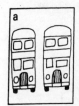   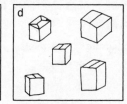 

two buses

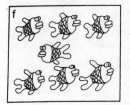 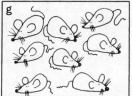 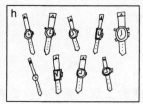 

_____ _____ _____ _____

C 把左欄與右欄相關的部分連成句子：

1 Buses are   very hard all year.
2 The bus is   a Rolex.
3 Women   made of paper.
4 That woman is   invented a long time ago.
5 Watches were   about geography on my desk.
6 My watch is   going to the station now.
7 Most students work   from near Buenos Aires.
8 A student in my class comes   work as well as men.
9 Books are   cheaper than taxis.
10 There is a book   my neighbour.

D 用以下單詞完成疑問句：

months days day hours hour minutes week weeks year year

1 'How many _____ are there in a _____ ?'   'Seven'

2 'And how many _____ are there in a _____ ?'   '52'

3 'How many _____ are there in a _____ ?'   '24'

4 'How many _____ are there in an _____ ?'   '60'

5 'How many_____ are there in a _____ ?'   '12'

第一編

17 單數名詞、複數名詞和集體名詞
Singular, plural and collective nouns

1 許多普通名詞是單數名詞，就是説它們只能用作單數形式：

a 有時，有些單數名詞所指的事物在世上是獨一無二的，這樣的單數名詞通常要與 the 連用：

the air the sun the moon the sky the dark the world the future the past
The sky is very cloudy. It's difficult to see **the sun**.

b 許多由動詞構成的名詞，被用作單數名詞來表述日常活動，它們通常與 a 連用：

a bath a fight a rest a wash a shower
'Do you want **a drink**?' 'Yes, great. But I need **a** quick **wash** first.'

2 有些名詞被稱作複數名詞，是因為它們沒有單數形式，或是在複數形式下有特殊含義，這樣的名詞通常要與the或物主代詞如 my、his 連用：

your clothes her feelings the pictures my travels
the sights his likes and **dislikes the police**

The police are coming. They'll be here in a minute.
I've met a lot of interesting people on **my travels**.

In three days we saw all **the sights** of London.

3 一些由兩個相似部分組成的工具或服裝是複數名詞：

glasses trousers pants tights jeans pyjamas shorts scissors binoculars scales tweezers

Where are my **jeans**? What colour are your **pyjamas**?

也可用 "a pair of ＋複數名詞＋單數動詞" 來表示：
A large **pair of scissors** was on the table.

4 指特定人群或事的名詞是集體名詞，這樣的名詞既可用單數動詞，也可用複數動詞，因為可以把群體看成一個概念，也可以把它們看成是許多個個體：

army audience company enemy family gang government group public staff team

My **family is** in Brazil. His **family are** all strange. Do you know them?

36

17 練習 Practice

A 用以下單數名詞完成句子：

the sun   the sky   the moon   the past   the future
the dark   the air   the world

1 Travel was much slower in _____.
  Now everyone has fast cars.

2 It's a beautiful day. There isn't a cloud in _____ .

3 I sleep with the light on because I'm afraid of _____ .

4 What do you think cars will look like in _____ ?

5 The first astronauts to walk on _____ were American.

6 It's not good for your eyes to look directly at _____ .

7 Heathrow is the busiest airport in _____ .

8 There's a bad smell in _____ . Have you been cooking?

B 把左欄與右欄相關的部分連成句子：

1 I'm very thirsty. I'd love   a wash.
2 The doctor felt exhausted. He needed   a drink.
3 Mrs Small is taking her dogs for   a fight.
4 Listen to the shouts. Someone is having   a sleep.
5 We played tennis, then had   a walk.
6 My hands are dirty. I need   a shower.

C 玩文字遊戲 — 變位字。根據左頁第三點的插圖，按正確的字母順序拼寫出物品的名稱：

a pair of S R O S S I C S   a pair of W E Z E T E R S

a pair of C L I R A B O N U S   a pair of M A J A P Y S

a pair of S L A S G E S   a pair of S H I G T T

D 現在用習題 C 的答案完成以下句子：

1 Can I borrow _____ to cut this paper, please?

2 Jack went to the opticians to get _____ .

3 She wore _____ under her jeans to keep warm in winter.

4 He used _____ to get a small piece of wood out of his finger.

5 To keep warm in bed at night, many people wear _____ .

6 _____ will help you see things that are a long way away.

E 用 staff、team 和 audience 完成以下句子：

1 Which is the best football _____ in your country?

2 The _____ of this school is excellent.

3 I'm afraid no one can help you at the moment, the _____ are all in a meeting.

4 Are your _____ all professionals?

5 The _____ isn't very big tonight: there are only 10 people in the cinema.

6 The _____ were singing and dancing everywhere in the concert hall.

18 不具數名詞（一） Uncount nouns (1)

英語中大多數名詞具有單數形式和複數形式（如：one bed、two beds），但許多常見的事物是無法直接數出來的。這樣的名詞稱作不具數名詞(uncount nouns)。

1 不具數名詞的特點：

a 沒有複數形式：

We bought a lot of **food** at the supermarket.
There's going to be some **rain** at the weekend.
Milk is good for you.
If you need to change **money**, go to the bank.

b 使用單數動詞：

Electricity is dangerous.
Rice is the basic ingredient of Eastern cooking.
Water is more important than food in the desert.

c 不能與 a、an 或數字連用：

My uncle started **work** when he was fourteen.
Last winter we had **ice** on the lake.

d 與 the、this、that 和 my 等連用（但不能與 these 和 those 等複數詞連用）可談及特指的事物：

What's **the food** like in that restaurant?
I like **music**, but I didn't like **the music** we heard today.
I gave you **that money** for clothes, not chocolates!

We bought a lot of food at the supermarket.

2 不具數名詞與 some、much 和 any 連用可表述某些事物的數量：

Mrs Pick went out to buy **some bread**.
There's not **much petrol** in the car, so we'd better go to a garage.
We haven't had **any rain** here since April.

3 有些名詞既可是不具數名詞，又可是具數名詞。作不具數名詞時它們泛指某類事物；作具數名詞時，它們指的是這類事物的一個特定實例：

A shop near me sells 20 different **cheeses**. I hate **cheese**.

There's a **hair** in my soup! Val has long dark **hair**.

It's made of **glass**. I had a **glass** of Coca-Cola.

There's a **hair** in my soup.

練習 Practice

A 把以下不具數名詞歸入正確類別：

snow	dinner	petrol	toast	ice
food	milk	maths	lunch	coffee
wood	aerobics	butter	physics	breakfast
metal	glass	bread	gold	tea

1 substances: _snow_

2 liquids: _____

3 meals: _____

4 types of food: _____

5 sports/subjects: _____

B 現在用習題 A 的一些不具數名詞完成以下句子：

1 The car ran out of _____ a kilometre from our home.

2 We got up early, had _____ , then drove to the airport.

3 _____ is a very valuable metal.

4 A lot of people keep fit by doing _____ , which is exercising to music.

5 They say that the English drink a lot of _____ .

6 When we woke up, everything was white: the ground was covered with _____ .

C 用以下單詞或短語完成句子：

glass/glasses	paper/a paper	business/a business
two sugars/sugar	cheese/a cheese	a grey hair/hair

1 Sam went out to buy _____ to read.

2 _____ is made from trees.

3 They say that mice like _____ .

4 Camembert is _____ from France.

5 You don't always need a lot of money to

start _____ .

6 Do you prefer long or short _____?

7 I was very worried when I found I had _____ .

8 _____ is bad for your teeth.

9 'How do you like your tea?' 'White

with_____, please.'

10 After the accident the road was covered

with broken _____.

11 We had a coffee and two

_____ of mineral water.

12 '_____ is always good in the holidays, ' said the toy-shop owner.

19 | A, an, some

1 單數名詞可與 a 連用，在以下的單數名詞前加上 a：

_____ week	_____ book	_____ person	_____ tables
_____ sports	_____ people	_____ tomato	_____ cup
_____ dog	_____ house	_____ parents	_____ children

2 a 可以與具數名詞連用，但不能與不具數名詞連用。在以下的單數具數名詞前加上 a：

_____ box	_____ work	_____ job	_____ news
_____ banana	_____ honey	_____ traffic	_____ holiday
_____ teacher	_____ hat	_____ water	_____ furniture

3 首字母是 a、e、i、o、u 的單詞要與 an 連用。請把 an 加到應該加的地方：

| _____ elephant | _____ apple | _____ cat | _____ aunt |
| _____ beach | _____ test | _____ opinion | _____ idiot |

4 首字母是 h 但 h 不發音的單詞要與 an 連用。請比較：

an hour　**a hospital**　**an honour**　**a hope**　**an honest man**

5 首字母是 eu 或 u 的單詞，其第一個音發 /juː/ 時，要與 a 連用。請比較：

a European country　**a university**　**an ugly** face

6 首次談及一個人或物時，要用 a 或 an：

There is **a man** at the door. (=I don't know which man.)
I need to buy **a** new **shirt**. (=not one specific shirt)

7 談論職業要用 a 或 an：

My father is **an engineer** now, but he was **a soldier** before.
I worked as **a secretary** last summer. This year I want to be **a shop assistant**.

8 a 或 an 可代替 one 與某些數字連用：

a hundred pounds　half **a kilo**　**a million people**
a litre of wine　**an hour**　**a thousand times**

9 當數字不重要時，some 與複數名詞或不具數名詞連用，可談及一個以上的事物：

I want **some apples, some wine, some potatoes** and two **oranges**.

Some friends gave me some information about good hotels.

19 練習 Practice

A 把左欄與右欄相關的部分連成句子：

1 I've been waiting for you for	a hundred people.
2 This car can do 140 miles	half an hour.
3 Those apples cost 50p	a few times.
4 We're having a party for about	a lot to do.
5 Sue has been to Germany	a month.
6 We're very busy in the office.	There's a kilo.
7 We normally go to the cinema once	an hour.

B 請看圖，圖中有些甚麼人？用以下單詞完成句子：

a student   a nurse   a tourist   a musician   students   nurses   tourists   singers

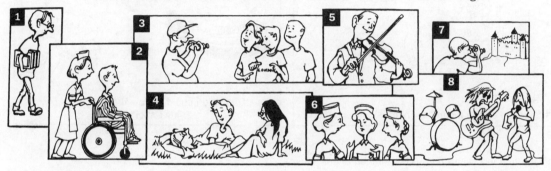

1 He looks like _____.

2 I think she is _____.

3 They look like _____.

4 I think they are _____.

5 He's _____.

6 They are _____.

7 She is _____.

8 They are _____.

C 請看圖，用 a、an 或 some 和相關詞彙寫出完整句子：

如：There – telephone – living room. *There's a telephone in the living room.*

1 There – small table – kitchen.

2 There – lot of pictures – living room.

3 There – flowers – living room.

4 There – lamp – corner of the living room.

5 There – TV – living room.

6 There – plants – both rooms.

7 There – guitar – living room.

8 There – people – living room.

20 The

1 複習第十九單元有關 a 或 an 的內容。

2 當與你交談的人知道你所講的是哪一個人或哪一件事時，單數名詞前要加 the：

I had a book and a magazine with me. I read **the book** first. (=the book I had with me)
He bought a new shirt and a tie. **The tie** was very expensive. (=the tie he bought)
I spoke to **the headmaster** at school this morning. (=the headmaster of my school)

'Is there life on **the moon**?' (=There is only one moon.)

'Dad said I could borrow **the car** tomorrow.'
(=my father's car)

I left the fruit in **the kitchen**. (=the kitchen in our house)
The president is coming next week. (=the president of our country)
She went into her room and locked **the door**. (=the door of her room)
Who is **the woman** next to Mary?
She was talking to **the man** who lives next door.

當與你交談的人知道你所講的是哪一類人或哪一類事時，複數名詞前要加 the：

Where are **the children**? (=our children)
He bought two shirts and a tie. **The shirts** were quite cheap. (=the shirts he bought)
Have you washed **the cups and saucers**? (=the cups and saucers we have been using)

3 談論一個系統或一項業務時要用 the：

I spoke to her on **the telephone** yesterday. I heard it on **the radio**.

4 對某事作一般陳述時，單數名詞前要加 the：

The tiger is a very dangerous animal. My favourite flower is **the rose**.

(注意) 用複數名詞作一般描述，或對一個不具數名詞作一般描述時不能用 the：

Tigers are dangerous animals. **Roses** are my favourite flowers.
Rice is very expensive in England. **Platinum** is more valuable than gold.

20 練習 Practice

A 填上 a、an 和 the 完成以下句子：

1 I was speaking to _____ *a* _____ friend on _____ *the* _____ telephone.

2 _____ headmaster is moving to _____ new school.

3 My sister is taking _____ children to _____ party.

4 He ate three sandwiches and _____ large cake. _____ cake was filled with cream.

5 I heard _____ great programme on _____ radio this morning.

6 The first man on _____ moon was _____ American.

7 There's some hot water in _____ kettle. Can you make _____ cup of tea?

8 'Help! There's _____ snake in _____ garden.'

9 'Look, there's _____ big kite in _____ sky.'

B 用 a、an 或 the 填空：

Police have been looking for (1) _____ eight-year-old boy who tried to hold up (2) _____ sweet shop with (3) _____ gun, writes David Ward.

The boy threw (4) _____ carrier bag at (5) _____ shopkeeper and ordered her to fill it up. 'I don't know whether he wanted me to fill (6) _____ bag with sweets or money,' said (7) _____ shopkeeper. 'I am not sure if (8) _____ gun was real or not, but I don't think it was (9) _____ toy gun.' The boy went into the shop and bought (10) _____ bar of chocolate for 25p. 'He gave me (11) _____ 50p piece and as I gave him his change (12) _____ man came in. (13) _____ boy waited until (14) _____ man went. Then he threw (15) _____ plastic carrier bag at me, pointed (16) _____ gun at me and said: 'Put everything in.'

21 The 的其他用法 Other uses of *the*

1 有些地方名與 the 連用：

a 帶 Union、Kingdom、States、Republic 的地名要加 the：

The United States   The United Kingdom   The People's Republic of China

b 山脈、群島名要加 the：

The Alps   The Rockies   The Canaries

c 河流、海和大洋名要加 the：

The Thames   The North Sea   The Atlantic Ocean

d 酒店、影院、劇場和博物館名要加 the：

The Hilton Hotel   The Odeon   The British Museum

2 地理方位要加 the：

It's much colder in **the north** of England than in **the south**.

A: Where do you come from? B: I'm from **the north-east**, near Newcastle.

3 形容詞與 the 連用可指某類人，常被這樣使用的形容詞有：

the rich   the poor   the young   the old   the blind   the disabled   the dead

Life nowadays is very difficult for **the poor** and **the disabled**.

There was a garden for **the blind**. All the flowers had a very strong scent.

4 最高級要加 the（參見第六十四單元）：

She is **the oldest daughter**. It was **the best film** I had ever seen.

5 the 可用來指一個家族：

The Kennedys are probably the most famous family in the USA.

We live next door to **the Browns**.

6 the 還可以用來：

a 與樂器連用：

He's learning **the guitar** and **the piano**.

b 與方位連用：

in the corner	*at the top*
	in the middle	
on the left	*on the right*
	at the bottom

注意 談及一件特指的樂器時不能用 the：

We bought Helen **a new violin** for her birthday.   A: What's that? B: It's **a trombone**.

A 根據以下疑問句找出相關答案：

the Ritz   the Andes   the Nile   the Clintons   the guitar   the Odeon   the south west

1 Which instrument does Paul McCartney play? _____

2 What's the nearest cinema to your house? _____

3 Which part of the country do you live in? _____

4 What's the longest river in your country? _____

5 Who are your neighbours? _____

6 Which is the biggest hotel in your town? _____

7 Which are the biggest mountains in your country? _____

B 加上 the 來完成以下句子。第一個句子中必須加一個 the，第二個句子中必須加兩個 the，第三個句子中必須加三個 the，依此類推：

1 Excuse me, can you tell me time please?

2 What's name of nearest cinema?

3 We went to cinema last night. Unfortunately we were late so we missed start of film.

4 Name of river that flows through middle of London is Thames.

5 Weather in north of England will get worse on Thursday and Friday. At weekend temperature will be 3 degrees and there will be snow during night.

6 We live near sea in south of England. Every day in afternoon we walk dogs in woods for a couple of hours. Scenery is so beautiful.

7 I read in encyclopaedia you gave me that Mount Everest in Himalayas is highest mountain in world. Longest river in world is Nile in Africa.

8 I was thinking of girls we met in street when we were going to a party in house next to restaurant where Michael works. One came from Republic of Ireland. We invited them to party but they couldn't go because they were flying to United States next day.

22 物主詞 Possessives

1 你能把以下的物主形容詞和相關的代詞連起來嗎？

their　your　her　his　our　my　your　its

I _____ It _____ You _____ We _____

He _____ You _____ She _____ They _____

2 物主詞可以用來：

a 表述某物屬於某人：

'That's **my** car.'

They showed us **their** holiday photographs.

b 談及人們之間的關係：

Sarah is **my sister**. Have you met **their father**? What's **your friend** called? He hasn't seen **his parents** today.

c 談及人體部位：

Arlene broke **her arm** last week, did you know? **My head** hurts.

d 談及衣物：

Take **your** hands out of **your pockets**! Have you seen **my jeans**? I can't find them.

3 也可以用 "名詞＋ 's" 的方法來表示：

a 與名稱連用：

I was in **Mark's** new house last night. Sidney is **Jane's** brother.

b 與單數名詞（通常與人有關）連用：

It's my **uncle's** birthday next Monday.
Sam asked if he could borrow his **friend's** car.

c 與不規則複數名詞連用：

Children's clothes are expensive.

d 用於談及人們的住宅和一般商店：

I slept at **David's** last night. He went to the **chemist's**.

4 用於規則性複數名詞時，只需在該名詞後面加一撇號 "'"：

Sinatra was my **parents'** favourite singer.

Colston College is the best **boys'** school in the region.

22 練習 Practice

A 用物主詞完成以下句子：

1 I don't live with _____ parents now.

2 Rosa wanted to give_____ father a CD for _____ birthday.

3 Jessica went upstairs and started to wash _____ hair.

4 I know the Spencers but I've never met _____ son.

5 We're having a party in _____ house on Friday. Can you come?

6 Good morning, ladies and gentlemen. Can I have _____ attention, please?

7 France is famous for _____ wine and _____ cheese.

8 I don't know much about the Amazon and _____ history.

B 哪兒錯了？每幅圖裏都有一個錯，找出它們並完成以下句子：

1 He's forgotten _____ . (trousers)

2 The cup is missing _____. (handle)

3 They've lost _____ . (keys)

4 Patricia can't remember _____ . (number)

5 'Excuse me, is this _____ ?' (animal)

6 'Excuse me, can you give us _____ back?' (ball)

C 改寫以下疑問句：

例如：What's the name of your mother? _What's your mother's name?_____

1 What's the name of your best friend? _____

2 What's the favourite colour of your mother? _____

3 What's the address of your neighbour? _____

4 Do you know the first name of your teacher? _____

5 What is the main export of your country? _____

6 What food is the speciality of your region? _____

D 用以下的詞作開頭，按真實情況回答上面的疑問句：

1 My _____.

2 My _____.

3 My _____.

4 His/Her _____.

5 My _____.

6 My _____.

23 指示形容詞 Demonstrative adjectives

1 談及的物品為單數時，距離較近的用 this，距離較遠的用 that：

This water tastes strange. **That building** is 200 years old.

'Have you got **this shirt** in **that colour**?'

'**This coffee** isn't mine!'

2 談及的物品為複數時，距離較近的用 these，距離較遠的用 those：

I don't like **these shoes** much. **These chocolates** are very nice!

'Can I have some of **those apples**, please?'

'Aren't **those people** strange!'

3 this 與 morning、afternoon、evening（不能用 night）、week、month、year 和 century 連用，表述的是現在；that 與這些詞連用，表述的是過去：

Are you busy **this evening**? We could go out.
I'm afraid the doctor can't see you **this week**.
Is next week OK?

4 表達式 these days 用來泛指現在，表達式 those days 用來泛指過去：

It's difficult to find good quality products **these days**.
These days every office has a fax, a photocopier and its own computer.

In **those days** people had quite big families.

5 數詞和形容詞要置於 this、that、these 和 those 之後，名詞之前：

I bought **these two books** second hand for just £1. My mother doesn't like **these plastic cups**.
How much are **those new CD players**?

23 練習 Practice

A 找出與圖相關的句子來：

1 How much is this plate, please?
2 Can you pass me that plate, please, Tom?
3 This bird is called 'Geronimo'. It's an owl.
4 What is that bird over there? Is it an owl?
5 Excuse me, are these shoes yours?
6 Excuse me, where did you buy those shoes?
7 I saw that film last week.
8 This film is great, isn't it?

B 用 this、that、these 或 those 完成以下句子：

1 He's so busy that I don't see much of him ＿＿＿＿＿＿＿＿ days.
2 We haven't got enough money to go on holiday ＿＿＿＿＿＿＿＿ year.
3 What's the name of ＿＿＿＿＿＿＿＿ man we met ＿＿＿＿＿＿＿＿ morning?
4 Have you been in ＿＿＿＿＿＿ new supermarket in the ＿＿＿＿＿＿ centre?
5 The price of petrol ＿＿＿＿＿＿＿＿ days is incredible!
6 Who are ＿＿＿＿＿＿＿＿ people over there?
7 Listen! Do you know ＿＿＿＿＿＿＿＿ song?
8 ＿＿＿＿＿＿＿＿ exercise is very easy!

9 When I was a child, I played a lot of sport.
In ＿＿＿＿＿＿＿＿ days I was very active.

C 參照例句改寫下面的句子，可做必要的改動：

如：This is my favourite hat. _This hat is my favourite._

1 This is my mother's favourite song. ＿＿＿＿＿＿＿＿＿＿＿＿
2 That was a terrible joke! ＿＿＿＿＿＿＿＿＿＿＿＿
3 This is a delicious cake. ＿＿＿＿＿＿＿＿＿＿＿＿
4 These are comfortable shoes. ＿＿＿＿＿＿＿＿＿＿＿＿
5 That is a fashionable colour. ＿＿＿＿＿＿＿＿＿＿＿＿
6 Those are my best trousers. ＿＿＿＿＿＿＿＿＿＿＿＿
7 These are very popular books. ＿＿＿＿＿＿＿＿＿＿＿＿
8 That was a great party. ＿＿＿＿＿＿＿＿＿＿＿＿
9 Those are beautiful paintings. ＿＿＿＿＿＿＿＿＿＿＿＿

24 人稱代詞 Personal pronouns

1 下面是兩組人稱代詞，你能找出與主語人稱代詞相關的賓語人稱代詞嗎？

賓語人稱代詞：us, me, you, them, her, it, him

主語 人稱代詞	賓語 人稱代詞	主語 人稱代詞	賓語 人稱代詞
I	_____	it	_____
you	_____	we	_____
he	_____	they	_____
she	_____		

2 主語人稱代詞用作動詞的主語：

I like your hat. **You live** near here, do you? **He's** my boss.
She's on holiday. **We were** in London yesterday. **They come** from Nigeria.

3 賓語人稱代詞可以：

a 用作動詞的賓語：

Could you **help us** with this, please? She **gave me** £5.
I **told them** to be here at 6 o'clock. She **saw him** in town.

b 置於介詞之後：

She was waiting **for us.** I talked **to him** yesterday.
Can you take me **with you**?

I don't know anything **about him**.

c 置於動詞 to be 之後：

This **is us** in Greece, and this **is us** in Italy last year, and this **is me** in Paris.

Hello, John, it**'s me**.

4 用 you 或 they 泛指人們，用 we 談及的人群包括説話者本人：

They have good food in this restaurant. **You** can buy this book anywhere. **We** drink a lot of tea in England.

5 首次提到某人或某事後，用代詞可避免重複：

I spoke to Mary this morning. **She** said **she** was very busy.
Patrick lives near the coast. **He** has a lovely house.

50

24 練習 Practice

A 在以下句子裏的主語人稱代詞下面加上底線：

1 I can't forget the last time we went to that restaurant. The food made me ill, and it wasn't cheap, either.
2 Do you know where we can buy an English newspaper? Someone told us there was a shop near here.
  Can you help?
3 I got a letter from Simon today. I hadn't heard from him for ages. He's working in Milan now, apparently.
4 Val invited me to her party, but I'm not sure if I can go. She lives miles away, and I've got a million things
  to do.

B 再請看上面的句子。每個句子裏都有一個實語人稱代詞，看看你能不能找到？

C 把左欄與右欄相關的句子連成對話：

1 Do you know Mr and Mrs James?	It's in Africa, I think.
2 Where's Timbuctoo?	He's in hospital now.
3 Mike had an accident on Sunday.	It's boring.
4 That's a brilliant film.	They eat a lot of pasta.
5 I'm not interested in football.	We met them last week.
6 Where did you buy those shoes?	I've seen it three times.
7 What's the food like in Italy?	Paul gave them to me.

D 請看圖。在以下句子中填上人稱代詞，然後把代表圖中説話者的字母正確地填到相關句子後的括號裏：

1 Do you know Sue? _____ 's a top
  model. (　)

2 I made her dress. Do you like _____? (　)

3 I think I'm in love with _____ , but _____'s
  not very interested in _____ . (　)

4 We are her assistants. _____ are always very
  busy. She travels everywhere with _____. (　)

5 Don't bring flowers in here. Sue doesn't like
  _____ . (　)

6 I'm her manager. _____ have to talk to
  _____ if _____ want an
  interview with _____ . (　)

7 _____ gave us these photographs of
  _____ ! (　)

51

25 This, that, these, those, one, ones

1 this（單數）和these（複數）可用於：

a 介紹別人：

Mary, **this** is John.

These are my neighbours, Mr and Mrs Baxter.

b 談及距離自己較近的人或物：

This is really good coffee.

These are the books I bought from Jane.

c 開始電話交談：

Hello. **This** is Sally; can I speak to Jane, please?

Tom, **this** is Barbara. How are you?

This is the BBC World Service ...

2 that（單數）和those（複數）可用於：

a 談及距離自己不太近的人或物：

This is my house, and **that** is John's over there.

Is **that** a bird or a plane up there?

b 確認看不到的人是誰：

Is **that** you, David?

Hi, is that **Sally**?

Those are expensive shoes. Buy these, they're cheaper.

3 可用 this、that、these 和 those 來回答某人說過的話。最常用的是 that：

'Coffee?'　'**That**'s a good idea.'

'Is **that** the London train?'　'Yes, **that**'s right.'

'I've got a new job in the city.'　'**That**'s fantastic!'

4 用one（單數）和 ones（複數）可避免重複使用一個名詞，它們可以：

a 置於形容詞之後：

My car is the **blue one**. (= the blue car)

Your question is a **difficult one**. (= a difficult question)

b 置於 the 之後：

Our house is **the one** in the middle.

She gave me a lot of books. **The ones** I really enjoyed were love stories. (= the books I enjoyed)

c 在疑問句裏置於 which 之後：

We've got lots of tapes. **Which one** do you want to listen to?

I need batteries for my personal stereo. Which ones are best?

25 練習 Practice

A 改寫下面句子，為避免重複，請用 one 或 ones：

1 I love cakes, especially the cakes my mother makes!
2 Our car is the black car at the end of the road.
3 I'm not sure if I need a big bottle or a small bottle.
4 He lost his umbrella, so he wants to buy a new umbrella.
5 The hotel is a modern hotel on the coast.
6 The books I bought are the books on the table.
7 I always have two pens with me, a blue pen and a red pen.

8 Is this museum the museum you were talking about?

B 根據以下疑問句找出適當答案：

1 'Would you like a coffee?'   'The brown ones on the desk.'
2 'Which gloves are yours?'   'Sure. Which one?'
3 'Which shirt should I wear to the party?'   'Thanks, I'd love one.'
4 'Have you seen my new photos?'   'Your new cotton one.'
5 'Can I borrow a book?'   'The ones of Spain? Yes.'

C 用以下句子完成簡短對話：

> That's a lot.   That's all right.   That's why you're tired.   That's great.

1 a I'm sorry I broke your cup.   3 a We're getting married!

  b _____   b _____

2 a These boots cost £90.   4 a We danced all night.

  b _____   b _____

D 用 this、that、these 或 those 完成以下對話：

1 a Bill, _____ is Wolfgang.   3 a Is _____ Jane?

  b Oh! Are you German?   b Yes, speaking. Who's _____?

  a Yes, _____ 's right.   a _____ is Tom from next door.

Bill, _____ is Wolfgang.

Is _____ Jane?

2 a I'm going to Greece on holiday.   4 a Where are my shoes?

  b _____ 's nice.   b Are _____ yours over there?

第
一
編

26 物主代詞 Possessive pronouns

1 物主代詞有以下幾個：

I like your car. **Mine** is very old; **yours** looks very fast.

The red umbrella is **hers**.

Thanks for your address. Let me give you **ours**, too.

This isn't my shirt, it's **his**.

注意 it 沒有領屬形式。 Yours 既是單數又是複數。

'Which team won?' '**Theirs.**'

2 使用物主代詞可避免重複：

如： That book is my book. (=That book is mine.)

That book is **mine**, and the pictures are **mine**, too.
The jazz records are **hers**, the rock records are **his**.
All the new furniture is **ours**.

'Excuse me, is this newspaper **yours**?

3 物主代詞可置於 of 之後：

He was an old friend of **mine** (not: 'of me').
The teacher was talking to a student of **his**.
Listening to music is a hobby of **ours**.

Can I borrow that map of **yours**?
Are the Smiths friends of **hers**?
I think the dog is one of **theirs**.

4 物主代詞可用作以 whose 開頭的疑問句的省略回答：

練習 **Practice**

A 參照例句完成以下句子：

如：Have you got a blue pen?　No, _mine is red._ _____ (red)

1　'Has David got a new car?'　'No, _____ (very old).'
2　'Did Sheila say she has a Japanese camera?'　'No_____ (German).'
3　'Is this your coffee?'　'No, _____ (over there).'
4　'Is your house bigger than this one?'　'No, _____ (smaller).'
5　'Do they have a colour TV?'　'No, _____ (black and white).'
6　'Will we have first class tickets?'　'No, _____ (second class).'

B 參照例句，用 a...of...代替有底線的詞來改寫以下句子：

如：This is one of his paintings. _This is a painting of his._

1　Susan is one of our friends. _____
2　The small man is one of our neighbours. _____
3　Is singing one of your hobbies? _____
4　Hamid is one of my students. _____
5　Pink is one of her favourite colours. _____
6　I am one of their fans. _____
7　Roast beef is one of my favourite meals. _____

C 完成以下句子：

'Whose car is that?' 'It's _____.'

'Whose is this?' 'It's _____.'

'Excuse me, is this _____?'

'I haven't got a pen on me.'
'Here, you can borrow _____.'

第一編

27 時間狀語 Adverbials of time

1 以下表達式用來表述某事要在何時發生或已在何時發生：

the day before yesterday   the week before last   yesterday
last week   today   this week   tomorrow   next week
the day after tomorrow   the week after next
I have an important meeting **the day after tomorrow**.

與 month 和 year 連用的表達式和 week 的一樣，例如：
the month before last   last year
this month   the year after next

2 ago 與簡單過去時態連用，表示所談之事
是在多久之前發生的：

I'll be leaving school **the year after next**.

The game **started ten minutes ago**. The bus **went an hour ago**.

ago 要與 five minutes、an hour、three weeks、four months 和 a few years 等時間表達式連用。下
面是最常用的表達式：

ages ago   a long time ago   some time ago   not long ago   a short time ago

注意 ago 不能與現在完成時態連用，不能說：I have seen him two minutes ago.

3 頻度狀語用來表述某事有多經常地發生：

Always	frequently	occasionally
never	hardly ever	normally
often	sometimes	usually
rarely		

We don't **often** swim in the sea.

I'm **always** sick when I travel by sea.

頻度狀語通常置於主要動詞之前：
I **hardly ever watch** TV.   You can **sometimes waste** a lot of time.

但是當 am、is、are、was 和 were 用作主要動詞時，頻度狀語要置於它們之後：
She **is usually** very late.   You **are probably** right.

有些頻度狀語（如 sometimes、occasionally、normally、usually）可以置於句首：
Sometimes I go swimming at the weekend.
Normally I go swimming on Thursday night.

27 練習 Practice

A 按真實情況回答以下疑問句：

1 When did you last go swimming? _I last went swimming three months ago._

2 When did you last go to the cinema? _____

3 When did you start school? _____

4 When were you born? _____

5 When was your mother born? _____

6 When did you have breakfast today? _____

7 When were you last ill? _____

8 When did you start learning English? _____

B 回答以下疑問句：

1 What is the date the day after tomorrow? _____

2 What day was it the day before yesterday? _____

3 What month was it the month before last? _____

4 How old will you be the year after next? _____

5 How old were you the year before last? _____

C 用頻度狀語根據自己的真實情況造句：

1 I am late for lessons. _I am often late for lessons._

2 I get up late on Sunday. _____

3 I watch TV in the evening. _____

4 I play tennis in the summer. _____

5 In my country it is cold in winter. _____

6 I read in bed before I go to sleep. _____

再請根據一位朋友的真實情況寫出三個句子：

7 _____

8 _____

9 _____

D 看看這些陳述句是對（T）還是錯（F）？

1 Adverbials of frequency never come at the beginning of a sentence. (_F_)

2 'Sometimes' can come at the beginning of a sentence. (　)

3 'Always' often comes at the beginning of a sentence. (　)

4 Adverbials of frequency usually come before the main verb. (　)

5 You always use the present perfect tense with 'ago'. (　)

6 In conversations we often use short questions. (　)

28 較大可能性狀語和程度狀語
Adverbials of probability and degree

1 較大可能性狀語用來表述對某事的確定程度：

certainly   definitely   probably   perhaps   possibly   maybe

I **definitely** saw her yesterday. The driver **probably** knows the quickest way.

所有的較大可能性狀語（maybe 除外）都要置於主要動詞之前：
He can **probably answer** your question. They will **certainly help** you.

但是：當 am、is、are、was、were 用作主要動詞時，要置於它們之後：
I **am certainly** very tired.   You **are probably** right.

有些較大可能性狀語可置於句首：

perhaps   maybe   probably   possibly

Maybe Annette can tell you. **Perhaps** he has forgotten.
Probably they'll come later. **Possibly** she didn't understand.

2 常用的程度狀語和頻度狀語：a lot、(not) much 和 very much。

有時這些詞可用作頻度狀語：
The baby cries **a lot**. (a lot = very often)   We do**n't** go out **much**. (not much = not often)

有時這些詞可用作頻度副詞：
Did it rain **very much** last night? (very much = very heavily)

a lot、(not)much 和 very much 通常置於其所在從句的句尾：
Things have**n't** changed **much**. They always shout **a lot**.
We enjoyed the film **very much**. Do you play football **very much**?

但有時它們後面要跟一個時間表達式或地點表達式：
We enjoyed the film **very much last night**. Things have**n't** changed **much here**.

注意 much 不能用於肯定句，不能説：I liked it much.
而説：I liked it **a lot**. 或説：I liked it **very much**.

28 練習 Practice

A 根據真實情況，用較大可能性副詞寫出以下句子（需要時請加 not）：

1 The USA will win the next football World Cup.

The USA will definitely not win the next football World Cup.

2 My country will win the next football World Cup. _____

3 I am the oldest person in my class. _____

4 I will go away for a holiday this summer. _____

5 It will rain tomorrow. _____

6 The next leader of my country will be a woman. _____

7 I will get married next year. _____

8 I will get most of these sentences right. _____

B 下面的句子中有六個句子是正確的，五個句子有錯。找出錯句，把正確的句子寫在橫線處：

1 Nearly I have finished this exercise. ✗ _____ *I have nearly finished this exercise.*

2 I cut myself this morning, and it hurt a lot. _____

3 I like a lot your new dress. _____

4 We don't work very much at the weekend. _____

5 This is a very good book. I enjoyed it much. _____

6 He is very lazy. He doesn't help very much his parents. _____

7 I have almost finished this exercise. _____

8 People say that it rains a lot in England. _____

9 I always enjoy very much the weekend. _____

10 I don't work much at the weekend. _____

11 They are very noisy children. They shout a lot. _____

29 持續狀語 Adverbials of duration

1 for 可用來表示某事持續了多長時間:

I've been working here **for fifteen years**. I hadn't eaten **for ten hours**.
I will be away **for three weeks**. We stayed in Paris **for a couple of days**.

請注意 for 的後面要跟一個表明某事持續了多久的時間段:
fifteen years   ten hours   three weeks   a couple of days

2 用 since 表示一個活動開始的時間:

I've been working here **since 1980**. I hadn't eaten **since eight o'clock**.

請注意 since 後面要跟一段時間:
1980   eight o'clock   this morning   yesterday   last week

或跟一件事:

I've been working here **since the war**. I hadn't eaten **since breakfast**.

或跟一個從句:

I've been working here **since I left school**.
I hadn't seen him **since I was a child**.

Since 通常要與現在完成時態或過去完成時態連用。

當提及的時間延續到當前時,since 要與現在完成時連用:
We **have lived** here **since we were children**. (=and we still live here.)

當提及的時間延續到過去一個指定時間時,since 要與過去完成時連用:
It was 1973. Elizabeth **had been** queen **since 1953**. (=and in 1973 she was still queen.)

常用的表達式還有: "It's...since +簡單過去時" 和 "It was...since +過去完成時":
It's a long time **since I saw** Jeff.   It was five years **since we had last met**.

3 from...to 或 from...till/until 可用來表述某事開始於何時,結束於何時:

The shops will be open **from nine until five thirty**.
The winter season lasts **from December to March**.
We worked non-stop **from six in the morning till nine at night**.

till 和 until 後面可跟從句:
We can watch television **till Dad gets home**.
I lived in Manchester **until I went to university in 1987**.

29 練習 Practice

A 用 since 從句完成以下句子：

1 He hasn't played football   a ever since we first met.
2 We have been good friends   b since she started secondary school.
3 She hasn't written to us   c since seven o'clock this morning.
4 He has been out at work   d ever since supper time.
5 She has been learning English   e since he hurt his leg last week.
6 I have been feeling hungry   f since she sent that letter on your birthday.

B 加上 for、since、from 或 until 來完成以下句子：

1 There has been a university in Oxford ____for____ more than eight hundred years.

2 They have been married _____ 1966.

3 The First World War lasted _____ 1914 _____ 1918.

4 _____ 1992 _____ last year we had a flat in the centre of town.

5 Can you wait for a few minutes _____ I'm ready?

6 I haven't spoken to Bill _____ we were at school.

7 We usually stop for lunch _____ one _____ two thirty.

8 It has been raining _____ early this morning.

9 It's nearly five years _____ Jenny left school.

10 She was at college _____ two years and she's been working here _____ almost three years.

C 根據真實情況完成以下句子：

1 I have been learning English since _____ .

2 I have lived in _____ for _____ .

3 I have an English lesson today from _____ until _____ .

4 I usually sleep from about _____ to about _____ in the morning.

5 It's _____ since I had my breakfast.

6 I haven't been to the cinema since _____ .

30 In、on 和 at（用於時間） In, on, at (time)

1 at 可用於：

a 時間：at ten o'clock, at midnight

b 三餐：at breakfast

c 節日：at Christmas, at Easter

請注意下面這些特殊表達式：

at the weekend **at** the moment **at** that time **at** night **at** the end of the month

2 in 可用於：

a 月份：in January, in September

b 年份： in 1988, in the year 2001

c 世紀： in the fourteenth century, in the last century

d 一天的時間： in the morning, in the evening

e 季節： in the spring, in winter

It often snows in winter.

3 on 可用於：

a 星期：on Monday, on Sunday

b 特定日期的時間：on Tuesday evening

c 特別日期：on New Year's Day, on Christmas Eve

d 日期：on Friday 13th, on the ninth of May

e 特別時刻：on my birthday, on our anniversary

...on my birthday.

4 in 還可用來談及會在將來發生的事情：

I'm busy now, so I'll talk to you **in** ten minutes.

They say he will be an important person **in** a few years.

The London train leaves **in** two minutes.

注意 在 this、next、last、every、today 和 tomorrow 之前不能用 at、in 和 on：

We'll see you next week sometime.

What are you doing this weekend, John?

We go camping almost every summer.

30 練習 **Practice**

A 請看下面的幾組詞，每組詞裏有一個不應該歸入該類別的詞或表達式，原因是它所跟的介詞不同。你能找出它嗎？

例如：...night, Tuesday, Christmas, the end of the morning.

我們説 at night、at Christmas 和 at the end of the morning，但是不説 at Tuesday，所以 Tuesday 要排除在外。

1 the morning, July, 1999, nine o'clock
2 May 31st, Friday morning, the weekend, Sunday
3 my sister's birthday, eight fifteen, the weekend, lunch
4 the twentieth of August, winter, Wednesday evening, Friday
5 December, the late afternoon, 1956, five o'clock

B 用 at、in 或 on 完成以下句子：

1 I was born _____ 1975.
2 My birthday is _____ September.
3 My mother's birthday is _____ the seventeenth
   of January.
4 I wake up most mornings _____ half past seven.
5 Last year we went on holiday _____ July.
6 I work best _____ the morning.

7 Yesterday I went to bed _____ midnight.

C 選用最合邏輯的詞或表達式來完成以下句子：

at the moment   at the end of the month   at dinner   on my birthday   on the first of April   on Monday morning
in the morning   in the next century   in August

1 Do you think life will be very different _____ ?
2 I was given this watch _____ .
3 It's traditional to play jokes on people _____ .
4 My grandmother would always wear her best clothes _____
5 It's very hot here _____ so most people go away on holiday.
6 Jeff slept badly so he felt very tired _____ .
7 I'm afraid Mr Markham is busy _____ . Can you wait a few minutes?

複習　第一編 **1 - 30** 單元

這是第一個單元複習。

如果你已經學習了第 1 - 30 單元，本複習會：

a 幫助你看到自己有多大進步。
b 幫助你複習已學過的知識。
c 幫助你判斷哪些單元應該再複習一次。

如果你還沒有學習第 1 - 30 單元，本複習會：

a 告訴你現在已經掌握多少知識。
b 幫助你判斷哪些單元對你最有用。

本複習的練習題從哪裏開始做都可以。如果對自己所做的回答沒有把握，可查看問題所在單元的語法解釋。

各種時態：

第三單元：簡單現在時 Present simple

A 完成以下句子：

1 January _____ one of the coldest winter months.

2 Hi, my name _____ Carlos. I _____ from Peru.

3 Where _____ you from?

4 My father _____ doctor.

5 What _____ your father _____ ?

6 I _____ two brothers and a sister.

7 _____ you _____ any brothers or sisters?

8 My hobbies _____ reading, swimming and going to the cinema.

B 用以下詞彙構成疑問句：

如： you/like/spaghetti? *Do you like spaghetti?*

1 you/want/go/cinema? _____

2 your father/work/an office? _____

3 your friend/speak/English? _____

4 you/know/that man? _____

5 your mother/have/job? _____

6 you/want/travel abroad? _____

複習　第一編 **1 – 30** 單元

第二單元：現在進行時 Present continuous

C 用現在進行時構成以下疑問句：

如：what/you/think? *What are you thinking?*

1　What/you/wear/today? _____

2　Where/you/go/tonight? _____

3　What/you/do/now? _____

4　Where/you/sit/at the moment? _____

5　you/listen/music/now? _____

6　you/go on holiday/with your family/this year? _____

7　you/wear/a watch? _____

8　you/have/lunch/now? _____

第五、六單元：現在完成時 Present perfect

D 用括號裏的動詞構成以下疑問句：

Have you ever ...?

1　(visit) Bath? _____

2　(break) your arm or leg? _____

3　(cook) for more than 5 people? _____

4　(see) a crocodile? _____

5　(take) a photograph? _____

6　(meet) a famous person? _____

E 請看下面這些事情，然後寫出你今天是否做了它們：

have breakfast　have a shower　read a newspaper　do your homework
eat lunch　finish work　watch TV　speak English
do the washing-up　talk to a friend

1　I have ...

_____

_____

2　I haven't ...yet.

_____

_____

Cycle 1

F 他們在做甚麼？用以下動詞完成對話：

revise for my exams   cut onions   wait for two hours   play football

1 Why are you crying? _____

2 Why are you so tired? _____

3 Why are you angry? _____

4 Why are you so dirty? _____

第七單元：Was, were

G 用 was 或 were 完成下面的段落：

We 1 _____were_____ in a hurry because we 2 _____ late. Our flight 3 _____ at 7.30, and Steve 4 _____ worried that we might miss the plane. It 5 _____ not easy to find a taxi at that time of the morning. We eventually got one, and because there 6 _____ n't a lot of traffic, the drive 7 _____ quite quick. It 8 _____ 7.15 when we finally arrived at the airport. There 9 _____ only 15 minutes left before take-off! We 10 _____ the last people on the plane, of course.

H 多項選擇題。用適當的時態完成以下句子：

1 We _____ our cousins this weekend.

   a visit   b are visiting   c have visited

2 My dog _____ five years old.

   a has   b are   c is

3 Patrick is very active. He _____ sport every day.

   a is playing   b plays   c play

4 'Have you heard the new record by Madonna?' '_____'

   a Yes, I did.   b No, I didn't.   c No, I haven't.

5 I'll telephone you as soon as I _____ home.

   a get   b will have got   c am getting

6 Where _____ you yesterday?

   a were   b did   c was

7 _____ you go abroad on holiday last year?

    a Did   b Do   c Were

8 I _____ hot food.

    a am liking   b like   c liking

9 Tomorrow _____ the thirty-first of May.

    a is   b are   c is going to be

10 Do you think it _____ tomorrow?

    a rains   b will rain   c is raining

11 There _____ a man, a woman and some children in the garden.

    a was   b were   c are

12 What _____ this sign means?

    a you think   b think you   c do you think

13 Why _____ that?

    a said you   b did you say   c you said

14 'We've got a new teacher.' 'Really? _____ ?'

    a How is he   b What's he like   c How is he like

第八、九單元：簡單過去時和過去進行時 Past simple and past continuous

用以下動詞的簡單過去時或過去進行時完成下面的段落：

shop need find out be surprise know come wear see play walk be

The other day I (1) _found_ out something that (2) _____ me while I (3) _____ in the city centre. I (4) _____ down the High Street when someone I (5) _____ (6) _____ out of a very expensive clothes shop. The surprising thing (7) _____ that she (8) _____ terrible old jeans and a dirty T-shirt. Later on I (9) _____ that those were the clothes she (10) _____ for her job: she (11) _____ an actress who (12) _____ the part of a punk in a new film!

用以下動詞完成疑問句：

buy   speak   pay   do   go   understand

1 '_____ to a restaurant yesterday?' 'No, we went last week.'

2 'Where _____ your sunglasses?' 'I didn't. They were a present.'

3 'How much _____ for your camera, Sandra?'

4 'What _____ at ten o'clock last night?' 'We were talking with some friends.'

5 '_____ what he said?' 'No, he _____ Italian, I think.'

Cycle 1

第十一單元：現在時態表示將來 Present tenses used for the future

K 用簡單現在時或現在進行時完成以下句子：

1　Today is Monday 21st, so the day after tomorrow _____ the 23rd.

2　This morning I got up at 5 a.m. Tomorrow _____ at 7 a.m.

3　Today I flew to Paris. On Friday _____ to Acapulco.

4　Last night we had a pizza. Tonight _____ fish and chips.

5　We went to a disco last month, and we _____ to another one next week.

6　The first train left at 8.30; the next train _____ at 11.25.

7　The film I saw last night began at 6. Tonight the film _____ at 8.15.

第十二單元：Will and going to

L 選擇正確答案：

1　'There's someone at the door.' 'Ok, I go/I'll go.'

2　My neighbours will have/are having a barbecue tonight.

3　I am going to/will help you if you want.

4　Look at those clouds. I think it will/is going to rain soon.

5　According to the timetable, the next bus goes/will go at 6.

6　We will meet/are going to meet Bill and Patty tomorrow.

M 請看圖。用 will 或 going to 完成以下句子：

1　He _____ have a shower.

2　They _____ see a play.

3　They _____ have a crash.

4　'I think I _____ have the omelette.'

5　'We _____ see you on Sunday, then.'

第十三、十四、十五單元：There 、 what 和 wh- 疑問句 There, what and wh-questions

N 完成以下對話：

1　' _____'s the matter? You look worried.'

　　' _____'s a spider on my desk!'

　　' _____ is it exactly? I can't see it.'

　　'It's on my books.'

　　'Well, it isn't _____ now.'

2　'Excuse me. _____ can I buy a newspaper near here?'

　　' _____'s a newsagent on Park Street.'

　　' _____'s that?'

　　'Just round the corner.'

3 'Hi, Mark! _____*How*_____ How are you?'

  'Fine. _____ are you going?'

  'We're off to the centre.'

  'Sorry, _____ did you say?'

  'I said we're going to the centre.'

  '_____ ? '

  _____'s happening?'

  '_____'s a sale on at Debenhams.'

第十六、十七、十八單元：名詞 Nouns

O 選擇正確答案：

1 How many brother/brothers and sister/sisters do you have?

2 Man/men and woman/women can do the same jobs.

3 I like your jeans. Is it/Are they new?

4 Sheila's having her hairs/hair cut this afternoon.

5 Don't worry. The police is/are coming.

6 There aren't so many bus/buses after 8 p.m.

7 They say that eating carrot/carrots will help you see well in dark/the dark.

第十九、二十和二十一單元：A, an, some and the

P 在必要的地方加上 the、a、an 或 some：

1 Would you like _____ piece of _____ cake I made yesterday?

2 Yes, that'd be nice. But just _____ small piece.

3 A lot of people think that New York is _____ capital of _____ United States.

4 You're working too hard. You need _____ holiday.

5 Do you drive on _____ left or on _____ right-hand side of _____ road in your country?

6 You often have to wait for _____ hour or more before you can see _____ doctor.

7 'I'm going to _____ supermarket. Do you want anything?' 'Yes, can you get me _____ can of soup and _____ eggs, please?'

8 'What time are you going to _____ match tomorrow?' 'I've told you _____ hundred times, at two o'clock.'

第二十二 ── 二十六單元：物主詞、指示詞和代詞
Possessives, demonstratives and pronouns

Q 填上以下句子所缺的字詞：

1 _____ is a photo of _____ and a friend of _____ in front of _____ first car.

2 'Excuse _____. Is _____ luggage, sir?'

3 'Do _____ want a lift?' ' _____ 's very kind of _____ .'

4 I need a coffee. I haven't had _____ for hours.

5 'We have hundreds of umbrellas, sir. Can _____ describe what _____ looks like?'

6 'A piece of cake, please.' 'Certainly, which _____?'

7 'Who can tell _____ the answer?' _____!'

8 '_____ £ 10 note is this?' ' _____!'

9 '_____ skirt is a little short. Do you have a longer _____?'

10 'I think I preferred the first _____ you showed _____ .'

第二十七、二十八和二十九單元：狀語 Adverbials

R 選用最適當的狀語完成以下句子：

1　What was the weather like　next week/last week?
2　They eat fish and chips　always/a lot in England.
3　We enjoyed the party　much/a lot.
4　It's ages　until/since　the holidays start.
5　It's ages　until/since　we last went to the sea.
6　They are　probably/maybe　going to get married in May.
7　If you phone them now they'll　possibly/probably be there.
8　This park is so popular you can　occasionally/hardly ever find a place to sit down.

第三十單元： In、on 和 at（用於時間） In, on, at (time)

S 根據需要在空白處填上 in、 on 或 at：

1　We're having our holiday _____ the autumn this year.
2　What did you do _____ the weekend?
3　It snowed _____ Christmas Eve last year.
4　Our first lesson is _____ the morning.
5　School finishes _____ 3.30 in England.
6　A lot of people are too worried to go out _____ night.
7　The announcement said our plane will take off _____ half an hour.
8　Do you want to come with us _____ next week?

9　Can you imagine what life was like _____ the seventeenth century?
10　I've felt sick _____ every morning this week.

31 May 和 might（用於表達可能性）
May, might (possibility)

1 談及某事的可能性但又不能確定時，可用 may 或 might：

a 表達現在的可能性：

'Where is Sue?' 'She **might** be at the office.'

'Is Chris Sutton a football player?' 'He **might** be, I'm not sure.'

'I'm sure his wife's name is Elise.' 'You **may** be right.'

b 表達將來的可能性：

'What are you doing tonight, John?' 'I **might** go to the pub.'

'Is it going to rain tomorrow?' 'It **may**. I haven't seen the weather forecast.'

'Valerie **might** not come to school tomorrow. She's a bit ill today.'

2 請注意 may 和 might 與所有情態動詞一樣，只有一種形式，用在 he、she 和 it 後面時詞尾不要加 -s：

I **might** go to the party tonight.

You **might** meet my mother if you come tomorrow.

He **might** be French. I don't know.

Ask that woman where the post office is. She **might** know.

It **might** rain later, so take an umbrella.

注意 不定式在 may 和 might 後面不要帶 to：

They **might be** angry if we are late. (不能用：might to be)

It **may be** true, I don't know. (不能用：may to be true)

3 might 的否定式是 might not 或 mightn't；may 的否定式是 may not（沒有縮略形式）：

'We **might not** be able to sell these chairs.'

'The traffic is bad, so I **mightn't** be back before 10 or 11.'

4 may 和 might 在意思上沒有重大區別，但 might 表示的不確定性較 may 稍大：

Take some paper and pens. They **might** be useful.

Take some paper and pens. They **may** be useful.

31 練習 **Practice**

A 判斷以下句子是指將來可能發生的事（F），還是指現在可能發生的事（P）：

1 I might be able to visit you this Friday. _____

2 John may be back home now. Give him a ring. _____

3 you may know the answer to this question already. _____

4 They might be politicians, it's hard to say. _____

5 We might be going to France this year. _____

6 You may be wrong about her age. She doesn't look 50. _____

7 Try this cheese. You might like it! _____

8 Chinese may be the most important language next century. _____

B 用 may 或 might 改寫以下句子：

如：Perhaps he is at the party. _He might be at the party._

1 Perhaps the shops are closed now. _____

2 Perhaps they are on holiday. _____

3 Perhaps the weather will be good tomorrow. _____

4 Perhaps I will get married before I am 30. _____

5 Perhaps they will go to the disco tonight. _____

6 It's nice here. Perhaps I'll stay an extra week. _____

7 Perhaps we will go to see the new play at the theatre. _____

8 They've trained a lot. Perhaps they will win the match. _____

C 你是如何想的？根據下面的陳述句寫出你的意見：

如：It'll rain tomorrow. _Yes, I think it will._
No, I don't think it will.
I'm not sure. It might.

1 The next leader of your country will be a woman. _____

2 You will go to the cinema this month. _____

3 You will receive a letter this week. _____

4 The price of your favourite drink will go up this year. _____

5 Someone will ask you a difficult question today. _____

6 You will eat in a restaurant next week. _____

7 There will be some very good news tomorrow. _____

8 You will go to a party this weekend. _____

9 The weather will be better next month than it is now. _____

10 You will listen to music this evening. _____

32 Can、could 和 be able to (用於表達可能性和能力)
Can, could, be able to (possibility and ability)

1 can (否定式是 cannot 或 can't) 可用於：

a 表達某事的可能性：
Swimming after eating **can** be dangerous.
Making mistakes **can** be a good way of learning.
Smoking **cannot** be good for you!

b 表達某人懂得做某事：
My brother **can** drive.
Can you speak French?

c 表達某人有能力做某事：
She's a great driver: she **can** drive almost any car.
I **can't** eat fish.
Anyone **can** become a qualified teacher.

d 可與 see、hear、feel、smell、remember、recognise 和 imagine 一類的動詞連用：
She **can't** remember the name of the book.
I **can't** see the reason for doing that.
Can you imagine living in a palace?

除了 a 項外，can 都可以用 be able to 替代。
但 can 較為常用，較不正式：
My brother **is able** to drive. I **am not able** to eat fish.
She **isn't able** to remember the name of the book.

I **can't** spell very well.

'Don't shout! We **can** all hear you.'

2 could (否定式是 could not 或 couldn't) 可用於：

a 談及某人過去的能力：
He **could** run faster than any of us. She **could** tell the most incredible jokes.
A lot of them **couldn't** read or write.

b 與 see、hear、smell、feel、remember、recognise 和 imagine 一類的動詞連用，表示過去的能力：
You **could** see they weren't happy. The policeman **could** smell gas.
He **couldn't** see them, but he **could** hear them in the dark.

c 表述不能完全確定某事的可能性：
There's a lot of traffic. That **could** explain why he's late.
There **could** be a storm tonight: look at the clouds!

3 以下情況可以用 be able to 代替 can：

a 在另一個情態動詞之後 (will、must、might 等)：
I **might be able to** help you later on. You should be able to buy some cheese in that shop.

b 當要用 -ing 形式或用 to- 不定式小句時：
It's nice **to be able to** get some exercise. He complained about not **being able to** go to London I enjoy **being able to** get up late at the weekend.

c 談論某人在過去特定條件下有能力做某事 (否定式是 wasn't able to、weren't able to 或 couldn't)：
Were you **able to** buy everything on the list? They **were able to** save enough money to buy a car.
I **wasn't able to** finish the meal. (=I couldn't finish it.)

A 改寫以下疑問句，用 can 或 can't 代替 know how to：

1 Do you know how to drive? _____

2 Do you know how to play the piano? _____

3 Where could we find someone who knows how to repair clocks? _____

4 Do any of your friends know how to use a word processor? _____

B 請看圖。用框中的動詞寫出 Jack 能做些甚麼，如下例：

1 *Jack can drive. I don't know if he can cook.*

| drive cook play chess sing play the guitar paint ski |
| speak Spanish play tennis type skate ride a horse |

2 寫出你能做的事和不能做的事，如下例：

I can ski, but I can't cook.

3 寫出你何時學會了做這些事情，如下例：

I can drive now, but I couldn't two years ago.

C 用以下的詞完成句子：

can could can't couldn't were able to will be able to won't be able to

1 I don't think we _____ travel to Mars before 2010.

2 Luckily the weather was great, so we _____ have a picnic.

3 My cousin _____ swim when he was three, but I still _____ .

4 The music was so loud that I _____ hear what you were saying.

5 If we don't finish early, we _____ see the programme on TV.

6 Anyone _____ do that!

哪個句子可能有一個以上的答案？

D 用 be able to 改寫以下句子，如下例：

I can get up late. I enjoy being able to get up late.

The reasons I enjoy holidays ...

1 I can wear casual clothes.   *I enjoy*

2 I can watch TV when I want. _____

3 I can see my friends._____

4 I can travel abroad. _____

5 I can stay up late. _____

第二編

33 Can、could、will 和 would（用於表達主動幫助和提出請求）
Can, could, will, would (offers and requests)

1 can I 或更有禮貌的 can I possibly 或 could I（possibly）可用於：

a 提出要為某人做某事：

Can I help you, sir?

Could I carry your suitcase for you, sir?

b 詢問是否可以做某事：
Can I take the last biscuit?
Could I borrow £10 from you, Sam? I'll pay you back soon.

2 可用 I'll 提議要做某事，但遠不如 can I 或 could I 正式：

I'll take you into town if you want.
I'll answer the door for you.

3 可用 can you 或更為禮貌的 could you
提出請求：

Can you help me with the washing-up, Harry, please?

可用 would you mind + -ing 提出請求；用 would you
mind not + -ing 請求某人停止做某事：

Would you mind answering a few questions, please?
Would you mind not smoking?
Would you mind not talking during the examination, please?

'**Could you** come here, please? I need some help.'

4 一個地位較他人重要的人用 would you 提出要求時，要比用 will you 顯得更有禮貌。
Would you 比 will you 更有禮貌：

Jane, **would you** open the letters on my desk, please?
Will you be quiet for a moment, please?

5 可用 would you like 向某人提議做某事：

Hugh, **would you** like another drink?
Would you like to come to Scotland with us?

33 練習 **Practice**

A 用 could 把下面的陳述句改寫成禮貌疑問句：

1 I want to have another cup of coffee. _____?
2 Give me a cigarette. _____?
3 Tell me when the train leaves. _____?
4 We want to have a table near the window. _____?
5 I want to have a ticket to London. _____?
6 I want to go home early today. _____?

B 用 would you like 把以下疑問句改寫成禮貌疑問句：

1 Do you want to watch TV now? _____?
2 Do you want soup with your meal? _____?
3 Do you want to go home now or later? _____?
4 Do you want sugar in your tea? _____?
5 Do you want me to type these letters? _____?
6 Do you want us to help you plan the meeting? _____?
7 Do you want a single or a double room? _____?
8 Do you want me to start work early tomorrow? _____?

C 參照例句，用 Would you mind...? 提出請求：

如：I'm hot. (open the window) _Would you mind opening the window?_

1 It's cold in here. (close the door) _____?
2 I can't concentrate. (turn the music down) _____?

3 I've got a (not smoke) cough.
_____?

4 We can't understand you. (not speak French)
_____?

5 The manager is busy at the moment. (wait a minute) _____?
6 I'm sorry, Simon's not here now. (leave a message) _____?

34 Would like 和 want（用於表達需要與願望）
Would like, want (wants and wishes)

1 談及需要某事時，可用 would like：

a would like to + 不定式：
   I **would like to be able** to speak several languages.
   They **would like to know** what time we'll be back home.

b would like + 名詞：
   They **would like seats** in the non-smoking section.
   We **would like an English-German dictionary**, please.

2 would 在代詞後面時，可用縮略形式 'd：

We**'d like** to go now, please.
He**'d like** to see you again on Thursday, if possible.
I**'d like** you to do this for homework, please.

3 否定式是 would not like 或 wouldn't like：

Don't be late. The boss **wouldn't like** that.

'I **wouldn't like** to meet him on a dark night.'

4 強調形式：would like 的強調形式是 would love；wouldn't like 的強調形式是 would hate：

I**'d love** another ice-cream!
You know what I**'d love**? I**'d love** to travel around the world.
We**'d hate** to live somewhere cold.

5 談及需要或渴望某事時用 want to：

a want to + 不定式；否定式是 "don't want to + 不定式"：
   I **wanted to be** a pilot when I was young.
   We **don't want to go** shopping this afternoon.
   Do you **want to come** with us?

b "want + 名詞"；否定式是 "don't want + 名詞"：
   Do you **want a cup of tea**?
   Who **wants another piece of cake**?
   I **don't want dogs** in my house.

注意 人們通常不用 I want 索要某物。這種用法不禮貌。
在商店裏不要説：'I want a packet of chewing gum.'
最好説：'**Can/could I have** a packet of chewing gum?'
或者説：'I**'d like** a packet of chewing gum, please.'

'I **'d like** a packet of chewing gum, please.'

34 練習 Practice

A 圖裏的人物想要些甚麼？根據圖的內容，找出與他們為何作出這樣的要求：

1 'Can I have a packet of cigarettes and a box of matches?'
2 'How much does it cost to stay in that hotel in France?'
3 'Where is Park Street, please?'
4 'Can I be excused, please?'
5 'I need flour, eggs, sugar, butter, milk and apples.'
6 'Please be quiet.'
7 'Could I ask you a few questions, Prime Minister? '
8 'Is this seat free?'

A He wants to leave the room.
B She wants to sit down.
C She wants to make a cake.
D They want to go to a party.
E She wants to get some information.
F They want a holiday.
G He wants to study.
H He wants to smoke.

B 請看這個清單。用 I'd like to...、 I'd love to...、 I wouldn't like to...或 I'd hate to...提出你對此清單的想法：

如：I'd love to learn how to fly.
I wouldn't like to wake up at 4 a.m. every day.

'I'd _____ to find a spider in my bed.'

speak English fluently
speak several languages well
be able to cook
meet your favourite singer
be famous
go to New York next week
be very rich
have a sports car
find a spider in my bed
be 100 years old
be in hospital
live in a haunted house
live in another country
work in a noisy factory
be a teacher/politician/stuntman
wake up at 11 a.m. every day

35 Have to、have got to、must 和 mustn't（用於表達責任義務）
Have to, have got to, must, mustn't (obligation)

1 表達某人有必要做某事，或者某事對某人很重要時，可用 must。否定式是 mustn't：

a 用於表達現在：

I **must** go now, I don't want to be late.

B 用於表達將來：

I **must** talk to him tomorrow afternoon.
You **mustn't** forget to phone me.

2 就非常重要的事情提出意見，或提出強烈建議，或向某人發出邀請，可用 must：

You **must** go and see the new Spielberg film. It's great.
This **is** a book that you really **must** read.
You **must** visit us.

3 表達不做某事很重要時，可用 must not 或 mustn't：

You **mustn't** take photos in the gallery, it's bad for the paintings.
I **mustn't** forget to write a cheque for the rent today.

4 談及某事必會發生，如某條法例，或某人認為某事很重要時，可用 has to 或 have to：

Because Sandra is an au-pair, she **has to** get up early and help with the children's breakfast.
Val won't be in work today. She **has to** see the doctor.

5 表達不必要做某事時，可用 don't have to：

You **don't have** to do the whole exercise.
Tomorrow is Sunday, so I **don't have to** get up early.

6 must 和 have to 的過去時都是 had to 或 didn't have to：

I **had to** go to London yesterday for a meeting.
The doctor told me I **had to** stop smoking.
'**Did** you **have to** wait long for the bus?'

7 do、does 和 did 與 have to 和 not have to 連用，可構成疑問句：

'When **does** Dave **have to** go back to work?'
'**Do** you **have to** book a table in that restaurant?'
'**Did** everyone **have to** wear a uniform before?'

8 在非正式英語中可用 have got to 代替 have to：

It's late. We**'ve got to** go.
Where **have you got to** send that letter?

A 你是一家公司的經理，正和一位新僱員談話。請在你最看重下屬的那些特點旁打勾（✓）：

work hard	speak good English	be smart	know how to type	
have long hair	be polite	arrive early	be punctual	be organized

現在用 must 向新僱員交代工作：

1 _____   3 _____

2 _____   4 _____

B 請看以下標誌。它們傳遞的全都是你必須做甚麼和不得做甚麼的信息。用 must 或 mustn't 完成以下句子：

如：This sign means you mustn't drive over 30 mph.

1 This sign means you _____.
2 This sign means you _____.
3 This sign means you _____.
4 This sign means you _____.
5 This sign means you _____.
6 This sign means you _____.
7 This sign means you _____.
8 This sign means you _____.

C 你年輕時的學校生活是怎樣的？用 had to 或 didn't have to 完成以下句子：

1 _____ stand up when the teacher came into the room.
2 _____ wear a uniform.
3 _____ do a lot of homework.
4 _____ have short hair.
5 _____ study languages.
6 _____ eat at school.
7 _____ take a lot of exams.

D 用 has to 或 have to 完成以下句子：

1 Because Jill is a student she _____ read a lot of books.
2 Frank's a sportsman. He _____ keep very fit.
3 If you want to be a pilot you _____ have good eyesight.
4 Before you can drive a car you _____ take a test.
5 You _____ be 18 or over to see some films.
6 If you break something in a shop you _____ pay for it.

再請用 has got to 或 have got to 重寫上面的句子。

36 Should、ought 和 had better（用於表達提建議）
Should, ought, had better (advice)

1 談及在某一情況下應做的事時，可用 should 或 ought to：

Jane's in hospital. We **should** visit her.
You **should** go and see that film. It's great.
We **ought to** leave now, it's getting late.
You **ought to** be polite to people you don't know.

談及在某一情況下不應做某事時，可用 should not（或 shouldn't）和 ought not to：

Children **shouldn't** go to bed late.
You **shouldn't** eat too much chocolate, it's bad for you.
If you don't like people, you **ought not to** be a teacher.

2 建議某人要做甚麼事時，可用 should 或 ought to：

You **should** see a doctor if you are in pain.
You **ought to** buy a new car. Yours is dangerous.
You **should** spend your money carefully.

建議不要做甚麼事時，可用 shouldn't 或 ought not to：

You **shouldn't** drink and drive.
You **ought not to** smoke so much.

3 要發表意見時，可用 I think...should 和 I think...ought to。否定式是 I don't think...should 或 I don't think...ought to：

I think we ought to go now.
Do you think I should buy the red or the blue dress?
My friends don't think I should go to Britain next year.

4 提出意見或建議時，也可用 "had better + 不定式" 或 "'d better"。否定式是："had better not +不定式"：

We'd better leave now, or we'll be late.

You'd better not go out. It's raining.

36 練習 Practice

A 把左欄與右欄相關的部分連成句子：

1 If you feel hot	you should put the heating on.
2 If you are cold	you ought to see a doctor.
3 If you feel hungry	you should see a dentist.
4 If you feel sleepy	you should go to bed now.
5 If you don't feel well	you ought to open the window.
6 If your teeth hurt	you should have something to eat.
7 If you don't understand something	you should ask for help.

B 根據以下的詞彙，分別用 should 和 shouldn't 寫出一個肯定建議和一個否定建議：

1 In a hospital (be calm) (make a lot of noise)

_____   _____

2 At work (arrive late) (work hard)

_____   _____

3 On the motorway (drive carefully)   (drive close to the car in front)

_____   _____

4 In the library (play music) (work in silence)

_____   _____

再請用 ought to 和 ought not to 回答一次。

C 請看圖。然後用 I think you should... 或 I don't think you should...向朋友提出建議：

1 I've got an exam tomorrow morning. What should I do?

_____

3 I found a small sum of money on the ground this morning. What should I do?

_____

5 I've been invited to a party by a group of people I don't really know. But my favourite film is on TV. What should I do?

_____

2 I saw someone driving dangerously in town. What should I do?

_____

4 The person next to me in the exam was cheating. What should I do?

_____

6 I need a holiday. I have enough money for either a weekend in New York, or a week in Scotland, I can't decide. Where should I go?

_____

37 | 非人稱代詞 it　Impersonal *it*

1 it 可用來談及時間或日期：

What time is **it**?	**It's one o'clock.**	**It's nearly two o'clock.**
What day is **it** today?	**It's Monday.**	**It's the first of January.**

2 "it + since" 可用來表述某事是多久以前發生的：

It's two weeks **since** I washed the car. **It**'s nearly a year **since** our last holiday.
It's a long time **since** you last wrote to me.

3 it 可用來談及天氣：

It's very cold. It'll be nice and warm. It was very hot in Brazil.
I think **it's going to rain. It's** often **very windy** in autumn.

4 "it + 形容詞 + ...ing" 或 "it + to- 不定式小句..."，可用來表達一般想法：

It's great living in London. **It's dangerous driving** fast at night.
It's difficult **to** learn a foreign language. **It's** not safe **to** go out at night.

可以用 It is/was...of you/him/her to...表達想法：

It was clever **of you to** remember my name. **It is** kind **of you to** write to me.

也可以用 It is/was for...to...表達想法：

It's easy **for** anyone **to** make a mistake. **It**'s hard **for** me **to** get up early in the morning.

5 It + (that) ...可用來發表意見：

It's great **that** she has passed her exams. **It**'s surprising Alan didn't send you a birthday card.

六個特別常用的表達式：

It's lucky ...　　It's nice ...　　It's a good thing ...　　It's a pity ...　　It's possible ...　　It's funny ...

It's lucky it's not raining. **It's a pity** it's so cold. **It's possible** that we'll get a letter tomorrow.
It's funny we haven't met before. **It's a good thing** you can speak English.

6 可用 I like it、I don't like、I hate it... 來表達意見：

I like it here. **I hate it** when you leave.

7 可用 Who is it？來詢問某人是誰。可用 It's 來確認某人的身份：

A Who's that over there? B **It's** Bill.

8 一些與 it 連用的常用表達式：

It doesn't matter ...　　It takes ages ...　　It takes a week ...

A I'm afraid I'll be a bit late.
B Don't worry. **It doesn't matter.**

A How long does it take to get to London?
B **It takes** about an hour by train.

37 練習 Practice

A 用 It's a pity、It's lucky 和 It's a good thing... 完成以下句子：

1 ___It's a pity___ English is such a difficult language.

2 Everything's very expensive. _____ we brought plenty of money with us.

3 There's nothing to eat. _____ we had a big breakfast.

4 It's nice to see you, but _____ Ian isn't here too.

5 It's awfully cold in here. _____ we are wearing warm clothes.

6 It's very crowded in here. _____ we didn't come earlier.

7 He's a very clever boy. _____ he's so lazy.

B 用以下表達式完成對話：

> Oh, it's great being in London.   Hello, it's me, Angela.   it's ages since I saw you.   Who is it?
> It's nice to talk to you.   Well, it's a bit cold, but it's not too bad.

A: Hello. _Who is it?_ _____

A: Oh, hi! What's it like in England?

A: What about the weather?

A: _____

B: _____

B: _____

B: _____

_____

B: Well, _____

用以下的表達式繼續對話：

> I didn't like it very much on the plane.   it was a very long journey.   it's four o'clock in the morning.
> Was it very uncomfortable?   Eight o'clock.   I didn't know it was so late.   It's really nice to hear from you.

A: Did you have a good journey?

A: Why not?

A: What time is it over there?

A: Well, _____

_____ here in Singapore.

A: Don't worry. _____

B: Not really. _____

B: No, it was comfortable, but _____

_____

B: _____ why?

B: Oh, I'm sorry. _____

85

38 雙賓語動詞 Verbs with two objects

1 有些動詞常有兩個賓語 —— 一個間接賓語，一個直接賓語：

I'll buy **some chocolates** (direct object) **for the children** (indirect object).
I'll buy **the children** (indirect object) **some chocolates** (direct object).

She wrote **a long letter** (direct object) **to her mother** (indirect object).
She wrote **her mother** (indirect object) **a long letter** (direct object).

2 以下動詞的間接賓語通常置於 for 的後面：

| book | get | buy | keep | bring | make |
| cook | pour | cut | prepare | find | save |

They kept a place **for Jack**.

Will you bring something **for the children**?

Could you pour a cup of coffee **for your mother**?

I'll book a room in the hotel **for you**.

She cooked a great meal **for us**.

I bought some flowers **for her**.

Save a piece of cake for me too please.

3 以下動詞的間接賓語通常置於 to 的後面：

| give | post | tell | lend | promise | write | pay |
| hand | read | offer | sell | pass | show | teach |

They say they posted the letter **to you** last week. He promised it **to me**.
Show it **to Bill** when you've seen it. Do you think you could lend it **to us**?

4 非常短的間接賓語可直接放在動詞的後面：

Give **Mary** my love. She sent **her sister** a birthday card.
He cooked **them** a wonderful meal. Ken bought **his teacher** a present.

A 改寫以下句子，把間接賓語換成 him、her 或 them：

1 He cooked a nice meal for all his friends. _He cooked them a nice meal._

2 She lent some money to her grandmother. _____

3 Hand that plate to your brother. _____

4 Who'll read a story to the children? _____

5 I've made some coffee for father. _____

6 Jack's gone to get some water for his mother. _____

7 He offered the job to a young girl. _____

B 改寫以下句子，把間接賓語置於 to 或 for 之後：

1 I have booked them seats. (the children) _I have booked seats for the children._

2 Can you make them a cup of tea? (everyone) _____

3 I've written her a letter. (my sister) _____

4 Who's going to cook them supper? (the family) _____

5 We can show them our photographs. (all the visitors) _____

6 Could you cut them some bread? (your brothers and sisters) _____

7 I sold her my old skis. (your friend) _____

C 完成以下句子，描述 Diana 送給家人的是些甚麼禮物：

1 She bought a bicycle _for her little brother, Simon._

2 She gave Helen. _____.

3 She bought a pipe _____.

4 She sent some flowers _____.

5 She bought _____ a box of chocolates.

6 She gave a dictionary _____.

7 She bought a nice new teapot _____.

8 She gave _____ a pullover.

合上書本，看看 Diana 的禮物你記住了多少。

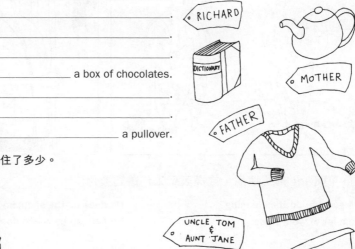

RICHARD

DICTIONARY

MOTHER

FATHER

LITTLE SIMON

GRANDFATHER

HELEN

UNCLE TOM & AUNT JANE

CHOCOLATES

GRANDMOTHER

39 | Make and do

1 make 可與表示以下內容的名詞連用：

計劃 (Plans)： appointment arrangement choice decision plan
旅遊 (Travel)： journey tour trip visit
談話與聲音 (Taking and sounds)：comment noise point promise sound speech suggestion
食物與飲料 (Food and drink)：breakfast a cup of tea some coffee a meal a sandwich

I think I **made the wrong decision**.
In 1978 she **made a trip** to America.
If you **make a promise** you have to keep it.

Let's **make a plan**.
We'll **make a short visit** if we have time.
Don't **make too much noise**.

2 我們説 make something，意思是造出某種新的東西：

Sheila **makes** all her own clothes. You can **make** petrol from coal.

3 一些與 make 連用的常見表達式：

make friends (with) — **make** a mistake — **make** some money
make a difference — two and two **make** four — I think Pedro would **make** a good teacher

4 do 可與 -ing 形式連用，或與表示工作的詞連用：

Who's going to **do the cleaning**?
I have **a lot of work** to do.

He **does** all **the shopping** and I **do the washing**.
He gets up early and **does a hard day's work**.

5 如果一個名詞能明確表達一個動詞的意思，那麼 do 與該名詞連用，就可以代替這個動詞：

You must **do your teeth** before you go to bed.
I'll **do the kitchen** if you **do the flowers**.

Have you **done the dishes** yet?
Do I need to **do my hair**?

6 一些與 do 連用的常見表達式：

do well　**do** badly　**do** your homework　**do** an exercise

39 練習 Practice

A 用 make 或 do 完成以下句子：

1 Don't forget to _____ your homework.
2 Read your book carefully and _____ the exercise on page 52.
3 If you want to see Mr. Brown you must _____ an appointment.
4 I have to _____ a speech at the meeting tomorrow.
5 The baby is going to sleep. Try not to _____ a noise.
6 I'll _____ the garden if you _____ the house.
7 We have to _____ a long journey. We should try to leave early.
8 Some pop stars and sports stars _____ a lot of money.

9 'Don't be frightened. He just wants to _____ friends.'

B 完成以下疑問句：

1 Have you ever had to _____ a speech?
2 Who _____ most of the washing-up in your house?
3 If you _____ a promise, do you always keep it?
4 Do you _____ friends easily?
5 Was it easy to _____ this exercise?

合上書本，看看你記住了多少個疑問句。

10 'Just be careful and try not to _____ a mistake.'

C 用 make 或 do 完成以下對話：

1

A: What work do you want to _____ when you leave school?
B: If I _____ well in my exams I'd like to be a doctor.
A: Then you would _____ a lot of money.
B: I don't mind about the money. I just want to _____ an interesting job.

2

A: Are you going to _____ a cup of coffee?
B: I have to _____ the dishes first.
A: Ok then. I'll _____ the coffee, while you _____ the washing-up.
B: Right. While we have coffee we can _____ plans for our holiday this year.

第二編

不具數名詞(二)(有關不具數名詞的內容參見第十八單元)
Uncount nouns (2) (See Unit 18 for patterns with uncount nouns)

1 複習第十八單元：

不具數名詞沒有複數形式，不能與 a 和 an 連用，但可以與 some 連用：

I bought **some rice** and **some milk**.

2 有些名詞在英文裏是不具數名詞，如：

advice	homework	machinery
baggage	information	money
equipment	knowledge	news
furniture	luggage	traffic

She gave me **a lot of useful advice**.
There's **not much traffic** in town at midday.

'Do you think you could help me
with my **luggage**?'

3 如果想按複數含義使用上面的詞，通常要
用到下面這兩個詞：

bit: She gave me a few **bits of advice**. I have a couple of **bits of news** for you.
piece: They had only a few **pieces of furniture**.

如果想表明所談及的是單數物品時，可以用 a piece of 或 a bit of：

A calculator is **a useful piece of equipment**. That's a **heavy bit of luggage**.

4 以 -ing 結尾的名詞是不具數名詞：

Living at home is much cheaper. **Skiing** is an expensive hobby.

5 許多抽象名詞都是不具數名詞，下面是一些最常用的抽象名詞：

time trouble weather love fun travel work happiness music

We had lovely **weather** in Spain and Greece.

Travel by train isn't always comfortable.

6 有些名詞有兩個含義，一種含義是可數的，另一種則是不可數的：

Hurry up. We haven't **much time**. I've been to Athens **three times**.

40 練習 **Practice**

A 用以下的詞完成句子：

advice information news homework money traffic furniture equipment

1 I want to buy some stereo equipment. I wonder if you could give me some _____ .

2 Did you hear the _____ on the radio this morning?

3 I can't go out tonight. I have too much _____ .

4 They bought a lot of new _____ for the dining room.

5 He has two computers and lots of other electronic _____ .

6 I'd like some _____ about trains to Oxford please.

7 How much _____ will we need for the journey?

8 There's always a lot of _____ in the rush hour.

B 用括號裏的詞改寫以下句子：

1 Let me give you some advice. (a piece)
   Let me give you a piece of advice.

2 There was some old furniture in the room. (a few bits of)
   _____

3 I have some homework to do. (a couple of bits)
   _____

4 The fire destroyed some expensive machinery. (a piece)
   _____

5 I wonder if you could help me with some information. (a bit)
   _____

6 I have some good news for you and some bad news. (a piece; a bit)
   _____

7 A computer is very expensive equipment. (a piece of)

8 They had a lot of luggage. (more than a dozen pieces)
   _____

C 用以下的詞完成句子：

fun music trouble happiness weather travel work

1 If you behave badly you will get into a lot of _____ .

2 We have lovely _____ in summer and autumn.

3 I've got a lot of _____ to do before I can go home tonight.

4 We had a lot of _____ when we went out last night.

5 That piano sonata is one of my favourite pieces of _____ .

6 Money doesn't always bring _____ .

7 I enjoy foreign _____ .

第二編

41 量詞（一）與 of 連用的結構
Quantifiers (1) — patterns with *of*

1 談及一特定人群或一特定類事物時，要用下面的結構：

All of the children enjoyed the party.   **All of** us enjoyed the party.
They didn't eat **all of** the cakes.   They didn't eat **all of** them.
We picked **some of** the flowers.   We picked **some of** them.

2 談及兩個人或兩件事時，要用 both：

Both of the girls stayed at home.   **Both of** them stayed at home.

要用 neither 進行否定：
Neither of the boys stayed at home.   **Neither of** you stayed at home.

3 下面的結構可與數字和分數連用：

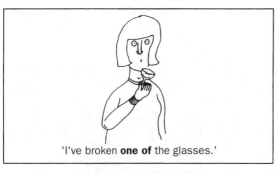

'I've broken **one of** the glasses.'

'I've read about **a quarter of** it.'

About half of the pupils are girls.   **Two of** them were very big, and one was quite small.

4 下面這些表達式還可以用來：

表達較大的數字或數量：a lot of lots of many of plenty of
I've read **lots of** the books in the library. I've read **lots of** them.

表達半數以上：I know **most of** the people in your class.

表達較小的數字或數量：I've got some new magazines. Would you like to borrow **a few of** them?

表達甚麼都沒有：none of   not ... any of

None of us enjoyed the programme.

She did**n't** like **any of** them.

5 上面各項中的表達式全都可以和物主詞連用：

I'm going to invite **all of my** friends. I've read **most of your** books.

A 根據真實情況完成以下句子：

1 _____ the people in my country speak English.

2 _____ the children in my country must go to school until they are _____ .

3 _____ the young people in my country go to university.

4 _____ the people in my country live in large towns or cities.

5 _____ the people in my country live in villages.

6 _____ my classmates are men/boys.

7 _____ the TV programmes at the weekend are interesting.

8 _____ my friends live in my town/village.

B 用 one、two、all、both、some、most、none 和 neither 完成以下句子：

1 _Two of_ _____ the men are wearing suits.
2 _____ the boys are playing.
3 _____ the boys are reading.
4 _____ the women is sitting down.
5 _____ the men are sitting down.
6 _____ the adults are standing up.
7 _____ the children are reading.

8 _____ the women are wearing suits.
9 _____ the girls are playing.
10 _____ the girls are reading.
11 _____ the women are standing up.
12 _____ the women are wearing dresses.
13 _____ the children are playing.
14 _____ the men is wearing a pullover.

根據上圖的內容造六個句子，三個句子要根據事實，三個句子不用根據事實：

1 _____

2 _____

3 _____

4 _____

5 _____

6 _____

合上書本，看看圖中的內容你能記住多少。

42 量詞（二）（複習第四十一單元的結構。該單元所有的例句都是與具數名詞連用的。）
Quantifiers(2)(Review the patterns in Unit 41. All the examples there are with count nouns.)

1 以下詞彙可與不具數名詞連用：

all of   some of   a lot of   lots of   plenty of   most of   none of   a bit of

'Don't hurry, we have **plenty of time**.'

He earns **a lot of money**.

We've finished **most of** the bread. Could you buy some more?

2 可以用 they/them all...、you all...、we/us all...、they/them both...、we/us both...：

After the game **they both** went home together. I know them and I like **them both**.

We all live in a yellow submarine. There is plenty of room for **us all**.

All 和 both 要置於主要動詞之前：

We will **all miss** the train. They have **both missed** the bus.

或置於 is、was、were 之後：

We missed the train and we **were all** late. They **were both** tired.

3 在第四十一單元我們已學過表述一特定群體的結構：

如用作泛指時，這些結構不要與 of the 連用：

All children enjoy a good party. We picked **some** flowers.
Most children start school quite young. **Many** people all over the world learn English.

4 也可以用 a lot of...、lots of...、plenty of...：

A lot of children start school at the age of five.
Lots of people all over the world learn English.

42 練習 Practice

A 用以下詞彙完成句子。有時要用單數形式，有時要用複數形式：

traffic　　shop　　bread　　car　　　luggage　　advice　　subject　　house　　help
animal　　building　furniture　country　idea　　　friend　　weather　　rice

1 Would you like some ___*bread*___ and butter?

2 There were a lot of _____ on the road.

3 I have left most of my _____ in the car.

4 Most of the University _____ in Cambridge seem to be quite old.

5 We saw some interesting _____ in the zoo.

6 My grandfather gave me a lot of good _____ when I was a child.

7 We visited a lot of different _____ last year.

8 We had a lot of really bad _____ last winter.

9 They have built a lot of new _____ in the last few years.

10 Would you like some more _____ with your meat?

11 Plenty of my _____ live near London.

12 I enjoyed most of the _____ I studied at school.

13 Most of the _____ will be closed for the holiday.

14 We need to buy some new _____ for the bedroom.

15 She's very clever. She has lots of good _____ .

16 There is a lot of _____ in town around lunch time.

17 Andrew was very kind. He gave us a lot of _____ .

B 用 all of them/us 、 both of them/us 改寫以下句子：

1 I like them both.　　　　　　　　*I like both of them.*

2 There is room for them all.　　_____

3 They all wanted to come.　　_____

4 We both stayed at home.　　_____

5 They wanted to see us both.　_____

6 They all live in a yellow submarine.　_____

7 We both come from Liverpool.　_____

8 There is room for us both.　_____

43 量詞（三）few、a few 和 any
Quantifiers (3) — few; a few; any

1 a few 的含義和 some 一樣：

We were quite tired so **a few** of us went to bed early.

Red Riding Hood picked **a few** flowers for her grandmother.

few 的含義和 not many 一樣：

They were all very excited. **Few** of them went to bed before midnight.

It was a dreadful accident. **Few** passengers survived.

2 Any 可與具數名詞和不具數名詞連用：

當指某一個或任何一個都無所謂時，any 可用於肯定陳述句：

You can buy it at **any** book shop. You can hire a car at almost **any** airport.

Any ten-year-old knows how to use a computer. I'd like **any** book by Jane Austen.

由於 any 有這層含義，所以也常用在否定句和疑問句裏：

There aren't **any** tomatoes left. There's some sugar, but there isn't **any** rice.

'Have you got **any** children?'

Are they in **any** danger?

但我們一般用 some 來提要求或建議，因為要求或建議是用於特定的事物。

Could you lend me **some** money? Could I have **some** tomatoes please?

Would you like **some** tea? Here, have **some** cake.

練習 Practice

A 用 some、a few 或 not many、few 完成以下句子：

1 We invited a lot of people to the meeting but ___*not many/few*___ came.
2 I am going to buy _____ things for supper.
3 There are lots of girls in my class but _____ boys.
4 Nobody wanted to go out in the rain, but _____ people had to.
5 We all wanted to go home early but _____ people had to stay behind and work.
6 We saw lots of interesting animals and _____ birds.
7 Lots of us wanted to go skiing but _____ of us could spare the time.

8 I don't like dangerous sports but _____ of my friends do.

B 用 some 或 any 填空：

1 Would you like ___*some*___ coffee?
2 We've got plenty of rice, but we haven't ___*any*___ potatoes.
3 I'd like _____ apples and _____ oranges please.
4 You can buy stamps at _____ post office.
5 I think _____ child who has a bicycle should have lessons in road safety.
6 No thanks, I don't want _____ coffee, but I'd like_____ tea please.
7 We bought _____ fish but we didn't buy _____ meat.
8 She likes _____ film about animals.
9 I would like to go with you, but I haven't _____ time to spare.
10 You can get your car mended at _____ good garage.
11 It's a very common word. You will find it in _____ dictionary.
12 A: Can you lend me _____ money?
   B: I'm sorry. I haven't _____ .
13 Almost _____ bank will change traveller's cheques.

14 _____ children are quite dangerous on their bicycles.

名詞修飾其他名詞 Nouns to describe other nouns

1 英語中，常把一個名詞置於另一個名詞之前，以便對後一個名詞作更多説明：

A What sort of dress was she wearing?　　A Did you leave it in the dining room?

B It was a beautiful **silk dress**.　　B No. It's on the **kitchen table**.

2 這種做法的目的是：

a 表述某物由甚麼材料造成：

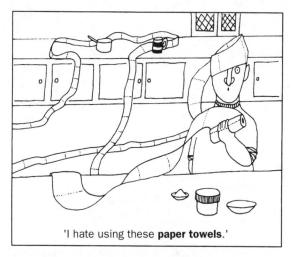

'I hate using these **paper towels**.'

They were kept in a **glass case**. He put it in a **cardboard box**. She wore an expensive **silk dress**.

注意 有些用木頭製成的東西，通常用 wooden 來表述：

He put it in a **wooden box**. There was an old **wooden table** in the corner.

b 表述某物在何處：

Put these flowers on the **dining-room table**. It's in the **kitchen cupboard**.
London hotels are very expensive.

c 表述某事開始的時間：

Are you going to the **six o'clock class**? Let's have a **Christmas party**.

d 表述某物的尺寸或重量：

She bought some milk in a **one litre carton**. There was a **ten foot wall** round the house.

e 表述某物的價格：

He wore a **fifteen hundred dollar suit**. She bought a **five dollar ticket**.

f 表述某物是關於哪方面的：

Where's my **history book**? I'm listening to the **sports news**.

3 常用名詞是由動詞加 -er 構成的：

He got a job as a **window cleaner**. She's a **good language learner**.

注意 第一個名詞幾乎從來不用複數形式。如：

A man who cleans windows is a window cleaner.
A cheque for a hundred pounds is a hundred pound cheque.

但 sports 一詞例外，如要説："一個運動場地"，就要説成 "a sports field"。

44 練習 Practice

A 寫出下面是甚麼樣的事物。在括號中標示它們屬於本單元的哪一種用法：

1	a belt made of leather	_a leather belt (2a)_

2 a handkerchief made out of paper

3 a table made of wood

4 a bag made out of plastic

5 a chair in the kitchen

6 furniture used in the garden

7 seats found in an aeroplane

8 a meeting on Thursday

9 a party on someone's birthday

10 an appointment at two o'clock

11 a traveller's cheque for fifty pounds

12 a note worth ten pounds

13 a bag weighing on hundred kilos

14 a baby weighing three kilos

15 a book about cookery

16 a magazine about fashion

17 the page about sports

18 someone who sells newspapers

19 someone who teaches languages

20 someone who plays cards

注意 名詞修飾名詞的用法在英語中太普遍了，所以不可能將所有的情況一一列出。

有時，由於兩個名詞經常一起使用，以致後來變成了一個詞，如：You dry your hair with a <u>hairdryer</u>.。

B 你能把下面的詞和圖連起來嗎？

1 a story teller	2 a dishwasher	3 a tin opener	4 an ice cube
5 a cigarette lighter	6 an egg-timer	7 a petrol station	8 a dog kennel
9 a carpet sweeper	10 a hairdryer		

45 地點表達式 Expressions of place

1 地點介詞可用來表述某物在何處。最常用的地點介詞有：

above　behind　below　beside　between　in　near　on　opposite　over　under

There's a poster **on** the wall **above** the bed.
You can see some shoes **under** the bed.
The lamp is **on** the small table **beside** the bed.
The table is **between** the bed and the door.
The boy's clothes are **in** the wardrobe.
There is a tennis racket **behind** the wardrobe.
The wardrobe is **near** the window.
The window is **opposite** the door.
He has put his coat **over** the arm of the chair.
His books are **on** the shelf **below** the window.

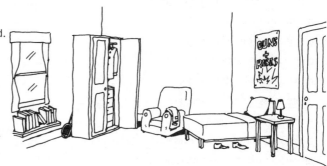

2 有些介詞是由一個以上的詞構成的：

I was standing **in front of** Jim.
Jim was **next to** Jane.

3 也可以用副詞或副詞短語表述某人或某物在何處：

abroad　away　downstairs　upstairs　here　indoors　outdoors
there　anywhere　everywhere　somewhere　nowhere

Paddy doesn't live in England now. He lives **abroad**.
I'm sorry, you can't talk to Mr Smith. He is **away** just now.
The kitchen is **downstairs**, but the dining-room is **upstairs**.
Sarah was **here**, but now she has gone.

I'd love to visit the United States.
I've never been **there**.

'Mummy, I can't find my shirt **anywhere**!'
'I've looked **everywhere**.'
'Well, it must be **somewhere**.
Shirts don't just disappear.'
'It's **nowhere** I can think of.'

I want a job where I can work **outdoors**. I need fresh
air, and I don't want to stay **indoors** all day.

45 練習 Practice

A 請看圖A及圖B，然後讀下面的句子並標示它們描寫的是圖A還是圖B：

1 The TV is on a table in the corner. _____
2 There is a video below the TV. _____
3 There are books on the shelf above the table. _____
4 The flowers are in a vase on the table next to the window. _____
5 The painting is opposite the sofa. _____
6 There is a cat under the table. _____
7 There is a poster of Paris on the wall. _____
8 The flowers are between two photographs. _____
9 The light switch is next to the door. _____
10 The TV is between the window and the door. _____
11 The cat is on the rug between the table and the sofa. _____
12 There are some books behind the sofa. _____
13 The light is above the sofa. _____
14 There is a crack in the ceiling above the TV. _____

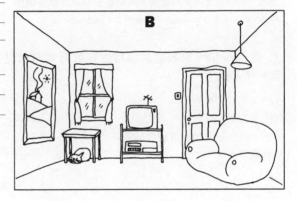

B 用括號裏的詞完成以下句子：

1 I haven't always lived _____ you know. I've also lived _____, in France, Germany and Thailand. (abroad/here)

2 It's very difficult to buy Italian ice-cream _____, that's why I always eat lots of it when I am _____ on holiday. (there/here)

3 I am going to be _____ in the office for a few hours now, but you won't be able to see me tomorrow, because I shall be _____ at a conference. (away/here)

4 Frances and Jonathan live _____, on the ground floor; my flat is on the first floor, and Mr Jones lives _____, on the second floor. (downstairs/upstairs)

5 I enjoy working _____, except when it is raining. Then I prefer to be _____. (indoors/outdoors)

C 用以下幾對詞彙完成以下句子：

under/beside   on/under   behind/next to

1 Keep your shoes _____ the bed, not _____ it!

2 If you want to see, put the desk _____ the light, not _____ it.

3 I prefer to sit _____ my friends not _____ them.

101

46 時間表達式 Expressions of time

1 可用 during（或 in）來表述：

a 某事發生在某一時間段：

The phone rang **during** the interview.
I went out once **during** the morning.

b 某事經常發生在一個階段的開始至結束，或發生在這個階段內的某一時間：

We put the radiators on **during** the winter.
We were very busy **during** the holidays.

We were very busy
during the holidays.

注意 不能用 during 來表述某事持續了多久。During 表述的是某事發生於何時，而不是某事持續的時間。

注意 during 後面要跟名詞，不能跟數詞或介詞。例如：
My parents were in Dublin ~~during~~ for two weeks.

2 可用 before 來表述某事發生在某時或某事之前，可用 after 來表述某事發生在某時或某事之後：

We will finish **before** six o'clock.
Turn the light off **before** you leave.

提示：before 和 after 可與名詞或短語連用。

> Can I talk to you after the lesson?

3 可用 from...until、from...till、from...to 來表述某事開始於一個時間，結束於另一時間：

I waited for you **from** 4 **to** 6 o'clock! The shops are open **from** 9 **until** 5.

4 可用 by 來表述某事會在某時或早於某時發生：

I must be home **by** seven tonight. (= not later than 7)
Give me your work **by** Friday lunch-time. (=Wednesday or Thursday would be better, but Friday morning is possible.)

5 可用 about 或 around 來表示籠統時間或大概時間：

> I'll see you at about eleven.

> Someone called at around half-past six.

A 用以下短語完成句子：

by six   during the holidays   by now   during the storm   by 2020   during the morning
by the end of the week   during the demonstration   by bedtime   during the lesson

1 All the lights went out _____.

2 Give him a ring. He should be home _____.

3 I had a lazy time. I didn't do much _____.

4 The forecast said that the weather will get better _____.

5 If we catch the next train we can be in Cardiff _____.

6 Colin fell asleep _____.

7 The population of England will probably reach 65 million _____.

8 The police said that no one was arrested _____.

9 Please call after 12.30, because we are always busy _____.

10 I'm staying in a Youth Hostel and I have to be in _____.

B 選用正確的時間表達式來完成以下句子：

1 The postman comes *at around/from* eight in the morning.

2 It rained *after/during* the night.

3 *Before/By* the end of the week the group had visited all
   the most important sights of the capital.

4 I think the film starts *at about/from* 6.45 tonight.

5 Eva could speak quite well *during/after* two weeks in the
   country.

6 Put your boots on *before/after* you go out!

C 用 from、before、after、until 完成以下句子：

1 What are you going to do _____ school today?

2 The skiing season is _____ October _____ April.

3 Have I got time for a bath _____ we go out?

4 The coach leaves at 5.20, so get to the station _____ that.

5 The banks are only open _____ Monday _____ Friday.

6 You should always wash your hands _____ you eat.

7 My grandparents often have a short sleep _____ lunch.

8 Most people feel a little nervous _____ an examination.

D 參照下面列舉的事情，把你平常在上午以及在晚上要做的事情寫成句子：

read a paper have a shower get dressed watch TV go out with friends
go to work/school write letters brush your teeth polish your shoes relax

47 方式副詞 Adverbs of manner

1 大多數方式副詞都是在形容詞後面加 -ly 構成的：

bad — **badly**　quick — **quickly**　beautiful — **beautifully**　slow — **slowly**　careful — **carefully**

2 構成副詞後拼寫有時會有少許變化：

-le 變成 -ly：　　　　gentle — **gently**
-y 變成 -ily：　　　　easy — **easily**
-ic 變成 -ically：　　automatic — **automatically**
-ue 變成 -uly：　　　true — **truly**
-ll 變成 -lly：　　　　full — **fully**

3 像 friendly 和 lonely 這樣已經以 -ly 結尾的形容詞沒有副詞形式，可以用
in a friendly way 或 in a friendly manner 這兩種方式來表述：

He smiled at me **in a friendly way**.

4 方式副詞可用來表述某人是如何做某事的，
或某事是如何發生的：

I'm afraid I sing very **badly**.
The children sat and waited **quietly** for the dentist.
Read these instructions **carefully**.

Sarah drives very **slowly**.

5 提示：形容詞提供有關名詞的信息，副詞提供有關動詞的信息：

There was heavy rain all day: It rained **heavily** all day.
He's a quick reader: He reads **quickly**.

6 與形容詞 good 相對應的方式副詞是 well：

Luke is a good tennis player. He played **well** in the match.
I'm not a good skier: I don't ski very **well**.

7 有些方式副詞和形容詞同形。最常見的是 fast、hard、late、loud、early：

They drove down the motorway **fast**.

The class started **late** and finished **early**.

47 練習 Practice

A 先把下面的形容詞變成副詞，再把它們正確歸類：

1 -ly	2 -ily	3 -ically	4 -lly
____	____	____	____
____	____	____	____
____	____	____	____

polite happy soft angry comfortable helpful fluent
nice sudden sad frantic reasonable dramatic dull

B 現在用上面的副詞完成以下句子：

1 I know someone who can speak three languages _____ .

2 This is a very popular shop because everything is _____ priced.

3 Classical music was playing _____ in the background in the restaurant.

4 'Get out of my office!' the manager shouted _____ .

5 'Do you mind if I smoke?' he asked _____ .

6 The train stopped _____ and I nearly fell out of my seat.

7 'Did you find the money you lost?' I asked. Jim shook his head _____ and said no.

8 The teacher waited until we were sitting _____, and then began her lesson.

C 回答以下疑問句，如下例：

Do you know anyone who is a good tennis player?
Yes, my brother (father, friend). He plays very well.

或：

No, I don't know anyone who plays well.

你知道誰是……（Do you know anyone who ...）？：

1 is a quick reader?
2 is a good dancer?
3 is a slow eater?
4 is a dangerous driver?
5 is a good singer?
6 is a fast talker?

你做得如何？哪些事你能做好？哪些事你做不好？

D 在每句選出一個詞彙完成句子：

1 Unemployment is a *serious/seriously* problem now.

2 The train went *slow/slowly* through the mountains.

3 I didn't realize that you were *good/well* friends with Jack.

4 It rained *heavy/heavily* all day.

5 We heard some *loud/loudly* noises upstairs.

6 The countryside here is *beautiful/beautifully*.

48 At 和 in（用於地點） At, in (place)

1 可用 at 來表述：

a 特定場所：
I was **at my friend's house**.
We waited **at the bus stop** for ages.
Neil wasn't **at work**. I think he's ill.
Let's stay **at home** tonight.

b 地址：
She lives **at 5, Regent Street**.

c 公共場所或機構：
I'll be **at the station** at nine.
We met **at university** in 1985.

d 商店或工作場所：
He's **at the doctor's** now.

e 有組織的社交活動：
Were you **at Steve's party**?
He spoke **at the conference** last year.
We were **at the theatre** last night.

They arrested him **at the airport**.

f 旅途中的一個地方：
Does this bus stop **at Sainsbury's**?
The London train calls **at Bath and Reading**.
We stopped **at Oxford** on the way home.

g 某地方的某些部分，可與 back、front、top、bottom、end 等連用：
The Smiths live **at the end of the road**.
The bathroom is **at the top of the house.**
The answers are **at the back of the book.**

2 可用 in 來表述：

a 國家或地區：
They're **in Spain** now.
We took these photos **in the mountains**.

b 城鎮、鄉村或較大的地方：
My parents used to live **in Bath**.
They were walking **in the park**.
The college is **in Brighton**.
What shops are **in the area**?
The group are playing **in Leicester** tonight.

c 公路或街道：
They live **in Kingsdown Road**.
There are lots of shoe shops **in that street**.

d 在房間或建築物內：
It was very cold **in the school**.
I thought I heard a noise **in the kitchen**.

e 容器或液體：

There's a fly **in my coffee**.

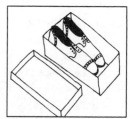

The shoes were **in a box**.

We spent the afternoon swimming **in the sea**.

48 練習 Practice

A 把左欄和右欄連成句子：

1 The title of the story was	in the corridor.
2 I bought the souvenir when I was	at the top of the page.
3 The train stops	in bed.
4 I keep my money	in the garden.
5 You'll find the telephone	at Exeter and Plymouth.
6 I spend about 38 hours a week	in a box in my room.
7 The weather's so lovely, let's eat	in Paris last year.
8 Pauline's not feeling well. She's	at work.

B 下面是我房子的描述，請在空白處填上 in 或 at：

We live (1) _____ an old house (2) _____ the end of a quiet street (3) _____ Birmingham. There are four rooms downstairs. I have my study on the left (4) _____ the front of the house. There are a few chairs (5) _____ the room and (6) _____ one corner there is a table with a computer – that's where I do most of my work. The sitting room is also (7) _____ the front of the house, on the right as you come in. The kitchen is (8) _____ the back. It looks out over the garden. There is another small sitting room (9) _____ the back of the house. There are four bedrooms upstairs, two (10) _____ the front and two (11) _____ the back. There's a bathroom (12) _____ the end of the corridor.

C 現在請描述一下你的住所：

1 Which rooms are at the front? _____

2 Which rooms are at the back? _____

你家裏有電視機、電話、電腦和洗衣機嗎？它們擺放在你家裏的甚麼位置？

D 用 at 或 in 完成以下句子：

1 Hamid works _____ a restaurant _____ Oxford.

2 We live _____ number 32 Redland Road now.

3 We had a wonderful week _____ Madrid.

4 The accident happened because the driver didn't stop _____ the traffic lights.

5 There's a supermarket _____ the end of the street.

6 We had great fun last night _____ Mick's party.

7 Are there any fish _____ this river?

8 It's too cold to go out. I'm staying _____ home tonight.

49 與交通方式連用的介詞
Prepositions with forms of transport

1 當泛指時，by 可以與大多數交通方式連用：

I always go to work **by car**.
It's quicker to go to Birmingham **by train**, you know.
When the weather's good, more people travel **by bike**.

2 可用 "in + my"、"in + your"、"in + the..." 來談及特指的汽車 (car)、客貨車 (van)、貨車 (lorry)、計程車 (taxi) 或救護車 (ambulance)：

We all went to the party **in Jim's car**.
You haven't been **in my new car**, have you?
They went to hospital **in the ambulance**. I followed **in the car**.

3 "on + my"，"on + your"，"on + the..." 可與特指的自行車 (bike)、馬匹 (horse)、長途公共汽車 (coach)、公共汽車 (bus)、輪船 (ship)、火車 (train) 或飛機 (plane) 連用：

You can buy something to drink **on the train**.

I met an interesting man **on the bus** this morning.

'Excuse me, is there somewhere I can lie down **on the ship**?'

4 要步行到某處可用 on foot 來表述：

Take a taxi – it's too far to go **on foot**.

5 行程開始或結束時，可用 get in、get into 或 get out of 分別表述上車下車，可以是小汽車（car）、客貨車（van）、卡車（lorry）、計程車（taxi）或救護車（ambulance）：

We paid the driver and **got out of the taxi**.

It was difficult for Chris to **get into the car**.

6 行程開始或結束時，可用 get on、get onto 或 get off 分別表述搭乘或離開某種交通工具，如飛機（plane）、公共汽車（bus）、長途公共汽車（coach）、火車 (train) 和輪船（ship）：

Everyone wanted to **get off the ship** as soon as possible. Please do not smoke until you have **got off the plane**. We **got onto the train** and looked for a seat.

49 練習 **Practice**

A 把下面相關的短語連成合邏輯的句子：

1 Everyone	by car	felt very nervous.
2 I first travelled	on the coach	when I was 14.
3 It's cheaper	by coach	than by train.
4 The nurse	by bicycle	gave me an injection.
5 We watched a video	on the plane	on the way to the airport.
6 If more people went	by plane	there'd be less pollution.
7 I'll take the shopping	in our car	if it's not too heavy.
8 We can take 5 people	on my bicycle	if necessary.
9 When I go	in the ambulance	I take a map.

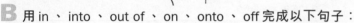

B 用 in、into、out of、on、onto、off 完成以下句子：

1 We all got ＿＿＿＿＿＿ the train and walked out of the station.

2 Sally parked and got ＿＿＿＿＿＿ the car quickly.

3 We can get ＿＿＿＿＿＿ the bus here and walk to my house. It's not far.

4 The Prime Minister got ＿＿＿＿＿＿ the Rolls Royce and returned to Downing Street.

5 There was a queue of people in the rain patiently waiting to get ＿＿＿＿＿＿ the coach.

6 The driver jumped ＿＿＿＿＿＿ the lorry and ran to see if he could help the people who had been injured in the crash.

7 Mike put the shopping ＿＿＿＿＿＿ the car and drove home.

C 用與 go 連用的表達式和一種交通方式改寫以下句子：

如：I drove to London. *I went to London by car.*

1 Tom is flying to Mexico tomorrow. ＿＿＿＿＿＿＿＿＿＿＿＿＿＿＿＿＿＿

2 Ian walked home after the party. ＿＿＿＿＿＿＿＿＿＿＿＿＿＿＿＿＿＿

3 We caught the train to Bristol. ＿＿＿＿＿＿＿＿＿＿＿＿＿＿＿＿＿＿

4 How much does it cost to take the coach to Paris? ＿＿＿＿＿＿＿＿＿＿

5 I used to cycle to school every day. ＿＿＿＿＿＿＿＿＿＿＿＿＿＿＿＿

6 Last year we drove to Scotland. ＿＿＿＿＿＿＿＿＿＿＿＿＿＿＿＿＿＿

7 Sarah always feels seasick when she goes on a ship. ＿＿＿＿＿＿＿＿

8 They took a taxi into the city. ＿＿＿＿＿＿＿＿＿＿＿＿＿＿＿＿＿＿

複習　第二編 **31 – 49**單元

第三十一 — 三十六單元：情態動詞 Modal verbs

A 用正確的情態動詞完成以下對話：

can　can　might　will　will　would　would

A (1) _____ I help you?

B I (2) _____ like to speak to Dr. Jones please.

A I'm afraid he's out. (3) _____ you mind waiting?

B Not at all. How long will he be?

A I don't know. I'm afraid he (4) _____ be quite a long time. I (5) _____ try to telephone him if you like.

B No, don't do that. (6) _____ I leave a message?

A Yes, of course. I (7) _____ give it to him when he gets back.

第三十七單元：非人稱代詞 it Impersonal *it*

B 用以下帶 it 的短語完成句子：

It's very expensive　　It looks like　　It was silly of me　　It was kind of you
It's nice to meet you　It's a pity　　It gets very cold

1 _____ to forget my keys.

2 _____ . My husband has told me a lot about you.

3 _____ Bridget.

4 _____ to remember my birthday.

5 _____ it's so late. I'm afraid we have to go home.

6 _____ travelling first class.

7 _____ in December and January.

第三十八單元：雙賓語動詞 Verbs with two objects

C 用括號裏的短語完成以下句子：

1 She invited her friends round and cooked a nice meal. (them)
   She invited all her friends round and cooked them a nice meal.

2 I posted the letter this morning. (to the bank)
   _____

3 Can you get a newspaper when you go to do the shopping? (for your father)
   _____

4 Karen showed her new dress. (me)
   _____

5 Her aunt is going to make clothes when it is born. (for the baby)
   _____

6 Will you keep some food if I'm too late for supper? (me)
   _____

7 I usually read a story before they go to sleep. (the children)
   _____
   _____

8 James handed the papers when he had finished writing. (to his teacher)
   _____

9 Mr. Wilson teaches English every Tuesday. (us)
   _____

10 I've lent my bicycle so he can cycle to school. (to my brother)
   _____

第三十九單元：Make and do

D 用 make 或 do 完成以下句子：

1 Mary has to _____ some work in the house before she goes to school.

2 Will you _____ a promise?

3 Twenty pounds and fifteen pounds – that will _____ thirty-five pounds altogether.

4 The sitting room is very untidy. Can you _____ a bit of cleaning up before you go out?

5 We are hoping to _____ a trip to Italy later this year.

6 Did you _____ any skiing over the holidays?

7 It was a dreadful match. Our team didn't _____ very well.

8 I promise I'll be very quiet. I won't _____ a sound.

9 Write very carefully and try not to _____ any mistakes.

10 Have you any toothpaste? I want to _____ my teeth before I go to bed.

第四十單元：不具數名詞 Uncount nouns

E 用括號中的詞完成以下句子，必要時把它們變成複數：

1　Ken and Sylvia both had a lot of ___*luggage*___ . (luggage)
2　Harry is very bright. He has a lot of good ___*ideas*___ . (idea)
3　My parents both gave me useful _____ . (advice)
4　Most big towns are full of _____ at the weekend. (traffic)
5　We are going on holiday next week. I hope we have plenty of good _____ . (weather)
6　We played lots of _____ when we were kids. (game)
7　Let's go out and have some _____ after school. (fun)
8　It was hard work. We had a lot of _____ . (problem)
9　They bought some expensive new _____ . (furniture)
10　They played some lovely _____ on the radio last night. (music)

第四十一、四十二單元：量詞 Quantifiers

F 選用正確的短語完成以下句子：

1　My father went out and bought *lot of/lots of* books.
2　I telephoned my two friends but *both them/both of them* were out.
3　*All/All of* students have to learn English.
4　There are two good films on but I've seen *both them/them both*.
5　Someone has opened my drawer and stolen *all my/my all* money.
6　There's *plenty/plenty of* milk. I've only drunk half *it/half of it*.

7　*Most/Most of* children in the class were girls.

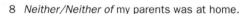

8　*Neither/Neither of* my parents was at home.
9　*Some/Some of* my friends left school last year.
10　*A few/A few of* our friends are coming to see us tomorrow.

第四十三單元：Few and a few

G 用 few 或 a few 完成以下句子：

1　We went out for a drive to visit _____ friends.
2　I bought some presents to take home and _____ things for myself.
3　It was very cold so _____ people came to the meeting.
4　I drank a glass of orange juice and ate _____ sandwiches.
5　A lot of us watched the programme, but _____ of us enjoyed it very much.

第四十三單元：Some and any

H 用 some 或 any 完成以下句子：

1 I'd like _____ biscuits please.

2 I bought _____ rice but I didn't buy _____ potatoes.

3 You could put an advertisement in _____ newspaper.

4 I'd like _____ sugar, but I don't take _____ milk in my coffee, thanks.

5 _____ taxi will take you to the University.

6 Can I have _____ more bread and butter please?

7 There's _____ water in the fridge, but there isn't _____ milk.

8 You can buy it at _____ good book shop.

9 I wanted _____ bananas, but our local shop didn't have _____.

10 Here you are. Have _____ grapes.

第四十四單元：名詞修飾其他名詞 Nouns to describe other nouns

I 請看第四十四單元的練習，看看你是否記住了以下事物被描述的方式：

1 a cookery book *a book about cookery* _____

2 a two o'clock appointment _____

3 a language teacher _____

4 a kitchen chair _____

5 a Thursday meeting _____

6 a newspaper seller _____

7 a leather belt _____

8 aeroplane seats _____

9 a fashion magazine _____

10 a ten pound note _____

第四十五單元：地點表達式 Expressions of place

J 請看圖並完成以下句子：

1 Dad is standing _____ Mum and Richard.
2 Mum is _____ Penny.
3 Sue is standing _____ Richard.
4 Dad is standing _____ Joe.
5 Richard is _____ Sue.

6 There is a _____ beside the computer.
7 The _____ is under the desk.
8 The book is _____ the desk.
9 There is a _____ in front of the computer.
10 Next to the desk there is a _____ .

第四十六單元：時間表達式 Expressions of time

K 請看時間表，用 about、by、during、from、at、after、to、until 表示準確時間及完成以下句子：

Monday	
0900 - 1030	History
1030 - 1100	Break
1100 - 1230	Maths
1230 - 1400	Lunch
1400 - 1530	English
1530 - 1700	Geography
1700 - 1830	French

1 We have maths *from eleven to twelve thirty* _____ .
2 We have history _____ o'clock _____ .
3 We can meet _____ the break _____ forty-five.
4 We have to be back in class _____ lunch _____ o'clock.
5 I asked permission to leave at six _____ the last lesson.
6 All our lessons last _____ an hour and a half.
7 We have _____ and a half hours of lessons every day.

L 完成以下對話，其中一句話要用 by，另一句話要用 until：

1 A The meeting will probably go on _____ nearly five o'clock.

　B Oh dear. I have to be home _____ five thirty.

2 A John and Jean will be here from the fifth _____ the twelfth.

　B Can they get here _____ ten o'clock on the fifth?

複習　第二編 **31－49**單元

第四十七單元：方式副詞 Adverbs of manner

M 先把下面的形容詞變成副詞，然後用這些副詞完成以下句子：

bad careful fast good hard happy sad sleepy slow

1 You should always drive _____, especially on wet roads.
2 Kim won the first game easily, but he played very _____ in the second.
3 The children were playing _____ together.
4 I'm very sorry, he said _____.
5 I'm sorry I can't understand when you speak _____. Could you speak more _____?
6 I'm tired. I had to work _____ all day, and I slept very _____ last night.
7 I tried hard, but I'm afraid I didn't do very _____.
8 Andrew woke up late and got out of bed _____.

第四十八單元：At 和 in（用於地點）
At, in (place)

N 用 in 或 at 完成以下句子：

1 I'll meet you _____ the bus stop.
2 We went to the Louvre while we were _____ Paris.
3 We couldn't find a supermarket _____ the main street.
4 I don't want to go out. I'd much rather stay _____ home.
5 There's a great film on _____ our local cinema.
6 There were hundreds of beautiful flowers _____ the garden.
7 Pisa is _____ northern Italy.
8 It's really cold _____ our house at this time of year.

9 Ron has finished school. He's _____ Art College now.

第四十九單元：與交通方式連用的介詞 Prepositions with forms of transport

O 用正確的介詞完成以下句子：

1 It's too far for me go to school _____ foot. I usually go _____ my bike, unless it's wet. Then I go _____ bus.
2 It was very hot when we got _____ the plane in Singapore.
3 I can't afford to go _____ taxi. I'll just have to go _____ the bus.
4 I had a bad leg so it was difficult getting _____ the car.
5 We got _____ the coach ready for the trip to Stratford.
6 There was a man with a really fierce dog _____ he train this evening.
7 If you are very ill they will take you to the hospital _____ ambulance. If not you will have to go _____ bus or _____ the car.
8 I got _____ the train at Northfield and did the rest of the journey _____ foot.
9 There's a video _____ the coach to help passengers pass the time.

總複習 **A**：第一編和第二編

A 根據右欄的答案提問（第一 — 十四單元）：

1 A: _How old are you?_____ B: I'm twenty-three.

2 A: _____? B: We live in Bromley, near London.

3 A: How long _____? B: We've lived there nearly six years.

4 A: _____ in Bromley? B: Yes, I like it very much.

5 A: _____ in Bromley? B: No, I work in London.

6 A: _____? B: No, I don't drive to work. I go by train.

B 填上動詞的正確時態來完成以下句子（第一 — 十二單元）：

1 I got very wet while I (wait) _____ for the bus.

2 We live in Birmingham. We (live) _____ here for five years.

3 You should take your umbrella. It (rain) _____ quite heavily.

4 It was my first visit to New York. I (never be) _____ to America before.

5 I'm sorry I can't come out. I (do) _____ my homework. We were very tired.

6 We (work) _____ for over three hours.

7 Mary (wave) _____ when she saw me.

8 We (prepare) _____ the salad when the telephone rang.

9 It's nearly ten o'clock. I (work) _____ since six o'clock this morning.

10 The next train (leave) _____ in half an hour.

C 在必要的地方填上介詞來完成以下句子（第四十五、四十六、四十八、四十九單元）：

1 We have an extra English class ____*at*____ two o'clock _____ tomorrow.

2 We can go to the cinema either _____ the evening or _____ Friday.

3 Are you going to town _____ bus or _____ your bike?

4 A Is your father _____ home?

   B No, I'm sorry. He's _____ work.

5 We stayed _____ a flat _____ the centre of Paris.

6 We will be _____ home _____ Christmas, but we'll be away _____ January.

7 Let's go _____ my car. It's too far to go _____ foot.

8 Are the Niagara Falls _____ Canada or the USA?

9 Part of Turkey is _____ Europe and part of it is _____ Asia.

10 George left home _____ half past six this morning.

11 I'll see you _____ next week _____ Friday.

12 Did you enjoy yourselves _____ the cinema?

13 I have to get _____ the bus _____ the next stop.

14 Can you hold the door so I can get _____ the car?

15 It's usually very cold _____ winter, but it was quite warm _____ this year.

總複習 A：第一編和第二編

D 改寫下面的句子，要把括號裏的狀語放在適當位置：

1 I have been to Portugal but I have been to Spain. (twice; never)

_____

2 I enjoyed his first book, but I didn't like his second. (a lot; very much)

_____

3 He was driving and that saved his life. (quite slowly; certainly)

_____

4 You have to work if you want to do. (hard; well)

_____

5 We play football but we play hockey. (sometimes; never)

E 選用單詞或短語完成以下對話：

A: Good morning. (1) *Will/Could* I have two kilos of (2)
potato/potatoes and half a kilo of (3) *rice/rices*?

B: Here you are. (4) *Do/Would* you like anything else?

A: Yes please. (5) *Will/Can* you give me (6) any/some
apricots – about half a kilo.

B: I'm sorry. We haven't (7) *some/any* apricots left.
We have (8) *few/a few* peaches though.

A: Thank you. I'll take one kilo please.

A: Hello. Where (9) *will you go/are you going*?

B: We are off to Italy.

A: (10) *Did you go/Have you been* there before?

B: Yes, we (11) *have gone/went* there last year.

A: How long (12) *you will be/will you* be away?

B: Two weeks. We'll be back (13) *in/on/at* the
second of August.

A: I hope you have (14) *good weathers/a good
weather/good weather*.

B: Oh yes. (15) *It/There* is always fine in Italy.

50 Should、ought、must 和 can't (用於表達可能性)
Should, ought, must, can't (probability)

1 要表述某事可能是真的，或要表述某事可能會發生，可用 should 或 ought to：

The sun is shining. It **ought to** be a nice warm day.
I think I can do that for you. It **shouldn't** be any problem.
It's eight o'clock. Father **ought to** be home soon.

注意 這兩種形式只能用於表述希望發生的事物。不能説：We've missed our bus. We ought to be late.

2 相當肯定某事是真實時，可用 must：

There's someone at the door. It **must** be the postman.
Hello. Nice to meet you. You **must** be Sylvia's husband.

3 肯定某事並非如此時，可用 cannot 或 can't：

He **can't** be very old. He's not more than forty, is he?

注意 肯定某事並非如此時，不能用 must not 或 mustn't。不能説：

That mustn't be true. You mustn't be tired already. ✗

'But we've just started. You (mustn't) be tired already.' ✗

'You've just had lunch. You can't be hungry again.' ✓

118

50 練習 Practice

A 用 should be 或 ought to be 與下面的一個短語連用來完成對話：

nice and quiet   very comfortable   a good game   an exciting trip   a nice day   really funny

1 A We're thinking of going to New York this summer.
   B Wow! That _____*ought to be an exciting trip.*_____

2 A Mum has just bought some nice new armchairs.
   B That's nice. They _____.

3 A I think the weather's going to be fine tomorrow.
   B Yes. It _____.

4 A I'm looking forward to the football match this weekend.
   B So am I. It _____.

5 A We are going to have a holiday in the mountains.
   B That sounds great. _____.

6 A There's a good film with Robin Williams. He always makes me laugh.
   B Yes. It _____.

B 用 must be 或 can't be 完成以下句子：

1 It's still early. Surely you _____*can't be*_____ tired already.

2 The dog is barking. There _____ someone at the door.

3 I hear your daughter's got a really good job. You _____ very proud of her.

4 It's not very expensive. It _____ more than twenty dollars.

5 There's no answer. They _____ out.

6 'You have just had lunch.
   You _____ hungry again.'

7 She's very short. She _____ taller than five feet.

8 It's getting dark. It _____ getting late.

9 But you look so young. You _____ Rebecca's father!

10 I'm sorry to hear your wife's in hospital. You _____ very worried.

11 Bob has been off work for six weeks. He _____ very ill.

12 I've eaten most of them. There _____ many left.

13 It's really freezing cold. It _____ the worst winter we've ever had.

51 Can、could、may 和 need (用於提出要求和請求同意)
Can, could, may, need (requests and permission)

1 可用 can 來表述某人已獲允許做某事；可用 cannot 或 can't 來表述某人不得做某事：

You **can** leave your coat here if you like. You **can** go now.

'We **can't** go in there. It's private.'

'You **can't** drive a car until you are seventeen.'

可用 You're allowed to... 或 You're not allowed to... 來進行一般性陳述：

In Britain **you're not allowed to** drive a car until you're seventeen,
but in some countries **you're allowed to** drive when you're only sixteen.

2 可用 may 或 may not 來表述某人已獲允許做某事，或不得做某事：

You **may** leave your coat here if you like. You **may** go now.
We **may not** go in there. It's private. You **may not** drive a car until you are seventeen.

提示：現在 may 的這種用法已相當正式。

3 可用 can 來提出要求或請求同意：

Can I ask a question, please? **Can** I use your telephone, please?

如果希望顯得正式或非常有禮貌，就要用 could：
Could I ask a question, please? **Could** I use your telephone, please?

也可用 may 來請求同意，但這種用法非常正式：
May I come in now, please? **May we** leave these things here?

4 當允許某人可以不做某事或建議某人不要做某事時，或表示某事沒有必要時，
可用 needn't、don't need to、don't have to：

You **don't need to** cook your own supper. You **don't need to** shout.

'You **don't have to** say anything if you don't want to.'

'You **don't have to** pay now.
You can send a cheque later.'

(注意) don't need 和 don't have 後面要跟 to；needn't 後面要直接跟動詞：
You **needn't** come to work today. You **needn't** write it out in full.

51 練習 Practice

A 下面這些人正在提出要求或請求同意。用 can 或 could 把他們說的話寫在圖的下面：

這些詞彙對你會有所幫助：borrow your pen; have another biscuit; play with you; go home early tonight; ask a question; have a kilo of bananas; take this chair; have a lift home 。

合上書本，看看上面的句子你記住了多少。

B 住在賓館裏，有些事情就不需要做或不必去做了。用 don't need to do 或 don't have to do 把這樣的事情寫在圖的下面：

這些詞彙對會你有所幫助：clean the windows; make your bed; clean the furniture; cook your own meals; lay the table; wash the dishes; tidy your room; clean the bath 。

合上書本，看看上面的句子你記住了多少。

52 喜歡、不喜歡和邀請 Likes, dislikes, invitations

1 下面的詞與 "動詞 + -ing" 結構連用，可用來表述喜歡做某事或不喜歡做某事：

enjoy like love feel like fancy dislike detest hate mind

Do you **enjoy skiing**?

My cousin **loves watching** football on TV.

It's raining. I don't **feel like going** out, thanks.

I **hated cooking** when I was younger, but I **liked eating** out.

I **fancy having** a night out tonight. What about you?

Do you **feel like coming** to the cinema with us, Dave?

2 要請某人做某事，可以用下面的結構：

a "How about + -ing" :

How about coming with us to the cinema?
How about having a meal with us later on in the week?

提示：這種結構也可與名詞連用：

How about another drink? How about a trip to London?

b "would you like + to- 不定式" :

Would you like to have something to eat?
Would you like to come to the party?

c "You must + 不帶 to 的不定式" :

You really **must have** some more ice-cream.

You must visit us when you're in Hong Kong.

d 向朋友發出非正式的邀請時也可使用祈使句，要特別強調時，可以在祈使句的主要動詞前加 do：

A '**Have** a sandwich.'   B 'I shouldn't.'
A 'Oh, **do take** one.'

A '**Come** any time you like. ' B 'We'll try.'
A 'Yes, **do come**.'

52

練習 Practice

A 用 "feel like + -ing" 的正確形式改寫以下句子：

如：Do you want to go out? Do you feel like going out?

1 Do you want to see that new film? _____

2 Don't you want to drive to the mountains this weekend? _____

3 They wanted to get a video. _____

4 It was a hot day and everybody wanted to go to the beach. _____

5 I really don't want to go home now. It's early. _____

6 Is there anything you particularly want to do? _____

再請用 fancy 改寫上面的句子。

B 請看圖，根據圖中的人物和他們的活動完成以下句子：

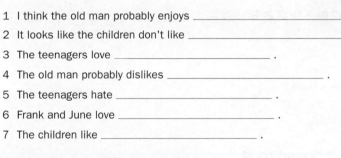

1 I think the old man probably enjoys _____ .

2 It looks like the children don't like _____ .

3 The teenagers love _____ .

4 The old man probably dislikes _____ .

5 The teenagers hate _____ .

6 Frank and June love _____ .

7 The children like _____ .

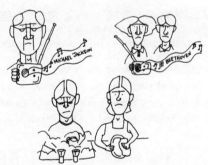

再用同樣的動詞表述你對這些活動的感受。

C 用 do 改寫以下句子：

如：Please have some more coffee. *Do have some more coffee.*

1 You must come in and relax for a moment. _____

2 You must let me buy you that picture. _____

3 You must spend the weekend with us. _____

4 Please write to me with your news. _____

5 Please tell me when you're bored. _____

再用 "How about... + -ing" 改寫上面的句子。

第三編

1 "動詞＋ to-不定式" 可與一些表示説話和思想的普通動詞連用：

agree   choose   decide   expect   hope   learn   plan   promise

> **She agreed to go to the cinema with me.**

'My son **hopes to study** medicine at university next September.'

They **promised to give** the books back on Friday.
We are **planning to have** a party next week.
I **learnt to drive** in a week. It was easy!

在 to 的前面加 not 可構成否定：

It was late so we **decided not to go out**.

I **agreed not to play** the guitar after midnight.

2 "動詞＋賓語＋ to-不定式" 的結構可與下面這些動詞連用：

advise   tell   ask   remind   order   expect

My teacher **advised me to buy** a dictionary.
'I **expect you to be** here at 9 o'clock,' his mother said.
The officer **ordered the soldiers to go back**.
They **told us to be** at the train station at 6 o'clock.

3 "動詞＋wh-詞＋ to-不定式" 可與下面這些動詞連用：

ask   explain   learn   understand   decide   forget   know   remember

I can't **explain how to do** it, I'm sorry.
We can't **decide what to eat**.
I didn't **know what to do**.
I can never **remember
how to spell** that word.

When did you **learn how to ski**?

53 練習 Practice

A 根據左欄的內容，完成右欄的句子：

1 'I'll have the red shirt, please.' He decided _____.
2 I started swimming when I was 9. I learnt _____.
3 We're going to visit Moscow this year. We plan _____.
4 I'll never be late again. He promised never _____.
5 She's sure she will be home at ten. She expects _____.

6 He's not going to swim after all. He decided _____.

B 用以下動詞完成以下句子：

remind   advised   asked   want   asked   told

1 The teacher _____ me to take the exam.

2 Who _____ you to come to the party?

3 A policeman _____ us not to park the car on the corner because it was dangerous.

4 'The train leaves at ten, so I _____ you all to be ready at halfpast nine'.

5 We were lost so we stopped and _____ someone to show us the way to the hotel.

6 Please _____ me to buy some milk on the way home.

C 用以下詞彙完成以下句子：

understand what   know how   remember what   forget how   decided when   explained how
understand how   know what   remember where   forgotten what   decide what   explained where

1 This exercise is difficult. I don't _____ to do.

2 Could you repeat that, please? I've _____ you said.

3 When I was young I didn't _____ to ski. Now I'm an expert.

4 We got lost because we couldn't _____ to turn off the motorway.

5 I went to the supermarket, but I couldn't _____ to buy for the cake.

6 Some people find it difficult to _____ to wear to parties.

7 A: Have you _____ to go on holiday? B: Yes, in April.

8 The situation was so embarrassing. I didn't _____ to do!

9 They say you never _____ to ride a bicycle.

10 The guide _____ to go to buy the best souvenirs.

11 It was difficult finding your flat. Fortunately, we met someone who _____ to get there.

12 A lot of people use computers nowdays, but very few actually _____ they work.

第三編

125

54 Make、let、help＋不帶 to 的不定式
Make, let, help + bare infinitive

1 Make 與不帶 to 的不定式連用，可用來：

a 表述某人或某事給你的感受：

The film was so sad. It **made** me **cry**. (= I cried because of the film.)

You always **make** me **feel** happy. (= I am happy because of you.)

I had to wait an hour to see the doctor. That **made** me **want** to complain.

(= I wanted to complain because of the wait.)

b 表述某人要求你或強迫你做某事：

He **made** me **sit down**. You can't **make** me **eat** it. They **made** me **wait** for hours. I didn't want to see the film, but they **made** me **go**.

2 Let 與不帶 to 的不定式連用，可用來：

a 表述某人允許另一人做某事：

He **let** me **go** home early.

Shut up and **let** me **talk**!

'**Let** me **help** you'.

When I was young, my parents never **let** me **go out** alone.

b 提議做某事：

Let's go to the theatre tonight.

Let's have an ice-cream.

Let's not walk, let's take a taxi.

3 help 可與不帶 to 的不定式連用：

Thanks for **helping** me **clean** the car, John. Your explanation **helped** me **understand** the problem.

help 也可以與帶 to 的不定式連用：

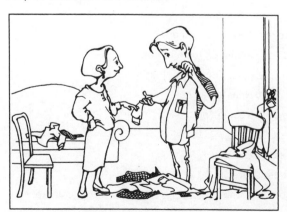

She **helped** me **to choose** a shirt.

'Thanks for **helping** me **to clean** the car.'

54 練習 Practice

A 你父母在你小的時候曾經讓你做過甚麼事？用 They let me... 或 They didn't let me...
把這些事寫出來：

1 go to bed after 10 p.m. _____
2 eat chocolate when I wanted _____
3 visit my friends' homes _____
4 buy my own clothes _____
5 ride my bike on the road _____
6 go shopping alone _____
7 travel alone _____

B 現在想一想老師們曾經要求你做過甚麼事？用 They made us... 或 They didn't make us...
把這些事情寫出來：

1 play sport _____
2 wear a uniform _____
3 do a lot of homework _____
4 stand up when they came into the classroom _____
5 sing songs _____
6 read newspapers and magazines _____
7 speak English _____

C 用 let's 和以下詞彙提建議，並完成句子：

have a rest   go for a drink   go and see it   go inside   do another exercise   ask someone for help

1 I'm thirsty. *Let's* _____
2 It's very hot. _____
3 There's a good film on at the cinema. _____
4 I need more practice. _____
5 I'm tired. _____
6 We're lost. _____

D 把左欄和右欄相關的內容連成句子：

1 The bad news   made us go inside.
2 The medicine   made me happy.
3 The bad food   made the cars stop.
4 Meeting you last weekend   made me depressed.
5 The policeman   made my father ill.
6 The rain   made my brother feel better.

E 把左欄和右欄相關的內容連成句子：

1 A dictionary can help you   find your way.
2 A map can help you   find what you want.
3 These pills will help you   understand a new word.
4 The shop assistant will help you   go to sleep.

127

感知動詞＋賓語＋不定式或 -ing
Verbs of perception + object + infinitive/-ing

1 以下動詞的後面可跟帶賓語的 -ing 從句：

see　hear　watch　notice　observe　smell　listen to　find　feel　look at

這種結構可用來表述某人正在做某事：

We **saw him crossing** the road.

They **heard someone playing** the guitar upstairs.

I **found an old man lying** on the floor, and called an ambulance.

She lay in bed, **listening to the rain falling**. The children **looked at the monkeys playing** in the zoo.

提示：這種結構所表述的活動在說話者未看到之前已開始了，說話者看到的只是活動的一部分。

2 下面這些感知動詞可與帶賓語但不帶 to 的不定式連用：

see　hear　watch　notice　observe　smell　listen to　feel （但 find 和 look at 不能這樣用。）

這種結構可用來表述一個完整的動作或行動：

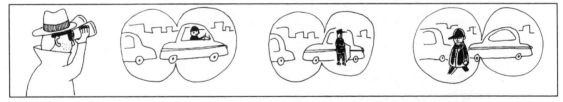

I **saw** him **park** the car, **open** the door, **get out** and **cross** the road. (= I saw the start and finish of each activity.)

The audience **listened to the group play** their latest hits. (= They heard the whole show.)

She **watched them steal** the car, and then she phoned the police. (= She saw everything.)

55 練習 Practice

A 判斷以下句子描述的是已經完成的動作 (F)，還是未完成的動作 (U)：

1 Did you see the police arrest the robber? _____

2 I heard the birds making their nest in the roof. _____

3 Everyone watched the plane land. _____

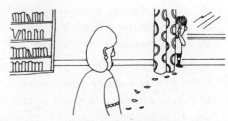

4 Mrs Jameson noticed someone hiding in the lounge. _____

5 We listened to the group play a few songs, then left. _____

6 Noriko felt something touch her leg when she was swimming. _____

B 下面的插圖講述一個故事，請給以下句子排出正確的順序：

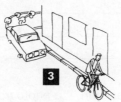

1 A tall man was getting onto his bicycle. I saw him. *1*

2 Then the car crashed into the traffic lights. We heard it. _____

3 A police car was coming to the scene of the accident.
   We heard it. _____

4 The children screamed. Everybody heard them. _____

5 The car tried to overtake the cyclist. We watched it. _____

6 A blue car turned into the street. My friend noticed it. _____

7 Some children were standing near the traffic lights.
   My friend noticed them. _____

8 He rode down the street. I watched him. _____

9 The car was driving very fast. We heard it. _____

10 The car knocked the man off his bike. We saw it. _____

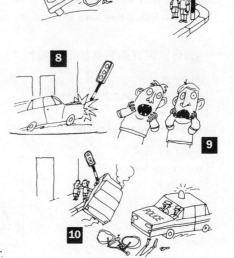

再改寫上面的句子，如下例：

He opened the door. I heard him: *I heard him open the door.*

He was opening the door. I heard him: *I heard him opening the door.*

第三編

56 乏詞義動詞 (give、take、have、go)
Delexical verbs (give, take, have, go)

1 have 與一些名詞連用，可用來表述下面幾方面常見的活動：

a 餐 (meals: breakfast, lunch, dinner, tea, meal, snack)：
We **have breakfast** at 8:30, all right?
When would you like to **have dinner**?

b 食物和飲料 (food and drink: a drink, a coffee, a taste, a sip etc)：
I think I'll **have a cheese salad**, please.
Can I **have a quick taste** of your ice-cream, Pat?

c 談話 (talking: a chat, a discussion, an argument, a conversation)：
Let's **have a chat**. Did you **have an argument** about work?
I was **having a conversation** with Sue when the phone rang.

d 盥洗 (washing: a wash, a bath, a shower)：
I want to **have a shower**.

'**Have you had a bath** today?'

e 休閒 (relaxation: a rest, a break, a holiday, a day off)：
Can I **have some time off** this week? I **haven't had a break** for ages. I think we all need to **have a rest**.

2 下面是一些與 give 連用的普通名詞，把它們正確歸類：

cry information kiss laugh warning kick whistle shout punch example
speech hug report caress interview answer push scream news

| 談與説 (talking and telling)： |
| 其他聲響 (other noises)： |
| 動作 (actions)： |

3 take 可與 care、a chance、a decision、a photograph、responsibility、a risk 和 time 連用：

I'll lend you my camera, but **take care** of it.
The tourists **took some photographs** of the city's sights.
The children **took a long time** to finish the exercise.

4 go 可以與許多常見的活動連用：

a "go + -ing"：
I'm **going shopping** this afternoon.
Let's **go camping**.
Yesterday I **went swimming**.

b "go for a + 名詞"：
I want to **go for a walk**.

They **went for a ride** on their bikes.

56 練習 **Practice**

A 用本單元第一項中帶 have 的表達式改寫以下句子，可做必要的改動：

如：They argued angrily. *They had an angry argument.*

1 We discussed it seriously. _____

2 They were chatting quietly in the reception room. _____

3 They eat dinner very late in Spain. _____

4 I washed quickly, then went to school. _____

5 Paula ate a hamburger for lunch. _____

6 Most people prefer to go on holiday in the summer. _____

7 I need to talk with you about Simon. _____

8 Mark enjoys lying in the bath for a long time after playing sport. _____

B 用 give 或 take 完成以下句子：

1 Check the oil, the petrol and the brakes before driving off on holiday. We don't want to _____ any chances of things going wrong.

2 Every time I see the woman who works in the newagent's she _____ me a big smile.

3 The President _____ the journalists a quick interview.

4 Let me _____ you an example of what I mean.

5 The terrorist group said it _____ responsibility for the bombing of the airport.

6 It will _____ a long time to finish repairing these houses.

7 When the home team scored, the spectators _____ a terrific shout.

8 The doctor _____ us a warning about the dangers of smoking.

C 用 go + -ing 的表達式改寫以下句子：

1 They decided to go for a swim in the river.

_____

2 If you feel hot why don't you go for a swim?

_____

3 When was the last time you went for a walk across the moor?

_____

4 I think I'll go for a jog.

_____

5 The lake is a great place to fish.

_____

1 英語中有許多動詞是由一個以上的詞構成的。通常這些動詞是由 "動詞＋小品詞" (in、on、out、off 等) 構成的。這樣的動詞叫做短語動詞。短語動詞的含義和構成它的基本動詞的含義是不一樣的：

基本含義：

Look here!

基本含義，帶強調語氣：

Look up here!

短語動詞：

Look it up in the dictionary.

I'll bring the newspaper.

Thanks. Bring it up here.

I'm bringing up the children.

2 短語動詞的常見結構是 "動詞＋小品詞"：

get by　go on　go away　grow up　keep on　meet up　watch out

I can speak a little French. I can **get by**.
I'm sorry I interrupted your story. Please **go on**.
The music was so bad we paid the musicians to **go away**.
We **grew up** in the countryside, but now we live in the city.
It's hard to succeed, but you must **keep on** trying.
They visited different shops, then **met up** at the library.

There's a policeman coming. **Watch out!**

有時短語動詞與單字動詞的含義是一樣的。上面例句中的短語動詞哪幾個帶有 continue 的含義，manage的含義或 leave 的含義？

3 另一個結構是 "動詞＋小品詞＋賓語"。你能在以下例句中的短語動詞下面加底線嗎？

Someone broke into my flat and stole my TV and video.
We've got an au-pair to look after the children.
I bumped into Chris and Annie in the centre.
The police are looking into the crime.

上面哪些句子的短語動詞有 investigate 和 meet 的含義？

4 一些短語動詞有三個單詞，即動詞後有兩個單詞。你能在以下句子中的短語動詞下面加底線嗎？

Mary left before me, but my car is faster, so I caught up with her very soon.
Parts of this cathedral date back to the tenth century.
We were so busy we didn't get round to watching the video until midnight!

Cycle 3

A 在以下句子中的短語動詞下面加底線:

1 Sue was so busy she stayed up all night to finish her work.
2 Laurence is so rude. How can you put up with him?
3 He took up skiing when he was 4. He was a champion at 16.
4 I'm like my mother, but my sister Sarah takes after our father.
5 If we start out now, we'll be there by nine o'clock.
6 Hurry up! I don't want to be late.
7 'Could you find out what time the train leaves, please?'
8 The soldiers carried out a dangerous raid.
9 If you are hot, take off your coat.

10 The car broke down on the motorway. We had to get help.

B 把習題 A 中的短語動詞歸類:

動詞＋小品詞	動詞＋小品詞＋賓語	三詞短語動詞
She stayed up.	He took up skiing.	How can you put up with him?

C 用以下短語動詞完成以下句子:

got by   grew up   stay up   watch out   hold on   play around

1 My parents _____ in Bulgaria, but they went to live in London when they were married.
2 They broke the window when they were _____ with a football.
3 Last night we _____ to watch the late film on TV.
4 'Can you speak Chinese?' 'No, when we were there we _____ with a few words and some sign language!'
5 'Can I speak to Paul, please?' ' _____, I'll just go and get him.'
6 _____! Don't touch the paint, it's wet!

D 改寫以下句子。用以下短語動詞代替有底線的動詞:

keep on   find out   got away   bumped into

1 The police followed the robbers, but they <u>escaped</u>.

_____

2 I'm trying to <u>discover</u> whose car this is.

_____

3 Most of the students said they wanted to <u>continue</u> studying.

_____

4 I <u>met</u> an old friend on the ferry. What a surprise!

_____

1 一些短語動詞可用於 "動詞＋實語＋小品詞" 的結構：

> answer back ask in call back catch out hand over invite in
> order about point out ring up take out take up tell apart

Paula was out when I rang her up, so I'll **call her back** later.

We'd like to **invite you out** to a restaurant.

'The house is a dreadful mess. We can't **invite
anyone in**.'

'The twins look exactly the same.
No one can **tell them apart**.'

2 許多短語動詞帶有實語。下面這些短語動詞的實語可置於小品詞之前或之後：

> add on bring up call up fold up hand over hand in knock over point out put down
> put away put up rub out sort out take up tear up throw away try out write out

She had to **bring up** the children on her own.	She had to **bring** the children **up** on her own.
He **folded up** his newspaper.	He **folded** his newspaper **up**.
I'll try to **sort out** the problem.	I'll try to **sort** the problem **out** for you.
He **took off** his shirt and lay in the sun.	He **took** his shirt **off** and lay in the sun.
He **rubbed out** all the mistakes.	He **rubbed** all the mistakes **out**.

注意 代詞作實語時必須置於小品詞之前：

He **knocked over** a little girl and her brother.	He **knocked** them **over**.
He **tore up** the letter and **threw** the pieces away.	He **tore** it **up** and **threw** it **away**.

'**Take out** the money and **hand** it **over**.'

'**Put down** your gun and **put up** your hands.'

58 練習 Practice

A 把以下單詞和短語按適當順序排成句子：

1 the people in the bank/told/the robbers/all their money/to hand over.
_____

2 were you/when you/how old/skiing/took up.
_____

3 a couple/he/pointed out/of mistakes.
_____

4 their papers/handed in/the students/of the exam/at the end.
_____

5 the shop assistant/in the bag/folded up/and put them/the clothes.
_____

B 把帶底線的詞換成代詞。必要時可改變詞的順序：

1 I was very surprised when they invited Pascal out to lunch.
_____

2 The student quickly rubbed out the mistakes and wrote the sentence out again.
_____

3 Please help me put away the plates and cups.
_____

4 I'm going to ring up the Carters and ask Angela round to dinner.
_____

5 George brought up all three children and kept his job at the same time.
_____

6 My doctor advised me to give up smoking.
_____

C 用以下短語動詞完成以下句子：

clean up   take up   knock over   point out   fold up   call back   tell apart   write out

1 I'm not very fit. I think I'll _____ jogging.

2 I can't talk to you now I'm afraid. Can you _____ later?

3 The guide will _____ all the interesting places on the route.

4 This is a great tent. It will _____ and fit into this tiny bag.

5 Parties are great. But it's no fun when you have to _____ afterwards.

6 Be careful you don't _____ the bottle.

7 They look almost the same. They are very difficult to _____.

8 Give me some paper and I'll _____ my address.

第
三
編

1 許多動詞常與某一個介詞連用。有些動詞與不同的介詞連用而有不同的含義：

動詞 + TO

Belong to: The house **belongs** to the Smiths.
Listen to: The audience **listened to** the music in silence.
Speak to: I haven't **spoken to** anyone about this.
Talk to: Could I **talk to** you for a minute, Sam?

Write to: Please **write to** us when you have time.

動詞 + ABOUT

Care about: I don't **care about** the cost. I want a new car.
Complain about: They **complained about** the terrible weather.
Dream about: I **dreamed about** you last night, Eva.
Speak about: They were **speaking about** their holidays.
Talk about: I'm going to **talk about** our new product.
Think about: What are you **thinking about**?

Write about: You should **write about** your travels.

Smile at: She's so friendly.
She **smiles at** everyone.

動詞 + AT

Laugh at: Nobody **laughs at** my jokes.
Look at: **Look at** me!
Shout at: He was angry, so he **shouted at** me to go away.

動詞 + FOR

Apologize for: I must **apologize for** being so late.
Apply for: I'd like to **apply for** the job you advertised.
Ask for: We finished the meal and **asked for** the bill.
Look for: 'What are you **looking for**?' 'My pen. I lost it.'
Pay for: I'll **pay for** the food, you can **pay for** the drink.

Wait for: Do you want me to **wait for** you?

動詞 + ON

Count on: You can **count on** me. I'll help you.
Depend on: I might go out. It **depends on** the weather.
Rely on: He's never late. You can **rely on** him.

動詞 + INTO

Bump into: I spilled the wine because someone **bumped into** me.
Crash into: The car **crashed into** the tree.

Drive into: The mechanic **drove** the car **into** the garage.

A 用 "動詞＋to" 或 "動詞＋about" 完成以下句子：

1 _____ me when I'm talking to you!

2 They asked the explorer to _____ his experience in the jungle.

3 'Is this your flat?' 'No, it _____ my sister.'

4 Since the service was so terrible, we _____ the manager.

5 The visitors wanted to see the manager to _____ the uncomfortable beds.

6 A lot of children _____ Father Christmas with a list of presents.

7 Today I want to _____ you _____ our business plans.

8 Biographers are writers who _____ famous people.

9 They went to sleep and _____ winning a lot of money.

10 We must _____ where to go on holiday this summer.

11 'Do you mind if I _____ the radio?'

12 'Who do these _____?'

B 用 "動詞＋at" 或 "動詞＋for" 完成以下句子：

1 Everyone _____ the comedian when he fell over. It was funny.

2 Simon _____ his watch and saw that he was late.

3 I hate _____ the bus in the rain.

4 When he lost his keys, Mark _____ them for an hour.

5 My secretary _____ me _____ a week off work to visit her sick mother.

C 用 "動詞＋on" 完成以下句子：

1 If someone is reliable, it means you can _____ them.

2 People who are not dependable are people you can't _____ .

3 We want to have a picnic tomorrow, but it _____ the weather.

4 I'd like to buy your painting, but it _____ the price.

60 反身代詞 Reflexives

1 請看下面的例子：

I hurt the cat by accident.

Bill fell and hurt himself.

反身代詞可用來表示自己對自己做了某事，或自己為自己做了某事：

I bought the car **for myself**. (= not for you. I will use it.)
He was talking **to himself**. (= not to anyone)

2 反身代詞的單數形式是 -self，複數形式是 -selves。把下面的反身代詞和相關的主語人稱代詞連起來：

I ...	It ...	yourselves	itself
You ...	We ...	himself	herself
He ...	You ...	ourselves	myself
She ...	They ...	yourself	themselves

3 在英語中，像wash和shave這樣的動詞通常不跟反身代詞。當它們使用反身代詞時則表示特別強調：

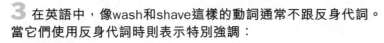

I **washed** very quickly and went downstairs.
We taught Harry to **wash himself** when he was two.
It was cold so we **undressed** quickly and got into bed.   It's very difficult to **undress yourself** with a broken arm.

4 反身代詞常與下面這些動詞連用：

blame   cut   dry   enjoy   help   hurt   introduce   teach

Helen **taught herself** Japanese from a book.
You mustn't **blame yourself** for the bad result: it wasn't your fault.
'Can I have a drink of water?' '**Help yourself.**'

The man **introduced himself** as 'Little John.'

5 反身代詞還可以用來強調做某事時是沒有別人幫助的：

I made the table **myself**! (=I didn't buy it.)
I'm not going to pay anyone to paint the house, I'll do it **myself**! (=I will paint the house.)
'What a lovely card! Did you make it **yourself**?'

如果説你做某事 by yourself，就是説你獨自完成了某事：
Paul was sitting **by himself** in a corner.

60 練習 Practice

A 用括號裏的詞完成以下句子：

1 Everyone looked at _____ when I fell over and hurt _____. (myself/me)

2 John often sings to _____. I think I'll ask _____ why he does it. (him/himself)

3 Unfortunately a lot of young people kill _____ because they think no one loves _____. (them/themselves)

4 Since nobody introduced _____ to the other people at the party, we had to introduce _____. (us/ourselves)

5 My daughter was four when I showed _____ how to dress _____. (herself/her)

6 This computer will program _____ when you switch _____ on. (it/itself)

7 I hope _____ will enjoy _____ tonight. (yourselves/you)

8 Help _____ to anything _____ want in the kitchen. (yourself/you)

B 把左欄與右欄相關的部分組連成簡短對話：

1 Can I borrow a pen and some paper?	No, I made it myself.
2 Where did you learn to paint?	Enjoy yourselves.
3 We're off to the party now.	Sure, help yourself.
4 What did you say? I didn't hear.	Let me introduce myself.
5 Sorry, who are you?	I taught myself, actually.
6 Did you buy that table?	I was talking to myself.
7 Why is he wearing a bandage on his finger?	I think they did it themselves.
8 Who cut their hair?	He burnt himself.

C 用 by myself、for yourself 或 to himself 等完成以下句子：

1 Can I help you with that?	No thanks, I want to do it _____.
2 Did Jim go with Paul?	No, he went _____.
3 Do you like holidays with friends?	No, we prefer holidays _____.
4 Who bought the books for him?	Actually, he bought them _____.
5 Are you self-employed?	That's right, we work _____.
6 Does she live with her parents?	No, she lives _____.
7 Will you order something for me, please?	No, you should order _____.
8 Let me buy you something.	No, keep your money _____.

61 -ing形容詞和-ed形容詞 -ing and -ed adjectives

Jill is **bored**. She has a very **boring** job.

Children can be very **annoying**. Mr. Brown is **annoyed**.

Mary is very **frightened**. It's a **frightening** film.

1 最常用的 -ing 形容詞是：

amusing interesting worrying annoying shocking disappointing
boring surprising exciting terrifying frightening tiring

如果某事令你產生興趣，你可以説它有趣。如果某事令你害怕，你可説它可怕，如此類推。
I got some **interesting** news this morning. There was a **frightening** film on TV last night.
There was a **shocking** story in the newspaper this morning. I'm going to bed early. I've had a **tiring** day.

2 最常見的 -ed 形容詞是：

annoyed finished tired bored frightened worried closed interested
broken delighted pleased disappointed excited surprised

如果某事令你不快，你可説你感到不快。如果某事令你產生興趣，你可説你感興趣，如此類推。

如果你打破了某物，那某物就是破碎的了。如果你做完某事，那某事就是完成的。

這些 -ed 形容詞通常跟在動詞 be 的後面，或跟在 feel、look、 seem 和 sound 等幾個動詞的後面。

The wolf **looked delighted** to see Little Red Riding Hood.

'I think it**'s broken**.'

61 練習 Practice

A 用 -ing 形容詞來表述你對下面事情的看法：

1 Horror films _____*frightening*_____   2 Computer games _____

3 English lessons _____   4 Football _____

5 Small children _____   6 Road accidents _____

7 Jogging _____   8 Pop music _____

B 請用 -ed 形容詞描述，如果發生了下面這些事情你會有甚麼感受：

1 If you were driving a car and you were stopped by the police _____

2 If you got an unexpected parcel in the post _____

3 If you heard that you had won a lot of money in a competition _____

4 If you broke your leg and were in hospital for three weeks _____

5 If you woke up in the night and heard burglars in the house _____

C 用由括號裏的動詞構成的 -ing 形容詞或 -ed 形容詞完成以下各組句子。
其中一個句子用 -ed 形容詞，另一個句子用 -ing 形容詞：

1 a Annette was _____*bored*_____ She had nothing to do. (bore)

   b She had a book to read but it was very _____*boring*_____ .

2 a I enjoyed our visit to the museum. It was really _____. (interest)

   b I like swimming but I'm not _____ in jogging.

3 a I didn't enjoy the film very much. The dinosaurs were too _____. (terrify)

   b The whole house was on fire. We were all _____.

4 a There are far too many accidents on the roads. It's very _____. (worry)

   b I thought we were lost. I was really _____.

5 a My brother always laughs at me. He's very _____. (annoy)

   b He wasted a lot of money. His father was extremely _____.

6 a We were all _____ to hear that the president had been killed. (shock)

   b I don't feel at all well. I've got a _____ cold.

7 a The first half was good but the second half wasn't very _____. (excite)

   b We were all very _____ when we heard the news.

8 a I knew what would happen. It wasn't at all _____. (surprise)

   b I was _____ to hear that Anna had failed her exam.

9 a It was _____ that there weren't more people at the concert. (disappoint)

   b There weren't many people at the theatre. The actors were very _____ .

10 a He told a few funny stories but they weren't very _____ . (amuse)

   b I don't think that's very funny. I am not _____ .

62 不定代詞 Indefinite pronouns

1 不定代詞有下面這些：

anybody	anyone	anything	everybody	everyone	everything
nobody	no one	nothing	somebody	someone	something

2 不定代詞總是要用動詞的單數形式：

Everybody knows that. **Everything was** fine.

'**Is anybody** there?'

'There**'s somebody** at the door.'

3 在不能確定是用 he 或 she；him 或 her；his 或 hers 的情況下，返指不定代詞時要用複數形式：

Somebody's been eating my porridge and **they**'ve eaten it all up.
Has **everyone** had as much as **they** want? **Anyone** will tell you if you ask **them**.

但是，如果知道所指的是一個男人或一個女人時，可以使用 someone 或 somebody 的單數形式：
Somebody called. **She** left a message.

4 在一個句子裏使用了反身代詞 nobody、no one 或 nothing 後，通常就不能在這個句子裏使用另一個否定詞了。

不能説：	There wasn't nobody there.	I didn't do nothing.	Nobody didn't come.
而要説：	There was **nobody** there.	I did**n't** do **anything**.	**Nobody** came.

5 也有不定副詞形式，如anywhere、everywhere、somewhere、nowhere：

There was **nowhere** to hide. I can't find Barbara **anywhere**.

6 在不定代詞後面加 else，可以指稱其他人或其他地方：

Everyone else is downstairs. I don't like it here. Let's go **somewhere else**.

7 也可以用在else後面加 "'s"（撇號＋s）的方式：

He was wearing **someone else's** jacket. This isn't mine. It's **somebody else's**.

62 練習 Practice

A 在正確的地方加上不定代詞或不定副詞來完成以下句子:

1 Shop at Binn's! There's __*something*__ for __*everybody*__. (everybody/something).

2 Get a free prize! _____ likes to get _____ for _____. (everybody/nothing/something)

3 _____ knows _____ but _____ knows _____. (everybody/everything/nobody/something)

4 _____ should do _____, but _____ ever does _____. (anything/nobody/something/somebody)

5 I know _____, because _____ ever tells me _____. (anything/nobody/nothing)

6 I've looked _____, but I can't find it. I've probably left it _____ else. (everywhere/somewhere)

B 用一個不定代詞或不定副詞與 else 或 else's 連用來完成以下句子:

1 I spoke to Janet but I didn't talk to __*anyone else*__.

2 He's not at home. He must have gone _____.

3 I saw three people. There was Ken and Sylvia and _____.

4 I was the only one there. There was _____.

5 I'm sorry we haven't any lemonade. Would you like _____?

6 Let's go to the cinema. There's _____ to do.

7 I'm really hungry. I'd like _____ to eat.

8 We stayed all the time in Athens. We didn't go _____.

9 That doesn't belong to me. It must be _____.

10 I had to borrow Stephen's jacket. _____ was big enough.

11 'It's not here. You must have left it _____.'

12 'You must get better. That's the most important thing. _____ matters.'

第三編

63 比較級 Comparatives

1 單音節詞在詞尾加 -er 可構成比較級，在詞尾加 -est 可構成最高級：

cheap → **cheaper** → **cheapest**
These shoes are much **cheaper** than those.

hard → **harder** → **hardest**
He works **harder** than most people.

以 "-e" 結尾的單音節詞，要分別加 -r 和 -st：

safe → **safer** → **safest**
This is the **safest** place.

large → **larger** → **largest**
You need something much **larger**.

單元音並以一個輔音結尾的詞，要將這個輔音雙拼：

big → **bigger** → **biggest**
It gets **bigger** every day.

hot → **hotter** → **hottest**
It's much **hotter** in summer.

2 雙音節並以輔音後跟 -y 結尾的形容詞，要先將 -y 變為 -i，再加 -er 或 -est：

busy → **busier** → **busiest**
Friday is the **busiest** day of the week.

happy → **happier** → **happiest**
You would be **happier** at home.

3 大多數雙音節形容詞和所有以 -ly 結尾的較長形容詞和副詞，比較級要用 more，最高級要用 most：

careful → **more careful** → **most careful**
You should be **more careful**.

seriously → **more seriously** → **most seriously**
You could have been **more seriously** injured.

4 下面這些常用的雙音節形容詞和副詞，既可以加 -er 和 -est，又可以用 more 和 most：

common cruel gentle handsome likely narrow pleasant polite simple stupid

You should try to be **gentler**. You should try to be **more gentle**.

請注意 quiet 和 clever 這兩個常用的形容詞通常只能加 -er 和 -est。這兩個形容詞一般不能用 more 和 most：

It's much **quieter** living here. She's **cleverer** than her brother.

5 有些常用形容詞和副詞的比較級形式和最高級形式是不規則的：

good/well	better	best
bad/badly	worse	worst
far	farther/further	farthest/furthest

You can ask him when you know him **better**. I feel much **worse** today.

6 比較級形式可用於：

與 than 連用，可對兩件事或兩個人作直接比較（見第六十四單元）：
These shoes are much **cheaper** than those. She's **cleverer** than her brother.

表示有某種變化：
It's much **quieter** living here. It gets **bigger** every day.

可將某事與某一個標準相比：
Bigger cars generally use a lot of petrol. The new computer games are **more exciting**.

63 練習 Practice

A 把以下形容詞歸入 A 組或 B 組：

certain careful cheap cold dark expensive famous full great green
hard high important interested interesting kind often small useful

A 組：單音節詞，比較級加 -er， 最高級加 -est：	B 組：較長的詞，比較級用 more， 最高級用 most：

從上面兩組各選出 4 個詞，分別在 A 組和 B 組中寫出它們的的比較級和最高級：

A 組：cheaper, cheapest	B 組：more famous, most famous

B 寫出以下各詞的比較級和最高級：

nice _____   busy _____

clever _____   late _____

happy _____   good _____

quiet _____   bad _____

big _____   hot _____

C 把以下的形容詞變成比較級，再把它們用在下面的句子裏：

young   easy   important   expensive   useful   bad   heavy

1 It's only a cheap bike. I couldn't afford anything _____ .

2 That small dictionary is all right, but a big one would be _____.

3 I used to enjoy all kinds of sports when I was _____.

4 Let me help you with your bag. It's much _____ than mine.

5 Luckily this year's exam is much _____ than last year's.

6 I know the children often behave badly, but they were much _____ a few years ago

   when they were _____.

7 Last winter was very cold but it seems this year will be even _____.

8 Which is _____, grammar or vocabulary?

9 My sister is three years _____ than me.

10 The weather has been awful – and it's getting _____.

11 Petrol is much _____ nowadays.

64 The -est; than; as ... as ...

1 最高級形容詞與名詞連用時，前面要帶 the：

It's **the best film** I've ever seen. Which is **the biggest city** in the world? I was **the youngest child** in my family.

one of the...-est...是常用的表達式：

Liverpool is **one of the biggest cities** in Britain.

物主詞也常與最高級形容詞連用：

Jack is **one of my oldest friends**. This is **London's oldest theatre**.

2 比較級形容詞與 than 連用，可以對兩個事物進行對比：

English is **more useful than** Latin. Tokyo is **bigger than** London.

3 程度副詞可以與比較級形容詞連用：

slightly a bit not much a lot far much

This pullover is **much nicer** than that one, and it's **a bit cheaper too**.
I'm coming home soon. I won't be **much longer**.

4 可用 as...as...來表述兩個事物或兩個人在某些方面相似：

Their house is **as small as** ours. I'm **as tired as** you are.

可用 not as...as...來表述兩個事物或兩個人在某些方面有所不同：

'I'm **not as young as** I used to be.'

'It's **not as easy as** you think.'

5 可用 the same as 來表述兩者在某些方面相似：

Your car is quite old. It's **the same as** ours. This book is **the same as** mine.
He's very funny – just **the same as** his brother.

6 可用 just 或 exactly 來表述二者完全一樣：

I'm **just as pleased as** you are. They are **just as bad as** when they were children.

7 可用 nearly、almost、not quite 來表述二者幾乎完全一樣：

It's **nearly as hot as** it was yesterday. This one is **not quite as good as** that.

A 請看圖，完成以下與 Tom、Helen、Anne 和 Bill 有關的句子：

1 Bill is as tall as _Helen_ , but he isn't as tall as _Tom_ .

2 Tom is a bit taller than _____ and
_____, and much taller than _____.

3 Helen is just as tall as _____, but she
isn't as heavy as he is.

4 Bill is a bit younger than _____ and
much younger than _____ and
_____ .

5 Both _____ and _____ are
younger than Helen.

6 _____ is the oldest and _____
is the youngest.

7 _____ isn't quite as old as _____ .

8 _____ is as tall as _____ , but she
isn't as tall as _____ .

9 _____ is just a bit older than _____ but he's much heavier than she is.

10 _____ is the youngest but _____ is the lightest.

Tom	Helen	Anne	Bill
20	19	14	12

B 用最高級形容詞改寫以下句子：

1 I have never seen such a big dog before. _It's the biggest dog I have ever seen._

2 I have never met such a nice person. _She's_

3 They had never heard such a funny story. _It was_

4 Mary had never read such a good book. _It was_

C 根據你了解的人或地方寫出與以下句子相似的句子：

1 London is a much bigger city than Leeds.   1 _____

2 Peter is a bit taller than Fred.   2 _____

3 Oxford is an older city than Birmingham.   3 _____

4 Emma is much older than her sister.   4 _____

D 你能回答下面的疑問句嗎？

1 What is the commonest word in English? _____

2 What is the highest mountain in the world? _____

3 What is the longest river in the world? _____

4 What is the tallest tower in the world? _____

65 | So, such

1 可用 so 和 such 來強調正在談論的事情：

You are kind.

You are **so** kind. (= very kind)

Jim's tall.　　He's **such** a tall person!

2 下面是一些常用的結構：

"so ＋形容詞"：
I feel **so good** today.　The weather's **so nice**.　He's **so young**.

"so ＋副詞"：
Everything happened **so quickly**. Why are you leaving **so soon**?

so many、so much、so few 和 so little：
There are **so many** wonderful shops here!　We had **so little** time.
I know **so few** people.　There's **so much** to do!

3 與 such 連用的幾種不同結構：

a "such ＋ a/an（＋形容詞）＋單數名詞"：
　Henry is **such a sweet person**. The dog made **such a mess**!

b "such（＋形容詞）＋不具數名詞"：
　I've never had **such good advice**. This is **such boring homework**.

c "such（＋形容詞）＋複數名詞"：
　He paints **such beautiful pictures**.

4 可用 "so...＋ that" 或 "such...
＋ that" 來表述結果：

It was **so cold that** we stayed at home.
It is **such a long book that** I couldn't finish it.

The train was **so crowded that** we couldn't move.

65 練習 Practice

A 用 such 和括號裏的詞改寫以下句子，可做必要的改動：

例如：I didn't know their house was so big. (place) *I didn't know their house was such a big place.*

1 Why were you in the shop for so long? (time) _____

2 I really like Sue. She's so nice. (person) _____

3 I can never hear him. He speaks so quietly. (in ... voice) _____

4 We saw you driving your BMW yesterday. It looks so powerful. (car) _____

5 Have you heard the new REM album? It's so good. (CD) _____

B 把左欄與右欄相關的部分連成句子，以達到最合情理的結果：

1 The food was so delicious ...	that all the hotels were full.
2 We had such good weather ...	that I couldn't stop to talk.
3 I was in such a hurry ...	that I didn't recognise it.
4 The town has changed so much ...	that we talked for hours.
5 The dog was barking so loudly ...	that we came back with tans.
6 It was such a long time since I'd seen him ...	that we cried.
7 There were so many tourists ...	that I helped myself to more.
8 The film was so sad ...	that we couldn't hear the TV.

C 檢查以下句子是對還是錯，把錯誤的地方改正過來：

1 The Smiths are so nice people. _____

2 You look so young in those clothes. _____

3 Thanks for the party. We had such good time. _____

4 It was such a boring film that we fell asleep.

_____

_____

5 He was driving so fast that he didn't notice the police car. _____

6 Bob's an expert. He knows such much about computers. _____

第五十單元：可能性 Probability

A 用以下情態動詞完成句子：

should　must　can't　ought to　must　can't

1　'You've been driving for 8 hours. You ＿＿＿＿＿ be tired.'

2　It's not far to Bristol, so we ＿＿＿＿＿ be there by 4 o'clock.

3　Finish all that work in one hour! You ＿＿＿＿＿ be serious!

4　No one is answering the phone. They ＿＿＿＿＿ all be out.

5　We did this exercise yesterday so it ＿＿＿＿＿ be easy.

6　'£25 for one coffee! That ＿＿＿＿＿ be right!'

完成以下句子，使其意思與習題A的第2、3、4、5、6小題的意思一樣：

7　We're nearly there now. It ＿＿＿＿＿ take much longer.

8　You ＿＿＿＿＿ be joking!

9　They ＿＿＿＿＿ be at home.

10　We ＿＿＿＿＿ be able to finish it quickly.

11　That ＿＿＿＿＿ be a mistake!

第五十一單元：提出要求和請求同意 Requests and permission

B 用 may 或 could 把以下陳述句改寫成禮貌疑問句：

1　I want to have another drink.

＿＿＿＿＿＿＿＿＿＿＿＿＿＿＿＿＿＿＿＿＿＿＿＿＿＿＿＿＿＿＿＿＿＿＿＿?

2　I want you to give me directions to the nearest bank.

＿＿＿＿＿＿＿＿＿＿＿＿＿＿＿＿＿＿＿＿＿＿＿＿＿＿＿＿＿＿＿＿＿＿＿＿?

3　Tell me when I can see Mr Smart.

＿＿＿＿＿＿＿＿＿＿＿＿＿＿＿＿＿＿＿＿＿＿＿＿＿＿＿＿＿＿＿＿＿＿＿＿?

4　I'd love some more chocolate cake.

＿＿＿＿＿＿＿＿＿＿＿＿＿＿＿＿＿＿＿＿＿＿＿＿＿＿＿＿＿＿＿＿＿＿＿＿?

5　The man wants you to tell him what time the film starts.

＿＿＿＿＿＿＿＿＿＿＿＿＿＿＿＿＿＿＿＿＿＿＿＿＿＿＿＿＿＿＿＿＿＿＿＿?

6　We'd like to leave now.

＿＿＿＿＿＿＿＿＿＿＿＿＿＿＿＿＿＿＿＿＿＿＿＿＿＿＿＿＿＿＿＿＿＿＿＿?

7　Janet wants to have a quick talk with the manager.

＿＿＿＿＿＿＿＿＿＿＿＿＿＿＿＿＿＿＿＿＿＿＿＿＿＿＿＿＿＿＿＿＿＿＿＿?

8　It's very hot. They want to take their jackets and ties off.

＿＿＿＿＿＿＿＿＿＿＿＿＿＿＿＿＿＿＿＿＿＿＿＿＿＿＿＿＿＿＿＿＿＿＿＿?

C 用 can't、doesn't need to、needn't、don't need to、are not allowed to 完成
以下句子：

1　You _____ leave your suitcase there. It's
　　dangerous.

2　You _____ smoke on the Underground
　　now. It's illegal.

3　They _____ do the whole exercise. Five
　　questions are enough.

4　'Your father _____ worry. I'm a very careful driver.'

5　We _____ get up early tomorrow.
　　It's Saturday.

6　'They _____ park their car there! It's my garden.'

第五十二單元：喜歡、不喜歡和邀請 Likes, dislikes and invitations

D 用動詞的正確形式完成以下句子：

1　My father /dislike/do/ the washing-up.

　　_____.

2　How about /go/ to the beach this weekend?

　　_____?

3　Young children normally /enjoy/watch/ adventure films.

　　_____.

4　Nature-lovers often /enjoy/go/ camping.

　　_____.

5　You must /tell/ us about your holiday.

　　_____.

6　How about /let me/do/ the cooking this evening?

　　_____?

7　I don't mind /listen/ classical music.

　　_____.

8　I /hate/sleep/ in the dark when I was a child.

　　_____.

9　Do you /fancy/come/ with us to the disco?

　　_____?

第
三
編

第五十三單元：説與想 Saying and thinking

E 用括號裏的詞完成以下句子：

1 'I'll buy you a present.'
He _promised to buy his wife_ _____ a present. (promise/wife)

2 'OK, I won't smoke in the house.'
My father _____ in the house. (agree)

3 'If we're lucky we'll get there before the match starts.'
The fans _____ before the start of the match. (hope)

4 Could you give me a hand with the shopping?
Sheila _____ with the shopping. (ask/husband)

5 We're not going abroad after all. It's too expensive.
We _____ go abroad after all. (decide)

6 You can't leave until the room is clean.
The officer _____ the room. (order/soldiers)

7 Use a dictionary to check new words.
The teacher _____ new words. (advise/students)

8 Don't show anyone your work.
He _____ his work. (tell/artist)

9 Can you ski?
Someone _____ . (ask/me/know)

第五十四單元：Make、let、help＋不帶 to 的不定式 Make, let, help + bare infinitive

F 用 make、let 或 help 的正確形式完成以下句子：

1 'Could you _____ me clean the house, please?'
2 'What shall we do tonight?' 'I know, _____'s go out.'
3 I don't think parents should _____ their children stay up late every night.
4 I'm afraid the pills didn't _____ me. I've still got a headache.
5 'When does the play start?' _____ me see ... At 8, I think.'
6 The heavy traffic _____ me miss my train.

7 Father: 'Go to bed!'
Son: 'You can't _____ me!'

8 The robbers _____ the bank clerk give them all the money.

Cycle 3

複習　第三編 **50 – 65**單元

第五十五單元：感知動詞 Verbs of perception

G 選擇以下動詞的正確形式：

1 Listen! You can hear the birds *singing/sing*.
2 Are you coming to watch the team *playing/play*?
3 We saw them *getting/get* into the car and drive off.
4 They saw hundreds of people *swimming/swim* as they drove along the coast.
5 I thought I heard you *coming/come* in at two o'clock.
6 If you notice someone *acting/act* suspiciously, phone the police.

第五十六單元：乏詞義動詞 Delexical verbs

H 用 give、take、have 或 go 的正確形式完成以下句子：

1 Your salad looks delicious. Can I _____*take*_____ a mouthful?

2 Let me _____ you an example of what I mean.

3 There's no hurry, so _____ your time.

4 The referee _____ the player a warning for playing dangerously.

5 When do you _____ breakfast here?

6 We _____ a wonderful holiday last year.

7 They decided to _____ for a ride in the country.

8 _____ care not to break anything!

9 They were _____ an interesting chat about their holidays.

10 Most sensible people don't like _____ risks.

第五十七、五十八單元：短語動詞 Phrasal verbs

I 把下面相關的小品詞和動詞連成短語動詞，然後用其正確形式完成句子：

find hurry look take stay keep go look   up out on on after up up up

1 You're so slow. _____*Hurry up.*_____

2 Can I _____ to watch the end of the film on TV?

3 Henry agreed to _____ the children while his wife was away on business.

4 My mother was really angry when she _____ that I hadn't gone to school.

5 I didn't know your phone number so I _____ it _____ in the phone book.

6 Don't let me disturb you. Please _____ with your work.

7 No one was listening, but he _____ speaking.

8 If you want to get fit, you should _____ a sport.

複習　第三編 **50 – 65** 單元

第五十九單元：與介詞連用的動詞 Verbs with prepositions

J 選擇正確的介詞：

1 He said he had dreamt *with/about* me the night before.
2 This house used to belong *on/to* Madonna, you know.
3 You'll never guess who I bumped *on/into* this morning.
4 I might go out tomorrow. It depends *of/on* how I feel.
5 You look worried. What are you thinking *about/on*?
6 If you break anything, you'll have to pay *for/about* it.
7 They had to ask the shop assistant *about/for* help.
8 They promised they would write *to/at* each other every week.

第六十單元：反身代詞 Reflexives

K 在必要的地方填上適當的反身代詞來完成以下句子：

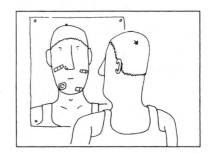

1 'That's a great dress. Where did you buy it?'
   'Actually, I made it _____ .'
2 'We're off to the concert now.' 'Fine. Enjoy _____ .'
3 'Can I go to the disco in jeans?' 'No, I think you should
   change _____ .'
   　　　　　　4 Neil was angry because he cut _____ while he was shaving _____ .
5 They say that people who talk to _____ are a little strange.
6 The washing machine will turn _____ off when it has finished. It's very handy.
7 Mrs Banks got up, washed _____ and went to work as normal.
8 I have two uncles who live by _____ .

第六十一單元：-ing 形容詞和 -ed 形容詞 -ing and -ed adjectives

L 選擇以下形容詞的正確形式：

We found the tour of the city (1) *fascinating/fascinated*. There
were so many (2) *interesting/interested* places to see. We
were both very (3) *impressing/impressed* by
the historic monuments, but the children, of course, began
to look (4) *boring/bored* quite quickly. They were more
(5) *interesting/interested* in the shops.
I wanted to have a (6) *relaxing/relaxed* evening in the
hotel, but the children insisted on going out, so
we bought a paper to see if there was an
(7) *amusing/amused* film on. They were quite
(8) *disappointing/disappointed* when they
realized they had already seen all the films.

Cycle 3

複習　第三編 **50 – 65** 單元

第六十二單元：不定代詞 Indefinite pronouns

M 選用括號裏的一個詞來完成以下句子：

1 Do you know ＿＿＿＿＿＿ who lives near here? (nobody/anybody)

2 Keep this a secret. Don't talk to ＿＿＿＿＿＿ . (nobody/anybody)

3 I want to ask you ＿＿＿＿＿＿ . (something/anything)

4 Are you sure that we haven't forgotten ＿＿＿＿＿＿? (nothing/anything)

5 If you get lost, ask anyone. ＿＿＿＿＿＿ will help you. (they/he)

6 He talked so fast that ＿＿＿＿＿＿ understood what he was saying. (somebody/nobody)

7 There's ＿＿＿＿＿＿ Ken doesn't understand about electronics. He's a genius. (everything/nothing)

8 You can put the book back ＿＿＿＿＿＿ on the shelf. It doesn't matter. (everywhere/anywhere)

第六十三單元：比較級與程度副詞 Comparatives with adverbs of degree

N 選用適當的狀語，並把它置於適當的位置來完成以下句子：

1 The video we watched last night was the funniest I have seen for a long time. (by far/a bit)

＿＿＿＿＿＿＿＿＿＿＿＿＿＿＿＿＿＿＿＿＿＿＿＿＿＿＿＿＿＿＿＿＿＿＿＿

2 It's hotter today than it was yesterday. (far/very)

＿＿＿＿＿＿＿＿＿＿＿＿＿＿＿＿＿＿＿＿＿＿＿＿＿＿＿＿＿＿＿＿＿＿＿＿

3 I feel more relaxed now. (quite/a good deal)

＿＿＿＿＿＿＿＿＿＿＿＿＿＿＿＿＿＿＿＿＿＿＿＿＿＿＿＿＿＿＿＿＿＿＿＿

4 This is the best book she's written. (slightly/by far)

＿＿＿＿＿＿＿＿＿＿＿＿＿＿＿＿＿＿＿＿＿＿＿＿＿＿＿＿＿＿＿＿＿＿＿＿

5 This exercise is more difficult than I thought. (rather/quite)

＿＿＿＿＿＿＿＿＿＿＿＿＿＿＿＿＿＿＿＿＿＿＿＿＿＿＿＿＿＿＿＿＿＿＿＿

6 More people went to the exhibition than expected. (a little/a lot)

＿＿＿＿＿＿＿＿＿＿＿＿＿＿＿＿＿＿＿＿＿＿＿＿＿＿＿＿＿＿＿＿＿＿＿＿

7 The things they sell in the shops nowadays are more expensive than last year. (much/many)

＿＿＿＿＿＿＿＿＿＿＿＿＿＿＿＿＿＿＿＿＿＿＿＿＿＿＿＿＿＿＿＿＿＿＿＿

8 I think it would be a better idea to go on holiday in the spring when there aren't so many tourists. (much/a lot)

＿＿＿＿＿＿＿＿＿＿＿＿＿＿＿＿＿＿＿＿＿＿＿＿＿＿＿＿＿＿＿＿＿＿＿＿

第三編

第六十四單元：The -est; than; as … as

O 用以下形容詞的原形、比較級形式或最高級形式來完成以下句子：

good big expensive long exciting lucky famous competitive

1 Can you think of anything _____ than
   flying by balloon?

2 All sports are _____ now than they used to be.

3 This is one of the _____ restaurants in the area.

4 'How _____ is that ring, please?'

5 You can keep my dictionary for as _____
   as you like.

6 Brazil is the _____ country in South America.

7 Thieves have stolen two of Picasso's _____
   paintings.

8 Mike is the _____ person I know.
   He escaped unhurt from a plane crash once!

9 'Today is my _____ day.'

10 'How are you?' 'I've never felt _____ .'

11 I'm afraid I can't wait any _____ .

12 One day we will be even _____
   than the Beatles!

第六十五單元：So, such

P 用 so 或 such 完成以下句子：

1 It's _____ kind of you to come and help me.

2 I've never stayed in _____ a comfortable hotel.

3 It's _____ a pity you can't come to our party.

4 There were _____ many people in the queue that we decided not to go to the cinema after all.

5 The room was in _____ a mess after the party.

6 No one had ever seen Mark look _____ worried.

7 Why are you driving _____ fast?

8 Have you ever heard _____ a ridiculous story?

9 We had _____ fantastic weather that we were on the beach every day!

10 'You say _____ wonderful things to me!'

A 用括號裏動詞的正確時態完成以下句子 (第一 — 十二單元)：

My friend Helena 1 (move) _____ to our city on the south coast last year. Before she 2 (come) _____ here, she 3 (go) _____ abroad for four months because she 4 (finish) _____ with her boyfriend and 5 (want) _____ to get out of London. She 6 (worry) _____ that there would be nothing to do, but she 7 (be) _____ totally wrong. There 8 (be) _____ a brilliant theatre and lots of restaurants and clubs. Also, she 9 (find) _____ that everything 10 (be) _____ much cheaper, and she 11 (make) _____ a lot of friends here. In fact she 12 (go) _____ on holiday with a group of new friends next month.

B 用以下動詞的正確時態和否定形式完成以下句子：(第四單元)

be be finish hear work rain be feel go arrive

1 Chris _____ to the cinema tonight because he's tired.
2 I'm sorry, I _____ what you said.
3 Could you buy some fruit? There _____ any left.
4 Paul _____ well lately, so he called the doctor for an appointment.
5 Boris _____ French, he's from Switzerland.
6 The lesson _____ yet, so stay where you are.
7 Don't put any money in that drinks machine. It _____ at the moment.
8 The flight from Tangiers was delayed, so I'm afraid that it _____ yet.
9 Leave your umbrella, it _____ now.
10 We had a lovely meal out, and it really _____ expensive.

C 在必要的地方加上適當的冠詞和代詞完成以下對話：(第十九 — 二十六單元)

'Jane, here's 1 ___*the*___ recipe for iced coffee 2 ___*you*___ asked 3 _____ for after 4 _____ meal 5 _____ had 6 _____ last week.'

'Great. Let 7 _____ just get 8 _____ piece of 9 _____ paper and 10 _____ pen to write everything down. OK. What are 11 _____ ingredients?'

'Well, 12 _____ need 13 _____ coffee, either ground or instant, of course, and 14 _____ sugar to make 15 _____ sweet, then 16 _____ ice and 17 _____ milk. You can use 18 _____ vanilla, too.'

'OK. What do 19 _____ do first?'

'Right. Put 20 _____ vanilla and 21 _____ coffee in 22 _____ small saucepan. Add about half 23 _____ litre of 24 _____ water, and boil 25 _____ all quickly. Then turn off 26 _____ heat and add 27 _____ sugar. Leave 28 _____ for 29 _____ few minutes. Then pour 30 _____ liquid through 31 _____ coffee filter into 32 _____ jug.'

'That sounds fine. What about 33 _____ ice?'

'Fill 34 _____ couple of 35 _____ glasses with as much of 36 _____ ice as possible, pour in 37 _____ coffee. When 38 _____ is cool, add 39 _____ milk and enjoy 40 _____ delicious drink.'

D 用物主詞、代詞或形容詞完成以下句子（第二十二 — 二十六單元）：

1 Where did you buy _____ painting?

2 _____ books are about literature, and _____ are about cooking.

3 Yesterday was one of _____ days when everything went wrong.

4 I need a new handbag. The _____ I've got is too small.

5 'I was talking to Patrizia this morning.' 'Who's _____?'

6 'We enjoyed _____ meal. I hope you enjoyed _____ .'

7 This is a photo of Jacky and _____ husband.

8 _____ time tomorrow we'll be on the beach.

E 完成以下疑問句形式（第十四、十五單元）：

1 'We're going to the cinema. Do you _____ with us?'

2 'What _____ see?' 'Blood Castle.'

3 'What sort _____?' 'A comedy, I think.'

4 'When _____?' 'At half-past seven.'

5 'And how long _____?' 'About 2 hours, I think.'

6 'Is _____ expensive?' 'No, not at all.'

7 'So, how much _____?' '£ 3.50.'

8 'Great. Where _____ showing?' 'At the Odeon.'

總複習 B：第一編

F 用以下單詞或短語完成以下句子（第二十七 — 三十單元）：

> since in very much ago from hardly ever since recently in until
> probably ago since in until until probably very much often hardly ever

1 We've been incredibly busy _____ .

2 The weather turned bad a couple of days _____ .

3 Hurry, the shops close _____ ten minutes.

4 If you see someone looking at a map, they are _____ tourists.

5 'Did you enjoy your holiday?'
   'Yes, _____ .'

6 'The party next door went on _____
   4 o'clock _____ the morning!'

7 I haven't had time to relax _____ I got up this morning.

8 Dinner is served _____ 7.00 _____ 11.30 every evening.

9 I'm _____ ill. I think I've only missed two days' school in my life.

10 It's ages _____ you did the washing-up! You're so lazy.

11 My father re-decorated the bathroom six months _____ .

12 I'm planning to retire _____ eight years.

13 Some of my classmates have been together _____ they were in kindergarten.

14 Children think most things are interesting. They are _____ bored.

15 I enjoy my work _____ .

16 The meeting went on _____ three o'clock in the afternoon.

17 I will _____ be a bit late home tonight.

18 It's good to be honest, but it's _____ better to remain silent.

總複習 C：第二編

A 用情態動詞完成以下句子（第三十一 — 三十六單元）：

1 £100 for a hamburger! You _____ be joking! You _____ be serious!

2 The accident happened when the driver _____ stop the car. People _____ jump out of the way of the car.

3 The last thing the driver _____ remember is turning the corner.

4 Take an umbrella. It _____ rain.

5 With your new glasses you _____ to read better. (2 modals)

6 _____ you mind staying late and helping me tonight, please?

7 The phone's ringing. That _____ be my mother.

8 You _____ wear a uniform in most schools nowadays.

9 The train leaves at 6 o'clock, so you _____ be late.

10 'I'm sorry I'm late.' 'Oh, you _____ apologize, We've only just started the meeting.'

11 If you _____ choose anywhere in the world, where _____ you most like to live?

12 What _____ you do if you saw a robbery?

B 用非人稱代詞 It 結構完成以下句子：（第三十六單元）：

1 This is my favourite place. I like _____

2 Can you tell me the time? What _____

3 Tomorrow the weather will be stormy. It _____

4 We haven't had a holiday for almost a year. It _____

5 Your sister was very kind. She lent me some money. It _____

6 Is that Joseph? Who _____?

7 What a pity they weren't here with us. It _____

8 Driving in a city can be frightening. It _____

C 先把括號裏的詞排成正確次序，再用它們完成以下句子（第四十單元）：

1 I'll _____ when they arrive. (your exam results/post/you)

2 Could you _____ when you go to the shops? (for me/something/buy)

3 Please _____ now. (that dictionary/to me/bring)

4 Their mother promised _____ . (them/to read/a story)

5 My father is trying _____ . (a present/to find/for my mother)

6 They spent the morning writing _____ . (to their friends/postcards)

7 The children told _____ . (to the policeman/their version/of what had happened)

8 Can I offer _____? (another piece of cake/you)

9 I never know _____ . (get/father/my/what/his/for/birthday/to)

10 His mother prepared _____ . (tea/cups/of/everyone/for)

D 用 make 和 do 的正確形式完成以下句子（第三十九單元）：

1 Don't put your dirty boots there! You'll _____ a mess.

2 I haven't had time to _____ my homework.

3 I'm just _____ some coffee. Do you want a cup?

4 We've _____ a decision. We're going to get married.

5 Do you know anyone who enjoys _____ the ironing?

6 You all _____ well to get here so early.

E 用括號裏的詞改寫以下句子，可做必要的改動（第四十 — 四十四單元）：

1 There were so many cars on the road that we arrived late. (traffic)

_____

2 Bournemouth is on the coast, so is Brighton. (both)

_____

3 My friends can't speak Japanese. (none)

_____

4 Most of the suitcases were already on the plane. (luggage)

_____

5 We bought one or two souvenirs for family and friends. (a few)

_____

6 You can buy stamps in every post office. (any)

_____

7 I've listened to almost all the records in the school library. (most)

_____

8 Everyone in our class has travelled abroad. (all)

_____

9 Many of the facts you gave me were wrong! (information)

_____

10 He wrote me a cheque for one hundred pounds. (pound)

_____

總複習 **C**：第二編

F 選用正確的詞彙完成以下句子（第四十五 — 四十八單元）：

1 Meeting you in town was a *really/real* surprise!

2 Someone has put the cups back *in/on* the shelf.

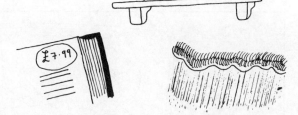

3 The price is written *in/at* the top of the page.

4 It's raining *hard/hardly*.

5 Do you know anyone who lives *at/in* the countryside?

6 The nearest supermarket is *opposite/in front of* the train station.

7 Tim put a pile of books *on/above* his desk.

8 It was only 6 a.m. but the manager was already *in/at* work.

9 A man was asking for money *next to/ out of* the theatre.

10 'I don't know anyone,' he said *lonely/in a lonely* manner.

163

總複習 D：第三編

A 選用正確的詞彙完成選段：

(1) *A/The* American President and (2) *his/her* wife (3) *arrived/have arrived* in London yesterday (4) *at/on* the beginning of (5) *their/theirs* six-day trip (6) *to/in* Europe. They (7) *can meet/ are going to meet* (8) *the/a* Prime Minister and other politicians for (9) *dinner/a dinner* this evening (10) *in/on* Downing Street.

B 選用正確的詞彙完成選段：

(1) *The/This* acrobat (2) *who/which* survived a 6,000 foot fall (3) *over/in* Shanghai (4) *when/how* his parachute (5) *doesn't/didn't* open (6) *other/the other* day was very lucky. Even (7) *luckier/luckiest* was Vesna Vulovic, (8) *a/an* Czech air hostess who (9) *come/came* down in the broken tail of (10) *a/the* Boeing 747. The plane (11) *explodes/exploded* at an altitude of 33,330 feet (12) *on/over* Czechoslovakia (13) *on/in* 1972. The Guinness Book (14) *of /for* Records says that her fall (15) *is/has been* the (16) *longest/longer* without (17) *the/a* parachute.

C 選用正確的詞彙完成選段：

(1) *On/In* October 12th, a woman driver (2) *has/had* her handbag (3) *taking/taken* when she (4) *waits/ was waiting* at traffic lights in Birmingham. She (5) *was feeling/felt* very angry, so she (6) *drove/drives* after the man who (7) *had/has* robbed her. Then the man (8) *had dropped/dropped* the handbag (9) *on/ in* the middle of the road, and the woman (10) *was getting/got* (11) *out of/off* her car to pick (12) *up it/ it up*, and was happy to find (13) *every/all* her money (14) *was/were* still inside it and that the man (15) *took/had taken* (16) *anything/nothing*. Unfortunately, when she (17) *looked/is looking* up, she (18) *has seen/saw* him jump (19) *onto/into* her car and drive away. The police (20) *was/were* unable to find the car.

總複習 D：第三編

D 請看圖，然後完成以下句子：

1 'Mary, you _____ clean the floor.' 'I did it yesterday.'

2 'That _____ be enough for the weekend.'

3 'You only got up an hour ago. You _____ be tired!'

4 '_____ make a suggestion?'

5 'How about _____ for a walk now?'

6 '_____ have some more of my home-made lemonade.'

7 'Do you feel like _____ that film?'

8 'I agree _____ you to the beach tomorrow if you promise _____ to bed right now.'

9 '_____ me go! Please, someone, _____ me escape!'

E 完成以下的選段：

I was (1) _____ to a nurse who works (2) _____ the local hospital. She (3) _____ me a very (4) _____ story about a man (5) _____ stole rings, money and other valuables from the nurses' room while he was waiting (6) _____ the doctor to treat (7) _____ broken arm. No one saw him (8) _____ the objects, but they found (9) _____ he was a thief when they (10) _____ the X-ray picture and saw the things in his pocket!

165

66 不能用於進行時態的動詞
Verbs not used in continuous tenses

1 有些動詞通常不能用進行時態。這些動詞通常表述:

思想 (thoughts): believe know remember think (= believe) understand want wish
I **know** Angela but I **don't know** her brother. I **think** English is very difficult.
It was very difficult. I **didn't understand** it. **Do** you **believe** in fairies?

喜歡和不喜歡 (likes and dislikes): dislike hate like love prefer
I **like** history but I **don't like** geography. I quite **liked** hockey, but I **preferred** basketball.

所屬 (possession): belong to have own possess
They **own** a big house in the country. Oh dear! I **don't have** any money with me.

感覺 (senses): look seem smell sound taste
The cake **tasted** very good.

'What's that? It **looks** very interesting.'

'Try this milk. It **smells** funny to me.'

2 這些動詞中有些還含有其他的意思。當它們用於其他的意思時就可以使用進行時態:

在下面的句子裏,have 不作所屬解:
She's **having** a shower. I'm **having** a drink.
They're **having** a party. We're **having** fun.

Think 不作 believe 解:
Be quiet I'm **thinking**. What are you **thinking** about?

有時兩種形式都可以使用:
You're **looking** very smart today. 或 You **look** very smart today.
She **looked** a bit tired. 或 She **was looking** a bit tired.

請看動詞 taste 的用法:

'I'm **tasting** the milk ... Mm it **tastes** bad.'

3 動詞 see 和 hear 通常不使用現在進行時態:

see 和 hear 通常與 can 連用: Please speak a bit louder. I **can't hear** you.
　　　　　　　　　　　　　Look over there. I **can see** Peter.

當 see 作 visit 解時,可以使用進行時態:
Little Red Riding Hood **was seeing** her grandmother.

4 動詞 be 通常不使用現在進行時態:

This **is** my friend, Michelle. **Is** there anyone at home?

A 用 think 或 believe 説出你對以下事物的看法：

1 _____ that some people can tell the future.
2 _____ that there is life on Mars.
3 _____ that some people are born lucky.
4 _____ that thirteen is an unlucky number.

5 _____ that our future is in the stars.
6 _____ that three is a lucky number.
7 _____ that Friday is an unlucky day.
8 _____ that animals have a language.

用 like、dislike、love 或 hate 説出你對下面這些事物的看法：

9 _____ getting up early in the morning.
10 _____ singing karaoke.
11 _____ cooking.
12 _____ rock and roll music.

13 _____ swimming.
14 _____ dancing.
15 _____ going to the dentist.
16 _____ classical music.

習題 A 中的兩項練習各説了 8 件事。每做完一項練習後就合上書本，看看你能記住多少。

B 用 look、smell、sound 或 taste 的正確形式完成以下句子：

1 Jack is only sixteen, but he _____ much older.

2 I spoke to Mary on the phone. She _____ very happy.

3 I like your perfume. It _____ wonderful.

4 These oranges _____ really sweet.

C 把括號裏的動詞變成簡單現在時或現在進行時來完成以下對話：

1 A Hello what (you/do) are you doing?

B Hi! (I/read) _____ this book.

A (That/look) _____ interesting.

B Yes. (It/be) _____ very good.

A (You/like) _____ reading?

B Yes, (I/love) _____ it.

2 A Can I borrow your pen?

B (I/be) _____ sorry. (I/use)

_____ it.

A What about this one? Who (this/belong to)

_____?

B (I/think) _____ it's Carol's.

(I/know) _____ (she/have)

_____ one like that. You can ask her.

(She/work) _____ in the next room.

3 A (You/remember) _____

Fred Johnson?

B Yes, (I/know) _____ him well.

Why?

A (I/write) _____ him a letter.

B Great! Say 'Hello' to him from me.

4 A (That coffee/smell) _____

great!

B Would you like some coffee or (you/prefer)

_____ tea?

A (You/make) _____ tea as well?

B I can make some tea if (you/like)

_____ .

A Thank you. (I/think) _____

a cup of tea would be very nice.

第四編

1 -ed 形容詞。在第五十九單元裏，我們學習了以 -ed 結尾的形容詞。

下面這些形容詞都是從動詞轉化來的：

annoyed	bored	closed	delighted	excited
finished	frightened	interested	pleased	surprised
tire	worried	broken	disappointed	shut

這些形容詞在意思上是被動的：

We always lock the door:
The door is always **locked**.

We'll finish the job before next week:
The job will be **finished** before next week.

When I was young spiders frightened me:
I was **frightened** of spiders.

2 被動語態動詞是由動詞 to be 和動詞過去分詞構成的：

They were serving lunch when we arrived:
Lunch **was being served** when we arrived.

They are going to build a lot of new roads:
A lot of new roads **are going to be built**.

People learn English all over the world:
English **is learned** all over the world.

3 把動詞 be 加到疑問句和否定句裏，可構成被動語態疑問形式和被動語態否定形式：

Nobody has sent the letters yet:
The letters **haven't been sent** yet.

They didn't invite Sandra to the party:
Sandra **wasn't invited** to the party.

Will they show that film on TV soon?:
Will that film **be shown** on TV soon?

'Have they delivered the mail yet?:'
'Has the mail **been delivered** yet?'

4 可用 by 談及施行動作的人或事：

A lot of damage **has been caused by the recent storms**.

67 練習 Practice

A 用 is、are、was、were 完成以下句子：

1 We _____ told to be ready at ten o'clock.
2 The police are looking for a man who _____ thought to be dangerous.
3 Guernica _____ painted by Picasso.
4 The 1948 Olympic Games _____ held in London.
5 Rice _____ grown all over Asia.
6 Most people _____ paid at the end of the month.
7 Thousands of gadgets _____ invented every year.
8 The concerts in England and America _____ watched by millions of fans.

B 用 be、being、been 完成以下句子：

1 A new museum has _____ opened in the city centre.
2 Can you drive me to town? My car is _____ repaired.
3 Many changes will have to _____ made to improve our image.
4 Most sportsmen and women hate _____ beaten.
5 Have you ever _____ invited to dinner by a stranger?
6 Our staff have _____ trained to use computers.

C 先把括號裏的動詞變成被動語態，再用它們完成以下句子：

1 The prices of all our products _____ in the sale this year. (reduce)
2 Three people _____ in a road accident yesterday. (kill)
3 I _____ by my grandparents. (bring up)
4 Dogs _____ in the shop. (not allow)
5 E.T. _____ by Steven Spielberg. (direct)
6 Cigarettes _____ in newsagents and supermarkets in Britain. (sell)
7 Today's match _____ because of the weather. (cancel)
8 Tickets for the concerts can _____ from the box office. (buy)

D 請看下面兩幅圖，然後用以下動詞完成以下句子，描述做了哪些事情，哪些事情還沒有做：

put away   do   wash   turn off   change   clean   empty

1 The washing-up
2 The radio
3 The dustbin
4 The windows
5 The pots and pans
6 The floor
7 The clock
8 The table

第四編

轉述過去 Reporting the past

1 間引結構可以用來提供人們所説或所想的信息。常見的轉述動詞可用於以下結構：

a 用於 that- 從句：

admit   agree   answer   complain   explain   promise   reply   say   think

He **agreed that** the exercise was difficult. They **explained that** they would be late.

Sally **replied that** she was busy.

b 用於 "動詞＋人稱賓語＋ that- 從句" 結構：

convince   inform   remind   tell

We **told them that** the work was important. I **reminded everyone that** it was Ben's birthday.

2 轉述時通常要改變説話者所用的時態：

説話者的話：	被轉述從句：
I'm so hungry I could eat a horse!	He said that he **was** very hungry.
We've just about finished; just one more page.	They said they **had** nearly **finished**.
The film was absolutely great.	They said the film **was** great.
	They said it **had been** great.
I'll be with you in a couple of minutes.	She said she **would be** here soon.

請注意，一般不必逐字逐句轉述説話者所説的話，只需轉述講話的主要意思。

3 轉述時情態動詞要有變化：

説話者的話：	被轉述從句：
Can I help you, sir?	The assistant asked if he **could** help me.
OK, it's time. You must stop now.	The examiner said we **had to** stop.

但是要小心：could、would、should、might、ought to 要保持不變：

We might need some help.　　They said that they **might** need help.

4 在下面的情況中，被轉述的句子可用現在時：

a 想説的事情仍是真實的：

My name is Henry.　　　　He said that his name **is** Henry. (或 'was')

b 談及的是將來的事情：

I'm having a party next Friday.

He told me he **is having** a party next Friday.

Cycle 4

68 練習 Practice

A 找出正確的轉述陳述句：

1 I really love jazz music.
   a She said she loved jazz music.
   b She said she would love jazz.

2 We were in France for a week.
   a They told us they had been in France for a week.
   b They told us they have been in France.

3 He's working hard.
   a She said he worked hard.
   b She said he was working hard.

4 I'll phone you.
   a You promised you phoned me.
   b You promised you would phone me.

5 But I can't swim!
   a He explained he couldn't swim.
   b He explained he won't swim.

6 She has read the book.
   a He told me she read the book.
   b He told me she had read the book.

7 You should know the answer.
   a She told me I knew the answer.
   b She told me I should know the answer.

Alice — *I'm meeting a client.*
Mary — *I would normally do it, but I must visit my mother in hospital.*
Mr Jones — *I can't because I will be in Glasgow.*
Linda — *I've already arranged something important.*
Geoff — *I stayed late the last time.*
Peter — *I don't think I will be able to; I already have too much work.*

B 一位經理因其部門業務繁忙，要求下屬在週五晚上加班。看看下屬們怎麼回答他，然後完成以下句子：

1 Alice explained that _____ client.
2 Mary said _____ hospital.
3 Mr Jones told the manger _____ Glasgow.
4 Linda replied that _____ important.
5 Geoff complained that _____ the last time.
6 Peter answered that _____ able to.

C 用 said、told、asked 或 thought 完成以下句子：

1 Someone _____ me the time. I _____ her that I didn't have a watch but _____ that it was about three o'clock.

2 When I was walking in the city, someone _____ me if I was a tourist. I _____ him that I lived here, then _____ him if he wanted some help.

3 'Have I _____ you the story of my first holiday abroad?'

4 The journalist _____ the policeman had _____ him about the murder.

69 省略回答 Short answers

1 在英語口語中，常用省略回答來回答問題。用省略回答比只用 Yes 或 No 禮貌。

a 當疑問句中有情態動詞時，回答時要重複這個情態動詞：

Would you like some more tea? Yes, **I would**.
Can you come tonight? Yes, **we can**.
No, I'm afraid **we can't**.

b 當疑問句中有助動詞時，回答時要重複這個助動詞：

Will your parents be at home tonight? Yes, **they will**.
Do you always work on Saturdays? No, **I don't**.

> **Have you finished?**
> **Yes, I have.**
> **No, you haven't.**

c 當 be 是疑問句的主要動詞時，回答時要用 be：

Are you married? Yes, **I am**.
No, **I'm not**.
Is there any more milk in the fridge? Yes, **there is**.

2 當疑問句是關於過去的事情時，省略回答要用過去時態：

Had they gone to bed when you got home?	Yes, **they had**.
Were they angry with you?	No, **they weren't**.
Did you have an argument?	No, **we didn't**.
Did I tell you that my father was a policeman?	Yes, **you did**.

3 要是想得到有關某事的更多信息，可以用 "where? why? when? how? which? ＋名詞" 進行提問：

Harry's at university now.	**Which university?** 或 **Which one?**
I'm going to town tomorrow.	**When?**
I think they live abroad.	**Where?**
The concert was cancelled.	**Why?**
She put your stuff by the door.	**Which door?**

4 在省略回答中，有些常用動詞和意見表達式可以與 so 連用：

	肯定	否定
Is this where they live?	**I think so.**	**I don't think so.**
Are the banks open now?	**I expect so.**	**I don't expect so.**
Will it rain tomorrow?	**I'm afraid so.**	**I'm afraid not.**
Is Jane coming tonight?	**I hope so.**	**I hope not.**

A 把相關的疑問句和省略回答連起來：

1	Do you see your friends often?	No, I'm not.
2	Are you new here?	Yes, you can.
3	Have you had breakfast today?	No, I don't.
4	Is the sun shining?	Yes, I do.
5	Are those your friends?	Yes, I have.
6	Do you know London well?	No, they aren't.
7	Can we go home early today?	Yes, it is.
8	Is there anything good on TV?	No, there isn't.

B 寫出以下疑問句的省略回答：

1 Can lions climb trees? _____

2 Is Bonn the capital of Germany? _____

3 Do they speak English in New Zealand? _____

4 Does rice grow in Wales? _____

5 Has the weather been good this week? _____

6 Was Marilyn Monroe an actress? _____

7 Did the Aztecs live in Spain? _____

8 Was the television invented by Einstein? _____

9 Were you born before 1950? _____

10 Are the Rocky Mountains in Europe? _____

C 下面每個陳述句都可以引出兩個不同的省略疑問句。找出與陳述句相關的省略疑問句：

例如：We met Paul recently. Where?/When?

Why?　Where?　When?　Which one?

1 I'm going on holiday soon. _____

2 We saw a brilliant video last night. _____

3 She refused to answer one of my questions. _____

4 Did you know that the last time I went abroad I was arrested? _____

5 My parents saw the Prime Minister in a restaurant last night. _____

6 Jack gave away all his books except one. _____

D 用括號裏的詞對以下疑問句作肯定回答：

1 Is this jacket expensive? (expect) _____

2 Are museums open on Sunday? (think) _____

3 Is the weather going to be the same tomorrow? (hope) _____

4 Was there any food left after the party? (afraid) _____

再對上面的疑問句作否定回答。

第四編

70 附加疑問 Question tags

1 用附加疑問可把陳述句變成疑問句：

You know Bill, **don't you**?
You didn't understand, **did you**?

在肯定陳述句後面通常要用否定附加疑問：
You are foreign, **aren't you**?
They left early, **didn't they**?

在否定陳述句後面通常要用肯定附加疑問：
She hasn't been here before, **has she**?
They didn't finish on time, **did they**?

2 附加疑問的幾種不同形式：

a 在有動詞 be 形式的主句後面，要用 be 構成附加疑問：

War and Peace wasn't written by an American, **was it**?
You are going to come to the cinema with us, **aren't you**?

b 在有助動詞或情態動詞（has、have、will、would、can、could 等）的主句後面，要用同一個助動詞或情態動詞構成附加疑問：

He will be there tonight, **won't he**?
They can't drive, **can they**?
The film hasn't started, **has it**?
He didn't go to Spain last year, **did he**?

c 在沒有助動詞或 be 的主句後面，要用 do、does、doing 構成附加疑問：

'It rains a lot here, **doesn't it**?'

'The war started in 1939, **didn't it**?'

3 附加疑問可用於：

a 在不知道答案的情況下，可以做出提問。提問時，必須在附加成分處提高語調：

You haven't got £5 I could borrow, **have you**?

b 要驗證某人是否與你的意見一致，或驗證你說的對不對時，語調必須下降：

It's Tuesday today, **isn't it**? She is beautiful, **isn't she**?

70 練習 Practice

A 選出正確的附加成分：

1 'The concert was great, *didn't it/wasn't it*?'

2 'You haven't finished already, *haven't you/have you*?'

3 'No one telephoned me, *didn't they/did they*?

4 'Not everyone can drive at eighteen, *can they/can't they*?'

  5 'There isn't room for another person, *isn't there/is there*?'

B 請看下面的陳述句，它們全都遺漏了附加成分。

a 在以下陳述句中的 be 動詞、情態動詞和助動詞下面加底線：

1 You're not from this country, _____

2 We're going to London tomorrow, _____

3 The weather was wonderful yesterday, _____

4 He was very angry because we were late, _____

5 It snowed last week, _____

6 Inflation used to be a big problem, _____

7 Young people should get as much exercise as possible, _____

8 You shouldn't be rude to people, _____

9 You know you shouldn't shout in restaurants, _____

10 Her friends from New York didn't visit you, _____

b 現在把下面的附加成分與上面帶情態動詞和助動詞的句子連起來：

  shouldn't they?   should you?   aren't we?   wasn't it?   are you?   wasn't he?

c 現在用 do 的正確形式作附加成分，把它們加到上面的其他陳述句裏。

C 你有多肯定？請看下面的疑問句，把你的答案寫出來，如下例：

Were Charles Haughey and John Lynch Prime Ministers of Britain or Ireland?
I think they were Prime Ministers of Ireland, weren't they?

1 Is the population of Oslo more or less than a million?

_____?

2 Were the 1976 Olympics held in Moscow or Montreal?

_____?

3 Did Henry Ford, the pioneer of the Ford automobile, die in 1947 or 1927?

_____?

4 Did the group Status Quo start playing in the 1960s or 1970s?

_____?

5 Are there 9, 10 or 11 players in a cricket team?

_____?

6 Which city is bigger, Istanbul or Berlin?

_____?

7 Does 'photophobia' mean that you have a fear of being photographed, or a fear of light?

_____?

第四編

175

71 Too, either, so, neither

1 把 too 置於從句後面，表示有關某人或某事的陳述同樣適用另一人或另一事：

He likes chocolate. I like it **too**. (= I like chocolate.)
The Smiths went by train. We did **too**. (= We went by train.)
Vincent was absent last week. He'll be away this week **too**.

注意 too 要用於肯定陳述句。在否定陳述句中要用 "否定動詞＋either"：

I didn't understand; my friend **didn't (understand) either**.
She can't come tomorrow, and she **can't come** on Friday **either**.

2 還可以使用肯定陳述句與 so 連用的結構。請注意在這種結構裏，詞序是："so＋動詞＋主語"：

a 在有動詞 be 的句子或從句後面，要用 "so + be"：

His shirt is new, and **so is his tie**. My sister is learning Greek; **so am I**. They were tired; **so was I**.

b 在 have 為助動詞的陳述句後面，要用 "so + have"：

'I've been to Iceland.' '**So have I**.'
Tania has bought a new car. **So has Steve**.
By ten o'clock the wind had stopped, **so had the rain**.

c 在使用 do 形式的陳述句後面，或在沒有助動詞的陳述句後面，要用 "so + do"：

I did like his last book; **so did my wife**.
The police came quickly; **so did the ambulance**.
The French produce a lot of wine, and **so do the Italians**.

d 在有情態動詞的陳述句後面，要用 "so＋情態動詞"：

Peter said he would love to go to Japan. **So would I**.
Sandra can cook wonderfully. **So can my friend Eva**.

3 在否定陳述句後面，要用 "neither＋肯定動詞＋主語"：

'I don't feel well'. '**Neither do I**.'
My father didn't go to college; **neither did my mother**.

'The fish isn't fresh, **neither are the vegetables**.'

'I haven't got time to go out tonight' '**Neither have I**.'

71 練習 Practice

A 把以下陳述句與正確的答案連起來：

1 They've been to Birmingham.	So did we.
2 She'll be away tomorrow.	So do you.
3 My neighbours are on holiday now.	So was I.
4 My sister drives a BMW.	So can I.
5 I was talking to the new Professor.	So are mine.
6 You look very healthy.	So does mine.
7 We worked hard last week.	So have we.
8 Chris can play the guitar.	So will I.

B 把以下的否定陳述句與正確的答案連起來：

1 I don't smoke.	Neither can mine.
2 We couldn't hear a thing.	Neither was I.
3 I haven't got a car.	Neither will I.
4 Most of my friends can't cook.	Neither do I.
5 I wasn't in bed early yesterday.	Neither have I.
6 I can't come tomorrow.	Neither can I.
7 We didn't do our homework.	Neither could we.
8 I won't tell anyone.	Neither did we.

C 改寫以下句子，如下例：

I like rock and roll. My sister does too.
I like rock and roll, so does my sister.

'I can't eat any more.' 'I can't either.'
'I can't eat any more.' 'Neither can I.'

1 Greenland is an island. Australia is an island, too. _____So is Australia._____

2 The whale is an endangered species. The rhino is, too. _____

3 My mother can't ski. My brother can't either. _____

4 Smoking isn't good for you. Eating a lot of chocolate isn't either. _____

5 The Beatles became famous in the 60's. The Rolling Stones did too. _____

6 Paul didn't write to me. Mandy didn't write to me either. _____

7 Mozart was a composer. Beethoven was a composer too. _____

8 Dictionaries aren't allowed in the exam. Computers aren't allowed either. _____

D 你的情況和下面的陳述句相似還是不同？根據真實情況回答下面的問題，如下例：

I live in a port. 或 — So do I. 或 — I don't.
I can't ski. 或 — Neither can I. 或 — I can.

1 I enjoy meeting people.
2 I don't live on the coast.
3 I get up early in the morning.
4 I didn't speak English yesterday.
5 I wasn't ill last week.

6 I don't drink alcohol.
7 I've been to London.
8 I was born in hospital.
9 I want to go home.
10 I've never been to the US.

第四編

72 限制性關係從句 Defining relative clauses

1 關係從句可用來確切説明正在談及的是何人或何事：

A: The girl got a three-week holiday in the US.

A: **The girl who won first prize.**

(**The girl who won first prize** got a three-week holiday.)

B: Which girl?

A: Do you remember the people?

A: **The people we met on holiday.**

(Do you remember **the people we met on holiday?**)

B: Which people?

A: Can I borrow that book?

A: **The book you told me about yesterday.**

(Can I borrow **the book you told me about yesterday**?)

B: Which book?

2 以 who 作主語的關係從句：

以 who 作主語的關係從句可用來説明正在談及的人是哪個人或哪些人。

who 要置於動詞之前：

The people **who live here** have a funny accent.

You are the only person **who can help us**.

We met someone **who used to work with your father**.

也可用 that 代替 who：

The people **that live here** have a funny accent.

'You are the only person **that can help us**.'

3 以 that 作主語的關係從句：

以 that 作主語的關係從句可用來説明正在談及的是哪件事或哪些事。 That 要置於動詞之前：

The car **that caused the crash** was going much too fast.

I need to catch the train **that leaves at 7.45**.

也可用 which 代替 that：

The car **which caused the crash** was going much too fast.

注意 在關係從句裏不能有第二個主語。

The people who ~~they~~ live next door are friendly. The things which ~~they~~ were stolen were very valuable.

4 以 that 作賓語的關係從句：

以 that 為賓語的關係從句可用來表述人或物。 That 要置於動詞的主語前面：

The car **that I wanted to buy** was not for sale.

Most of the people **that we met** were very friendly.

that 通常會被省略：

The car I **wanted to buy** was not for sale.

注意 在這種關係從句裏不能有第二個賓語。

The car that I wanted to buy ~~it~~ was not for sale. Most of the people that I met ~~them~~ were very friendly.

A 用 who、that 或 which 完成以下句子：

1 I don't know the names of the people _____ you talked to.
2 What's the name of the hotel _____ we stayed in last year?
3 I have read everything _____ Agatha Christie wrote.
4 Thanks for the postcard _____ you sent us.
5 Pierre has a brother _____ played football for France once.
6 We're taking the train _____ leaves at 10.15.
7 People _____ always think about money are sad, I think.

上面哪些句子不需要關係代詞？

B 用關係從句和以下詞彙填空：

cut/hair   sell/meat   sell/fruit and vegetables   write/newspaper articles
open/tins   protect you/from the sun

1 A barber is a man _____.
2 A woman _____ is called
   a hairdresser.
3 Someone _____ is a
   greengrocer.
4 A man or a woman _____
   is called a journalist.
5 A tin-opener is something _____.
6 A butcher is a man _____.

7 A parasol is something _____.

C 你知道某人……嗎？

完成以下句子，如下例：

I know someone who can speak 3 languages.
或 I don't know anyone who can speak 3 languages.

1 _____ has been to Iceland.
2 _____ can play the guitar.
3 _____ doesn't know how to swim.
4 _____ wants to be an actor or actress.

D 把下面每對句子合成一個句子，如下例：

I found a pen. You were looking for it.
I found the pen you were looking for.

1 Mr Davies is a dentist. My family goes to him.
2 Euro-net is a marketing company. My sister works for it.
3 Wine and cheese are the local products. This region is famous for them.
4 Simon is a friend of mine. He has just gone to New Zealand.

第四編

73 與 to-不定式小句連用的形容詞
Adjectives with to clauses

1 有些普通形容詞後面常帶有 to- 不定式小句。下面是通常意味某事的可能性的形容詞：

bound   due   likely   unlikely

而下面是意味某人想做某事或有能力做某事的形容詞：

able   prepared   ready   willing   unable   unwilling

The train is **due to arrive** at 7.50.

Your mum is **bound to be** angry when she sees what we've done.

It's **likely to rain** tomorrow.
The police were **unable to help** us.
Is anybody **prepared to stay** late and help me clean up?
I'm **willing to try** anything once.

2 to- 不定式小句與形容詞連用，可用來表述某人對某事是如何感受的：

afraid   disappointed   frightened   glad   happy   pleased   sad   surprised   unhappy

We were really **happy to see** everyone.
'Jack, this is Samantha.' 'I'm **pleased to meet** you.'

3 談及一人對另一人或另一事的感覺如何時，要用 that- 從句：

The teacher was **disappointed that** the students did so badly.
I'm **afraid that** you can't stay here.

也可用下面的形容詞和 that- 從句連用：

awful   bad   funny   good   important   interesting   obvious   sad   sorry   true

'I'm **sorry that I** was late'.
We were **sad that** you couldn't come to our wedding.
It's **true that** we didn't have much time to get ready.

4 也可以用下面的形容詞表達你對某人或某事的看法：

crazy   difficult   easy   impossible   mad   possible
right   stupid   wrong   important   essential   necessary

We were **mad to buy** this house.

The exercise was **difficult to finish**.
You were **wrong to criticize** them for something they didn't do.

5 在 it 後面的形容詞可與 to- 不定式連用：

It is **good** of you **to come** and see me.
It is **difficult** for my grandmother **to read** without glasses.

A 兩個一組，把下面的從句連起來：

1 It's unlikely	to go out tonight?
2 The football match is due	to save the patient's life.
3 Will your brother be able	to be late.
4 There's so much traffic, we're bound	to start at 3 p.m.
5 The price of petrol is likely	to do anything to get rich.
6 When will you be ready	to rain in August.
7 Some people are prepared	to go up next year.
8 The doctors were unable	to lend us some money?

B 用 it 和 "to- 不定式小句" 改寫以下句子：

1 Criticizing young people is easy. _It's easy to criticize young people._

2 Learning how to use a computer isn't easy. It isn't _____

3 Having a clean driving licence is essential. It's _____

4 Being polite to customers is important. It's _____

5 Arriving late is very rude. It's _____

6 Driving long distances when you're tired is stupid and dangerous. It's _____

7 Making everyone happy at the same time is difficult. _____

C 用 "to- 不定式小句" 改寫以下句子：

如：Jeremy met his girlfriend's parents. He was happy.
Jeremy was happy to meet his girlfriend's parents.

1 I didn't watch the film on my own. I was frightened. _____

2 My cousin didn't go home on foot. He was afraid. _____

3 I heard the bad news. I was sad. _____

4 We met an old friend in Japan. We were surprised. _____

5 The boys went home early. They were glad. _____

6 Eric did badly in the test. He was disappointed. _____

D 用 that- 從句改寫以下句子：

1 Everyone was on time. I was pleased. _I was pleased that everyone was on time._

2 We got home before dark. My parents were happy.

_____

3 The price of food is going up. The restaurant manager is worried.

_____

4 Henry couldn't find the right address. We were surprised.

_____

5 The weather wasn't very good. The tourists were disappointed.

_____

第
四
編

74 Too, enough

1 可用 enough 來表述某人擁有某物足夠的量。 Enough 可用於：

a 複數具數名詞之前：

We have got **enough sandwiches** for everyone.

The library doesn't have **enough books** on this subject.

b 不具數名詞之前：

Have you had **enough food**?

Fortunately we had **enough time** to visit both cathedrals.

We can't buy more magazines because we haven't got **enough money** with us.

2 還可以把 enough 用於形容詞和副詞之後：

You are **old enough** to know what is right. Can you hear? Am I speaking **loud enough**?

They missed the bus because
they didn't run **fast enough**.

'Is this water **warm enough** for your bath?'

3 請看下面這種有用的結構：

"（形容詞/副詞）＋enough（＋名詞）（為某人）＋ 做某事"：

(adj/adv) + enough (+ noun) (for someone) + to do something

I've cooked **enough cakes for everyone to have** some.

My French is **good enough for me to understand** people.

You are not **old enough to see** that film.

4 可用 too 來表示超過必需的程度，或超過可接受的程度：

a "too ＋形容詞／副詞"：

I like that picture, but I think it's **too expensive**.

You can't walk from here to the beach! It's **too far**.

I'm not surprised you feel sick. You ate **too quickly**!

b "too ＋ many/few ＋複數具數名詞"：

There were **too many people**. We couldn't sit down.

The hotel is closed in winter because we have **too few visitors**.

注意 不能用 "too ＋形容詞＋名詞"：

不要説：These are too expensive shoes. 而要説：These shoes are **too** expensive.

c "too ＋ much/little ＋不具數名詞"：

We didn't see the museum because we had **too little time**.

This tea is terrible. You put **too much sugar** in it!

'These jeans are **too big** for me.'

74 練習 Practice

A 用以下短語完成以下句子：

too many   too much   not enough   well enough   clearly enough   too many   enough   too little

1 Paul felt sick because he had eaten _____ sweets.

2 I'm not an expert, but I play _____ to be in the school team.

3 Don't spend _____ time doing the shopping. We are in a hurry.

4 The concert was cancelled because _____ people had bought tickets.

5 You should have finished by now. I gave you _____ time!

6 We didn't wait for the bus because there were _____ people in the queue.

7 You must speak _____ for everyone to understand.

8 I think I put _____ milk in this tea. It's still very black.

B 改寫以下句子，如下例：

He's very busy. He can't go to the theatre tonight.
He's too busy to go to the theatre tonight.

1 My brother's very young. He can't drive a car. _____

2 You look very tired. You shouldn't go out tonight. _____

3 That dress looks very expensive. I'm not going to buy it. _____

4 The book is very long. We can't finish it now. _____

5 It's very cold outside. They can't play football. _____

6 This is a very difficult question. We can't do it. _____

C 在以下各句中用 too 或 enough 填空：

1 I'm afraid the doctor can't see you today because he's _____ busy _____.

2 You don't look _____ old _____ to be married.

3 Did I put _____ sugar _____ in your coffee?

4 If you sit in the sun for _____ long _____ you'll get burnt.

5 The car isn't _____ big _____ for us all to go in.

6 'You're never _____ old _____ to rock and roll!' he shouted.

7 A workaholic is someone who works _____ much _____.

8 We invited _____ many _____ people to the party, and there wasn't _____ drink _____ for everybody.

9 There weren't _____ chairs _____ either. A lot of us had to stand up all night.

10 It's _____ soon _____ to know the results of the test.

第
四
編

1 請看以下句子中動詞的時態：

We will start **when we are ready.** I'll ask him **if I see him**.
I'll wait for you in the car tomorrow **while you are doing** the shopping.
We are going to get married **as soon as we have** enough money.

在與 if 連用的從句裏，或與時間詞 when、while、before、as soon as、after、until 連用的從句裏，通常用現在時表述將來。

請看以下句子。每句中的 if- 從句或時間從句是互相呼應的：

I will come round tomorrow **if I have time. If I see Jack** I will give him your message.

'**When Red Riding Hood comes**
I'm going to eat her up.'

'**If I don't hurry** it'll be dark **before I get to
Grandma's house.**'

You will break those glasses **if you're not careful.** I'm not coming **until I'm ready.**

2 下面這些帶 if 的表達式特別常用。應該練習使用這些表達式：

If I can   If I have time   If you like   If you want (to)

請注意下面這些短語全都是用現在時態表述將來：

A: Will you do the shopping?   B: Yes, if I **have** time.
A: Will you be home early tonight?   B: Yes, I will if I **can**.
A: Shall we go to the cinema?   B: Yes, we can if you **like**.
A: May I borrow this book?   B: Yes of course, if you **want** (to).

3 當認為某事可能發生，或認為某事在某方面可能很重要時，可用 What if...?
或 Suppose...? 與現在時連用的方式來表述：

What if it rains?   **What if** it breaks?   **Suppose** you hurt yourself?   **Suppose** you fall ill?

75 練習 Practice

A 把左欄與右欄相關的從句連成句子：

1 I'll take an umbrella	if you take a taxi.
2 I'm sure we will enjoy the match	as soon as your father gets home.
3 Would you like a hot drink	if it rains.
4 You will probably catch the train	before you go to bed?
5 We will have dinner	if anyone comes to the door.
6 You will hear the dog bark	if we can get tickets.

B 用以下詞彙改寫以下句子：

1 You will go to town tomorrow and I will look after the children.

When _*you go to town tomorrow I will look after the children.*_

2 Mary will be late. I will meet her at the station.

If _____.

3 Bill is going to write to me. I will tell you all his news.

_____ when _____.

4 You will go to the supermarket. You can buy some bread.

If _____.

5 I won't go to bed. Peter will get home at midnight.

_____ until _____.

6 She is going to finish her homework. She can't go out.

_____ until after _____.

7 The weather will probably be very bad next week. We will be on our holidays.

_____ while _____.

8 You will get your exam results next week. Then you can write to Mary.

When _____.

9 You won't get home till after midnight. Your mother will be very worried.

If _____.

10 I will pay you the money. I will get a job.

_____ as soon as _____.

再看上面的句子，在所有的 if- 從句和時間從句下面加底線。

C 用下面的句子編寫簡短對話：

A: Come round and see us tomorrow.	B: Yes, I will if I can.
A: Could you help me with this?	B: Sure, if you like.
A: Would you mind doing this?	B: Yes, of course, if you want me to.
A: Will you give this to Peter?	B: Yes, you can.
A: Can I borrow your pen?	B: No, I wouldn't.
A: Will you phone us when you get there?	

第
四
編

185

1 wish 後面接一過去時態的動詞，可用來表述你本希望某事會發生或本希望某事是真實的：

希望現在能做到某事：

It's cold. I **wish** it **was** a bit warmer. I'm hungry. I **wish** I **had** something to eat.

或希望過去能做到某事：

I forgot my overcoat. I **wish** I **had brought** it. I **wish** I **hadn't forgotten** it.

請注意時態的用法。要用過去時表述現在的事情，用過去完成時表述過去的事情。情態動詞也要用過去時。
不要用 can，而要用 could：

I'm tired. I **wish** I **could go** to bed. It's late. I **wish** we **could go** home.

希望某人做某事而某人不想做時，可用 I wish they would...來表述：

He's very silly. **I wish he would be** more careful.
They're very noisy. **I wish they wouldn't shout** so much.

常常只說 I wish they hadn't 或 I wish they wouldn't 就可以了：

They are making a dreadful noise. I **wish they wouldn't.**
He's gone out again. I **wish he hadn't.**

2 可用if-從句(條件從句)來表述沒有發生的事：

If I was a year older **I could drive** a car.
If I had enough money **I would buy** a new bike.

請注意要用過去時。最常見的是在 if- 從句中用過去時態，在另一個從句中用 would、could 或 might：

I'd (I would) certainly come and see you **if I had** time.
If you lived nearer **you could come** over on the bus.
If you left before breakfast **you might get** there before lunch.

注意 在 if- 從句中可用 were 替代 was：

If I **were** older I could drive a car.

不過除了 if I were you...外，這種用法非常正式，(見下面)。

3 下面是這種結構的一些特別常用的表達式：

常用 if I were you I'd...來提出建議：

A: I'm not very well. What should I do?　　B: **If I were you I'd see** a doctor.

常用 I would if I could...作為藉口：

A: Will you give me a lift?　　B: **I would if I could,** but I'm just too busy.

練習 **Practice**

A 把下面的句子改寫成表達意願的句子：

1 It's raining again. *I wish it wasn't raining.*

2 I don't know the answer. _____

3 Jack won't help us. _____

4 I didn't see Angela this morning. _____

5 We don't live here. _____

6 Mary never telephones. _____

7 Paul didn't write last week. _____

8 I haven't enough time. _____

B 把左欄與右欄的相關部分連成條件句：

1 If the weather was warmer   a   we could get there before lunch.

2 If you asked Peter   b   you could look it up.

3 If I had a better job   c   I would be much warmer.

4 If we got up early   d   we could go for a drive.

5 If we could borrow the car   e   we could go for a swim.

6 If I knew the answer   f   I would earn more money.

7 If you had a dictionary   g   I would tell you.

8 If I had a coat   h   he might help you.

C 把以下句子改寫成條件句：

1 I'm ill, so I can't play basketball. *If I wasn't ill I could play basketball.*

2 I haven't enough money, so I can't buy it. _____

3 She's not tired, so she won't go to bed. _____

4 We haven't much time so we can't wait for him. _____

5 He's so big it won't fit him.

If _____

6 'It's so cold we can't go out today.'

If _____

7 They haven't got a map so they can't find the way. _____

8 They don't know the way so they need a map. _____

9 Oh dear! I've got them all wrong. I'll do the exercise again. _____

第四編

187

77 目的和理由 **Purpose and reason**

1 可用...because I want to...或...because I wanted to...來解釋做某事的目的：

We are travelling overnight **because we want to get** there early tomorrow.

用 to 或 in order to 也可以起到同樣作用：

They locked the door **to keep** everybody out. **He gave up his job in order to spend** more time at home.

The wolf ran fast **because he wanted to get** there before Red Riding Hood.

Red Riding Hood stopped **in order to collect** some flowers for her Grandmother.

可用 so as not to... 或 because I didn't want to 來否定目的從句：

I spoke quietly **so as not to wake up** the baby.

I wrote his name in my notebook **so as not to forget** it.

'He always does that **because he doesn't want to be** left behind.'

2 可用 so 或 so that 來引導目的從句。這種方法通常要使用一個情態動詞，如 can、could、will、would：

I have drawn a map **so that you can get** here easily.
They put up a very large notice **so that everybody would see** it.

3 可用 because 來解釋某人為甚麼做某事，或解釋某事為甚麼會發生：

We went to bed early **because we were** very tired.
I spoke very slowly **because he didn't understand** English very well.

4 可用 so 來表述一個行動或情況的結果是甚麼：

We were very tired **so we went** to bed early. He couldn't understand English very well **so I spoke** very slowly.

下面是一首家喻戶曉的民歌歌詞：

I know an old lady who swallowed a fly.

I don't know why she swallowed the fly ... perhaps she'll die.

I know an old lady who swallowed a spider that wriggled and tickled and jiggled inside her.

She swallowed the spider to catch the fly, but I don't know why she swallowed the fly ... perhaps she'll die.

I know an old lady who swallowed a bird. Well how absurd — to swallow a bird.

She swallowed a bird _____ _____ _____ _____ that wriggled and tickled and jiggled inside her.
She swallowed the spider to catch the fly, but I don't know why she swallowed the fly ... perhaps she'll die.

I know an old lady who swallowed a cat. Well fancy that — she swallowed a cat.

I know an old lady who swallowed a dog. What a hog to swallow a dog.

I know an old lady who swallowed a goat. She just opened her throat and swallowed a goat.

I know an old lady who swallowed a cow. I don't know how she swallowed the cow.

I know an old lady who swallowed a horse — she died of course.

wriggle 扭動。如：*She wriggled her toes.*	absurd 荒唐，怪誕。如：*That hat looks absurd.*
tickle 搔癢	fancy 竟然。如：*Fancy that!*
jiggle 搖擺	hog 1 公豬 2 貪心的人（非正式用法）

合上書本，看看你是否能說出：

'She swallowed the cow because she wanted to catch the goat. She swallowed the goat because she wanted to catch the dog. She swallowed the dog ..... cat ...... bird ...... spider ...... fly — but I don't know why she swallowed the fly. Perhaps she'll die.'

你能用 in order to 再把這個故事講述一遍嗎？

以 Why did she swallow the dog？為例，進行提問和回答。

第四編

78 結果 Result

1 可用 so 或 such 後面跟 that 的結構來談及結果：

有關 so 和 such 的結構請看第六十五單元：

The food was **so delicious that** I helped myself to more. **(so + adjective + that)**

It was **such a nice day that** I had to go for a swim. **(such a + adj + count noun + that)**

We had **such good weather that** we came back with tans. **(such + adj + uncount noun + that)**

She made **such beautiful cakes that** they are all sold out. **(such + adj + plural noun + that)**

So 與副詞連用：

We arrived **so late** we almost missed the party.

He talked **so much** that she couldn't get a word in edgeways.

與量詞連用的結構：so much（與不具數名詞連用）；so many（與具數名詞連用）；so few（與具數名詞連用）；such a lot of（可與具數名詞或不具數名詞連用）：

We had **so many things** to carry that we had to ask Sophie to help us.

There were **such a lot of people** that we couldn't get a seat.

There was **so much food** left we had to throw some away.

2 enough 常與形容詞、副詞或名詞連用。Enough 要置於形容詞或副詞之後：

A: Are those shoes comfortable? B: Not really. They're not **big enough**.

I can't hear him. He never speaks **loud enough**.

Enough 要置於名詞之前：

A: How is your orange juice? B: It's very nice, but there's not **enough sugar** in it.

Ok. Let's start the meeting. There are **enough people** here now.

這些結構後面跟 to- 不定式，可用來談及結果：

The children are **old enough to go** to school. We ran **fast enough to catch** him.

I haven't **enough money to buy** a new car. There's **enough time to have** lunch.

副詞如 nearly、just、easily 可與 enough 連用：

We have **just enough time** to have lunch. They're **easily old enough** to go to school.

3 enough 可單獨用作代詞：

I've got **enough** to worry about. **Enough** has been said about this already.

4 too 與形容詞或副詞連用，常用來談及否定的結果：

A: Have the children started school yet? B: Oh no. They're still **too young**.

A: Let's go out for a meal. B: Oh no. It's **much too expensive**.

They were **too tired** to walk any further. (They were so tired that they could not walk any further.)

78 練習 **Practice**

A 用 so...that 或 such...that 把下面各題中的兩個句子連成一句：

1 He was very pleased. He wrote a letter to thank me for my help.
   He was so pleased that he wrote a letter to thank me for my help.

2 They worked very hard. They finished everything in one afternoon.
   _____

3 She is very kind. She will help anyone who asks her.
   _____

4 It's a nice day. We should go out for a walk in the fresh air.
   _____

5 She had a very bad cold. She could not possibly go to work.
   _____

6 He had a big car. There was plenty of room for everybody.
   _____

7 The flat was very small. Three of us had to share a room.
   _____

8 They have a lot of friends. They go out almost every evening.
   _____

B 用 enough 或 too 完成以下句子：

1 I won't be able to come tomorrow. I'm afraid I'm _____*too busy*_____. (busy)
2 Katherine can go to school by herself. She's certainly _____. (old)
3 You shouldn't go out without an overcoat. It's much _____. (cold)
4 We won't telephone you when we get back. It will be _____. (late)
5 You can walk there in about ten minutes. It's _____. (close)
6 You can't drive there in a day. It's _____. (far)
7 She cycles to the shops every day. She's still _____. (fit)
8 We can't afford to stay in a hotel. It's _____. (expensive)

再用 too...to...或 enough...to...重寫上面的句子：

1 *I'm afraid I'll be too busy to come tomorrow.* _____
2 _____
3 _____
4 _____
5 _____
6 _____
7 _____
8 _____

第
四
編

79 對比和比較 Contrast and comparison

1 可用 although 或 even though 對兩個陳述句進行對比：

Although he was late he stopped to buy a sandwich.
He went to work every day **even though** he was very ill.

有時可用 still 來強調這一對比：
I **still** like Anna, **even though** she is sometimes very annoying.
He was **still** cheerful, **even though** he was very ill.

2 另一種對比方法是將 in spite of 與名詞連用：

He is still very fit **in spite of his age**.
She worked very hard **in spite of the difficulties**.

In spite of 後面常跟 -ing 形式：
He still failed his exams **in spite of working** really hard.
He won the race **in spite of being** the youngest competitor.

3 比較級形容詞與 than 連用，或用 as....as，也可對事物進行比較（請看第六十四單元）：

This pullover is **much nicer than** that one, and it's **a bit cheaper** too.
Their house is **as big as** ours. It's **not as easy as** you think.

4 like 與少數幾個動詞連用，可用來談及在某方面幾乎相同的事物：

Ken **is just like** his father. New York **is like** London in many ways.
An okapi **looks like** a small giraffe. Who's that? It **sounds like** Henry.

下面這幾個動詞常和 like 連用：
be feel look seem smell sound taste

疑問句與 like 連用極為常見（請看第十四單元）：
What's it **like**? What does it look **like**? What did it sound **like**?

有些程度副詞可與 like 連用，如：
exactly just rather a bit a little bit nothing

He looks **exactly like** his father.

'They sound **a bit like** the Beatles.'

A 用以下的短語完成以下句子：

we drove very fast	we were really hungry	I was very angry
they didn't hear us	I haven't finished it yet	he was looking very well
we are very good friends	we don't see her very often	he looked very fierce
it's much more expensive	he still didn't earn very much	the sun was shining

1 Although _____ *we were really hungry* _____ there was no time to stop and eat.

2 _____ even though we have only just met.

3 Although he worked very long hours _____ .

4 _____ even though she lives next door.

5 The journey took over four hours even though _____ .

6 _____ even though he had just been ill.

7 Although _____ I tried to speak quietly and calmly.

8 This coat doesn't look as smart as that even though _____ .

9 It was still bitterly cold even though

_____ .

10 He was really quite friendly, although

_____ .

11 I must take this book back to the library even though _____ .

12 _____ even though we knocked very loudly.

B 用 in spite of 改寫以下句子：

1 We arrived on time although we got lost on the way.
   We arrived on time *in spite of getting lost on the way.* _____

2 He still takes a lot of exercise even though he is over seventy.
   He still takes a lot of exercise _____ .

3 Although she was injured she still finished the match.
   _____ she still finished the match.

4 He looks just like his brother although he's much younger.
   He looks just like his brother _____ .

5 She still has a job although she has three children to look after.
   She still has a job _____ .

第
四
編

80 描述性從句 Describing clauses

1 請看第七十二單元有關從句的內容。使用關係從句可以確定正在談及的是何人或何事:

A: I saw a friend of yours today. B: Who was that?

A: That man **who worked with you in Manchester**. B: Oh, you mean George.

A: Have you seen my shirt? B: Which shirt?
A: The one **I wore at the party last week**. B: Oh yes. It's here, in the drawer.

2 使用關係從句可進一步提供所談及的人或物的信息:

Once upon a time there was a little girl called Red Riding Hood, **who lived in a little house in the forest with her mother and father**.

There was a wicked wolf, **who wanted to catch Red Riding Hood and eat her up**.

I bought the car from Professor Jones, **who lives just across the road**.

They go to the King's School, **which is quite close to home**.

上面這些關係從句是描述性從句。描述性從句總是要由一個關係代詞引導。who用來引導人物,which 用來引導事物:

She works with Alex, **who used to go to school with her brother**.

I teach at the University, **which is in the centre of town**.

注意 在描述性從句裏不能使用 that。

3 在描述性從句中,可用 when 和 where 來談及時間和地點:

We haven't seen them since January, **when we were on holiday together**.

They live in Birmingham, **where Rebecca was born**.

4 以 which 引導的描述性從句可用來表述一個情景:

I've lost my key, **which is very annoying**. He shouted at us, **which was very rude**.

80 練習 Practice

A 用 who、which、when、where 完成以下句子：

1 Tomorrow we are going to Leeds, _____*where*_____ William and Jenny live.

2 On Tuesday it's the carnival, _____ everybody gets dressed up in a fancy costume.

3 We'll meet at Wendy's house, _____ is about a couple of miles out of town.

4 This is the store room, _____ we keep most of our equipment.

5 I'll introduce you to Monica, _____ has the office next to mine.

6 It's time for our coffee break, _____ we meet everyone in the canteen.

7 He stays at home and looks after the children, _____ is very hard work.

8 This is Dan, _____ works here on Mondays and Wednesdays.

B 把左右兩欄相關的內容連成句子。有些句子容易理解，有些很難理解：

1	We spent a week in Stratford-on Avon,	a where we saw the Parthenon.
2	I am reading about Marconi,	b which is a kind of cheese.
3	They live in Brussels,	c who discovered America.
4	John Logie Baird was a Scotsman,	d when we celebrate carnival.
5	You could come in December,	e where William Shakespeare was born.
6	It's a haggis,	f who discovered radium.
7	Valladolid is the birthplace of Cervantes,	g which is a very popular dish in Scotland.
8	We change planes in Canberra,	h who invented the radio.
9	We stopped off in Athens,	i when we celebrate Christmas.
10	This book is about Christopher Columbus,	j where the European Parliament is.
11	This is gorgonzola,	k who wrote Don Quixote.
12	I've just seen a film about Marie Curie,	l who invented television.
13	It's a microscope,	m which is the capital of Australia.
14	Next week is Mardi Gras,	n which is used to study very small objects.

C 用 who、which、when、where 把下面各題中的兩個句子改寫成一句：

1 My grandfather was born in 1914, _____*when the First World War started.*_____
   (The First World War started in 1914.)

2 He lived most of his life in Newcastle, _____.
   (He was born in Newcastle.)

3 When he was at university he met my grandmother, _____.
   (She was studying mathematics.)

4 They got married in 1938, _____.
   (They left university in 1938.)

5 My mother was born in Bournemouth, _____.
   (Bournemouth is in the south of England.)

第四編

複習　第四編 **66 – 80**單元

第六十六單元：不能用於進行時態的動詞 Verbs not used in continuous tenses

A 用動詞的簡單現在時或現在進行時完成以下對話：

A　What (you/cook?)
(1) _____? It (smell)
(2) _____ wonderful.

B　I (make) (3) _____ a chocolate cake.
　　(You like?) (4) _____ chocolate cakes?
A　Yes, I (love) (5) _____ it. Mmm, it
　　(taste) (6) _____ good.

A　(Be) (7) _____ this your bike?
B　No. I (think) (8) _____ it (belong)
　　(9) _____ to my neighbour's daughter.
　　I (know) (10) _____ she (have)
　　(11) _____ one like that.

B 用正確形式的動詞完成以下句子：

1　Mary's upstairs. She (a) *has/is having* a rest.
2　Be quiet. I (b) *think/am thinking* I (c) *am hearing/can hear* someone downstairs.
3　We were out very late last night because we (d) *saw/were seeing* some old friends.
4　Jack (e) *doesn't like/isn't liking* maths because he (f) *doesn't understand/isn't understanding* it very well.
5　Ivan was very rich. He (g) *owned/was owning* a big car and a house in the country.
6　Can you turn the TV down please? I (h) *try/am trying* to do some work. I (i) *think/am thinking* about my
　　homework.
7　A: That (j) *looks/is looking* interesting? What is it?
　　B: It's a cigarette lighter. It (k) *belonged/was belonging* to my grandfather.
8　A: Where's Jenny?
　　B: She's at the Arts Centre. She (l) *learns/is learning* to paint.
　　A: That (m) *sounds/is sounding* interesting.

第六十七單元：被動語態　The passive

C 把以下句子改寫成被動語態：

1 We keep the glasses in this cupboard.

The glasses _are kept in this cupboard._____

2 Someone found Jim's wallet lying in the street.

Jim's wallet _____.

3 You can obtain this book at your local library.

This book _____.

4 Someone told me to park my car outside in the street.

I _____.

5 They sold their house for over £ 200,000.

Their house _____.

6 Nobody has heard of John since he went to live in America.

John _____.

7 They sell newspapers at most corner shops.

Newspapers _____.

8 They do not allow you to borrow more than three books.

You _____.

9 Someone gave her a computer for her birthday.

She _____.

10 You must wear protective clothing in the factory.

Protective clothing _____.

D 選用正確的動詞形式：

1 A Birmingham woman (1) *attacked/was attacked* with a knife on her way home from work. Mrs Fung (2) *had just left/had just been left* her shop in South Street when she (3) *stopped/was stopped* by a young man who (4) *tried/was tried* to snatch her handbag. When Mrs Fung (5) *was fought/fought* back, the man (6) *took/was taken* out a knife. Mrs. Fung's face (7) *badly cut/was badly cut* and she (8) *took/was taken* to hospital.

2 Germany (9) *were won/won* the football World Cup in 1990, when they (10) *beat/were beaten* Argentina. In 1994 the Germans (11) *beat/were beaten* by Bulgaria in the quarter final, and the cup (12) *won/was won* by Brazil.

3 John F. Kennedy (13) *born/was born* in 1973. He (14) *elected/was elected* President of the US in 1960. On 22 November, 1963, he (15) *shot/was shot* dead by Lee Harvey Oswald, during a visit to Dallas, Texas. Two days later Oswald himself (16) *shot/was shot* and killed.

第六十八單元：轉述過去 Reporting the past

E 請看下面的對話：

A Hi Ken! Where are you going?
B I'm going into town to do some shopping. Why?
A Can you give me a lift? I'm late for work.
  My car has broken down. It won't start.
B I'm sorry, I'm not going into town,
  but I can give you a lift to the railway station.

填寫正確時態的動詞來完成以下轉述：

As I (1) (get) _____ into my car my neighbour (2) (shout) _____ out of

his front window and (3) (ask) _____ me where I (4) (go) _____ .When I

(5) (tell) _____ him I (6) (go) _____ to town he (7) (ask) _____

if I (8) (can) _____ give him a lift into work. He (9) (be) _____ afraid he

(10) (be) _____ late for work because his car (11) (break down) _____ and it

(12) (not start) _____ . I explained that I (13) (not/go) _____ into town

but I (14) (can) _____ give him a lift to the railway station.

F 再按上面的方法完成以下轉述：

'Tell me why do you want to
be a computer programmer?'

A: Tell me, why do you want to be a computer
   programmer?
B: Well I've always been interested in computers.
A: When have you used them before?
B: Well, we used computers for some of our work at
   school. And in my last job all the records were
   kept on computer.
A: Yes, but do you have any experience as a
   programmer?
B: No, not yet. But I have read a lot and I have been
   studying programming at night school.
A: I see. And do you have any qualifications?
B: Not yet. But I'm going to take my certificate exam
   next month.

Annette was asked why she (1) _____ to be a computer programmer. She said that

she (2) _____ always been interested in computers. She said she (3) _____

them at school and also in her last job, where all the records (4) _____ computerised.

She (5) _____ any experience as a programmer, but she (6) _____

programming at night school. Although she (7) _____ no qualifications she

(8) _____ to take her exam the next month.

第六十六、六十七、六十八單元

G 用括號裏適當的動詞形式完成下面的故事：

'Do you think you could take my carpets too?'

One day as Mrs. Jackson (1) *was looking/had looked* out of the window she (2) *saw/was seeing* two men in the garden next door. They (3) *carried/were carrying* some expensive carpets down the path towards a large van. Mrs Jackson (4) *called out/was calling out* and (5) *asked/asking* them what they (6) *are doing/were doing/do did*. One of the men (7) *explained/was explaining* that the carpets (8) *are taking/were taking/are being taken/were being taken* away to be cleaned.

Mrs. Jackson (9) *was thinking/thought* she (10) *will like/would like/liked* her carpets cleaned too and asked the two men if they (11) *can/could* put them on the van. The men agreed and explained that they (12) *will return/would return* the carpets in three weeks' time. A week later the neighbours came back and found that their carpets (13) *have stole/had stolen/have been stolen/had been stolen*. Poor Mrs. Jackson realised that she (14) *has given/had given* the thieves her carpets too.

第六十九單元：省略回答 Short answers

H 寫出以下疑問句的省略回答：

1 Mrs. Jackson saw two men, didn't she? *Yes she did.*

2 Were they carrying a carpet? _____

3 Were they thieves? _____

4 Did Mrs. Jackson call the police? _____

5 Did Mrs. Jackson want her carpets cleaned? _____

6 Could they put the carpets on the van? _____

7 Would the neighbours be happy? _____

8 Was Mrs. Jackson silly? _____

第
四
編

複習　第四編 66 – 80 單元

第七十單元：附加疑問 Question tags

I 為以下疑問句加上附加成分：

1 You live quite near here, _____?
2 I'm not late, _____?
3 Columbus discovered America, _____?
4 You're not tired, _____?
5 You'll come with us, _____?
6 We haven't met before, _____?
7 There's plenty of time, _____?
8 You've been to Britain, _____?
9 You went there last year, _____?
10 You can't lend me a pound, _____?
11 He looks unhappy, _____?
12 It isn't going to rain, _____?
13 You didn't enjoy it much, _____?
14 I'm next, _____?
15 You should work harder, _____?
16 We have to go soon, _____?
17 You won't forget, _____?
18 We'll all be late, _____?

第七十一單元：Too, either, so, neither

J 用 too、either、so、neither 完成以下句子：

1 There were lots of children at the circus, and quite a lot of adults _____.
2 We didn't enjoy the film much and _____ did our friends.
3 My mother is a wonderful cook, and _____ is my father.
4 I didn't see Jill and I didn't see her sister _____.
5 She bought a new dress, and some new shoes _____.
6 I haven't booked a seat for the theatre yet and I haven't bought a ticket _____.
7 I know Jane will be happy to see you, and _____ will her family.

第七十二單元：限制性關係從句 Defining relative clauses

K 以下面 1(b)為例造句：

1 (a) He was carrying an old bag. It looked really heavy.
　 (b) The old bag _he was carrying looked really heavy._
2 (a) Some people drive too fast. They are really dangerous.
　 (b) People _____.
3 (a) We went to a concert in London. It wasn't very good.
　 (b) The concert _____.
4 (a) I'd like to buy that red dress. I saw it in your shop yesterday.
　 (b) I'd like to buy that red dress _____.
5 (a) We know some people. They live very near to you.
　 (b) We know some people _____.

第七十四單元：Too, enough

L 用 too much 、 too many 、 enough 完成以下句子：

1 I'm sorry I can't help. I just don't have ___*enough*___ time.

2 I can't drink this coffee. There's _____ sugar in it.

3 I hate shopping on Saturday. There are always _____ people in town.

4 David can't drive the car yet. He's not old _____.

5 If we are going camping we must take _____ food for three days.

6 Everything is very wet. We have had _____ rain over the weekend.

7 There are _____ people. We haven't got _____ chairs for everybody.

8 I don't feel very well. I think I've had _____ to eat.

第六十九 — 七十四單元

M 請讀下面的對話，在正確答案下面加底線：

Travel Agent: Good morning. What can I do for you?

Helen: Good morning. We are looking for a holiday in the sun. We'd like to go next week We're not (1) *very late/_too late_/late enough* (2) *aren't we/are we/is it*?

Travel Agent: No. I think I can help you. What about the Greek Islands?

Susan: No, we've been to Greece, (3) *have we/haven't we/don't we* Helen?

Helen: Yes, we (4) *go/have gone/went* to Crete last year.

Travel Agent: I see. You want a country (5) *which you haven't visited it/you haven't visited* before. And you want somewhere sunny, (6) *is it/are you/do you*? Well Portugal isn't (7) *expensive enough/too expensive*, and it's certainly (8) *enough warm/warm enough* at this time of year.

Helen: (9) *Is it/does it* really? I haven't heard much about Portugal.

Travel Agent: (10) *Have you/Haven't you*? Well it's a popular place nowadays, with plenty of good resorts.

第四編

第七十五單元：現在時態與 if、when 等連用 Present tense with if, when etc.

N 填寫正確時態的動詞來完成以下句子：

a If it (1) *is/will be* fine tomorrow we (2) *have/can have* lunch in the garden ...

... but if it (3) *will rain/rains* we (4) *eat/will eat* in the house.

b I (5) *get/will get* home early tonight if I (6) *catch/will catch* the train at seven thirty.

c If you (7) *will want to/want to* you (8) *can stay/stay/will stay* with us when you (9) *come/will come* to London.

d I (10) *look after/am looking after/will look after* the children while you (11) *go/will go* to work.

e Joe says he (12) *comes round/will come round* tonight if he (13) *has/will have* time.

f The children are tired out. They (14) *fall/will fall* asleep as soon as they (15) *will get/get* home.

第七十六單元：條件從句和意願 Conditional sentences and wishes

O 填寫正確時態的動詞來完成以下句子：

1 What *would you do/will you do* if you *are/were* the richest person in the world?

2 I don't know where Anne lives. If I *know/knew* I *would go/will go* to see her.

3 A Oh dear. I've forgotten my pen.

B Never mind. You *can/could* borrow mine if you *haven't/hadn't* got one.

4 A Do you know what time the train goes?

B No, I'm sorry. If I *am/was/were* you *I'll/I'd* telephone the station and find out.

5 A I'm hungry.

B Okay. If you *are/were* hungry we *will/would* go out and get something to eat.

6 I wish Jack *would telephone/telephoned/had telephoned* yesterday.

7 A I wish Marie *is/will be/was* here.

B Yes, if she *is/will be/was* here she *will know/knows/would know* what to do.

8 If you *see/will see/saw* Henry tomorrow *will you give/did you give/do you give* him a message, please?

複習　第四編 **66 – 80** 單元

第七十七單元：目的和理由 Purpose and reason

P 用 used...to...改寫以下句子：

1　She opened the bottle with a corkscrew.
　She used a corkscrew to open the bottle.

2　I found what the word meant in a dictionary.
_____

3　He mended the chair with a piece of string.
_____

4　She polished her shoes with a wet cloth.
_____

5　I caught the mouse with a trap and a big piece of cheese.

6　Our teacher always marked our books with a red pen.
_____

7　She looked at the leaf under a microscope.
_____

8　He bathed the baby in a bucket.

第七十八單元：結果 Result

Q 用 so...that...或 such...that...改寫以下句子：

1　I couldn't work any more because I was very tired.
I was so tired that I couldn't work any more.

2　We couldn't go out because it was a very wet day.
_____

3　My bicycle was very old. It was always breaking down.
_____

4　Don is a very good friend. He will always help me if I ask him.
_____

5　My father lives a long way from his office. He has to drive to work every day.
_____

6　It was dark when we arrived because the journey took a very long time.
_____

7　He was very angry. He wouldn't speak to me.
_____

8　I was very frightened. I didn't know what to do.
_____

第七十九單元：對比和比較 Contrast and comparison

R 用 because 或 even though 完成以下句子：

1　She speaks good English _____ she hasn't been learning it very long.

2　I switched on the TV _____ I wanted to listen to the news.

3　We enjoyed the game _____ we didn't win.

4　He never goes out _____ he's always playing computer games.

5　He's very tall _____ he's only fourteen.

6　Katy didn't look very happy _____ it was her birthday.

7　Don was saving up _____ he wanted to buy a camera.

第八十單元：描述性從句 Descriptive clauses

S 用 who、which、where、when 把下面的句子連起來：

1　We are going on holiday to Brighton. My mother was born in Brighton.
We are going on holiday to Brighton, where my mother was born.

2　I'll telephone you at six o'clock. I get home at six o'clock.

_____

3　She comes from Sofia. Sofia is the capital of Bulgaria.

_____

4　This is my old friend, Tom. Tom is staying with us this week.

_____

5　I'm reading a book about Ronald Reagan. He used to be President of the USA.

_____

6　This is the garage. We keep all the garden furniture.

7　Pele is a famous footballer. He played for Brazil at the age of seventeen.

_____

8　We visited Buckingham Palace. The royal family lives in Buckingham Palace.

_____

第四編

第七十五 ─ 八十單元

T 用 and、although、because、enough、if、so、who、to 來完成下面的故事。

This story is about the Hodja, (1) _____ is a well-known character in the Middle East. One day the Hodja went to his neighbour's house (2) _____ he wanted to borrow a cooking pot. 'A lot of my relatives are coming to stay and my wife doesn't have a big (3) _____ pot,' he explained. '(4) _____ you can lend me a big pot I will bring it back next week,' he promised. Although the neighbour did not trust the Hodja he agreed to lend him a pot, (5) _____ the Hodja went off happily. After two weeks the neighbour went to see the Hodja (6) _____ the pot had not been returned. 'I am sorry,' said the Hodja. 'I have been looking after your pot very carefully (7) _____ I realised it was pregnant. The baby was born yesterday. Here it is.' He gave his neighbour the big pot and also a small one. (8) _____ the neighbour was very surprised he took the pots and went home happily. A week later the Hodja went to his neighbour's house again (9) _____ borrow another large pot. 'I will lend you the same pot again,' his neighbour said, '(10) _____ you promise to bring it back next week.' The Hodja promised and off he went with the pot. Again two weeks went by (11) _____ the neighbour went to the Hodja's house (12) _____ ask for his pot. 'I am very sorry,' said the Hodja. 'I cannot give you your pot (13) _____ it has died.' The neighbour was (14) _____ angry that he shouted at the Hodja. 'Don't think I am foolish (15) _____ to believe a story like that. Everyone knows that cooking pots don't die.' 'Please don't be angry,' said the Hodja. '(16) _____ you believed me when I said your pot was pregnant you should certainly believe me (17) _____ I tell you it has died.'

總複習 E

A 動詞的時態（第一 — 二十二單元、第六十六、七十五、七十六單元）

填入以下動詞的正確時態：

1　We (live) _____ in England for nearly five years now. We came here when I

　(be) _____ ten years old.

2　'Can you be quiet please?

　I (try) _____ to listen to the

　radio.'

3　'Janet's not at home.

　She (just go) _____ to school.

　She (go) _____ out ten minutes

　ago.'

4　Jim was very tired when he (get) _____ home. He (travel) _____ for over

　eight hours.

5　It was ten o'clock and I still (not finish) _____ my homework.

6　It (be) _____ my birthday tomorrow.

7　We are going to be late if we (not hurry) _____.

8　I met your brother the other day while I (wait) _____ for the bus.

9　If I (be) _____ seventeen I (can drive) _____ my father's car.

10 I wish I (can) _____ come to your party.

11 We (go) _____ to London for our holidays this year.

12 I (not play) _____ football since I (break) _____ my leg six weeks ago.

13 I (learn) _____ Greek ten years ago while I (work) _____ in Athens.

14 I (telephone) _____ Bill as soon as I (get) _____ home this evening.

15 It was eleven o'clock and we (just go) _____ to bed when the telephone (ring)

　_____.

16 A: Aren't you enjoying the film?

　B: No I (not like) _____ these horror films.

17 I (see) _____ that word yesterday, but I (not remember) _____ what it means

　now.

18 I wish we (live) _____ a more interesting place.

總複習 E

B 疑問句（第十四、十五單元）

根據答案寫出疑問句並完成下面的對話：

1 A: _____?

   B: It's nearly six o'clock.

2 A: _____?

   B: I'll be seventeen next month.

3 A: _____?

   B: No, there's no milk in the fridge, but there's a bottle on the table.

4 A: _____?

   B: No, I've never met Marie, but I know her brother well.

5 A: _____?

   B: Jack? He looks just like his father.

6 A: _____?

   B: I'll probably stay at home and do some gardening.

7 A: _____?

   B: We've got an old Ford.

8 A: _____?

   B: 21, North Street, Misson.

9 A: We're going on holiday next week.

   B: _____?

   A: Spain.

10 A: We'll come round and see you.

   B: _____?

   A: Probably next week.

C 介詞（第三十、四十八、四十九單元）

在必要的地方填上介詞來完成以下句子：

1 Do you go to school _____ your bicycle or _____ foot?

2 The match starts _____ ten o'clock _____ Thursday.

3 John's not very well. He's not _____ work today.

4 The weather is usually warm _____ summer, but it can be very cold _____ December.

5 Jan went to Manchester _____ bus, but I went _____ my friend's car.

6 We will get _____ the bus at the next stop.

7 Dad always reads the newspaper _____ breakfast.

8 We'll come and see you _____ tomorrow.

9 They sell sandwiches _____ the train.

10 We stay with my parents _____ every Christmas.

總複習 E

D 狀語的位置（第二十七、二十八、四十七單元）

把括號裏的詞放在適當的位置來完成以下句子：

1 We go to the cinema at the weekend. (often)

_____

2 George can tell you what you want to know. (certainly)

_____

3 I don't play football now (very much), but I play tennis. (a lot)

_____

4 I saw Fred but he isn't here now. (a while ago)

_____

5 It rained last night. (quite a lot)

_____

6 The door was locked when I went out. (definitely)

_____

7 We watch television at the weekend. (hardly ever)

_____

8 It is one of the best films I have seen. (ever)

_____

9 I didn't enjoy the film (very much), but I enjoyed the play. (a lot)

_____

10 I met Helen a week, but I haven't seen her since then. (ago)

_____

11 I read the instructions on the medicine bottle. (carefully)

_____

12 We see Richard when we are in Oxford. (always)

_____

E 一些常用動詞（第三十九、五十六單元）

使用正確的動詞來完成以下句子：

1 I've had a long journey. I'm going to _____ a shower.

2 Do you _____ the cooking in your family?

3 Keep very quiet and try not to _____ any noise.

4 Stand still a moment. I want to _____ a photograph.

5 Are you going to _____ a holiday this year?

6 Jan has her examination tomorrow. I'm sure she will _____ very well.

7 I'm sure you will _____ a lot of friends at your new school.

8 What time do you _____ breakfast in the morning?

9 There's Barbara over there. _____ her a smile.

10 Did you _____ much fishing on holiday?

總複習 E

語法練習

F 從括號裏選出合適的動詞形式，來完成以下故事：

One day a friend of mine (1) (a) *who he was driving* (b) *who driving* (c) *who was driving* home late at night saw a young woman (2) (a) *stand* (b) *stood* (c) *standing* by the side of the road. (3) (a) *A friend* (b) *The friend* (c) *My friend* stopped (4) (a) *to* (b) *for* (c) *and* give her a lift. (5) (a) *A young woman* (b) *Young woman* (c) *The young woman* got (6) (a) *on* (b) *into* (c) *to* the car and closed (7) (a) *the door* (b) *a door* (c) *door*. She (8) (a) *told to my friend* (b) *told* (c) *told my friend* she lived (9) (a) *at* (b) *in* (c) *on* 26 North Street, (10) (a) *which* (b) *where* (c) *that* was just near my friend's house.

The young woman talked happily as they drove along but after ten minutes she fell silent. My friend (11) (a) *looked* (b) *was looked* (c) *was looking* round to see if she was all right. To his astonishment[1] the young woman (12) (a) *vanish*[2] (b) *has vanished* (c) *had vanished*. At first my friend (13) (a) *did not know* (b) *was not knowing* (c) *has not known* what to do. Finally he decided (14) (a) *going* (b) *to go* (c) *go to* 26, North Street to see if anyone there (15) (a) *was knowing* (b) *knew* (c) *knows* the woman.

He went up to (16) (a) *a* (b) *the* house and knocked on the door. It (17) (a) *opened* (b) *was opened* by a middle-aged woman. My friend explained how he (18) (a) *was meeting* (b) *has met* (c) *had met* the young woman and (19) (a) *giving* (b) *given* (c) *give* her a lift. He (20) (a) *told to* (b) *told the* woman (21) (a) *who had answered* (b) *who she had answered* (c) *answered* the door that the young woman had said she lived (22) (a) *at* (b) *in* 26, North Street.

I (23) (a) *know* (b) *am knowing* the story said the woman at the door. A young woman who lived here fifteen years ago (24) (a) *killed* (b) *was killed* by a car on that road. It happened exactly (25) (a) *since ten years* (b) *ten years ago* (c) *before ten years*. Every year since then the young woman (26) (a) *had seen* (b) *had been seen* on the road and asked for a lift home to 26, North Street.

1　令⋯⋯驚訝的是⋯⋯
2　突然消失。

拼寫 Spelling

動詞

A 除了情態動詞之外，大多數動詞在第三人稱單數時要加 "-s"：

drink — He drinks a lot.

want — She wants to see you now.

like — The dog likes water.

break — Glass breaks easily.

以 -sh、-ch、-ss、-x、-z、-o 結尾的動詞，要加 -es：

finish — It finishes at 8.

watch — He watches everything.

pass — The train passes here, but it doesn't stop.

mix — This colour mixes well.

buzz — The bell buzzes.

go — She goes every Friday.

以輔音 + -y 結尾的動詞，要變 -y 為 -ies：

try — He tries very hard.

worry — He worries too much.

study — She studies in France.

cry — It cries a lot.

以元音 + -y 結尾的動詞，只加 -s：

play — She plays with us sometimes.

say — Who says so?

B 大多數規則動詞的過去式和過去分詞，要加 -ed：

finish — We finished early.

clean — Who cleaned this?

以 -e 結尾的動詞，要加 -d，而<u>不是</u>加 -ed：

dance — We danced all night.

move — They moved in last week.

以輔音 + -y 結尾的動詞，要變 -y 為 -ied：

try — They tried to help.

study — We've studied hard.

以單元音和單輔音（如 -ip、-op、-an）結尾的單音節動詞，要將最後一個輔音雙拼後，再加 -ed：

drop — He dropped the ball.

drip — The tap dripped all night.

plan — They planned it well.

stop — We stopped at Dover.

有一個元音並以輔音 -y、-w、-x 結尾的動詞，只加 -ed：

play — We haven't played with the children.

mix — She mixed the ingredients for the meal.

一個音節以上的動詞，以單元音和單輔音結尾時，如果重音在最後一個音節時，要將最後一個輔音雙拼後，再加 -ed：

refer — I referred to it.

prefer — She preferred my cake.

如果重音不在最後一個音節上，只需加 -ed：

offer — They offered to pay.

develop — It developed fast.

例外：在英式英語中，動詞如果以 -l 結尾時，即使重音不在最後一個音節，也要將 -l 雙拼：

travel — He's travelled a lot.

有許多常用的動詞是不規則動詞，它們的過去式或過去分詞不加 -ed。下表列出了一些不規則動詞：

原形	過去式	過去分詞
be	was/were	been
become	became	become
begin	began	begun
break	broke	broken
bring	brought	brought
build	built	built
buy	bought	bought
catch	caught	caught
choose	chose	chosen
come	came	come
cost	cost	cost
cut	cut	cut
drink	drank	drunk
drive	drove	driven
eat	ate	eaten
fall	fell	fallen
feel	felt	felt
find	found	found
fly	flew	flown
forget	forgot	forgotten
get	got	got
go	went	gone
have	had	had
hear	heard	heard
hide	hid	hidden
hold	held	held
keep	kept	kept
know	knew	known
leave	left	left
let	let	let

拼寫 Spelling

lose	lost	lost
make	made	made
mean	meant	meant
meet	met	met
pay	paid	paid
put	put	put
read	read	read
ride	rode	ridden
rise	rose	risen
run	ran	run
see	saw	seen
sell	sold	sold
send	sent	sent
shut	shut	shut
sing	sang	sung
sit	sat	sat
sleep	slept	slept
speak	spoke	spoken
stand	stood	stood
steal	stole	stolen
swim	swam	swum
take	took	taken
teach	taught	taught
think	thought	thought
understand	understood	understood
wear	wore	worn
write	wrote	written

C 大多數動詞的 -ing 形式或現在分詞，只在詞尾加 -ing：

do — What are you doing?

sleep — He's sleeping.

sing — Who's singing?

finish — We're finishing soon.

cry — Someone's crying.

play — They're playing now.

以-e結尾的動詞，要去掉-e，再加-ing：

dance — He's dancing now.

hope — We're hoping for the best.

以 -ee 結尾的動詞，只需在詞尾加 -ing，如 see、agree、disgree 要變成 seeing、agree、disagreeing。

以單元音和單輔音結尾的單音節動詞，要將最後的輔音雙拼後，再加 -ing：

begin — It's beginning now.

get — He's getting the car.

重音在最後一個音節的較長單詞，要將最後一個輔音雙拼後，再加 -ing：

refer — I'm not referring to you.

名詞、形容詞和副詞

A 大多數具數名詞在詞尾加 -s 可構成複數形式， -s 讀作 /s/ 或 /z/：

a cat — two cats

one table — two tables

a tree — many trees

a day — several days

名詞以 -se、-ze、-ce、-ge 結尾的，要在詞尾加 -s，但要讀作 /iz/，因此讀音要比單數形式多出一個音節：

a rose — a bunch of roses

the prize — We all won prizes.

a service — the services

a cage — Animals hate cages.

名詞以 -sh、-ch、-ss、-x、-s 結尾的，要在詞尾加 -es，也讀作 /iz/：

bush — They cut the bushes.

watch — He bought us all watches.

pass — The mountain passes are blocked with snow.

box — Where are those boxes?

bus — Take one of the buses.

名詞以輔音＋-y 結尾的，要變 -y 為 -ies：

lady — Good evening, ladies.

city — the cities of Europe

名詞以 -f、-fe 結尾的，要變 -f、-fe 為 -ves：

knife — Careful with those knives!

shelf — Paco is putting up shelves.

wife — The officers and their wives had a special party.

許多以 -o 結尾的名詞，詞尾只加 -s：

a photo — Here are your photos, sir.

my radio — Those radios look expensive.

但下面這些以 -o 結尾的名詞，複數形式要加 -es：

a tomato — sun-ripened tomatoes

an echo — the sound of echoes

potato — a kilo of potatoes

hero — He's one of my heroes.

拼寫 Spelling

B 要構成大多數形容詞的比較級和最高級形式，需在形容詞的詞尾加 -er 和 -est：

soon — sooner — soonest
cheap — cheaper — cheapest

以 -e 結尾的形容詞，只需要加 -r 和 -st：

late — later — latest
wide — wider — widest

以 -y 結尾的形容詞，要變 -y 為 -ier 和 -iest：

dry — drier — driest
dirty — dirtier — dirtiest
happy — happier — happiest
silly — sillier — silliest

注意 對 shy 來說，要保留 -y。它的比較級是 shyer，最高級是 shyest。

以一個元音和一個輔音結尾的形容詞，除了 w，所有的輔音都要雙拼：

fat — fatter — fattest
big — bigger — biggest

但是 slow 的比較級是 slower，最高級是 slowest。

C 要構成副詞，通常需在形容詞詞尾加 -ly：

slow — slowly
late — lately
cheap — cheaply

以 -l 結尾的形容詞，要變 -l 為 -lly：

real — really
hopeful — hopefully

以 -y 結尾的形容詞，要變 -y 為 -ily：

happy — happily
easy — easily

以 -le 結尾的形容詞，要變 -le 為 -ly：

simple — simply
idle — idly

以 -ic 結尾的形容詞，要加 -ally，而不是 -ly，但讀音和 -ly 一樣：

artistic — artistically
automatic — automatically
specific — specifically

D 大寫字母：

以下情況必須用大寫字母：

1 每個句子的第一個單詞的第一個字母。

2 人名和地名：

This is Arlene. She works in the Education Department.
Have you met Rajan? He's from Malaysia, I think.

3 星期或月份：

See you on Monday or Tuesday. I love September.

4 國籍和語言稱謂的形容詞或名詞：

He's not French or Belgian. He's Swiss.
Can you speak Russian? I met an American last night.
Most people seem to drive Japanese cars nowadays.

5 某些人名字前的頭銜：

Do you know Professor Blum? This was Queen Victoria's home.

6 代詞 I：

I know I told you that I was busy.

E 常見的拼寫問題：

以下所列的是許多學生都認為很難拼寫的單詞：

accommodation	government	responsible
across	holiday	science
address	language	secretary
argument	library	separate
beautiful	medicine	succeed
beginning	necessary	surprise
blue	occasion	though
businessman	occurred	through
calendar	parliament	tomorrow
embarrassing	professor	vegetable
February	recommend	Wednesday
foreign	referred	

讀音 Pronunciation

1 元音

1. /ɑː/   **far**; **start**; **large**[1]; **fa**ther.
2. /æ/   h**a**ve; f**a**t; b**a**d.
3. /e/   **e**gg; b**e**d; h**ea**d.
4. /ɪ/   s**i**t; g**i**ve; s**i**ng.
5. /iː/   m**e**; **ea**t; agr**ee**d; p**ie**ce.
6. /ɒ/   h**o**t; l**o**st; l**o**ng.
7. /ɔː/   s**aw**; m**o**re; f**ou**r. [1]
8. /ʊ/   c**ou**ld; g**oo**d; w**ou**ld.
9. /ʌ/   b**u**t; c**u**t; bl**oo**d.
10. /uː/   y**ou**; **u**se; f**oo**l; d**o**.
11. /ɜː/   l**ear**n; th**ir**d; w**or**d. [1]
12. /ə/   moth**er**; **a**bout; forg**e**t. [1]
13. /i/   cit**y**; ver**y**; jock**ey**.

A 從以上第一至十三找出以下單詞，並把它們拼寫出來：

1. /hæv/ _have_
2. /fɑː/ _____
3. /lɜːn/ _____
4. /fuːl/ _____
5. /iːt/ _____
6. /lɒst/ _____
7. /fəget/ _____
8. /bʌt/ _____
9. /sɔː/ _____
10. /sɪt/ _____
11. /get/ _____
12. /gʊd/ _____
13. /blʌd/ _____
14. /duː/ _____
15. /wɜːd/ _____
16. /əbaʊt/ _____
17. /gɪv/ _____
18. /piːs/ _____
19. /stɑːt/ _____
20. /əgriːd/ _____

2 輔音

14. /b/   **b**ed; **b**ig; **b**rother.
15. /d/   **d**id; **d**og; be**d**.
16. /f/   **f**ive; i**f**; co**ff**ee.
17. /g/   **g**ood; le**g**; pi**g**.
18. /h/   **h**at; **h**ave; **wh**o.
19. /j/   **y**ou; **y**ellow; **y**oung.
20. /k/   **c**an; ki**ck**ing; lu**ck**y.
21. /l/   **l**eg; ye**ll**ow; o**l**d.
22. /m/   **m**e; **m**oney; su**mm**er.
23. /n/   **n**o; mo**n**ey; ca**n**.
24. /p/   **p**ut; ha**pp**y; u**p**.
25. /r/   **r**un; hu**rr**y.
26. /s/   **s**ee; hit**s**; ma**ss**.
27. /t/   **t**ime; pu**t**; win**t**er.
28. /v/   **v**an; ha**v**e; lo**v**ely.
29. /w/   **w**ith; **wh**ite; **w**oman.
30. /z/   **z**oo; no**s**e; run**s**; ea**s**y.
31. /ʃ/   **sh**ip; **s**ugar; wi**sh**.
32. /ʒ/   plea**s**ure; mea**s**ure.
33. /ŋ/   si**ng**; runni**ng**; si**ng**er.
34. /tʃ/   **ch**eap; wa**tch**; rea**ch**ing.
35. /θ/   **th**in; **th**ick; ba**th**.
36. /ð/   **th**en; wea**th**er.
37. /dʒ/   **j**oy; **j**udge; **g**eneral.

B 從以上第十四至三十七找出以下單詞，並把它們拼寫出來：

1. /weðə/ _weather_
2. /jʌŋ/ _____
3. /lʌvli/ _____
4. /hæt/ _____
5. /dʒʌdʒ/ _____
6. /pleʒə/ _____
7. /dɒg/ _____
8. /mʌni/ _____
9. /wɪntə/ _____
10. /kɪkɪŋ/ _____
11. /θɪk/ _____
12. /wɒtʃ/ _____
13. /leg/ _____
14. /hʌri/ _____
15. /brʌðə/ _____
16. /sʌmə/ _____
17. /rʌnɪŋ/ _____
18. /rʌnz/ _____
19. /sɪŋə/ _____
20. /siː/ _____
21. /kɒfi/ _____
22. /hæpi/ _____
23. /riːtʃɪŋ/ _____
24. /wʊmən/ _____

C 能拼寫出下面這些單詞並把它們按順序排列嗎？

1. /sevən/ _seven_
2. /wʌn/ _____
3. /sɪks/ _____
4. /ten/ _____
5. /fɔː/ _____
6. /tuː/ _____
7. /θriː/ _____

哪三個數字沒有列出來？ _____ 和 _____

[1] 在標準英式英語中，這些詞的 /r/ 是不發音的。在大多數美式讀音和一些英國方言中，會聽到發 /r/ 音，如：/fɑːr/、/stɑːrt/ 和 /lɑːrdz/。

讀音 Pronunciation

3 雙元音

38 /aɪ/ **fi**ve; **ni**ne; al**i**ve; wh**y**
39 /aɪə/ **fi**re; h**i**gher
40 /aʊ/ **ou**t; d**ow**n; s**ou**nd
41 /aʊə/ fl**ow**er; s**ou**r
42 /eɪ/ s**ay**; **ei**ght; p**ai**nt; ag**ai**n

43 /eə/ th**ere**; h**air**; wh**ere**; b**ear**
44 /ɪə/ h**ear**; n**ear**ly
45 /oʊ/ g**o**ing; s**o**; sl**ow**ly
46 /ɔɪ/ b**oy**; t**oi**let; c**oi**n
47 /ʊə/ p**oor**; s**ure**

D 從上表中找出這些單詞並把它們拼寫出來：

1 /ðeə/ ___*there*___
2 /peɪnt/ _____
3 /əlaɪv/ _____
4 /nɪəlɪ/ _____

5 /flaʊə/ _____
6 /goʊɪŋ/ _____
7 /saʊnd/ _____
8 /kɔɪn/ _____

9 /haɪə/ _____
10 /ʃʊə/ _____
11 /əgeɪn/ _____

E 把A和B；C和D；E和F中相關的詞用線連起來：

A	B	C	D	E	F
/lʌndən/	/ɒstreɪljə/	/red/	/kɒfi/	/bred/	/tʃɪps/
/pærɪs/	/iːdʒɪpt/	/griːn/	/grɑːs/	/sɒlt/	/bʌtə/
/mədrɪd/	/ɪŋglənd/	/braʊn/	/mɪlk/	/ʃuːz/	/ɪŋk/
/lɪzbən/	/frɑːns/	/waɪt/	/ðə skaɪ/	/pen/	/pepə/
/toʊkjoʊ/	/griːs/	/bluː/	/ɪŋk/	/fiʃ/	/sɒks/
/mɒskoʊ/	/ɪndəniːzjə/	/blæk/	/ðə sʌn/		
/wɒʃɪŋtən/	/ɪtəli/	/jeloʊ/	/ə təmɑːtoʊ/		
/æθənz/	/dʒəpæn/				
/roʊm/	/dʒɔːdən/				
/æmɑːn/	/pɔːtjəgəl/				
/dəmæskəs/	/rʌʃə/				
/kænbrə/	/speɪn/				
/kaɪroʊ/	/sɪrɪə/				
/dʒəkɑːtə/	/ðə juːnaɪtɪd steɪts/				

4 混元音

英語中最常用的元音是 /ə/，/ə/ 通常也被稱為混元音。

F 請看下面的單詞。你以前已讀過這些單詞，能把它們拼寫出來嗎？

1 /bənɑːnə/ ___*banana*___
2 /sɪstə/ _____
3 /lesənz/ _____
4 /elɪfənt/ _____
5 /lʌndən/ _____
6 /pleʒə/ _____

7 /æpəl/ _____
8 /fɑːðə/ _____
9 /taɪgə/ _____
10 /ɒstreɪljə/ _____
11 /sʌmə/ _____
12 /meʒə/ _____

13 /brʌðə/ _____
14 /mʌðə/ _____
15 /lɪzbən/ _____
16 /dʒəpæn/ _____
17 /weðə/ _____
18 /mɪstə/ _____

讀音 Pronunciation

G 請讀以下句子。在與你情況相符的句子後面打上 ✓，不相符的句子後面打上 ✗：

1 /aɪm ə tiːtʃə/
2 /aɪm ə bɔɪ/
3 /aɪ əm mærɪd/
4 /aɪ hæv ə sɪstə/
5 /aɪ lɪv ɪn ə haʊs/

6 /aɪm ə stjuːdənt/
7 /aɪm ə gɜːl/
8 /aɪ əm nɒt mærɪd/
9 /aɪ hæv ə brʌðə ənd sɪstə/
10 /aɪ laɪk ɪŋglɪʃ lesənz/

11 /aɪ lɪv ɪn lʌndən/
12 /maɪ neɪm ɪz piːtə/
13 /aɪ hæv ə brʌðə/
14 /aɪ lɪv ɪn ə flæt/
15 /aɪ dəʊnt laɪk ɪŋglɪʃ lesənz/

H 把下面的詞分成 6 組，每組 3 個詞。每組選出一個詞，用音標把它們寫出來：

/kaʊ/ /desk/ /treɪn/ /æpəl/ /taɪgə/ /fɜːt/ /tʃeə/ /elɪfənt/ /hɔːs/

/bənɑːnə/ /dʒækɪt/ /teɪbl/ /bʌs/ /ɒrɪndʒ/ /kɑː/ /blaʊz/ /laɪən/ /ʃiːp/

_____ _____ _____ _____ _____ _____

_____ _____ _____ _____ _____ _____

_____ _____ _____ _____ _____ _____

5 定冠詞

定冠詞 the 只有一種書寫形式：

Give me **the** money. This is **the** end.

但是 the 卻有兩種讀音：

Give me **the** money. /ðə/
This is **the** end. /ði/

在輔音前 the 讀作 /ðə/：

/ðə mʌni/ /ðə bənɑːnə/ /ðə dɒg/ /ðə kæt/ /ðə laɪən/ /ðə taɪgə/

在元音前 the 讀作 /ði/：

/ði end/ /ði æpəl/ /ði ɑːnsə/ /ði iːvnɪŋ/ /ði aɪdɪə/ /ði ɒfɪs/ /ði əʊld mæn/

I 根據 /ðə 和 /ði/ 的讀音把下面的詞分成兩組：

/ðə/	/ði/
the name	*the ink*
_____	_____
_____	_____
_____	_____
_____	_____

elɪfənt   kɑː   deɪ

ɒrɪndʒ   neɪm   ədres

kɔɪn   aɪ   mæn   ɪŋk

你能寫出這些單詞嗎？

讀音 Pronunciation

6 不定冠詞

不定冠詞有兩種形式：a/ə/ 和 an/ən/ 。/ə/ 用於輔音前面，/ən/ 用於元音前面。

J 根據 a/ə/ 或 an/ən/ 的用法把下面的詞分成兩組：

/ə/	/ən/
a glass	*an apple*
_____	_____
_____	_____
_____	_____
_____	_____

æpəl   bɔɪ   endʒɪn   baɪk   æktə   haʊs   glɑːs   ɒfɪs   eg

你能寫出這些單詞嗎？

7 重音

一個音節以上的英語單詞，有一個音節要重讀。重音可能：

落在第一個音節上：

famous /feɪməs/　person /pɜːsən/　secretary /sekrətəri/　yesterday /jestədeɪ/　difficult /dɪfɪkəlt/　definitely /defɪnətli/

落在最後一個音節上：

behind /bɪhaɪnd/　before /bɪfɔː/　understand /ʌndəstænd/　cigarette /sɪɡəret/

落在倒數第二個音節上：

important /ɪmpɔːtənt/　excitement /eksaɪtmənt/　decision /dɪsɪʒən/　determined /dɪtɜːmɪnd/

以 -tion/ʃən/ 結尾的詞，重音要落在倒數第二個音節上：

nation /neɪʃən/　examination /eɡzæmɪneɪʃən/　information /ɪnfəmeɪʃən/　repetition /repɪtɪʃən/

K 寫出下面的單詞：

1 /ɪnʌf/ *enough* _____
2 /ekspləneɪʃən/ _____
3 /dʒenrəl/ _____
4 /evrɪθɪŋ/ _____

5 /endʒɔɪmənt/ _____
6 /juːnɪvɜːsəti/ _____
7 /ɪntenʃən/ _____
8 /tʃɪldrən/ _____

9 /keəfəl/ _____
10 /dɪsembə/ _____
11 /wensdeɪ/ _____
12 /ɡʌvənmənt/ _____

L 先標示以下各詞的重讀音節，再把它們拼寫出來：

1 /bɒrəʊ/ *borrow* _____
2 /ɪmpɔːtəns/ _____
3 /mæɡəziːn/ _____
4 /pəzɪʃən/ _____

5 /evrɪbɒdi/ _____
6 /nesəsəri/ _____
7 /fəɡɒtən/ _____
8 /æksənt/ _____

9 /əmerɪkən/ _____
10 /prɒbəbli/ _____
11 /septembə/ _____
12 /sɪləbəl/ _____

讀音 Pronunciation

8 兩個詞連在一起時的讀音：

當兩個詞連在一起使用時，它們的讀音有時會發生變化：

/n/ → /m/	/braʊm bred/ (brown bread)
/nd/ → /m/	/braʊm bred əm bʌtə/ (brown bread and butter)
/n/ → /ŋ/	/teŋ griːm bɒtəlz/ (ten green bottles)
/d/ → /b/	/ɡʊb bɔɪ/ (good boy)
/d + j/ → /dʒ/	/wʊdʒuː/ /kʊdʒuː/ /dɪdʒuː/ (would you, could you, did you)
/t + j/ → /tʃ/	/wəʊntʃə/ /dəʊntʃə/ (won't you, don't you)
/t + m/ → /pm/	/lep mɪ/ /pʊp mɪ daʊn/ /ɡep mə bʊk/ (let me, put me down, get my book)

M 嘗試快讀以下句子：

1 /ðə wə teŋgriːm bɒtəlz hæŋɪŋ ɒn ðə wɔːl/ (There were ten green bottles hanging on the wall.)
2 /wʊdʒuː laɪk səm braʊm bred əm bʌtə?/ (Would you like some brown bread and butter?)
3 /ðɪʃ ʃɒp selz ɡʊb braʊm bæɡz/ (This shop sells good brown bags.)
4 /kɑːntʃə lem mɪ ə paʊnd?/ (Can't you lend me a pound?)
5 /kæn jə ɡep mɪ ə kʌpə tiː?/ (Can you get me a cup of tea?)

9 弱讀式：

英語中有些特別常用的詞在連讀時常常要弱讀。弱讀形式有時可以在書面語中表現出來：

I am tired → I'm tired   She is not here → She's not here → She isn't here
She did not know → She didn't know   They have gone → They've gone
We will come tomorrow → We'll come tomorrow   He would help → He'd help

大多數弱讀式都使用混元音 /ə/。經常用於弱讀式的詞有以下幾類：

助動詞和情態動詞：

I was there.	/aɪ wəz ðeə/
They were friends.	/ðeɪ wə frenz/
I could come.	/aɪ kəd kʌm/
She would know.	/ʃiː wəd nəʊ/
You can go.	/juː kən ɡəʊ/
What have you done?	/wɒt əv juː dʌn/

代詞：

I was there.	/aɪ wəz ðeə/
You can go.	/juː kən ɡəʊ/
Tell them a story.	/tel ðəm ə stɔːri/

介詞：

A glass of water.	/ə ɡlɑːs ə wɔːtə/
I'm from England.	/aɪm frəm ɪŋɡlənd/
Is that for me?	/ɪz ðæt fə miː/
I'm going to bed.	/aɪm ɡəʊɪŋ tə bed/

讀音 Pronunciation

將 A 和 B 中相關的句子連起來，再把 B 的句子讀出來：

	A		B
1	Who was that?	a	/wʊdʒə laɪk ə glɑːs ə mɪlk?/
2	Where were you going?	b	/kʊd aɪ hæv ə kʌp ə tiː pliːz?/
3	What do you want?	c	/wiː wə weɪtɪŋ fər ə bʌs/
4	Could I have a cup of tea please?	d	/jə kən goʊ ɪf jə laɪk/
5	Do you know who it is?	e	/wɒdʒə wɒnt?/
6	Would you like a glass of milk?	f	/weə wə jə goʊɪŋ/
7	We were waiting for a bus.	g	/dʒə noʊ huː ɪt ɪz?/
8	You can go if you like.	h	/huː wəz ðæt?/

10 常用短語：

英語中有些短語很常用，以至組成這些短語的幾個詞，讀音都連成一體，讀起來非常快：

Would you mind → /wʊdʒəmaɪnd/. Do you mind → /dʒəmaɪnd/. Do you think → /dʒəθɪŋk/.
Don't you think → /dʌntʃəθɪŋk/. I don't know → /aɪdənoʊ/. Did you know → /dɪdʒənoʊ/.
Where's the ... → /weəzə .../. What's the matter → /wɒzəmætə/.
What's the matter with you → /wɒzəmætəwɪju:/. Who's that → /huːzæt/.
I want to → /æwɒnə/. I'm going to → /æmgənə/.

O 你能讀出下面的句子嗎？能用國際音標把它們全都拼寫出來嗎？

1	/weə dʒə lɪv?/	1	_Where do you live?_
2	/wɒtʃə gənə duː təmɒrə/	2	
3	/tel əm tə kʌm ət fɔːr ə klɒk/	3	
4	/aɪ wɒnə goʊ hoʊm/	4	
5	/aɪ dɪdn noʊ wɒdə duː/	5	
6	/wɒ dʒə wɒnə duː/	6	
7	/aɪ dənoʊ wɒtʃə miːn/	7	
8	/huː zæt oʊvə ðeə/	8	
9	/aɪ hæftə goʊ hoʊm naʊ/	9	
10	/jə kən duː wɒtʃə wɒnt/	10	
11	/aɪv gɒtə lɒtə mʌni/	11	
12	/aɪm gənə getə kʌpə tiː/	12	
13	/huː dʒə wɒnə siː/	13	
14	/aɪl tel jə wɒt aɪ wɒnt/	14	
15	/haʊ dʒə noʊ/	15	

數詞 Numbers

A 基數詞 1、2、3、4等:

1 數字0有幾個不同的稱謂。在計數或在數學中,0讀作 nought:

The substance weights nought point five grams (0.5 grams)

在大部分體育項目中,0讀作 nil:
We lost five - nil (5-0)

在網球比賽中,0讀作 love:
Becker leads forty - love (40-0)

談及溫度時,0讀作 zero:
In the winter it can get as cold as twenty-five degrees below zero.

談及電話號碼時,號碼要一個一個單獨讀出,0讀作 oh:
Oh two seven two five five oh nine
0 2 7 2 5 5 0 9

讀日期或比1小的數位時,0讀作 oh:
Nineteen oh one (1901)
Nought point oh oh five (0.005)

2 百和其他數字之間要加 and:
two hundred and fifty (250)
one hundred and twenty-one (121)
three thousand nine hundred and ten (3910)

3 當百、千和百萬是確切數字時,不用複數形式,不要加 -s:
Three million two hundred thousand four hundred and one (3200401)
There were millions of people at the concert.
They say this tree is a hundred years old.
I've told you hundreds of times, you mustn't smoke in here!

4 常常採用"數位+單數名詞"的方式,把數字轉變成複合形容詞。數字和單數名詞之間通常用連字符"-"連接:
The team played with ten men: It was a ten-man team.
The watch cost forty pounds: It's a forty-pound watch.

B 序數詞:第1、第2、第3等:

1 序數詞可用來表示某人或某物在一個序列或一組中的位置:
We lived on the fifth floor.
He was second in the race.
This is the tenth time I've seen the film.

2 序數詞可以與基數詞連用,序數詞要放在基數詞的前面:
The first five rows are the most expensive.
The first three people who come in to the shop will win £100, the second five will win £50.

3 日期要用序數詞表示。書寫日期時可用縮略形式,如 1st、2nd、3rd、4th等:
Today is the first of May (May 1st).
The play opens on the twenty-second of March (March 22nd).

C 可用 once、twice 來表示某人做某事的經常程度,兩次以上可用 three times、four times 等表示:

I've read that book twice.
The clock struck four times.
You must take this medicine three times a day.

數詞練習 Numbers Practice

A 請看下面的比賽結果，用以下序數詞給賽跑者排名次：

first   second   third   fourth   fifth   sixth

1 Team A finished in 49 seconds.
2 Team B finished in 51 seconds.
3 Team C finished last.
4 Team D finished in 48 seconds.
5 Team E finished in 55 seconds.
6 Team F finished in 50.5 seconds.

B 請讀下面的句子，判斷 0 在各個句子中該屬哪種稱謂：

oh   zero   nought   nil   love

1 The area code for Bath is 01225.
2 Germany won the match 2-0.
3 My great-grandfather was born in 1909, I think.
4 The score here at Wimbledon is 40-0 to Lendl.
5 In rugby you sometimes have scores of 70-0!
6 We want to reduce inflation to 0.5% this year.
7 0.004 milligrams of this substance can poison a man.
8 It was very cold. The temperature was below 0.

C 用複合形容詞完成以下句子：

如：The book has 120 pages.
   It's a one hundred and twenty page book.

1 The pass lasts for three days.
   It's a _____ pass.
2 The speed limit here is 80 miles per hour.
   There's an _____ speed limit here.
3 The baby weighed five pounds when she was born.
   She was a _____ baby.
4 The journey to Cornwall takes 3 hours by train.
   It's a _____ train journey to Cornwall.
5 My new shirt cost £22.
   This is a _____ shirt.
6 The meal we ate had three courses.
   We had a _____ meal.

D 請看 Bob 的活動計劃，然後用 once、twice、three times 等完成以下句子：

	Mon	Tues	Wed	Thurs	Fri	Sat	Sun
shopping		✔	✔		✔	✔	
swimming	✔			✔			
gardening					✔	✔	✔
watch TV		✔	✔	✔	✔		✔
eat in a restaurant						✔	

1 Last week Bob went shopping _____ .
2 He went to the swimming pool _____ .
3 Bob watched TV _____ last week.
4 He only went out for a meal _____ .

字母 Letters

A 英文字母表中有 26 個字母。你能把它們正確排列出來嗎？

Q W E R T Y U I O P A S D F G H J K L Z X C V B N M

1		8		15		22	
2		9		16		23	
3		10		17		24	
4		11		18		25	
5		12		19		26	
6		13		20			
7		14		21			

B 英語中有些字母的發音和其他語言的發音不一樣，下面是英語語音的音標：

元音：

/iː/	tree		/ʊ/	good
/ɪ/	big		/uː/	moon
/e/	get		/ʌ/	cut
/æ/	hat		/ɜː/	bird
/ɑː/	car		/ə/	father
/ɔː/	door		/ɒ/	pot
			/i/	very

雙元音：

/eɪ/ day
/oʊ/ no
/aɪ/ my
/aʊ/ now
/ɔɪ/ boy
/ɪə/ near
/eə/ hair
/ʊə/ sure
/aɪə/ fire
/aʊə/ flower

輔音：

/p/	pen	/f/	fall	/h/	hello
/b/	book	/v/	very	/m/	mum
/t/	tea	/θ/	thin	/n/	not
/d/	did	/ð/	then	/ŋ/	sing
/k/	can	/s/	so	/l/	leg
/g/	go	/z/	zoo	/r/	red
/tʃ/	cheap	/ʃ/	she	/j/	yes
/dʒ/	job	/ʒ/	vision	/w/	wet

C 下面的音標是字母表中的哪些字母？

1	/zed/	7	/biː/	13	/aɪ/	20	/dʒeɪ/
2	/eɪtʃ/	8	/eɪ/	14	/es/	21	/en/
3	/dʒiː/	9	/keɪ/	15	/ef/	22	/diː/
4	/iː/	10	/eks/	16	/em/	23	/piː/
5	/dʌbəljuː/	11	/el/	17	/juː/	24	/ɑː/
6	/waɪ/	12	/kjuː/	18	/siː/	25	/viː/
				19	/tiː/	26	/oʊ/

1 _____ 7 _____ 13 _____ 20 _____
2 _____ 8 _____ 14 _____ 21 _____
3 _____ 9 _____ 15 _____ 22 _____
4 _____ 10 _____ 16 _____ 23 _____
5 _____ 11 _____ 17 _____ 24 _____
6 _____ 12 _____ 18 _____ 25 _____
                      19 _____ 26 _____

D 你如何讀下面這些常見的縮略語？

1	UK	6	CD	11	EC
2	GB	7	DJ	12	USA
3	a.m.	8	BBC	13	VIP
4	p.m.	9	TV	14	UFO
5	PTO	10	NATO	15	WWF

1 _____ 6 _____ 11 _____
2 _____ 7 _____ 12 _____
3 _____ 8 _____ 13 _____
4 _____ 9 _____ 14 _____
5 _____ 10 _____ 15 _____

答案 Answer Key

Unit 1 Practice

Suggested Answers

A
1 I'm 16 years old.
2 I'm not a teacher.
3 I'm at home.
4 It's morning.
5 It's cold.
6 It's Monday.

B
1 tick ✓
2 tick ✓
3 cross ✗
4 tick ✓
5 tick ✓
6 tick ✓
7 tick ✓
8 cross ✗

C
1 The big book isn't on the table. It's on the chair.
2 The shoes aren't on the chair. They're under the chair.
3 The exercise book isn't on the chair. It's on the table.
4 The ruler and the pen aren't on the chair. They're on the table.
5 The pencil isn't next to the ruler. It's next to the pen.
6 The ball and the big book aren't on the floor. They're on the chair.

D Suggested Answers
1 My name isn't Kim, it's John.
2 I'm not three years old. I'm 14 years old.
3 I'm not from Scotland, I'm from Hong Kong.
4 I'm not a pop singer, I'm a student.
5 I'm not English, I'm Chinese.
6 His/Her name isn't Kim, it's Peter/Jenny.
7 He's/She's not three years old, he's/she's 15 years old.
8 He's/She's not from Scotland, he's/she's from Hong Kong.
9 He's/She's not a pop singer, he's/she's a teacher.
10 He's/She's not English, he's/she's Chinese.

Unit 2 Practice

A
1 PA
2 FP
3 PA
4 FP
5 PA
6 FP
7 PA
8 PA or FP
9 PA

B
1 I'm wearing jeans./ I'm not wearing jeans.
2 I'm studying English./ I'm not studying English.
3 I'm sitting at home./ I'm not sitting at home.
4 I'm watching TV./ I'm not watching TV.
5 I'm smoking a cigarette./ I'm not smoking a cigarette.
6 I'm talking with friends./ I'm not talking with friends.
7 I'm relaxing./ I'm not relaxing.
8 I'm listening to music./ I'm not listening to music.

C
1 The boy is eating sweets.
2 The businessman is walking across the road.
3 It's a fine day. The sun is shining.
4 A jogger is listening to music on a personal stereo.
5 The man at the bus stop is reading a newspaper.
6 The woman in the park is pushing a pram.
7 No one in the picture is wearing a hat.
8 Some customers are buying fruit.

D
1 To Malta probably.
2 I'm watching a video.
3 Because it's useful.
4 We're going camping.

Unit 3 Practice

A
1 have
2 lives, go
3 like
4 has/does
5 goes
6 do
7 does
8 live
9 likes

B
1 reads
2 listens
3 travels
4 live
5 comes
6 cost
7 speaks
8 knows

C Suggested Answers
1 I get up at half past seven.
2 I go to bed at eleven o'clock.
3 I play sports once a week.
4 I visit my friends on Sundays.
5 I like pop music.

Unit 4 Practice

A Suggested Answers
1 I study English.
2 I don't play cricket.
3 I don't speak French.
4 I don't study Japanese.
5 I don't go to England every year.
6 I don't like jazz.
7 I live in a flat.
8 I don't live in a house.

B Suggested Answers
1 She doesn't study English.
2 She plays cricket.
3 He speaks French.
4 She studies Japanese.
5 He doesn't go to England every year.
6 She doesn't like jazz.
7 He doesn't live in a flat.
8 She lives in a house.

C
1 Do you watch television every day?
2 Do you buy a newspaper every day?
3 Do you go abroad on holiday every year?
4 Do you work in an office?
5 Do you live alone?
6 Do you like rock music?
7 Do you play the piano?
8 Do you live in a big city?

Suggested Answers
9 I don't watch TV every day.
10 I buy a newspaper every day.
11 I go abroad on holiday every year.
12 I don't work in an office.
13 I don't live alone.
14 I don't like rock music.
15 I play the piano.
16 I live in a big city

D
1 I haven't any friends in England.
2 Have they a big house?
3 He hasn't much money.
4 They haven't any pets.
5 Has she any nice new clothes?
6 I haven't got any friends in England.
7 Have they got a big house?
8 He hasn't got much money.
9 They haven't got any pets.
10 Has she got any nice new clothes?

Unit 5 Practice

A 1c, 2f, 3a, 4d, 5h, 6b, 7e, 8g

B Suggested Answers
1 I haven't been to Brazil.
2 I haven't read Don Quixote.
3 I haven't been to Honolulu.
4 I've heard of Andre Agassi.
5 I've heard of Emilio Zapata.
6 I've read Oliver Twist.
7 I haven't been to Madrid.
8 I've heard of Charlie Chaplin.

C
a He's eaten too much.
b She's broken her arm.
c They've lost their way.
d She's won a prize.
e He's caught a fish.
f He's fallen down.
g He's had an accident.
h He's lost all his money.

Unit 6 Practice

A
1 When I have finished Oliver Twist I will read Don Quixote.
2 You can do the shopping after you have made the beds.
3 Don't go out before you have done your homework.
4 I'm going to stay in class until I have finished my essay.

B
1 Has your sister passed her exams? I don't know. She hasn't got the results.
2 Has your brother gone to America? No, he hasn't gone yet.
3 Has Peter started school? No, he hasn't started yet.
4 Have you read the newspaper? No, I haven't read it yet.

C
a He's been waiting for a bus.
b They've been skiing.
c She's been playing tennis.
d He's been swimming.
e She's been reading.
f He's been eating.

答案 **Answer Key**

Unit 7

4 Exercise (as table below)

	Present	Past (positive)	Past (negative)	Question
I	am busy	was busy	wasn't busy	Was I busy?
He	is busy	was busy	wasn't busy	Was he there?
She	is busy	was angry	wasn't busy	Was she there?
It	is cold	was angry	wasn't busy	Was it there?
We	are cold	were angry	weren't busy	Were we late?
You	are sad	were angry	weren't busy	Were you late?
They	are sad	were angry	weren't at home	Were they late?

Unit 7 Practice

A 1 I was in town.
2 No, I was with a friend.
3 It was really hot.
4 No, I was fine, but my brother was ill.
5 I was in bed, but I wasn't asleep.

B **Suggested Answers**
1 I was at school.
2 No, I was with a friend.
3 It was windy.
4 Yes, I was ill.
5 Yes, I was asleep.

C 1 was   2 was   3 were   4 were   5 was

D 1 False. Tony Blair is the Prime Minister of Britain.
2 False. Charlie Chaplin was a famous silent movie star.
3 False. Cities are larger now than in 1900.
4 False. The world record for the 100 metres sprint is less than 10 seconds.
5 True.
6 False. English is the most useful international language.

E 1 were, was
2 was, was
3 was
4 was, was
5 Was
6 weren't

Unit 8

3 begin, began; break, broke; buy, bought; come, came; do, did; drink, drank; drive, drove; eat, ate; find, found; get, got; give, gave; go, went; have, had; make, made; pay, paid; say, said; see, saw; take, took; tell, told; write, wrote;

Unit 8 Practice

A 1 saw
2 bought
3 went
4 ate
5 wrote
6 gave
7 broke
8 did

B The police are looking for a man who <u>stole</u> £25 and a jacket from a crowded fashion shop in Brighton last week. The man, who <u>was</u> between 20 and 25, with short brown hair, <u>took</u> the jacket from a staff changing-room. 'I'm not worried about the money, really,' <u>said</u> the victim, Sally Walker, 25, who works in the shop. 'But the jacket <u>cost</u> me £150. I <u>got</u> it when I was on holiday in Turkey.' The police do not think the man is dangerous, but <u>warned</u> the public to be careful.

C 1 When <u>did she buy</u> the jacket?
2 Where <u>did she go</u> on holiday?
3 What <u>did he</u> steal?
4 Where <u>did he steal them</u> from?
5 How <u>much did the jacket</u> cost?

D She bought a paper and a magazine for her mother.
She had a meeting with the bank manager.
She called Export International.
She didn't have time to write a letter to Gerry but she wrote a letter to the Directors of XYZ to confirm a meeting.
She talked with Jan and John about new products for the company.
She didn't have time to send a fax to ISB in Munich.
She didn't have time to meet David for lunch.
She took a taxi home, packed a suitcase and took a train to London.

Suggested Answers
I had a shower yesterday.
I didn't cook a meal yesterday.
I read a paper yesterday.
I made a phone call to a friend yesterday.
I didn't play a sport yesterday.
I didn't speak English yesterday.
I listened to music yesterday.
I went out yesterday.
I didn't visit a museum yesterday.

Unit 9 Practice

A 1 met, was shopping
2 were walking, began
3 hurt, was working

4 was staying, went
5 was doing, forgot
6 were living, was
7 was working, saw
8 went, were staying

B 1 hurt, went
2 heard, began
3 were listening, came
4 heard, began
5 was talking, went
6 was having, rang
7 had, got
8 were playing, arrived

Unit 10 Practice

A 1b, 2a, 3h, 4c, 5d, 6e, 7f, 8g

B 1e, 2g, 3a, 4h, 5i, 6b, 7j, 8c, 9d, 10f

C 1 went, had finished
2 had gone, was
3 had lived, was
4 had eaten, ordered
5 felt, had caught
6 took, had read

Unit 11

* There is no 30th February!

Unit 11 Practice

Dear Monica,

Many thanks for your letter. I <u>am</u> pleased you <u>are enjoying</u> your holiday. When (<u>do you come</u>) home? It will be great to see you again.
(We <u>are going</u>) to Greece this year – next Friday in fact. I <u>am trying</u> to get everything ready in time, but it <u>is</u> very difficult with three small children. Our plane (<u>leaves</u>) at six o'clock on Friday morning, so we (<u>are taking</u>) a taxi to the airport at four o'clock in the morning – I <u>hope</u> the children (<u>behave</u>) themselves and (<u>get</u>) ready quickly without too much trouble. Peter (<u>has</u>) three weeks holiday this year so when we (<u>get</u>) back from Greece we (<u>are staying</u>) with his mother in Brighton for a week. She <u>has</u> a big flat in a block right next to the sea. The children <u>love</u> it.
Lydia (<u>is starting</u>) school this September. I <u>hope</u> she (<u>likes</u>) it. Jimmy <u>hates</u> going to school. He <u>shouts</u> and <u>screams</u> every morning. Perhaps he will be better when Lydia (<u>starts</u>). Thank you for your news. I <u>am</u> very pleased to hear that Isabel has done so well at University. What (<u>is she doing</u>) next year? Has she decided yet? What about the twins? When (<u>do they leave</u>) school?
Give my love to Norman. I <u>am</u> sorry about his accident. I <u>hope</u> he (<u>gets</u>) better soon.
Much love, Teresa.

答案 Answer Key

B Suggested Answers

1 My next birthday is on a Friday.
2 This lesson finishes at ten o'clock.
3 I am visiting a friend tomorrow morning.
4 I have eight English lessons next week.
5 It is Thursday the day after tomorrow.
6 It is the sixth of April next Thursday.
7 I am having chicken for supper tonight.
8 I am playing football after my lesson.
9 It is in October.
10 I am 14 years old next birthday.

Unit 12 Practice

A 1c, 2e, 3a, 4f, 5b, 6d

B 1 will you lend
2 are going to have
3 are going to see
4 will not get back/won't get back
5 are you going to do
6 will share
7 are going to borrow
8 Will there be
9 are not going to come
10 are going to take
11 are going to stay with
12 will be
13 will have/are going to have

C a I will open the door for you.
b I will write a letter to you every day.
c Help! I'm going to fall!
d We are going to get wet.
e I will cook/I'm going to cook the supper.
f I think I'm going to get into trouble.

Unit 13 Practice

A Suggested Answers
1 There are thirty people in my class.
2 There are ten people in the room.
3 There are two pictures on the walls.
4 There is a pen on my desk.
5 There are four people in my family.
6 There were two big beds and a little bed in the room.

B 1 There's an English class every day.
2 There will be a meeting at three o'clock.
3 There was an accident this morning.
4 There were a lot of people at the concert.
5 There were three books on the desk.
6 There will be lots of children at the party.
7 There is nothing to eat or drink.
8 There were three people waiting in the shop.

C A Is there anything good on TV tonight?
B No, I don't think there'll be anything very interesting.
A Do you think there's a good film on at the cinema?
B I don't know. There wasn't anything

last week.
A Shall we go round and see Joe and Pamela?
B Let's telephone first. Last time we went there was nobody at home.

Unit 14 Practice

A 1 What are they going to do?
2 What work does he do?
3 What does it mean?
4 What time will they arrive?
5 What colour does she want?

B 1d, 2a, 3e, 4b, 5c

C 1 sort 2 time 3 size 4 day 5 colour
6 language 7 kind 8 work

D 1e, 2d, 3a, 4b, 5f, 6c

Unit 15 Practice

A A: Let's go and see Peter and Mary some time.
B: When?
A: Well, we could go this weekend.
A: They live in that big house on the corner.
B: Who?
A: You know – those friends of Michael's.
A: We could probably get there quite quickly.
B: How?
A: Well, we could take a taxi.
A: I'm afraid I've lost it.
B: What?
A: My library book. I don't know where it is.
A: I think they're away on holiday.
B: Where?
A: Italy, I think.

B 1 I wonder what she's like.
2 I wonder what she meant.
3 I wonder who this belongs to.
4 I wonder why they're so late.
5 I wonder what he wants.
6 I wonder how old he is.
7 I wonder where they have gone.
8 I wonder what they will say.

C Possible questions include:
1 When did she arrive?
2 Where is she now?
3 How much is it?
4 Where did he go?
5 When does she leave?
6 How do I get there?
7 Where can I find him?
8 Where did he go?
9 Where shall I put this?
10 Where do you live?
11 Where are you going?

D 1 How long will it take?
2 How much will it cost?
3 What does it mean?

4 Where do they come from?
5 When will they arrive?
6 Where has he gone?

Unit 16

4 child, children; fish, fish; sheep, sheep; foot, feet; man, men; tooth, teeth; mouse, mice; person, people; woman, women

Unit 16 Practice

A baby, babies; box, boxes; child, children; shoe, shoes; shop, shops; day, days; church, churches; foot, feet; radio, radios; sandwich, sandwiches; city, cities; story, stories

B a two buses   f seven fish
b three photos   g eight mice
c four sheep   h nine watches
d five boxes   i ten teeth
e six babies

C Buses are cheaper than taxis.
The bus is going to the station now.
Women work as well as men.
That woman is my neighbour.
Watches were invented a long time ago.
My watch is a Rolex.
Most students work very hard all year.
A student in my class comes from near Buenos Aires.
Books are made of paper.
There is a book about geography on my desk.

D 1 days, week   4 minutes, hour
2 weeks, year   5 months, year
3 hours, day

Unit 17 Practice

A 1 the past   5 the moon
2 the sky   6 the sun
3 the dark   7 the world
4 the future   8 the air

B 1 a drink   4 a fight
2 a sleep   5 a shower
3 a walk   6 a wash

C scissors, binoculars, glasses, tweezers, pyjamas, tights

D 1 a pair of scissors
2 a pair of glasses
3 a pair of tights
4 a pair of tweezers
5 a pair of pyjamas
6 A pair of binoculars

E 1 team   4 team
2 staff   5 audience
3 staff   6 audience

答案 Answer Key

Unit 18 Practice

A
1 snow, wood, metal, glass, gold, ice
2 milk, petrol, coffee, tea
3 dinner, lunch, breakfast, tea
4 food, butter, bread, toast
5 aerobics, maths, physics

B
1 petrol   4 aerobics
2 breakfast   5 tea
3 Gold   6 snow

C
1 a paper   7 a grey hair
2 Paper   8 Sugar
3 cheese   9 two sugars
4 a cheese   10 glass
5 a business   11 glasses
6 hair   12 Business

Unit 19

1 a week, a book, a person, a tomato,
a cup, a dog, a house

2 a box, a job, a banana, a holiday,
a teacher, a hat

3 an elephant, an apple, an aunt,
an opinion, an idiot

Unit 19 Practice

A
1 half an hour.
2 an hour.
3 a kilo.
4 a hundred people.
5 a few times.
6 a lot to do.
7 a month.

B
1 a student   5 a musician
2 a nurse   6 nurses
3 tourists   7 a tourist
4 students   8 singers

C
1 There's a small table in the kitchen.
2 There are a lot of pictures in the
living room.
3 There are some flowers in the living
room.
4 There's a lamp in the corner of the
living room.
5 There's a TV in the living room.
6 There are some plants in both rooms.
7 There's a guitar in the living room.
8 There are some people in the living
room.

Unit 20 Practice

A 1 a, the 2 The, a 3 the, a 4 a, The
5 a, the 6 the, an 7 the, a 8 a, the
9 a, the

B 1 an, 2 a, 3 a, 4 a, 5 the, 6 the,
7 the, 8 the, 9 a, 10 a, 11 a,
12 a, 13 The, 14 the, 15 the, 16 the

Unit 21 Practice

A
1 the guitar   5 the Clintons
2 the Odeon   6 the Ritz
3 the south west   7 the Andes
4 the Nile

B
1 Excuse me, can you tell me the time
please?
2 What's the name of the nearest
cinema?
3 We went to the cinema last night.
Unfortunately we were late so we
missed the start of the film.
4 The name of the river that flows
through the middle of London is the
Thames.
5 The weather in the north of England
will get worse on Thursday and Friday.
At the weekend the temperature will
be 3 degrees and there will be snow
during the night.
6 We live near the sea in the south of
England. Every day in the afternoon
we walk the dogs in the woods for a
couple of hours. The scenery is so
beautiful.
7 I read in the encyclopaedia you gave
me that Mount Everest in the
Himalayas is the highest mountain in
the world. The longest river in the
world is the Nile in Africa.
8 I was thinking of the girls we met in
the street when we went to a party in
the house next to the restaurant
where Michael works. One came
from the Republic of Ireland. We
invited them to the party but they
couldn't go because they were flying
to the United States the next day.

Unit 22

1 I, my; he, his; it, its; you, your; you,
your; she, her; we, our; they, their

Unit 22 Practice

A
1 my   5 our
2 her, his   6 your
3 her   7 its, its
4 their   8 its

B
1 his trousers.   4 her number.
2 its handle.   5 your animal.
3 their keys.   6 our ball.

C
1 What's your best friend's name?
2 What's your mother's favourite
colour?
3 What's your neighbour's address?
4 What's your teacher's first name?
5 What's your country's main export?
6 What's your region's speciality food?

D **Suggested Answers**
1 My best friend's name is Jacky.
2 My mother's favourite colour is red.
3 My neighbour's address is Room

203, Flat 8, Rose Garden, Kowloon,
Hong Kong.
4 His/Her first name is Mei Ling.
5 My country's main export is rice.
6 My region's speciality food is sweet
and sour pork.

Unit 23 Practice

A 1b, 2f, 3e, 4a, 5g, 6d, 7h, 8c

B
1 these   6 those
2 this   7 that
3 that, this   8 This
4 that   9 those
5 these

C
1 This song is my mother's favourite.
2 That joke was terrible.
3 This cake is delicious.
4 These shoes are comfortable.
5 That colour is fashionable.
6 Those trousers are my best ones.
7 These books are very popular.
8 That party was great.
9 Those paintings are beautiful.

Unit 24

1 I, me; you, you; he, him; she, her; it, it;
we, us; they, them

Unit 24 Practice

A
1 I, we, it   3 I, I, He
2 you, we, you   4 I, I, She, I

B 1 me 2 us 3 him 4 me

C
1 We met them last week.
2 It's in Africa, I think.
3 He's in hospital now.
4 I've seen it three times.
5 It's boring.
6 Paul gave them to me.
7 They eat a lot of pasta.

D
1 She (e)
2 it (c)
3 her, she, me (d)
4 We, We, us (a)
5 them (f)
6 You, me, you, her (b)
7 They, her (g)

Unit 25 Practice

A
1 I love cakes, especially the ones my
mother makes!
2 Our car is the black one at the end
of the road.
3 I'm not sure if I need a big bottle or
a small one.
4 He lost his umbrella, so he wants to
buy a new one.
5 The hotel is a modern one on the
coast.

226

6 The books I bought are the <u>ones</u> on the table.
7 I always have two pens with me, a blue <u>one</u> and a red <u>one</u>.
8 Is this museum the <u>one</u> you were talking about?

B 1 'Thanks, I'd love one.'
2 'The brown ones on the desk.'
3 'Your new cotton one.'
4 'The ones of Spain? Yes.'
5 'Sure. Which one?'

C 1 That's all right.
2 That's a lot.
3 That's great.
4 That's why you're tired.

D 1 this, that   3 that, that, This
2 That   4 those

Unit 26 Practice

A 1 his is very old
2 hers is German
3 mine is over there
4 mine is smaller / ours is smaller
5 theirs is black and white
6 ours are second class

B 1 Susan is a friend of ours.
2 The small man is a neighbour of ours.
3 Is singing a hobby of yours?
4 Hamid is a student of mine.
5 Pink is a favourite colour of hers.
6 I am a fan of theirs.
7 Roast beef is a favourite meal of mine.

C a 'Whose car is that?'
'It's his.'
b 'Whose is this?'
'It's his.'
c 'Excuse me, is this yours?'
d 'I haven't got a pen on me.'
'Here, you can borrow mine.'

Unit 27 Practice

Suggested Answers
A 1 I last went swimming three months ago.
2 I last went to the cinema three days ago.
3 I started school a long time ago.
4 I was born thirteen years ago.
5 My mother was born fifty years ago.
6 I had breakfast an hour ago.
7 I was last ill two weeks ago.
8 I started learning English a few years ago.

Suggested Answers
B 1 the fifth of March
2 Monday
3 February
4 I will be fifteen years old.
5 I was ten years old.

Suggested Answers
1 I am often late for lessons.
2 I often get up late on Sunday.
3 I sometimes watch TV in the evening.
4 I usually play tennis in the summer.
5 In my country it is occasionally cold in winter.
6 I often read in bed before I go to sleep.
7 He is often late for lessons.
8 She often gets up late on Sunday.
9 He sometimes watches TV in the evening.

D 1 (F) 2 (T) 3 (F) 4 (T) 5 (F) 6 (T)

Unit 28 Practice

Suggested Answers
A 1 The USA will definitely not win the next football World Cup.
2 My country will probably win the next football World Cup.
3 I am possibly the oldest person in my class.
4 I will certainly go away for a holiday this summer.
5 It will probably rain tomorrow.
6 The next leader of my country will possibly be a woman.
7 I will definitely get married next year.
8 I will certainly get most of these sentences right.

B 1 X I have nearly finished this exercise.
2 correct
3 X I like your new dress a lot.
4 correct
5 X This is a very good book. I enjoyed it very much.
6 X He is very lazy. He doesn't help his parents very much.
7 correct
8 correct
9 X I always enjoy the weekend very much.
10 correct
11 correct

Unit 29 Practice

A 1e, 2a, 3f, 4c, 5b, 6d

B 1 for   6 since
2 since   7 from, until
3 from, until 8 since
4 From, until 9 since
5 until   10 for, for

C **Suggested Answers**
1 I started kindergarten.
2 Hong Kong, twelve
3 two o'clock, three o'clock
4 eleven o'clock, seven o'clock
5 a long time
6 last week

Unit 30 Practice

A 1 nine o'clock is the odd one out. It takes at. The others take in.
2 the weekend is the odd one out. It takes at. The others take on.
3 my sister's birthday is the odd one out. It takes on. The others take at.
4 winter is the odd one out. It takes in. The others take on.
5 five o'clock is the odd one out. It takes at. The others take in.

B 1 in 2 in 3 on 4 at 5 in 6 in 7 at

C 1 in the next century
2 on my birthday
3 on the first of April
4 at dinner
5 in August
6 in the morning
7 at the moment

Review: Cycle 1 – Units 1-30

A 1 is   5 does, do
2 is, am   6 have
3 are   7 Do, have
4 is   8 are

B 1 Do you want to go to the cinema?
2 Does your father work in an office?
3 Does your friend speak English?
4 Do you know that man?
5 Does your mother have a job?
6 Do you want to travel abroad?

C 1 What are you wearing today?
2 Where are you going tonight?
3 What are you doing now?
4 Where are you sitting at the moment?
5 Are you listening to music now?
6 Are you going on holiday with your family this year?
7 Are you wearing a watch?
8 Are you having lunch now?

D 1 Have you ever visited Bath?
2 Have you ever broken your arm or leg?
3 Have you ever cooked for more than 5 people?
4 Have you ever seen a crocodile?
5 Have you ever taken a photograph?
6 Have you ever met a famous person?

E **Suggested Answers**
1 had breakfast
had a shower
read a newspaper
done my homework
eaten lunch
2 finished work
watched TV
spoken English
done the washing-up
talked to a friend

F
1 I've been cutting onions.
2 I've been revising for my exams.
3 I've been waiting for two hours.
4 I've been playing football.

G
1 were 2 were 3 was 4 was 5 was
6 was 7 was 8 was 9 were 10 were

H
1b, 2c, 3b, 4c, 5a, 6a, 7a, 8b,
9a, 10b, 11a, 12c, 13b, 14b

I
1 found out
2 surprised
3 was shopping
4 was walking
5 knew
6 came
7 was
8 was wearing
9 saw
10 needed
11 was
12 was playing

J
1 Did you go
2 did you buy
3 did you pay
4 were you doing
5 Did you understand, spoke/was speaking

K
1 is
2 I'm getting up/ I get up
3 I'm flying
4 we are having
5 are going
6 leaves
7 begins

L
1 I'll go
2 are having
3 will
4 is going to
5 goes
6 are going to meet

M
1 is going to
2 are going to
3 are going to
4 will
5 will

N
1 What, There, Where, there
2 Where, There, Where
3 how, Where, what, Why, What, There

O
1 brothers, sisters
2 Men, women
3 Are they
4 hair
5 are
6 buses
7 carrots, the dark

P
1 a, the
2 a
3 the, the
4 a
5 the, the, the
6 an, a / the
7 the, a, some
8 the, a

Q
1 This, me, mine, my
2 me, this, your
3 you, That, you
4 one
5 you, yours
6 one
7 me, Me
8 Whose, Mine
9 This, one
10 one, me

R
1 last week
2 a lot
3 a lot
4 until
5 since
6 probably
7 probably
8 hardly ever

S
1 in
2 at
3 on
4 in
5 at
6 at
7 in
8 No preposition needed.
9 in
10 No preposition needed.

Unit 31 Practice

A 1 (F) 2 (P) 3 (P) 4 (P) 5 (F) 6 (P)

7 (F) 8 (F)

B
1 The shops may/might be closed now.
2 They may/might be on holiday.
3 The weather may/might be good tomorrow.
4 I may/might get married before I am 30.
5 They may/might go to the disco tonight.
6 It's nice here. I may/might stay an extra week.
7 We may/might go to see the new play at the theatre.
8 They've trained a lot. They may/ might win the match.

C Suggested Answers
1 No, I don't think it will.
2 Yes, I think I will.
3 No, I don't think I will.
4 I'm not sure. It might.
5 I'm not sure. Someone might.
6 Yes, I think I will.
7 I'm not sure. There might be.
8 No, I don't think I will.
9 No, I don't think it will.
10 Yes, I think I will.

Unit 32 Practice

A
1 Can you drive?
2 Can you play the piano?
3 Where could we find someone who can repair clocks?
4 Can any of your friends use a word processor?

B Suggested Answers
1 Jack can play chess. I don't know if he can sing.
Jack can play the guitar. I don't know if he can sing.
Jack can speak Spanish. I don't know if he can paint.
Jack can type. I don't know if he can skate.
Jack can ride a horse. I don't know if he can play tennis.
2 I can cook, but I can't drive.
I can play the guitar, but I can't sing.
I can paint, but I can't speak Spanish.
I can type, but I can't skate.
I can play tennis, but I can't ride a horse.
3 I can play the guitar now, but I couldn't three years ago.
I can paint now, but I couldn't two months ago.

C
1 will be able to
2 were able to
3 could, can't
4 couldn't
5 won't be able to/can't
6 can/could

D
1 I enjoy <u>being able to wear casual clothes</u>.
2 I enjoy <u>being able to watch TV when I want</u>.

3 I enjoy <u>being able to see my friends</u>.
4 I enjoy <u>being able to travel abroad</u>.
5 I enjoy <u>being able to stay up late</u>.

Unit 33 Practice

A
1 Could I have another cup of coffee, please?
2 Could I have a cigarette, please?
3 Could you tell me when the train leaves, please?
4 Could we have a table near the window, please?
5 Could I have a ticket to London, please?
6 Could I go home early today, please?

B
1 Would you like to watch TV now?
2 Would you like soup with your meal?
3 Would you like to go home now or later?
4 Would you like sugar in your tea?
5 Would you like me to type these letters?
6 Would you like us to help you plan the meeting?
7 Would you like a single or a double room?
8 Would you like me to start work early tomorrow?

C
1 Would you mind closing the door?
2 Would you mind turning the music down?
3 Would you mind not smoking?
4 Would you mind not speaking French?
5 Would you mind waiting a minute?
6 Would you mind leaving a message?

Unit 34 Practice

A 1h, 2f, 3d, 4a, 5c, 6g, 7e, 8b

B Suggested answers
I'd like to speak English fluently.
I'd love to speak several languages well.
I'd like to be able to cook.
I'd love to meet your favourite singer.
I'd like to be famous.
I'd like to go to New York next week.
I'd love to be very rich.
I'd love to have a sports car.
I'd hate to find a spider in my bed.
I'd like to be 100 years old.
I wouldn't like to be in hospital.
I'd hate to live in a haunted house.
I'd like to live in another country.
I wouldn't like to work in a noisy factory.
I'd like to be a teacher/politician/stuntman.
I'd like to wake up at 11 a.m. every day.

Unit 35 Practice

Suggested answers
A ✓work hard   ✓speak good English
✓be polite   ✓be punctual
1 You must work hard.
2 You must speak good English.

3 You must be polite.
4 You must be punctual.

B 1 mustn't park.
2 mustn't use cameras/
take photographs.
3 must be quiet.
4 mustn't smoke.
5 mustn't take dogs here.
6 must carry children.
7 must stop here.
8 must keep off the grass.

C **Suggested Answers**
1 had to   5 had to
2 had to   6 didn't have to
3 had to   7 had to
4 didn't have to

D 1 has to   7 has got to
2 has to   8 has got to
3 have to   9 have got to
4 have to   10 have got to
5 have to   11 have got to
6 have to   12 have got to

Unit 36 Practice

A 1 you ought to open the window.
2 you should put the heating on.
3 you should have something to eat.
4 you should go to bed now.
5 you ought to see a doctor.
6 you should see a dentist.
7 you should ask for help.

B 1 In a hospital you should be calm.
You shouldn't make a lot of noise.
2 You shouldn't arrive late at work.
You should work hard.
3 On the motorway you should drive
carefully. You shouldn't drive close
to the car in front.
4 You shouldn't play music in the
library. You ought to work in silence.
5 In a hospital you ought to be calm.
You ought not to make a lot of noise.
6 You ought not to arrive late at work.
You ought to work hard.
7 On the motorway you ought to drive
carefully. You ought not to drive
close to the car in front.
8 You ought not to play music in the
library. You ought to work in silence.

C 1 I think you should study hard.
2 I don't think you should keep it.
3 I think you should watch your
favourite film.
4 I think you should call the police.
5 I think you should tell the teacher.
6 I think you should go to New York.

Unit 37 Practice

A 1 It's a pity
2 It's a good thing/It's lucky
3 It's a good thing/It's lucky
4 it's a pity
5 It's a good thing/It's lucky

6 It's a pity
7 It's a pity

B A: Hello, Who is it?
B: Hello, it's me, Angela.
A: Oh, hi! What's it like in England?
B: Oh, it's great being in London.
A: What about the weather?
B: Well, it's a bit cold, but it's not too bad.
A: It's nice to talk to you.
B: Well, it's ages since I saw you.
A: Did you have a good journey?
B: Not really. I didn't like it very much
on the plane.
A: Why not? Was it very uncomfortable?
B: No, it was comfortable, but it was a
very long journey.
A: What time is it over there?
B: Eight o'clock. Why?
A: Well, it's four in the morning here in
Singapore.
B: Oh, I'm sorry. I didn't know it was so
late.
A: Don't worry. It's really nice to hear
from you.

Unit 38 Practice

A 1 He cooked them a nice meal.
2 She lent her some money.
3 Hand him that plate.
4 Who'll read them a story?
5 I've made him some coffee.
6 Jack's gone to get her some water.
7 He offered her the job.

B 1 I have booked seats for the children.
2 Can you make a cup of tea for
everyone?
3 I've written a letter to my sister.
4 Who's going to cook supper for the
family?
5 We can show our photographs to all
the visitors.
6 Could you cut some bread for your
brothers and sisters?
7 I sold my old skis to your friend.

C 1 for her little brother, Simon.
2 a doll.
3 for her grandfather.
4 to her aunt and uncle.
5 her grandmother.
6 to Richard.
7 for her mother.
8 her father.

Unit 39 Practice

A 1 do 2 do 3 make 4 make 5 make
6 do, do 7 make 8 make 9 make
10 make

B 1 make 2 does 3 make 4 make 5 do

C 1 do, do, make, do
2 make, do, make, do, make

Unit 40

2 homework   machinery
baggage   money
equipment   furniture
luggage

Unit 40 Practice

A 1 advice   5 equipment
2 news   6 information
3 homework   7 money
4 furniture   8 traffic

B 1 Let me give you a piece of advice.
2 There were a few bits of old furniture
in the room.
3 I have a couple of bits of homework
to do.
4 The fire destroyed a piece of
expensive machinery.
5 I wonder if you could help me with a
bit of information.
6 I have a piece of good news for you
and a bit of bad news.
7 A computer is a very expensive piece
of equipment.
8 They had more than a dozen pieces
of luggage.

C 1 trouble   5 music
2 weather   6 happiness
3 work   7 travel
4 fun

Unit 41 Practice

A **Suggested Answers**
1 Some of   5 A few of
2 All of, five years old 6 Some of
3 Some of   7 Some of
4 Most of   8 All of

B 1 Two of
2 Neither of
3 Both of
4 One of
5 None of
6 Most of
7 Two of
8 None of
9 Both of
10 Neither of
11 Most of
12 All of
13 Two of
14 One of

1 Two of the men are wearing ties. (T)
2 One of the men is wearing eye-
glasses (T)
3 Two of the children are playing dices. (T)
4 Two of the women is sitting down. (F)
5 One of the men is sitting down. (F)
6 One of the women is wearing a
pullover. (F)

答案 Answer Key

Unit 42 Practice

A
1 bread
2 cars
3 luggage
4 buildings
5 animals
6 advice
7 countries
8 weather
9 houses
10 rice/bread
11 friends
12 subjects
13 shops
14 furniture
15 ideas
16 traffic
17 help

B
1 I like both of them.
2 There is room for all of them.
3 All of them wanted to come.
4 Both of us stayed at home.
5 They wanted to see both of us.
6 All of them live in a yellow submarine.
7 Both of us come from Liverpool.
8 There is room for both of us.

Unit 43 Practice

A
1 not many/few
2 some/a few
3 not many/few
4 some/a few
5 some/a few
6 some/a few
7 not many/few
8 some/a few

B
1 some
2 any
3 some, some
4 any
5 any
6 any, some
7 some, any
8 any
9 any
10 any
11 any
12 some, any
13 any
14 Some

Unit 44 Practice

A
1 a leather belt (2a)
2 a paper handkerchief (2a)
3 a wooden table (2a)
4 a plastic bag (2a)
5 a kitchen chair (2b)
6 garden furniture (2b)
7 aeroplane seats (2b)
8 a Thursday meeting (2c)
9 a birthday party (2c)
10 a two o'clock appointment (2c)
11 a fifty pound traveller's cheque (2d)
12 a ten pound note (2d)
13 a one hundred kilo bag (2d)
14 a three kilo baby (2d)
15 a cookery book (2f)
16 a fashion magazine (2f)
17 the sports page (2f)
18 a newspaper seller (3)
19 a language teacher (3)
20 a card player (3)
an ice cube, a carpet sweeper, a dog kennel, a dishwasher, a petrol station a story teller, a cigarette lighter, a hairdryer, a tin opener, an egg-timer

Unit 45 Practice

A 1A, 2B, 3A, 4A, 5B, 6B, 7A, 8A, 9B, 10B, 11A, 12A, 13B, 14A

B
1 here, abroad
2 here, there
3 here, away
4 downstairs, upstairs
5 outdoors, indoors

C
1 under, on
2 under, beside
3 next to, behind

Unit 46 Practice

A
1 during the storm
2 by now
3 during the holidays
4 by the end of the week
5 by six
6 during the lesson
7 by 2020
8 during the demonstration
9 during the morning
10 by bed-time

B
1 at around
2 during
3 By
4 at about
5 after
6 before

C
1 after
2 from, until
3 before
4 before
5 from, until
6 before
7 after
8 before

D **Suggested Answers**
I read a paper during the evening.
I have a show during the evening.
I get dressed after breakfast.
I watch TV during the evening.
I go out with friends during the evening.
I go to work/school after breakfast.
I write letters during the evening.
I brush your teeth before breakfast.
I polish my shoes during the evening.
I relax during the evening.

Unit 47 Practice

A 1 -ly: politely, softly, comfortably, helpfully, fluently, nicely, suddenly, sadly, reasonably
2 -ily: happily, angrily
3 -ically: frantically, dramatically
4 -lly: dully

B
1 fluently
2 reasonably
3 softly
4 angrily
5 politely
6 suddenly
7 sadly
8 comfortably

C
1 Do you know anyone who is a quick reader?
Yes, my sister. She reads very quickly.
2 Do you know anyone who is a good dancer?
Yes, my friend Jenny. She dances very well.
3 Do you know anyone who is a slow eater?
No, I don't know anyone who eats slowly.
4 Do you know anyone who is a dangerous driver?
Yes, my brother. He drives dangerously.
5 Do you know anyone who is a good singer?
Yes, my classmate Jenny. She sings very well.
6 Do you know anyone who is a fast talker?
No, I don't know anyone who talks very fast.

D
1 serious
2 slowly
3 good
4 heavily
5 loud
6 beautiful

Unit 48 Practice

A
1 at the top of the page
2 in Paris last year
3 at Exeter and Portsmouth
4 in a box in my room
5 in the corridor
6 at work
7 in the garden
8 in bed

B
1 in
2 at
3 in
4 at
5 in
6 in
7 at
8 at
9 at
10 at
11 at
12 at

C **Suggested Answers**
1 The sitting room and my bedroom are at the front.
2 The kitchen and the bathroom are at the back.

D 1 at, in 2 at 3 in 4 at 5 at 6 at 7 in 8 at

Unit 49 Practice

A
1 Everyone on the plane felt very nervous.
2 I first travelled by plane when I was 14.
3 It's cheaper by coach than by train.
4 The nurse in the ambulance gave me an injection.
5 We watched a video on the coach on the way to the airport.
6 If more people went by bicycle there'd be less pollution.
7 I'll take the shopping on my bicycle if it's not too heavy.
8 We can take 5 people in our car if necessary.
9 When I go by car I take a map.

答案 Answer Key

B 1 off 2 out of 3 off 4 into 5 onto
6 out of 7 into/in

C 1 Tom is going to Mexico by plane tomorrow.
2 Ian went home on foot after the party.
3 We went to Bristol by train.
4 How much does it cost to go to Paris by coach?
5 I went to school by bicycle every day.
6 Last year we went to Scotland by car.
7 Sarah always feels seasick when she goes by ship.
8 They went into the city by taxi.

Review: Cycle 2 – Units 31-49

A 1 Can 2 would 3 Would 4 might
5 will/can/could 6 Can/may 7 will

B 1 It was silly of me
2 It's nice to meet you.
3 It looks like
4 It was kind of you
5 It's a pity
6 It's very expensive
7 It gets very cold

C 1 She invited all her friends round and cooked them a nice meal.
2 I posted the letter to the bank this morning.
3 Can you get a newspaper for your father when you go to do the shopping?
4 Karen showed me her new dress.
5 Her aunt is going to make clothes for the baby when it is born.
6 Will you keep me some food if I'm too late for supper?
7 I usually read the children a story before they go to sleep.
8 James handed the papers to his teacher when he had finished writing.
9 Mr. Wilson teaches us English every Tuesday.
10 I've lent my bicycle to my brother so he can cycle to school.

D 1 do 2 make 3 make 4 do 5 make
6 do 7 do 8 make 9 make 10 do

E 1 luggage 6 games
2 ideas 7 fun
3 advice 8 problems
4 traffic 9 furniture
5 weather 10 music

F 1 lots of 6 plenty of,
2 both of them half of it
3 All 7 Most
4 them both 8 Neither of
5 all my 9 Some of
10 A few of

G 1 a few 2 a few 3 few 4 a few 5 few

H 1 some 6 some
2 some, any 7 some, any

3 any 8 any
4 some, any 9 some, any
5 Any 10 some

I 1 a book about cookery
2 an appointment at two o'clock
3 someone who teaches languages
4 a chair in the kitchen
5 a meeting on Thursday
6 someone who sells newspapers
7 a belt made of leather
8 seats found in an aeroplane
9 a magazine about fashion
10 a note worth ten pounds

J 1 between 6 lamp
2 behind 7 dog
3 in front of 8 on
4 behind 9 book
5 behind 10 chair

K 1 from eleven to twelve thirty
2 from nine o'clock until/to half past ten
3 during the break at about ten forty-five
4 after lunch by two o'clock
5 during
6 about
7 about seven

L 1 A until
B by
2 A until
B by

M 1 carefully 5 fast, slowly
2 badly 6 hard, badly
3 happily 7 well
4 sadly 8 sleepily

N 1 at 2 in 3 in 4 at 5 at 6 in 7 in
8 in 9 at

O 1 on, on, by 2 on/off 3 by, on
4 into 5 on 6 on 7 by, by, in
8 off, on 9 on

General review A: Cycles 1 and 2

A 1 How old are you?
2 Where do you live?
3 How long have you lived there?
4 Do you like it in Bromley?
5 Do you work in Bromley?
6 Do you drive to work?

B 1 waited/was waiting
2 have lived/have been living
3 is raining
4 had never been
5 am doing
6 had been working
7 waved
8 were preparing
9 have been working
10 leaves/is leaving

C 1 at, no preposition needed
2 in, on

3 by, on
4 at, at
5 in/at, in
6 at, at/for, in/during
7 in, on
8 in
9 in, in
10 at/around
11 no preposition needed, on
12 at
13 off, at
14 into
15 in, no preposition needed

D 1 I have been to Portugal twice but I have never been to Spain.
2 I enjoyed his first book a lot, but I didn't like his second very much.
3 He was driving quite slowly and that certainly saved his life.
4 You have to work hard if you want to do well.
5 We sometimes play football but we never play hockey.

E 1 Could 9 are you going
2 potatoes 10 Have you been
3 rice 11 went
4 Would 12 will you be
5 Can 13 on
6 some 14 good weather
7 any 15 It
8 a few

Unit 50 Practice

A 1 ought to be/should be an exciting trip.
2 ought to be/should be very comfortable.
3 ought to be/should be a nice day.
4 ought to be/should be a good game.
5 ought to be/should be nice and quiet.
6 ought to be/should be really funny.

B 1 can't be 8 must be
2 must be 9 can't be
3 must be 10 must be
4 can't be 11 must be
5 must be 12 can't be
6 can't be 13 must be
7 can't be

Unit 51 Practice

A a Could I take this chair, please?
b Can/Could I borrow your pen?
c Could I have a lift home, please?
d Can I play with you?
e Could I ask a question, please?
f Can/Could I go home early tonight?
g Could I have another biscuit, please?
h Can/Could I have a kilo of bananas?

B You don't need to/you don't have to:
1 cook your own meals.
2 make your bed.
3 wash the dishes.
4 tidy your room.

5 clean the windows.
6 clean the furniture.
7 lay the table.
8 clean the bath.

Unit 52 Practice

A 1 Do you feel like seeing that new film?
2 Don't you feel like driving to the mountains this weekend?
3 They felt like getting a video.
4 It was a hot day and everybody felt like going to the beach.
5 I really don't feel like going home now. It's early.
6 Is there anything you particularly fancy doing?
7 Do you fancy seeing that new film?
8 Don't you fancy driving to the mountains this weekend?
9 They fancied getting a video.
10 It was a hot day and everybody fancied going to the beach.
11 I really don't fancy going home now. It's early.
12 Is there anything you particularly fancy doing?

B 1 fishing   5 housework
2 classical music   6 travelling
3 disco dancing   abroad
4 rock music   7 playing ball

C 1 Do come in and relax for a moment.
2 Do let me buy you that picture.
3 Do spend the weekend with us.
4 Do write to me with your news.
5 Do tell me when you're bored.
6 How about coming in and relaxing for a moment.
7 How about letting me buy you that picture.
8 How about spending the weekend with us.
9 How about writing to me with your news.
10 How about telling me when you're bored.

Unit 53 Practice

A 1 He decided to have the red shirt.
2 I learnt to swim when I was 9.
3 We plan to visit Moscow this year.
4 He promised never to be late again.
5 She expects to be home at ten.
6 He decided not to swim after all.

B 1 advised   4 want
2 asked   5 asked
3 told   6 remind

C 1 understand what
2 forgotten what
3 know how
4 remember where
5 remember what
6 decide what
7 decided when
8 know what

9 forget how
10 explained where
11 explained how
12 understand how

Unit 54 Practice

A **Suggested Answers**
1 They didn't let me go to bed after 10 p.m.
2 They didn't let me eat chocolate when I wanted.
3 They let me visit my friends' homes.
4 They let me buy my own clothes.
5 They didn't let me ride my bike on the road.
6 They didn't let me go shopping alone.
7 They didn't let me travel alone.

B 1 They didn't make us play sport.
2 They made us wear a uniform.
3 They made us do a lot of homework.
4 They made us stand up when they came into the classroom.
5 They didn't make us sing songs.
6 They made us read newspapers and magazines.
7 They made us speak English.

C 1 Let's go for a drink.
2 Let's go inside.
3 Let's go and see it.
4 Let's do another exercise
5 Let's have a rest.
6 Let's ask someone for help.

D 1 made me depressed
2 made my brother feel better
3 made my father ill
4 made me happy
5 made the cars stop
6 made us go inside

E 1 understand a new word
2 find your way
3 go to sleep
4 find what you want

Unit 55 Practice

A 1 (F) 2 (U) 3 (F) 4 (U) 5 (F) 6 (F)

B Correct Sequence is: 1, 8, 6, 9, 5, 10, 7, 2, 4, 3
1 I saw him get on to his bicycle.
2 I watched him ride down the street.
3 My friend noticed it turn into the street.
4 We heard it driving very fast.
5 We watched it try to overtake the cyclist.
6 We saw it knock the man off his bike.
7 My friend noticed them standing near the traffic lights.
8 We heard it crash into the traffic lights.
9 Everybody heard them scream.
10 We heard it coming to the scene of the accident.

Unit 56

2 talking   information, warning,
and telling: example, speech, report,
                interview, answer, news
other noises: cry, laugh, whistle,
                shout, scream
actions: kiss, kick, punch, hug,
                caress, push

Unit 56 Practice

A 1 We had a serious discussion.
2 They were having a quiet chat in the reception room.
3 They have dinner very late in Spain.
4 I had a quick wash, then went to school.
5 Paula had a hamburger for lunch.
6 Most people prefer to have a holiday in the summer
7 I need to have a talk with you about Simon.
8 Mark enjoys having a long bath after playing sport.

B 1 take   5 took
2 gives   6 take
3 gave   7 gave
4 give   8 gave

C 1 They decided to go swimming in the river.
2 If you feel hot why don't you go swimming?
3 When was the last time you went walking across the moor?
4 I think I'll go jogging.
5 The lake is a great place to go fishing.

Unit 57

2 go on (means continue)
get by (means manage)
go away (means leave)

3 broke into, look after
bumped into (means: meet),
looking into (means: investigate)

4 caught up with, date back to, get round to

Unit 57 Practice

A 1 stayed up   6 Hurry up
2 put up with   7 find out
3 took up   8 carried out
4 takes after   9 take off
5 start out   10 broke down

B *Verb + particle*
She stayed up
If we start out
Hurry up!
The car broke down

Verb + particle + obj
He took up skiing
Sarah takes after our father

答案 Answer Key

find out what time the train leaves

Three part Verbs
How can you put up with him?

C
1 grew up
2 playing around
3 stayed up
4 got by
5 Hold on
6 Watch out!

D
1 The police followed the robbers, but they <u>got away</u>.
2 I'm trying to <u>find out</u> whose car this is.
3 Most of the students said they wanted to <u>keep on</u> studying.
4 I <u>bumped into</u> an old friend on the ferry. What a surprise!

Unit 58 Practice

A
1 The robbers told the people in the bank to hand over all their money.
2 How old were you when you took up skiing?
3 He pointed out a couple of mistakes.
4 The students handed in their papers at the end of the exam.
5 The shop assistant folded up the clothes and put them in the bag.

B
1 I was very surprised when they invited <u>him</u> out to lunch.
2 The student quickly rubbed <u>them</u> out and wrote <u>it</u> out again.
3 Please help me put <u>them</u> away.
4 I'm going to ring <u>them</u> up and ask <u>her</u> round to dinner.
5 George brought <u>them</u> up and kept his job at the same time.
6 My doctor advised me to give <u>it</u> up.

C
1 take up
2 call back
3 point out
4 fold up
5 clean up
6 knock over
7 tell apart
8 write out

Unit 59 Practice

A
1 Listen to
2 talk about/speak about
3 belongs to
4 complained to/spoke to
5 complain about
6 write to
7 tell about
8 write about
9 dreamt about
10 think about
11 listen to
12 belong to

B
1 laughed at
2 looked at
3 waiting for
4 looked for
5 asked for

C
1 count on/rely on
2 count on/rely on/depend on
3 depends on
4 depends on

Unit 60

2 I, myself; you, yourself; he, himself; she, herself; it, itself; we, ourselves; you, yourselves; they, themselves.

Unit 60 Practice

A
1 me, myself
2 himself, him
3 themselves, them
4 us, ourselves
5 her, herself
6 itself, it
7 you, yourselves
8 yourself, you

B
1 Sure, help yourself.
2 I taught myself, actually.
3 Enjoy yourselves.
4 I was talking to myself.
5 Let me introduce myself.
6 No, I made it myself.
7 He burnt himself.
8 I think they did it themselves.

C
1 by myself
2 by himself
3 by ourselves
4 for himself
5 for ourselves
6 by herself
7 for yourself
8 to yourself/ for yourself

Unit 61 Practice

A Suggested Answers
1 frightening
2 interesting
3 boring
4 exciting
5 annoying
6 shocking
7 relaxing
8 amusing

B
1 annoyed/worried/surprised
2 excited/surprised
3 delighted/excited/surprised
4 bored
5 frightened/worried

C
1 bored, boring
2 interesting, interested
3 terrifying, terrified
4 worrying, worried
5 annoying, annoyed
6 shocked, shocking
7 exciting, excited
8 surprising, surprised
9 disappointing, disappointed
10 amusing, amused

Unit 62 Practice

A
1 something, everybody
2 Everybody, something, nothing
3 Everybody, something, nobody, everything
4 Somebody, something, nobody, anything
5 nothing, nobody, anything
6 everywhere, somewhere

B
1 anyone else
2 somewhere else
3 someone else
4 nobody else
5 something else
6 nothing else
7 something else
8 anywhere else
9 somebody else's
10 Nobody else's
11 somewhere else
12 Nothing else

Unit 63 Practice

A

Group A	Group B
cheap	certain
cold	careful
dark	expensive
full	famous
great	important
green	interested
hard	interesting
high	often
kind	useful
small	

Group A
cheaper, cheapest
colder, coldest
darker, darkest
fuller, fullest
greater, greatest
greener, greenest
harder, hardest
higher, highest
kinder, kindest
smaller, smallest

Group B
more certain, most certain
more careful, most careful
more expensive, most expensive
more famous, most famous
more important, most important
more interested, most interested
more interesting, most interesting
more often, most often
more useful, most useful

B

nicer, nicest	busier, busiest
cleverer, cleverest	later, latest
happier, happiest	better, best
quieter, quietest	worse, worst
bigger, biggest	hotter, hottest

C
1 more expensive
2 more useful
3 younger
4 heavier
5 easier
6 worse, younger
7 worse/colder
8 more important
9 younger
10 worse
11 more expensive

答案 Answer Key

Unit 64 Practice

A
1 Helen, Tom
2 Helen and Bill, Anne
3 Bill
4 Anne, Tom, Helen
5 Anne, Bill
6 Tom, Bill
7 Helen, Tom
8 Helen, Bill, Tom
9 Tom, Helen
10 Bill, Anne

B
1 It's the biggest dog I have ever seen.
2 She's the nicest person I have ever met.
3 It was the funniest story they had ever heard.
4 It was the best book she had ever read.

C Suggested Answers
1 China is a much bigger country than Japan.
2 Jane is a bit taller than Mary.
3 This book is a bit cheaper than that one.
4 Jacky is much older than his brother.

D
1 The commonest word in English is 'the'.
2 The highest mountain in the world is Mount Everest.
3 The longest river in the world is the Amazon.
4 The tallest tower in the world is Canadian National Tower.

Unit 65 Practice

A
1 Why were you in the shop for such a long time?
2 I really like Sue. She's such a nice person.
3 I can never hear him. He speaks in such a quiet voice.
4 We saw you driving your BMW yesterday. It looks such a powerful car.
5 Have you heard the new REM album? It's such a good record.

B
1 that I helped myself to more.
2 that we all came back with tans.
3 that I couldn't stop to talk.
4 that I didn't recognise it.
5 that we couldn't hear the TV.
6 that we talked for hours.
7 that all the hotels were full.
8 that we cried.

C
1 The Smiths are such nice people.
2 correct
3 Thanks for the party. We had such a good time.
4 correct
5 correct
6 Bob's an expert. He knows so much about computers.

Review: Cycle 3 – Units 50-65

A
1 must
2 should
3 can't
4 must
5 ought to
6 can't
7 can't
8 must
9 can't
10 should
11 must

B
1 May/Could I have another drink, please?
2 Could you give me directions to the nearest bank, please?
3 Could you tell me when I can see Mr Smart?
4 May/Could I have some more chocolate cake?
5 Could you tell him what time the film starts?
6 Could/May we leave now?
7 Could Janet have a quick talk with the manager, please?
8 It's very hot. Could they take their jackets and ties off?

C
1 can't
2 are not allowed to
3 don't need to/needn't
4 needn't
5 don't need to/needn't
6 can't

D
1 My father dislikes doing the washing-up.
2 How about going to the beach this weekend?
3 Young children normally enjoy watching adventure films.
4 Nature lovers often enjoy going camping.
5 You must tell us about your holiday.
6 How about letting me do the cooking this evening?
7 I don't mind listening to classical music.
8 I hated sleeping in the dark when I was a child.
9 Do you fancy coming with us to the disco?

E
1 promised to buy his wife
2 agreed not to smoke
3 hope to get there
4 asked her husband to give her a hand
5 decided not to
6 ordered the soldiers not to leave
7 advised the students to use a dictionary to check
8 told the artist not to show anyone
9 asked me whether you know how to ski

F
1 help
2 let
3 let
4 help
5 Let
6 made
7 make
8 made

G
1 singing
2 play
3 get
4 swimming
5 come
6 acting

H
1 take
2 give
3 take
4 gave
5 have
6 had
7 go
8 Take
9 having
10 taking

I
1 Hurry up
2 stay up
3 look after
4 found out
5 looked up
6 go on
7 kept on
8 take up

J
1 about
2 to
3 into
4 on
5 about
6 for
7 for
8 to

K
1 Actually, I made it myself.
2 Enjoy yourselves.
3 No, I think you should change (no need to use reflexive pronouns).
4 ... he cut himself while he was shaving.
5 ... people who talk to themselves are a little strange.
6 The washing machine will turn itself off ...
7 Mrs Banks got up, washed (no need to use reflexive pronouns)and went to work as normal.
8 I have two uncles who live by themselves.

L
1 fascinating
2 interesting
3 impressed
4 bored
5 interested
6 relaxing
7 amusing
8 disappointed

M
1 anybody
2 anybody
3 something
4 anything
5 They
6 nobody
7 nothing
8 anywhere

N
1 The video we watched last night was by far the funniest I have seen for a long time.
2 It's far hotter today than it was yesterday.
3 I feel a good deal more relaxed now.
4 This is by far the best book she's written.
5 This exercise is rather more difficult than I thought.
6 A lot more people went to the exhibition than expected.
7 The things they sell in the shops nowadays are much more expensive than last year.
8 I think it would be a much better idea to go on holiday in the spring when there aren't so many tourists.

O
1 more exciting
2 more competitive
3 most expensive
4 expensive
5 long
6 biggest
7 best/most famous/most expensive
8 luckiest
9 lucky
10 better
11 longer
12 better/more famous

答案 Answer Key

P 1 so 2 such 3 such 4 so 5 such
6 so 7 so 8 such 9 such 10 such

General review B: Cycle 1

A
1 moved
2 came
3 had gone/went
4 had finished
5 wanted
6 was worried
7 was
8 is
9 has found
10 is
11 has made
12 is going

B
1 isn't going
2 didn't hear
3 isn't
4 hasn't felt/hasn't been feeling
5 isn't
6 hasn't finished
7 isn't working
8 hasn't arrived
9 isn't raining
10 wasn't

C
1 the   21 the
2 you   22 a
3 me   23 a
4 the   24 no article
5 we   25 it
6 no article   26 the
7 me   27 the
8 a   28 it
9 no article   29 a
10 a   30 the
11 the   31 a
12 you   32 a
13 some   33 the
14 some   34 a
15 it   35 no article
16 some   36 the
17 some   37 the
18 some   38 it
19 you/I   39 the
20 the   40 a

D
1 that   5 that/she
2 These, those 6 that, it
3 those   7 her
4 one   8 This

E
1 want to come
2 are you going to
3 of film is that
4 does it start
5 does it last
6 it
7 does it cost/will it cost
8 is it

F
1 recently   10 since
2 ago   11 ago
3 in   12 in
4 probably   13 since
5 very much   14 hardly ever

6 until, in   15 very much
7 since   16 until
8 from, until   17 probably
9 hardly ever   18 often

General review C: Cycle 2

A
1 must, can't   8 must/have to
2 couldn't, had to   9 mustn't
3 could   10 mustn't/
4 may/might   shouldn't
5 will be able   11 could, would
6 Would   12 should
7 may/might/
   could

B
1 I like it here.
2 What time is it?
3 It will be stormy tomorrow.
4 It is almost a year since we had a holiday.
5 It was very kind of your sister to lend me some money.
6 Who is it?
7 It is a pity they weren't here with us.
8 It can be frightening to drive in a city.

C
1 post you your exam results
2 buy something for me
3 bring that dictionary to me
4 to read them a story
5 to find a present for my mother
6 postcards to their friends
7 their version of what happened to the policeman
8 you another piece of cake
9 what to get my father for his birthday
10 cups of tea for everyone

D
1 make   4 made
2 do   5 doing
3 making   6 did

E
1 There was so much traffic on the road that we arrived late.
2 Both Bournemouth and Brighton are on the coast.
3 None of my friends can speak Japanese.
4 Most of the luggage was already on the plane.
5 We bought a few souvenirs for family and friends.
6 You can buy stamps in any post office.
7 I've listened to most of the records in the school library.
8 All the students in our class have travelled abroad.
9 Most of the information you gave me was wrong!
10 He wrote me a one hundred pound cheque.

F
1 real   6 opposite
2 on   7 on
3 at   8 at
4 hard   9 next to
5 in   10 in a lonely manner

General review D: Cycle 3

A
1 The   6 to
2 his   7 are going to meet
3 arrived   8 the
4 at   9 dinner
5 their   10 in

B
1 The   10 a
2 who   11 exploded
3 in   12 over
4 when   13 in
5 didn't   14 of
6 the other   15 is
7 luckier   16 longest
8 a   17 a
9 came

C
1 On   11 out of
2 had   12 it up
3 taken   13 all
4 was waiting 14 was
5 felt   15 had taken
6 drove   16 nothing
7 had   17 looked
8 dropped   18 saw
9 in   19 into
10 got   20 were

D
1 must   6 Do
2 will   7 seeing/watching
3 can't   8 to take, to go
4 Can/May   9 Let, help
5 going

E
1 talking   6 for
2 at   7 his
3 told   8 take
4 funny   9 out
5 who   10 looked at

Unit 66 Practice

A **Suggested Answers**
1 I think   9 I dislike
2 I believe   10 I love
3 I think   11 I like
4 I believe   12 I like
5 I think   13 I like
6 I believe   14 I like
7 I believe   15 I hate
8 I think   16 I like

B
1 looks   3 smells
2 sounded   4 smell/taste

C
1 A: Hello what are you doing?
   B: Hi! I'm reading this book.
   A: That looks interesting.
   B: Yes. It is very good.
   A: Do you like reading?
   B: Yes, I love it.
2 A: Can I borrow your pen?
   B: I'm sorry. I am using it.
   A: What about this one? Who does this belong to?
   B: I think it's Carol's. I know she has one like that. You can ask her. She works/is working in the next room.

3 A: <u>Do you remember</u> Fred Johnson?
　B: Yes, <u>I know</u> him well. Why?
　A: <u>I am writing</u> him a letter.
　B: Great! Say 'Hello' to him from me.
4 A: <u>That coffee smells</u> great!
　B: Would you like some coffee or <u>do you prefer tea</u>?
　A: <u>Are you making</u> tea as well?
　B: I can make some tea if <u>you like</u>.
　A: Thank you. <u>I think</u> a cup of tea would be very nice.

Unit 67 Practice

A　1 were　　5 is
　　2 is　　　6 are
　　3 was　　7 are
　　4 were　　8 were

B　1 been　　4 being
　　2 being　　5 been
　　3 be　　　6 been

C　1 have been reduced
　　2 were killed
　　3 was brought up
　　4 are not allowed
　　5 was directed
　　6 are sold
　　7 has been cancelled
　　8 be bought

D　Picture 1
　　1 The washing-up hasn't been done.
　　2 The radio hasn't been turned off.
　　3 The dustbin hasn't been emptied.
　　4 The windows haven't been cleaned.
　　5 The pots and pans haven't been washed.
　　6 The floor hasn't been cleaned.
　　7 The clock hasn't been changed.
　　8 The table hasn't been cleaned.

　　Picture 2
　　1 The washing-up has been done.
　　2 The radio has been turned off.
　　3 The dustbin hasn't been emptied.
　　4 The windows haven't been cleaned.
　　5 The pots and pans have been put away.
　　6 The floor has been cleaned.
　　7 The clock hasn't been changed.
　　8 The table has been cleaned.

Unit 68 Practice

A　1a, 2a, 3b, 4b, 5a, 6b, 7b

B　1 she was meeting a client
　　2 she had to visit her mother in hospital
　　3 he would be in Glasgow
　　4 she had already arranged something important
　　5 he had stayed late the last time
　　6 he didn't think he would be

C　1 asked, told, thought
　　2 asked, told, asked
　　3 told
　　4 said, told

Unit 69 Practice

A　1 Yes, I do./No, I don't
　　2 No, I'm not.
　　3 Yes, I have.
　　4 Yes, it is.
　　5 No, they aren't.
　　6 No, I don't./Yes, I do.
　　7 Yes, you can.
　　8 No, there isn't.

B　1 No, they can't.
　　2 No, it isn't.
　　3 Yes, they do.
　　4 No, it doesn't.
　　5 Yes, it has./No, it hasn't.
　　6 Yes, she was.
　　7 No, they didn't.
　　8 No, it wasn't.
　　9 No, I wasn't./Yes, I was.
　　10 No, they aren't.

C　1 Where? When?
　　2 Which one? Where?
　　3 Which one? Why?
　　4 Why? Where?
　　5 Which one? Where?
　　6 Why? Which one?

D　1 I expect so./ I don't expect so.
　　2 I think so./ I don't think so.
　　3 I hope so./ I hope not.
　　4 I'm afraid so./ I'm afraid not.

Unit 70 Practice

A　1 wasn't it　4 can they
　　2 have you　5 is there
　　3 did they

B　a　1 're
　　　2 're
　　　3 was
　　　4 was, were
　　　5 - (此處沒有 be 動詞、情態動詞和助動詞。)
　　　6 used to be
　　　7 should
　　　8 shouldn't be
　　　9 shouldn't
　　　10 didn't

　　b　1 are you?
　　　2 aren't we?
　　　3 wasn't it?
　　　4 wasn't he?
　　　5 - (此處不用 be 動詞、情態動詞和助動詞組成的附加成分，用 didn't it?)
　　　6 - (此處不用 be 動詞、情態動詞和助動詞組成的附加成分，用 didn't it?)
　　　7 shouldn't they?
　　　8 should you?
　　　9 should you?
　　　10 - (此處不用 be 動詞、情態動詞和助動詞組成的附加成分，用 did they?)

C　1 I think it is less than a million, isn't it?

2 I think they were held in Montreal, weren't they?
3 I think he died in 1947, didn't he?
4 I think they started playing in the 1960s, didn't they?
5 I think there are 11 players in a cricket team, aren't there?
6 I think Istanbul is bigger, isn't it?
7 I think it means a fear of light, doesn't it?

Unit 71 Practice

A　1 So have we.　　5 So was I.
　　2 So will I.　　　6 So do you.
　　3 So are mine.　7 So did we.
　　4 So does mine.　8 So can I.

B　1 Neither do I.
　　2 Neither could we.
　　3 Neither have I.
　　4 Neither can mine.
　　5 Neither was I.
　　6 Neither can I.
　　7 Neither did we.
　　8 Neither will I.

C　1 Greenland is an island. So is Australia.
　　2 The whale is an endangered species. So is the rhino.
　　3 My mother can't ski. Neither can my brother.
　　4 Smoking isn't good for you. Neither is eating a lot of chocolate.
　　5 The Beatles became famous in the 60's. So did the Rolling Stones.
　　6 Paul didn't write to me. Neither did Mandy.
　　7 Mozart was a composer. So was Beethoven.
　　8 Dictionaries aren't allowed in the exam. Neither are computers.

D　1 So do I./I don't.
　　2 Neither do I./ I do.
　　3 So do I./I don't.
　　4 Neither did I./I did.
　　5 Neither was I./I was.
　　6 Neither do I./I do.
　　7 So have I./I haven't.
　　8 So was I./I wasn't.
　　9 So do I./I don't.
　　10 Neither have I./I have.

Unit 72 Practice

A　1 who/that　　5 who
　　2 which/that　6 which/that
　　3 that　　　　7 who/that
　　4 which/that
　　* Sentences 1, 2, 3, and 4 do not need a relative pronoun.

B　1 who cuts hair
　　2 who cuts hair
　　3 who sells fruit and vegetables
　　4 who writes newspaper articles
　　5 which/that opens tins
　　6 who sells meat

答案 Answer Key

7 which/that protects you from the sun.

C 1 I know someone who
2 I don't know anyone
3 I know someone who
4 I don't know anyone who

D 1 Mr Davies is the dentist my family goes to.
2 Euro-net is the marketing company my sister works for.
3 Wine and cheese are the local products this region is famous for.
4 Simon is the friend of mine who has just gone to New Zealand.

Unit 73 Practice

A 1 It's unlikely to rain in August.
2 The football match is due to start at 3 p.m.
3 Will your brother be able to lend us some money?
4 There's so much traffic, we're bound to be late.
5 The price of petrol is likely to go up next year.
6 When will you be ready to go out tonight?
7 Some people are prepared to do anything to get rich.
8 The doctors were unable to save the patient's life.

B 1 It's easy to criticize young people.
2 It isn't easy to learn how to use a computer.
3 It's essential to have a clean driving licence.
4 It's important to be polite to customers.
5 It's very rude to arrive late.
6 It's stupid and dangerous to drive long distances when you're tired.
7 It's difficult to make everyone happy at the same time.

C 1 I was frightened to watch the film on my own.
2 My cousin was afraid to go home on foot.
3 I was sad to hear the bad news.
4 We were surprised to meet an old friend in Japan.
5 The boys were glad to go home early.
6 Eric was disappointed to do badly in the test.

D 1 I was pleased that everyone was on time.
2 My parents were happy that we got home before dark.
3 The restaurant manager is worried that the price of food is going up.
4 We were surprised that Henry couldn't find the right address.
5 The tourists were disappointed that the weather wasn't very good.

Unit 74 Practice

A 1 too many
2 well enough
3 too much
4 not enough
5 enough
6 too many
7 clearly enough
8 too little

B 1 My brother's too young to drive a car.
2 You look too tired to go out tonight.
3 That dress looks too expensive to buy.
4 The book is too long to finish now.
5 It's too cold outside to play football.
6 This question is too difficult to do.

C 1 too busy
2 old enough
3 enough sugar
4 too long
5 big enough
6 too old
7 too much
8 too many, enough drink
9 enough chairs
10 too soon

Unit 75 Practice

A 1 if it rains.
2 if we can get tickets.
3 before you go to bed?
4 if you take a taxi.
5 as soon as your father gets home.
6 if anyone comes to the door.

B 1 When you go to town tomorrow I will look after the children.
2 If Mary is late I will meet her at the station.
3 I will tell you all Bill's news when he writes to me.
4 If you go to the supermarket you can buy some bread.
5 I won't go to bed until Peter gets home at midnight.
6 She can't go out until after she finishes her homework.
7 The weather will probably be very bad next week while we are on our holidays.
8 When you get your exam results next week you can write to Mary.
9 If you don't get home till after midnight your mother will be very worried.
10 I will pay you the money as soon as I get a job.

C A Come round and see us tomorrow.
B Sure, if you like.

A Could you help me with this?
B Yes, of course, if you want me to.

A Would you mind doing this?
B No, I wouldn't.

A Will you give this to Peter?
B Yes, I will if I can.

A Can I borrow your pen?
B Yes, you can.

A Will you phone us when you get there?
B Yes, I will if I can.

Unit 76 Practice

A 1 I wish it wasn't raining.
2 I wish I knew the answer.
3 I wish Jack would help us.
4 I wish I had seen Angela this morning.
5 I wish we didn't live here.
6 I wish Mary would telephone.
7 I wish Paul had written.
8 I wish I had enough time.

B 1e, 2h, 3f, 4a, 5d, 6g, 7b, 8c

C 1 If I wasn't ill I could play basketball.
2 If I had enough money I could buy it.
3 If she was tired she would go to bed.
4 If we had more time we could wait for him.
5 If he was smaller it would fit him.
6 If it was warmer we could go out today.
7 If they had a map they would be able to find the way.
8 If they knew the way they wouldn't need a map.
9 If I hadn't got them all wrong I wouldn't do the exercise again.

Unit 77 Practice

A **Gaps in the song**
to catch the spider
In order to
She swallowed the dog to catch the cat.
She swallowed the cat to catch the bird.
She swallowed the bird to catch the spider.
She swallowed the spider to catch the fly.
She swallowed the cow in order to catch the goat.
She swallowed the goat in order to catch the dog etc.

Questions and answers
Why did she swallow the dog?
She swallowed the dog to catch the cat.
Why did she swallow the cat?
She swallowed the cat to catch the bird.
Why did she swallow the cow?
She swallowed the cow to catch the goat.

Unit 78 Practice

A 1 He was so pleased that he wrote a letter to thank me for my help.
2 They worked so hard that they finished everything in one afternoon.

3 She is so kind that she will help anyone who asks her.
4 It's such a nice day that we should go out for a walk in the fresh air.
5 She had such a bad cold that she could not possibly go to work.
6 He had such a big car that there was plenty of room for everybody.
7 The flat was so small that three of us had to share a room.
8 They have such a lot of friends that they go out almost every evening.

B 1 too busy
2 old enough
3 too cold
4 too late
5 close enough
6 too far
7 fit enough
8 too expensive

1 I'm afraid I'll be too busy to come tomorrow.
2 She's certainly old enough to go to school by herself.
3 It's much too cold to go out without an overcoat.
4 It will be too late to telephone you when we get back.
5 It's close enough to walk there in about ten minutes.
6 It's too far to drive there in a day.
7 She's still fit enough to cycle to the shops every day.
8 It's too expensive to stay in a hotel.

Unit 79 Practice

A 1 we were really hungry
2 We are very good friends
3 he still didn't earn very much
4 We don't see her very often
5 we drove very fast
6 He was looking very well
7 I was very angry
8 it's much more expensive
9 the sun was shining
10 he looked very fierce
11 I haven't finished it yet
12 They didn't hear us

B 1 in spite of getting lost on the way.
2 in spite of being over seventy.
3 In spite of being injured
4 in spite of being much younger.
5 in spite of having three children to look after.

Unit 80 Practice

A 1 where
2 when
3 which
4 where
5 who
6 when
7 which
8 who

B 1e, 2h, 3j, 4l, 5i, 6g, 7k, 8m, 9a, 10c, 11b, 12f, 13n, 14d

C 1 when the First World War started.
2 where he was born.
3 who was studying mathematics.

4 when they left university.
5 which is in the south of England.

Review: Cycle 4 – Units 66-80

A 1 are you cooking
2 smells
3 am making
4 Do you like
5 love
6 tastes
7 Is
8 think
9 belongs
10 know
11 has

B 1 (a) is having
2 (b) think
(c) can hear
3 (d) were seeing
4 (e) doesn't like
(f) doesn't understand
5 (g) owned
6 (h) am trying
(I) am thinking
7 (j) looks
(k) belonged
8 (l) is learning
(m) sounds

C 1 are kept in this cupboard.
2 was found lying in the street.
3 can be obtained at your local library.
4 was told to park my car outside in the street.
5 was sold for over £ 200,000.
6 has not been heard of since he went to live in America.
7 are sold at most corner shops.
8 are not allowed to borrow more than three books.
9 was given a computer for her birthday.
10 must be worn in the factory.

D 1 was attacked
2 had just left
3 was stopped
4 tried
5 fought back
6 took
7 was badly cut
8 was taken
9 won
10 beat
11 were beaten
12 was won
13 was born
14 was elected
15 was shot
16 was shot

E 1 was getting
2 shouted
3 asked
4 was going
5 told
6 was going
7 asked
8 could
9 was
10 was
11 had broken down
12 would not start
13 was not going
14 could

F 1 wanted
2 had
3 had used
4 had been
5 didn't have
6 had been studying
7 had
8 was going

G 1 was looking
2 saw
3 were carrying
4 called out
5 asked
6 were doing
7 explained
8 were being taken
9 thought
10 would like
11 could
12 would return
13 had been stolen
14 had given

H 1 Yes she did.
2 Yes, they were.
3 Yes, they were.
4 No, she didn't.
5 Yes, she did.
6 Yes, they could.
7 No, they wouldn't.
8 Yes, she was.

I 1 don't you
2 am I
3 didn't he
4 are you
5 won't you
6 have we
7 isn't there
8 haven't you
9 didn't you
10 can you
11 doesn't he
12 is it
13 did you
14 aren't I
15 shouldn't you
16 don't we
17 will you
18 won't we

J 1 too
2 neither
3 so
4 either
5 too
6 either
7 so

K 1 he was carrying looked really heavy.
2 who/that drive too fast are really dangerous.
3 we went to in London wasn't very good.
4 I saw in your shop yesterday.
5 that/who live very near to you.

L 1 enough
2 too much
3 too many
4 enough
5 enough
6 too much
7 too many, enough
8 too much

M 1 too late
2 are we
3 haven't we
4 went
5 you haven't visited
6 do you
7 too expensive
8 warm enough
9 Is it
10 Haven't you

N 1 is
2 can have
3 rains
4 will eat
5 will get
6 catch
7 want to
8 can stay
9 come
10 will look after
11 go
12 will come round
13 has
14 will fall
15 get home

O 1 would you do, were
2 knew, would go
3 can, haven't
4 were, I'd
5 are, will
6 had telephoned
7 was, was, would know
8 see, will you give

P 1 She used a corkscrew to open the bottle.
2 I used the dictionary to find what the word meant.
3 He used a piece of string to mend the chair.
4 She used a wet cloth to polish her shoes.
5 I used a trap and a big piece of cheese to catch the mouse.

答案 Answer Key

6 Our teacher always used a red pen to mark our books.
7 She used a microscope to look at the leaf.
8 He used a bucket to bathe the baby.

Q 1 I was so tired that I couldn't work any more.
2 It was such a wet day that we couldn't go out.
3 My bicycle was so old that it was always breaking down.
4 Don is such a good friend that he will always help me if I ask him.
5 My father lives such a long way from his office that he has to drive to work every day.
6 The journey took so long that it was dark when we arrived.
7 He was so angry that he wouldn't speak to me.
8 I was so frightened that I didn't know what to do.

R 1 even though   5 even though
2 because   6 even though
3 even though   7 because
4 because

S 1 We are going on holiday to Brighton, where my mother was born.
2 I'll telephone you at six o'clock, when I get home.
3 She comes from Sofia, which is the capital of Bulgaria.
4 This is my old friend Tom, who is staying with us this week.
5 I'm reading a book about Ronald Reagan, who used to be President of the USA.
6 This is the garage, where we keep all the garden furniture.
7 Pele is a famous footballer, who played for Brazil at the age of seventeen.
8 We visited Buckingham Palace, where the royal family lives.

T 1 who   10 if
2 because   11 so/and
3 enough   12 to
4 If   13 because
5 so/and   14 so
6 because   15 enough
7 because   16 If
8 Although   17 if/when
9 to

General review E

A 1 have lived, was
2 am trying
3 has just gone, went
4 got, had been travelling
5 had not finished
6 is
7 don't hurry
8 was waiting
9 was, could drive
10 could
11 went

12 have not played, broke
13 learnt, was working
14 will telephone, get
15 had just gone, rang
16 don't like
17 saw, don't remember
18 lived

B 1 What time is it?
2 How old will you be next birthday? or How old are you?
3 Is there any milk in the fridge?
4 Have you ever met Marie?
5 Who does Jack look like?
6 What are you doing tomorrow?
7 What kind of car have you got?
8 Where do you live? or What is your address?
9 Where to?
10 When?

C 1 on, on   7 at
2 at, on   8 no preposition
3 at   required.
4 in, in   9 on
5 by, in   10 no preposition
6 off   required.

D 1 We often go to the cinema at the weekend.
2 George can certainly tell you what you want to know.
3 I don't play football very much now, but I play tennis a lot.
4 I saw Fred a while ago but he isn't here now.
5 It rained quite a lot last night.
6 The door was definitely locked when I went out.
7 We hardly ever watch television at the weekend.
8 It is one of the best films I have ever seen.
9 I didn't enjoy the film very much, but I enjoyed the play a lot.
10 I met Helen a week ago, but I haven't seen her since then.
11 I read the instructions on the medicine bottle carefully./I carefully read the instructions on the medicine bottle.
12 We always see Richard when we are in Oxford.

E 1 take/have   6 do
2 do   7 make
3 make   8 have
4 take   9 Give
5 have   10 do

F 1c, 2c, 3c, 4a, 5c, 6b, 7a, 8c, 9a, 10a, 11a, 12c, 13a, 14b, 15b, 16b, 17b, 18c, 19b, 20b, 21a, 22a, 23a, 24b, 25b, 26b

Pronunciation

A 1 have   11 get
2 far   12 good
3 learn   13 blood
4 fool   14 do
5 eat   15 word
6 lost   16 about
7 forget   17 give
8 but   18 piece
9 saw   19 start
10 sit   20 agreed

B 1 weather   13 leg
2 young   14 hurry
3 lovely   15 brother
4 hat   16 summer
5 judge   17 running
6 pleasure   18 runs
7 dog   19 singer
8 money   20 see
9 winter   21 coffee
10 kicking   22 happy
11 thick   23 reaching
12 watch   24 woman

C 1 seven 2 one 3 six 4 ten 5 four
6 two 7 three
The right order is:
one, two, three, four, six, seven, ten
The three missing are:
five, eight and nine

D 1 there   7 sound
2 paint   8 coin
3 alive   9 higher
4 nearly   10 sure
5 flower   11 again
6 going

E A, B
London - England;
Paris - France;
Madrid - Spain;
Lisbon - Portugal;
Tokyo - Japan;
Moscow - Russia;
Washington - The United States;
Athens - Greece;
Rome - Italy;
Amman - Jordan;
Damascus - Syria;
Canberra - Australia;
Cairo - Egypt;
Jakarta - Indonesia.

C, D
red - tomato;
green - grass;
brown - coffee;
white - milk;
blue - the sky;
black - ink;
yellow - the sun.

E, F
bread - butter;
salt - pepper;
shoes - socks;
pen - ink;
fish - chips.

答案 Answer Key

F
1. banana
2. sister
3. lessons
4. elephant
5. London
6. pleasure
7. apple
8. father
9. tiger
10. Australia
11. summer
12. measure
13. brother
14. mother
15. Lisbon
16. Japan
17. weather
18. mister

G
1. I'm a teacher.
2. I'm a boy.
3. I am married.
4. I have a sister.
5. I live in a house.
6. I'm a student.
7. I'm a girl.
8. I am not married.
9. I have a brother and sister.
10. I like English lessons.
11. I live in London.
12. My name is Peter.
13. I have a brother.
14. I live in a flat.
15. I don't like English lessons.

H

cow	desk	train
horse	chair	bus
sheep	table	car
shirt	apple	tiger
jacket	banana	elephant
blouse	orange	lion

I
/ðə/ name coin man day car
/ði/ orange address eye ink elephant

J
/ə/ bike boy glass house
/ən/ apple office actor engine egg

K
1. enough
2. explanation
3. general
4. everything
5. enjoyment
6. university
7. intention
8. children
9. careful
10. December
11. Wednesday
12. government

L
1. borrow
2. importance
3. magazine
4. position
5. everybody
6. necessary
7. forgotten
8. accent
9. American
10. probably
11. September
12. syllable

N 1 -h; 2 -f; 3 -e; 4 -b; 5 -g; 6 -a; 7 -c; 8 -d.

O
1. Where do you live?
2. What are you going to do tomorrow?
3. Tell them to come at four o'clock.
4. I want to go home.
5. I didn't know what to do.
6. What do you want to do?
7. I don't know what you mean.
8. Who's that over there?
9. I have to go home now.
10. You can do what you want.
11. I've got a lot of money.
12. I'm going to get a cup of tea.
13. Who do you want to see?
14. I'll tell you what I want.
15. How do you know?

Numbers practice

A
1. second
2. fourth
3. sixth
4. first
5. fifth
6. third

B
1. oh
2. nil
3. oh
4. love
5. nil
6. nought
7. nought nought nought
8. zero

C
1. three-day
2. eighty-mile-per-hour
3. five-pound
4. three-hour
5. twenty-two-pound
6. three-course

D
1. four times
2. twice
3. five times
4. once

Letters

A

1 A	8 H	15 O	22 V
2 B	9 I	16 P	23 W
3 C	10 J	17 Q	24 X
4 D	11 K	18 R	25 Y
5 E	12 L	19 S	26 Z
6 F	13 M	20 T	
7 G	14 N	21 U	

C

1 Z	14 S
2 H	15 F
3 G	16 M
4 E	17 U
5 W	18 C
6 Y	19 T
7 B	20 J
8 A	21 N
9 K	22 D
10 X	23 P
11 L	24 R
12 Q	25 V
13 I	26 O

D
1. /ju: keɪ/
2. /dʒɪ: bɪ:/
3. /eɪ em/
4. /pi: em/
5. /pi: ti: oʊ/
6. /si: di:/
7. /di: dʒeɪ/
8. /bi: bi: si:/
9. /ti: vi:/
10. /neɪtoʊ/
11. /i: si:/
12. /ju: es eɪ/
13. /vi: aɪ pi:/
14. /ju: ef oʊ (ju:fəʊ)/
15. /dʌbəlju: dʌbəlju: ef/

附件 Appendices

目錄 **Contents**

規則動詞的時態 Regular Verb Tenses　　　　　　　　　244

名詞和可數性 Nouns and Countability　　　　　　　　246

形容詞的位置與順序 Position and Order of Adjectives　　248

介詞：in、on、at　Preposition: in, on, at　　　　　　　250

英式英語和美式英語 British and American English　　　　251

前綴和後綴 Prefixes and Suffixes　　　　　　　　　　253

英漢語法術語對照表 Glossary of Grammar Terms　　　　257

索引 Index　　　　　　　　　　　　　　　　　　　267

規則動詞的時態 Regular Verb Tenses

時態名稱	主動語態	被動語態	用法
現在進行時 （第 2 單元）	*he/she/it* **is helping** *her* *I* **am helping** *her* *you/we/they* **are helping** *her*	*he/she/it* **is being helped** *I* **am being helped** *you/we/they* **are being helped**	• 談及現在發生的事情 • 談及將來的計劃
簡單現在時 （第 3 單元）	*he/she/it* **helps** *her* *I/you/we/they* **help** *her*	*he/she/it* **is helped** *I/you/we/they* **are helped**	• 談及總是真實的事情 • 談及有規律的活動
現在完成時 （第 5,6 單元）	*he/she/it* **has helped** *her* / *you/we/they* **have helped** *her*	*he/she/it* **has been helped** *I/you/we/they* **have been helped**	• 談及某事發生在過去，但現在仍有影響
現在完成 進行時 （第 6 單元）	*he/she/it* **has been helping** *her* *I/you/we/they* **have been helping** *her*	*he/she/it* **has been being helped*** *I/you/we/they* **have been being helped***	• 談及某事於過去開始，但現在仍在起作用或剛剛結束
簡單過去時 （第 8 單元）	*I/you/he/she/it/we/they* **helped** *her*	*he/she/it* **was helped** *I/you/we/they* **were helped**	• 談及過去發生的事情 • 談及過去有規律的活動

* 不常使用

規則動詞的時態 Regular Verb Tenses

時態名稱	主動語態	被動語態	用法
過去進行時 （第 9 單元）	*I/he/she/it **was helping** her* *you/we/they **were** **helping** her*	*I/he/she/it **was** **being helped*** *you/we/they **were** **being helped***	• 談及過去沒有結束或中斷的活動
過去完成時 （第 10 單元）	*I/you/he/she/it/we/they* **had helped** *her*	*I/you/he/she/it/ we/they* **had been helped**	• 談及在過去一特定時間之前發生的事情
過去完成 進行時 （第 10 單元）	*I/you/he/she/it/we/they* **had been helping** *her*	*I/you/he/she/it/ we/they* **had been being helped***	• 談及在過去一特定時間之前的一段時間內發生的事情
將來時 （第 12 單元）	*I/you/he/she/it/we/they* **will help** *her*	*I/you/he/she/it/ we/they* **will be helped**	• 談及將來的事情

* 不常使用

名詞和可數性 Nouns and Countability

名詞的類型	例	限定詞	用單數形式或複數形式？	一些用法
單數具數名詞	*holiday, tooth, bus, potato, baby, child*	• 總是和限定詞如 a/an, the, this, every, another, 物主詞如 my, his 等或 one 連用	• 只用動詞單數形式： *A bus is coming.*	
複數具數名詞	*holidays, teeth, buses, potatoes, babies, children*	• 從不與 a/an 連用 • 有時與 the, these 和物主詞如 my, his 等或數詞連用 • 可以不用限定詞	• 只使用動詞複數形式： *The babies were crying.*	• 泛指人或物時不用限定詞： *I don't like spiders.*
單數名詞	*air, future, sun, chance, rest*	• 總是與限定詞 a/an, the 或物主詞 my, his 等連用	• 只使用動詞單數形式： *The sun was shining.*	• 常與 the 連用，指稱獨特的事物： *the air, the future* • 由動詞轉換而來的單數名詞，常用來表述一般活動： *a snooze, a rest*
複數名詞	*clothes, feelings, police, scissors*	• 通常與 the 或物主詞 my, his 等連用	• 只使用動詞複數形式： *The police are coming.*	• 常用來談及由兩個相似部分構成的工具或衣物： *trousers, glasses, scales*

名詞和可數性 Nouns and Countability

名詞的類型	例	限定詞	用單數形式或複數形式?	一些用法
集體名詞	team, audience, staff	• 通常與 the 或物主詞 my, his 等連用	• 使用動詞單數形式或複數形式: *Which team is winning?* *Our team are wearing red.*	• 用來指稱作為一個單位的群體: *My family **is** in Brazil.* • 或用來指稱一個單位中的許多個體: *His family **are** all strange.*
不具數名詞	food, electricity, music	• 從不與 a/an, these/those 或數詞連用 • 經常不用限定詞 • 可與 the, this/that 或物主詞 my, his 等連用	• 只使用動詞單數形式: *Electricity is dangerous.*	• 與 some, much 和 any 連用表示數量: *There's not much food in the house.* *I need to buy some bread.* • 常用來談及感情等抽象概念: *It was a year of sadness and happiness.*

形容詞的位置與順序 Position and Order of Adjectives

形容詞的位置

A 大多數形容詞可以置於名詞之前，作為名詞詞組的一部分。如果句子裏有限定詞或數詞時，形容詞要置於它們之後，但要置於名詞之前。

He had a **beautiful** smile.
She bought a loaf of **white** bread.
In the corner of the room there were two **wooden** chairs.

B 大多數形容詞可以用在 be、become、feel 等繫動詞之後。

I'm **cold**.
She felt **angry**.
Nobody seemed **happy**.

C 有些形容詞只能用在動詞 be 或其他繫動詞，如 become、seem、feel 之後。

例如：可以説 She was glad，但不能説 a glad woman。

此類形容詞舉數例如下：

| afraid | alive | alone | asleep | glad | ill |
| ready | sorry | sure | unable | well | |

I wanted to be **alone**.
We were getting **ready** for bed.
I'm not quite **sure**.
He didn't know whether to feel **glad** or **sorry**.

D 有些形容詞通常只能置於名詞前面。

比如，可以説 the main problem 但不能説 The problem was main。

此類形容詞舉數例如下：

| absolute | atomic | indoor | main |
| other | total | utter | |

Some of it was **absolute** rubbish.
The hotel has an **indoor** swimming pool.

E 有些描述大小或年齡的形容詞，可以跟在表示計量單位的名詞後面。

此類形容詞舉數例如下：

| deep | high | long | old |
| tall | thick | wide | |

He was about six feet **tall**.
The water was several metres **deep**.
The baby is nine months **old**.

F 少數有特殊含義的形容詞要緊跟在名詞後面。

此類形容詞舉數例如下：

| designate | elect | galore | incarnate |

She was now the president **elect**.
There are empty houses **galore**.

G 少數形容詞因放在名詞之前或之後而有不同含義。

比如，the concerned mother 意指一位憂心的母親；而 the mother concerned 指的是曾經提及的那位母親。

此類形容詞舉數例如下：

| concerned | involved | present | proper |
| responsible | | | |

I'm worried about the **present** situation. (= the situation that exists now)
Of the 18 people **present** (= the 18 people who were there), I knew only one.

形容詞的位置與順序 Position and Order of Adjectives

形容詞的順序

A 形容詞可用來描述不同的人或物。比如人們可能想談及他們的大小、形狀或是來自哪個國家。

描述性形容詞分為七大類，兩三種不同類別的形容詞往往同時使用。如果要使用一種以上的形容詞時，一般要按下面的順序排列：

1st	2st	3rd	4th	5th	6th	7th
意見	尺寸	年齡	形狀	顏色	國籍	材料
(opinion	size	age	shape	colour	nationality	material)
美麗的	大的	老的	圓的	黑的	中國的	木頭的
(beautiful	large	old	round	black	Chinese	wooden)

這就是說，如果想同時使用一個"年齡"形容詞和一個"國籍"形容詞時，就要把"年齡"形容詞放在前面。

*We met some **young Chinese** girls.*

同樣，"形狀"形容詞一般要放在"顏色"形容詞的前面。

*He had **round black** eyes.*

"尺寸"形容詞要放在"形狀"形容詞或"顏色"形容詞的前面，"形狀"形容詞或"顏色"形容詞要放在"材料"形容詞的前面。

*There was a **large round wooden** table in the room.*
*The man was carrying a **small black plastic** bag*

但是，如果同時使用兩個"顏色"形容詞時，它們之間就要用 and 連接。

*He was wearing a **long red** and **blue** t-shirt.*

同時使用三個"顏色"形容詞時，第一個形容詞後面加逗號（"，"），第二個形容詞和第三個形容詞之間要用 and 連接。

*France has a **red**, **white** and **blue** flag.*

B 可以使用一個以上的形容詞來修飾名詞，當使用兩個或更多形容詞修飾名詞時，一般把表達意見的形容詞放在只進行描述的形容詞的前面。

*You live in a **nice big** house.*
*He is a **naughty little** boy.*
*She was wearing a **beautiful pink** suit.*

C 當使用一個以上的形容詞提意見時，一般含義的形容詞，如 good、bad、nice、lovely，通常要放在有特定含義的形容詞，如 comfortable、clean、dirty 的前面。

*I sat in a **lovely comfortable** armchair.*
*He put on a **nice clean** shirt.*
*It was a **horrible dirty** room.*

D 比較級形容詞，如 cheaper、better 或最高級形容詞，如 hardest、best 通常要放在其他形容詞的前面。

*That plant has **larger** purple flowers.*
*Some of the **best** English actors have gone to live in Hollywood.*

E 在繫動詞如 be、seem、feel 後面使用兩個形容詞時，要用連詞如 and 連接這兩個形容詞。使用三個或更多形容詞時，要在最後兩個形容詞之間用連詞，在其餘的形容詞之間用逗號（"，"）。

*The day was **hot** and **dusty**.*
*The room was **large** but **square**.*
*We felt **hot**, **tired** and **thirsty**.*

介詞：in、on、at　Prepositions: in, on, at

英語中用來表述時間和地點的介詞使用頻率最高的就是 in、on、at 了。有時在個別的短語或句子裏，很難決定用哪一個介詞。下表所列的是本書中講述的這幾個介詞的最常見用法，並列舉了一些例子來幫助學習。

	in	**on**	**at**
時間	月份 / 年份： *in February* *in 1996* *in the last century* 一天的時間段： *in the morning* 季節： *in winter* *in (the) summer* 表述某事會在將來發生： *I'll talk to you in ten minutes.*	一星期中的某一天： on Monday 一星期中某一天 的時間段： *on Tuesday evening* 日期： *on the ninth of May* *on Friday 29th* 特殊日期： *on my birthday* *on Christmas Eve*	鐘錶時間： *at 10 o'clock* *at midnight* 三餐： *at breakfast* 節日： *at Christmas* *at Easter*
地點	地理區域： *in Spain* *in the mountains* 城市 / 大範圍的地方 *in York* *in the park* 公路 / 街道： *There are lots of shoe shops in that street.* 房屋 / 建築物： *I heard a noise in the kitchen.* *There's a wedding in the church.* 容器： *in a box* *in the fridge* 液體： *I'd like sugar in my coffee.*	表面： *on the wall/roof* *on the table/shelf* *on the first floor* *on a piece of paper* 公路 / 街道： *The bank is on Kings Road.*	特指地點： *at the bus stop* *at home/work* *at Amy's house* *at the back of the book* 地址： *She lives at 5, Regent Street.* 公共場所： *at the station/theatre* *at the doctor's* 商店： *at the supermarket* 事件： *at Steve's party* *at last year's conference*

英式英語和美式英語 British and American English

英式英語和美式英語在語法上有少許不同，其主要區別在於：

A 現在完成時態用法上的不同

和英式英語相比，美式英語較少使用現在完成時態 have/has(過去分詞，第五、六單元)。操美語的人常用簡單過去時（第八單元）替代現在完成時。

在下列情況下尤其是這樣：

(a) 在有 yet、just、already 的句子裏（第五單元）：

英式英語 / 美式英語	美式英語
A: Is your mother here?	A: Is your mother here?
B: No, she **has** just **left**.	B: No, she just **left**.
A: Is he going to the show tonight?	A: Is he going to the show tonight?
B: No. He**'s** already **seen** it.	B: No. He already **saw** it.
A: Can I borrow your book?	A: Can I borrow your book?
B: No, I **haven't finished** it yet.	B: No, I **didn't finish** it yet.

(b) 在表述過去發生的動作在當前仍有影響的句子裏（第五單元）：

英式英語 / 美式英語	美式英語
Arthur doesn't feel well.	Arthur doesn't feel well.
He's **eaten** too much.	He **ate** too much.
I can't find my glasses.	I can't find my glasses.
Have you **seen** them?	**Did** you **see** them?

B 在集體名詞用法上的不同

在英式英語中，用來指稱一些特定人群或物品的名詞，稱為集體名詞，它們既能使用動詞單數形式，又能使用動詞複數形式。因為可以把這個群體視作一個整體，也可以視作許多個個體（第十七單元）：

*My team **is** losing.*
*His team **are** all wearing red.*

而在美式英語中，集體名詞一般使用動詞單數形式：

*Which team **is** winning?*

C 在 needn't 用法上的不同

在英式英語中，表述某事沒有必要時，needn't 的用法與 don't need to 相同（第五十一單元）：

*You **don't need** to come to work today.*
*You **needn't** come to work today.*

在美式英語中，很少使用 needn't。經常使用的形式是 don't need to：

*You **don't need to** come to work today.*

D 在 have 和 take 用法上的不同

在英式英語中，have 與某些名詞連用表述常見的活動（第五十六單元）：

吃與喝（eating and drinking）：
Let's have a drink.

休閒（relaxation）：
I think we all need to have a rest.

盥洗（washing）：
She wants to have a shower first.

在美式英語中，不用 have 表示盥洗，美國人用 take 取而代之：

She wants to take a shower first.
Do you mind if I take a bath?

美國人通常也用 take 談及休閒：

Let's take a vacation.
I think we all need to take a rest.

E 在 do 作為助動詞時用法上的不同

英國人在回答問題時，有時把 do 作為助動詞使用，以替代疑問句裏的動詞：

*'Do you think you will vote in the future?' 'I might **do**.'*

美國人不這樣用 do：

'Do you think you might vote for Judith Ryan?' 'I might.'

英式英語和美式英語 British and American English

F 在 at、on、in 用法上的不同

在英式英語中，at 與許多時間表達式連用(第三十單元)：

at ten o'clock   **at** Easter
at the weekend

在美式英語中，談到 weekend 時，不用 at，而總是用 on：

Will he still be there **on** the weekend?
He'll be coming home **on** weekends.

美國人在談及大學或機構時，使用 in：
We both took calculus **in** university.

而在英式英語中則用 at：
Thomas Dane studied history of art **at** university.

G 在冠詞用法上的不同

指醫院時，美國人總是使用定冠詞 the：

I'm going to **the** hospital.

英國人則不這樣用 the：
I'm going to hospital.

H 在代詞 one 用法上的不同

英國人有時用 one 特指某人或泛指任何人：

'What can **one** say?' she whispered.

How can **one** know about things like that in advance?

美國人則用 a person、I、we 替代 one：

What can **I** say?
How can **a person** ask about a problem they don't know anything about?

I 在動詞過去式和過去分詞形式上的不同

在英式英語和美式英語中，有些動詞的簡單過去式和過去分詞的形式是不同的：

原型	過去式（英）	過去式（美）	過去分詞（英）	過去分詞（美）
burn[1]	burned/burnt	burned/burnt	burned/burnt	burned/burnt
bust	bust	busted	bust	busted
dive	dived	dove/dived	dived	dived
dream[1]	dreamed/dreamt	dreamed/dreamt	dreamed/dreamt	dreamed/dreamt
get	got	got	got	got/gotten
lean	leaned/leant	leaned	leaned/leant	leaned
learn	learned/learnt	learned	learned/learnt	learned
plead	pleaded	pleaded/pled	pleaded	pleaded/pled
prove	proved	proved	proved	proved/proven
saw	sawed	sawed	sawn	sawn/sawed
smell	smelled/smelt	smelled	smelled/smelt	smelled
spell	spelled/spelt	spelled	spelled/spelt	spelled
spill	spilled/spilt	spilled	spilled/spilt	spilled
spit	spat	spat/spit	spat	spat/spit
spoil[1]	spoiled/spoilt	spoiled/spoilt	spoiled/spoilt	spoiled/spoilt
stink	stank	stank/stunk	stunk	stunk
wake	woke	waked/woke	woken	woken

[1] 像 burn、dream、spoil 的不規則過去式（burnt、dreamt、spoilt）在美式英語中也被使用，但是和以 -ed 結尾的過去式相比，這種情況並不多見。

前綴和後綴 Prefixes and Suffixes

前綴是字的字首，有固定及可預計的含義。
後綴是字的字尾，通常加在字的後面，組成一個
詞類不同但意義相近的新字。

前綴

a- (構成形容詞) 表示 "無、沒有、相反"，例如：
atypical behaviour 反常行為。

aero- (構詞成分，尤其構成名詞) 表示 "空氣的、航空的"，例如：an *aeroplane* 飛機。

anti- (構成名詞、形容詞) 表示 "反對、對立"：an *anti-government* demonstration 反政府示威。

astro- (構詞成分) 表示 "宇宙的、外太空的"，例如：an *astronaut* 航天員。

auto- (構詞成分) 表示 "自己的、有關自己的"，例如：*autobiography* 自傳。

be- (用於帶 -ed 後綴的名詞後，構成形容詞) 表示 "穿戴的、佩戴的"，例如：*bespectacled* 戴眼鏡的。

bi- (構成名詞、形容詞) 表示 "雙的、兩個的"，例如：*bilingual* 雙語的，講兩種語言的。

bi- (構成形容詞、副詞) 表示 "兩次的、逢二的"，例如：*bimonthly* 每月發生兩次的或每兩個月發生一次的。

bio- (用於名詞、形容詞前) 表示 "有關人生的、生命的"，例如：*biography* 傳記。

co- (構成動詞、名詞) 表示 "共同、合作"：*co-write* 合著；*co-author* 合著者。

counter- (構成成分) 表示 "反對、反抗"，例如：*counter-measure* 反措施，對策。

de- (與某些動詞結合) 表示 "否定、相反"，例如：to *deactivate* a mechanism 關機，停機。

demi- (用於某些詞前) 表示 "一半、部分"，例如：a *demigod* 半神半人。

dis- (構詞成分) 表示 "相反"，例如：*dishonest* 不誠實的。

e- (構詞成分，是 electronic 的縮略語) 表示 "電子的"，例如：*e-business* 電子商務。

eco- (構成名詞、形容詞) 表示 "環境的、生態的"，例如：*eco-friendly* 環保的。

em- 是 en- 的其中一個形式。en- 用於 b-、m-、p- 之前的形式。見 **en-**。

en- (與某些詞構成動詞) 表示 "置於某種情況之中，處於某種狀態" 或構成形容詞和名詞，以描述這種狀態，例如：*endanger* 使遭受損害。

euro- (構詞成分) 表示 "歐洲的、歐盟的"，例如：*Eurocentric* 以歐洲為中心的。

ex- (構詞成分) 表示 "以前的、前任的"，例如：an *ex-policeman* 退役警官。

extra- (構成形容詞) 表示 "附加的、在某物之外的"，例如：Britain's *extra-European* commitments 英國對歐洲以外國家的承諾。

extra- (構成形容詞) 表示 "特別、格外"，例如：*extra-strong* 格外強壯的。

geo- (用於詞前) 表示 "地球的"，例如：*geology* 地質學。

great- (構成名詞) 表示 "隔一輩的"，例如：*great-aunt* 姨奶奶，姑奶奶。

hyper- (構成形容詞) 表示 "過度、過多"：*hyperinflation* 通貨膨脹過高。

il-、im-、in-、ir- (構詞成分) 表示 "不、相反、非"，例如：*illegal* 非法的；*impatient* 不耐煩的。

inter- (構成形容詞) 表示 "在兩個或以上的人或物之間的"：*inter-city* 市際間的。

ir- 見 **il-**。

kilo- (與某些詞構成新詞) 表示 "千"：*kilometre* 千米、公里。

macro- (構詞成分) 表示 "大、全"，例如：*macroeconomic* 宏觀經濟。

mal- (構詞成分) 表示 "不、壞、不當"，例如：*malfunction* 故障。

mega- (構詞成分) 表示 "百萬"，例如：*megawatt* 兆瓦，100萬瓦特。

micro- (構成名詞) 表示 "微、微小的"，例如：*micro-organism* 微生物。

mid- (構成名詞、形容詞) 表示 "在中間、在中部、在中段時間"，例如：*mid-June* 六月中旬。

milli- (構成名詞) 表示 "千分之一"，例如：*millimetre* 毫米。

前綴和後綴 Prefixes and Suffixes

mini-(構成名詞)表示"小的、微型的",例如:
minibus 小汽車。

mis-(構成動詞、名詞)表示"壞、錯":*miscalculate*
誤算。

mono-(構成名詞、形容詞)表示"單(一)、獨(一)":
monogamy 一夫一妻制。

multi-(構成形容詞)表示"多的":*multi-coloured*
多色的。

narco-(與某些詞構成新詞)表示"毒品的":
a *narco-trafficker* 毒販。

neo-(構成名詞、形容詞)表示"新式的、現代的":
neo-classical architecture 新古典主義建築。

neuro-(構詞成分)表示"神經、神經系統",例如:
neurology 神經病學。

non-(構成名詞、形容詞)表示"無、非、不",
例如:a *non-smoker* 不吸煙者; a *non-fatal*
accident 非致命事故。

non-(構成名詞)表示"無、拒絕",例如:*non-
attendance* 缺席(會議)。

out-(構成動詞)表示"超過、勝過",例如:
outswim 比某人游得快(遠)。

over-(構詞成分)表示"過於、過度",例如:*over-
cautious* 過於謹慎。

pan-(用於形容詞、名詞前)表示"總的、泛的",
例如:a *pandemic* 流行性疾病。

para-(構成名詞、形容詞)表示"類似、相近",例
如:*paramilitary* 準軍事的;*paramedic* 輔助醫
療的。

para-(構成名詞、形容詞)表示"超自然的",例如:
a *paranormal* event 超自然事件。

part-(構詞成分)表示"部分",例如:*part-baked*
部分烘烤的。

poly-(構成名詞、形容詞)表示"多",例如:
polysyllabic 多音節的。

post-(構詞成分)表示"發生在某日期或某事之
後",例如:a *post-Christmas* sale 聖誕節後大
減價。

pre-(構詞成分)表示"在某日期或某事之前",例
如:a *pre-election* rally 選前大會。

pro-(構成形容詞)表示"支持、親",例如:
pro-democracy 支持民主。

proto-(構成形容詞、名詞)表示"最初的",例如:
prototype 原型,樣本。

pseudo-(構成名詞、形容詞)表示"偽、假",例如:
a *pseudo-science* 偽科學。

psycho-(構詞成分)表示"精神的、心理的",例
如:a *psychoanalyst* 精神分析家。

re-(構成動詞、名詞)表示"再、重新",例如:
re-read 重讀。

semi-(構成名詞、形容詞)表示"半、部分",例如:
semi-conscious 半清醒的。

sub-(構成名詞、形容詞)表示"次要、分支",例如:
a *subcommittee* 小組委員會。

sub-(構成形容詞)表示"低於某人或某事","次於某
人或某事",例如:*substandard* 低於標準的。

super-(構成名詞、形容詞)表示"非常,極度",
例如:a *supertanker* 超級油輪;a *super-fit*
athlete 狀態極好的運動員。

techno-(用於名詞前)表示"技術的、工藝的",
例如:*technophobe* 技術恐懼。

trans-(構成形容詞)表示"橫越、穿過",例如:
transatlantic 橫越大西洋的。

trans-(構詞成分)表示"進入另一處,變成另一狀
態",例如:a blood *transfusion* 輸血。

tri-(構成名詞、形容詞)表示"三、三倍",例如:
a *tricycle* 三輪車。

ultra-(構成形容詞)表示"超、極端",例如:
an *ultra-light* fabric 超輕結構。

un-(構詞成分,表述相反之意)表示"不、非",
例如:*unacceptable* 不可接受的。

under-(構詞成分)表示"不足、過少",例如:
underweight 體重不足的,重量不足的。

vice-(用於級別和頭銜前)表示"副、代",例如:
a *vice-president* 副總統。

前綴和後綴 Prefixes and Suffixes

後綴

-ability and **-ibility** (取代形容詞後的 -able 和 -ible，構成名詞) 表示 "特點、性質"，例如：*reliability* 可靠性。

-able (構成形容詞) 表示 "有某種性質的"，例如：*readable* 可讀的，易讀的。

-al (構成形容詞) 表示 "與某物有關的"，例如：*environmental* problems 環境問題。

-ally (加在以 -ic 結尾的形容詞之後，構成副詞) 表示 "以某種方式做某事"：*enthusiastically* 熱情地，熱心地。

-ance, -ence, -ancy and **-ency** (構成名詞) 表示 "某種動作、狀況、性質"：*brilliance* 才華橫溢；*reappearance* 再次出現。

-ancy 見 **-ance**。

-ation, -ication, -sion and **-tion** (構成名詞) 表示某種 "狀態、過程、結果"，例如：the *protection* of the environment 環境保護。

-cy (構成名詞) 表示某種 "狀態、性質"，例如：*accuracy* 精確。

-ed (構成動詞過去式和過去分詞。過去分詞形式常用作形容詞) 表示 "具有某種特徵"：*cooked* food 熟食。

-ence 見 **-ance**。

-ency 見 **-ance**。

-er and **-or** 1. (構成名詞) 表示 "從事某種工作的人"，例如：a *teacher* 教師。 2. 表示 "有某種功能的工具 (機器)"，例如：a *mixer* 攪拌機。

-er 1. (與許多短的形容詞構成比較級)，例如：*nice* 的比較級是 *nicer*；*happy* 的比較級是 *happier*。 2. (與一些不以 -ly 結尾的副詞構成比較級)，例如：*soon* 的比較級是 *sooner*。

-est 1. (與許多短的形容詞構成最高級)，例如 *nice* 的最高級是 *nicest*；*happy* 的最高級是 *happiest*。 2. (與一些不以 -ly 結尾的副詞構成最高級)，例如 *soon* 的最高級是 *soonest*。

-fold (與數字共同構成副詞) 表示 "倍、重"，例如：increases *fourfold* 增長四倍。

-ful (構成名詞) 表示 "充滿所需之量"，例如：a *handful* of sand 一滿把沙子。

-ibility 見 **-ability**。

-ic (構成形容詞) 表示 "與某人或某物有關的"：*photographic* equipment 攝影設備。

-ication 見 **-ation**。

-icity (取代形容詞後的 -ic，構成名詞) 表示 "性質、狀態"，例如：*authenticity* 可靠性，真實性。

-ify (用於動詞之後) 表示 "使某人或某事變得不同、使某人某事有差異"：*simplify* 簡單化。

-ing (與動詞構成 -ing 形式或現在分詞) 1. (現在分詞形式常用作形容詞) 表示 "正在做某事"：a *sleeping* baby 正睡覺的嬰兒；an *amusing* joke 令人捧腹的笑話 2. (現在分詞形式常用作名詞) 表示 "活動"：like *dancing* 喜歡跳舞。

-ise 見 **-ize**。

-ish (構成形容詞) 表示 "有些、稍微"：*largish* 有些大，稍大；*yellowish* 淡黃的。

-ish (構詞成分) 表示 (時間或年齡) "在……左右，約……之數"，例如：*fortyish* 四十歲左右。

-ism (構成名詞) 表示 "主義、學說"，例如：*professionalism* 專業精神；*racism* 種族主義。

-ist (取代名詞後的 -ism，構成名詞、形容詞) 1. (構成名詞) 表示 "信仰某種主義的人"，例如：a *fascist* 法西斯分子。 2. (構成形容詞) 表示 "與某事有關，基於某種信仰的"。

-ist (構成名詞) 表示 "從事某種工作的人"，例如：a *geologist* 地質學家。

-ist (構成名詞) 表示 "演奏某種樂器的人"，例如：a *violinist* 小提琴家。

-ity (構成名詞) 表示 "特性、狀態"，例如：*solidity* 堅固，結實。

-ize (用於許多動詞之後) 表示 "使某人或某事變成一個新的狀態"，例如：*standardize* 標準化。有時也拼作 -ise，尤其用於英式英語。

-less (構成形容詞) 表示 "無、缺"，例如：*childless* 無子女。

-logical 見 **-ological**。

前綴和後綴 Prefixes and Suffixes

-logist 見 **-ologist**。

-logy 見 **-ology**。

-ly（構成副詞）表示"以某種方式做某事"，例如： whistles *cheerfully* 愉快地吹口哨。

-ment（構成名詞）表示"行為的過程或結果"， 例如：*assessment* 評估，評價。

-nd（除 12 之外，用於以 2 結尾的數字，構成序 數詞），例如：*22nd February* 2月22日；*2nd edition* 第 2 版。

-ness（構成名詞）表示"狀態、性質"，例如： *gentleness* 溫文爾雅。

-ological or **-logical**（用於取代名詞後的 *-ology* 或 *-logy*，構成形容詞）表示"某種學科的"： *biological* 地質學的。

-ologist or **-logist**（用於取代名詞後的 *-ology* 或 *-logy*，構成名詞）表示某種學科的專家"， 例如：a *biologist* 地質學家。

-ology or **-logy**（用於某些名詞之後）表示"某種學 科"，例如：*biology* 地質學；*sociology* 社會 學。

-or 見 **-er**。

-ous（構成形容詞）表示"具有某種品性的"，例如： *courageous* 勇敢的。

-phile（用於詞後）表示"喜愛某類人或某類事物的 人"，例如：an *Anglophile* 親英分子。

-phobe（用於詞後）表示"仇視某類人或對某事感到 恐懼的人"，例如： a *technophobe* 技術恐懼 者。

-phobia（用於詞後）表示"恐懼某事、憎惡某事"， 例如：*claustrophobia* 幽閉恐懼。

-phobic（用於詞後）表示"對某人或某事恐懼的；對 某人或某事憎惡的"：*claustrophobic* 幽閉恐懼 的。

-rd（除 13之外，用於以 3 結尾的數字，構成序數 詞），例如：*September 3rd* 9月3日；*the 33rd Boston Marathon* 第 33 屆波士頓馬拉松賽。

-sion, -tion 見 **-ation**。

-st（除 11 之外，用於以 1 結尾的數字，構成序數 詞），例如：*1st August 1993* 1993年8月1 日； *the 101st Airborne Division* 第101空降 師。

-th（用於以 4, 5, 6, 7, 8, 9, 10, 11, 12 或 13 結 尾的數字，構成序數詞），例如：*6th Avenue* 第六大街；*the 25th amendment to the American Constitution* 美國憲法第 25 條修正 案。

-y（構成形容詞）表示"某物滿是……的"，例如： *dirty* 骯髒的。

-y（構成形容詞）表示"像某物的，具有某物的性質 的"：*chocolatey* 巧克力味道的。

英漢語法術語對照表 Glossary of Grammar Terms

abstract noun 抽象名詞：
用於描述性質、思想、感覺或經歷而不是物質
事物的名詞，如 *size*、*reason*、*joy*。

active voice 主動語態：
主動語態指的是 gives、took、has made 等
動詞詞組，當使用它們時，其主語是做這個動
作的人或物，或對這個動作負責的人或物。比
較 **passive voice** 被動語態。

adjective 形容詞：
描寫人或物，如外貌、顏色、大小及其他屬性
的詞。
例如：*She was wearing a pretty blue dress.*

adjunct 附加狀語：
又稱 adverbial 狀語。

adverb 副詞：
能詳述某事在何時、何地、如何發生，或在甚
麼情況下發生的詞，如 *quickly*、*now*。

adverbial 狀語：
副詞、副詞短語、介詞短語或名詞詞組，能詳
述某事在何時、何地、如何發生，或在甚麼情
況下發生，作用與副詞一樣，如 *then*、*very*
quickly、*in the street*、*the next day*。

adverbial of degree 程度狀語：
表示感覺或屬性的程度或範圍的狀語。
例如：*She felt extremely tired.*

adverbial of duration 持續狀語：
表示某事進行或持續多久的狀語。
例如：*He lived in London for six years.*

adverbial of frequency 頻度狀語：
表示某事發生的經常性程度的狀語。
例如：*She sometimes goes to the cinema.*

adverb of manner 方式狀語：
表示某事發生的方式或怎樣做某事的狀語。
例如：*She watched carefully.*

adverbial of place 地點狀語：
能詳述位置或方向的狀語。
例如：*They are upstairs.*
Move closer.

adverbial of probability 可能性狀語：
能詳述某事確信程度的狀語。
例如：*I've probably lost it.*

adverbial of time 時間狀語：
能詳述某事發生於何時的狀語。
例如：*I saw her yesterday.*

adverb phrase 副詞短語：
指在一起使用的兩個副詞。
例如：*She spoke very quietly.*
He did not play well enough to win.

affirmative 肯定句：
不含否定詞如 not，也不是疑問句的從句或句
子。

apostrophe s 撇號和 s ('s)：
名詞後面加撇號和 s ('s) 表示領屬。
例如：*She is Harriet's daughter.*
He married the Managing Director's
secretary.

article 冠詞：
見 **definite article** 定冠詞；**indefinite article**
不定冠詞。

auxiliary 助動詞：
即 **auxiliary verb** 助動詞的另一個稱謂。

auxiliary verb 助動詞：
動詞 be、have、do 與主要動詞連用，構成
時態、否定句、疑問句時叫助動詞。有些語法
書也把情態動詞算作助動詞。

bare infinitive 不帶 **to** 的不定式：
指沒有 to 的不定式。
另見 **'to'-infinitive** to- 不定式。

英漢語法術語對照表 Glossary of Grammar Terms

base form 動詞原形：
指末尾沒有加任何其他字母，用作帶 to- 不定式和祈使句的動詞，如 *walk*、*go*、*have*、*be*。詞典裏的詞條形式就是原形。

cardinal number 基數詞：
用來計數的數詞，如 *one*、*seven*、*nineteen*。比較 **ordinal number** 序數詞。

clause 分句：
包含一個動詞的一組詞。
另見 **main clause** 主句；**subordinate clause** 從句。

collective noun 集體名詞：
指一類人或事物集合在一起的名詞，動詞可用單數形式又可用複數形式，如 *committee*、*team*、*family*。

comparative 比較級：
末尾加 -er 或前面加 more 的形容詞或副詞，如 *slower*、*more important*、*more carefully*。

complement 補足語：
指置於繫動詞 be 等之後，能詳述從句主語的名詞詞組或形容詞。
例如：*She is a teacher.*
She is tired.

complex sentence 複合句：
包含主句和從句的句子。
例如：*She wasn't thinking very quickly because she was tired.*

compound 複合詞：
兩個或兩個以上的名詞、形容詞或動詞合成的詞，如 *fat-cat corporate types*、*a stick of chewing gum*。

compound sentence 並列句：
由並列連詞 and、or、but 連接的兩個或多個主句的句子。

例如：*They picked her up and took her into the house.*

conditional clause 條件從句：
由 if、unless 引導的從句，常用來表述可能的情景或結果。
例如：*They would be rich if they had taken my advice.*
We'll go to the park, unless it rains.

conjunction 連詞：
連接兩個分句、詞組或單詞的詞，如 *and*、*because*、*nor* 等。

consonant 輔音：
發 p、f、n、t 的讀音。比較 **vowel** 元音。

continuous tense 進行時：
指動詞 be 的一個形式加上現在分詞構成的時態。
例如：*She was laughing.*
They had been playing badminton.
見 **tense** 時態。

contrast clause 對比從句：
由 although、in spite of the fact that 引導的從句，常用來和主句形成對比。
例如：*Although I like her, I find her hard to talk to.*

coordinating conjunction 並列連詞：
連接兩個主句的詞，如 and、but、or。

countable noun 可數名詞：
又稱 **count noun** 具數名詞。

count noun 具數名詞：
可有單數形式和複數形式的名詞，如 *dog/dogs*、*foot/feet*、*lemon/lemons*。比較 **uncount noun** 不具數名詞。

declarative 陳述句：
又稱 **affirmative** 肯定句。

英漢語法術語對照表 Glossary of Grammar Terms

defining relative clause 限制性關係從句：
指明所談及的人或物的關係從句。
例如：*I like the lady who lives next door.*
I wrote down everything that she said.

definite article 定冠詞：
指限定詞 the。比較 **indefinite article** 不定冠詞。

delexical verb 乏詞義動詞：
指本身詞義空乏的動詞，常與作為其所描述動作賓語的名詞連用。give、have、make、take 常用作乏詞義動詞。
例如：*She gave a small cry.*
I've just had a bath.

demonstrative 指示詞：
指 this、that、these、those 中的其中一個。
例如：*This woman is my mother.*
That tree is dead.
That looks interesting.
This is fun!

demonstrative adjective 指示形容詞：
又稱 **demonstrative** 指示詞。

descriptive adjective 描述性形容詞：
描述人或物，如大小、年齡、形狀、顏色，而不是表達對該人或物看法的形容詞。比較 **opinion adjective** 意見性形容詞。

determiner 限定詞：
指包括 the、a、some、my 在內的一組詞，用於名詞詞組的開頭。

direct object 直接賓語：
直接賓語是一個名詞詞組，用於主句中以表示受動詞動作所影響的人或物。比較 **indirect object** 間接賓語。
例如：*She wrote her name.*
I shut the windows.

direct speech 直接引語：
指直接引用某人的原話。比較 **indirect speech** 間接引語。

ditransitive verb 雙及物動詞：
指帶有兩個賓語的動詞，如 *give*、*take*、*sell*。
例如：*She gave me a kiss.*

double-transitive verb 雙及物動詞：
即 ditransitive verb 雙及物動詞的另一個稱謂。

-ed adjective -ed 形容詞：
與 -ed 形式的規則動詞或不規則動詞的過去分詞同形的形容詞，如 *boiled potatoes*，*a broken wing*。

-ed form -ed 形式：
規則動詞用於過去式和過去分詞的形式。

ellipsis 省略：
指在上下文清楚的情況下省去某些詞。

emphasizing adverb 強調副詞：
指用來修飾具極端特性的形容詞（如 *astonishing*、*wonderful* 等）的副詞，例如 *absolutely*、*utterly* 等。
例如：*You were absolutely wonderful.*

ergative verb 雙向動詞：
用作及物動詞和不及物動詞時意義相同的動詞。及物用法時的賓語是不及物用法時的主語。
例如：*He boiled a kettle.*
The kettle boiled.

first person 第一人稱：
見 **person** 人稱。

future tense 將來時：
見 **tense** 時態。

gerund 動名詞：
用作名詞的 -ing 形式的另一個稱謂。

英漢語法術語對照表 Glossary of Grammar Terms

if-clause if- 從句：
　　見 **conditional clause** 條件從句。

imperative 祈使：
　　用於給出命令或指示的動詞形式，與動詞原形同形。
　　例如：*Come here.*
　　　　　Take two tablets every four hours.
　　　　　Enjoy yourself.

impersonal 'it' 非人稱 it：
　　引出新信息的非人稱主語。
　　例如：*It's raining.*
　　　　　It's ten o'clock.

indefinite adverb 不定副詞：
　　指為數不多的副詞，包括泛指地點的 anywhere、somewhere。

indefinite article 不定冠詞：
　　限定詞 a 和 an。比較 **definite article** 定冠詞。

indefinite pronoun 不定代詞：
　　為數不多的一組代詞，包括不確指人或物的 someone、anything 等。

indirect object 間接賓語：
　　與雙賓語動詞連用的一個賓語。如在 I gave him the pen 和 I gave the pen to him 的句子中，him 是間接賓語，pen 是直接賓語。比較 **direct object** 直接賓語。

indirect question 間接疑問句：
　　指查詢資料或尋求幫助的疑問句。
　　例如：*Do you know where Jane is?*
　　　　　I wonder which hotel it was.

indirect speech 間接引語：
　　指轉述而不是引用某人所説的話。比較 **direct speech** 直接引語。

infinitive 不定式：
　　指動詞的原形。
　　例如：*I wanted to go.*
　　　　　She helped me dig the garden.

'-ing' adjective -ing 形容詞：
　　與動詞現在分詞同形的形容詞，如 *a smiling face*、*a winning streak*。

'-ing' form -ing 形式：
　　以 -ing 結尾的動詞形式，用於構成動詞的時態，充當形容詞或名詞。又稱 present participle 現在分詞。

interrogative pronoun 疑問代詞：
　　指用於提問的代詞，如 *who*、*whose*、*whom*、*what*、*which* 等。

interrogative sentence 疑問句：
　　指問句形式的句子。

intransitive verb 不及物動詞：
　　指不帶賓語的動詞。比較 **transitive verb** 及物動詞。
　　例如：*She arrived.*
　　　　　I was yawning.

irregular verb 不規則動詞：
　　指有三種或五種形式，或不按一般變化規則變化的動詞。比較 **regular verb** 規則動詞。

link verb 繫動詞：
　　帶補足語而不帶賓語的動詞。如 *be*、*become*、*seem*、*appear*。

main clause 主句：
　　不依附於另一個句子，也不屬於另一個句子其中的一部分。

main verb 主要動詞：
　　除助動詞或情態動詞之外的所有動詞。

英漢語法術語對照表 Glossary of Grammar Terms

manner clause 方式從句：
指描述某事完成方式的從句，通常由 as、like 引導。
例如：*She talks like her mother used to.*

modal 情態動詞：
在動詞詞組中總是首詞，後面要跟動詞原形的動詞，如 *can*、*might*、*will* 等。情態動詞用來表示要求、請求、建議、願望、意圖、禮貌、可能性、肯定性和義務等。
例如：*I might go after all.*

mood 語氣：
指動詞在從句中使用的方式，用來表明該從句是陳述句、命令句或疑問句。

negative 否定：
帶 not 等否定詞的否定從句、否定疑問句、否定句或否定陳述句，表示缺乏某物或它的反面，或說明某事並非如此。比較 **positive** 肯定。
例如：*I don't know you.*
I'll never forget.

negative word 否定詞：
指像 never、no、not、nothing、nowhere 的詞，用把從句、疑問句、句子或陳述句變成否定的意思。

non-defining relative clause 非限制性關係從句：
這種關係從句能對某人或某物進行詳述，但因已知那是何人或何物，故對所描述的人或物不起確指作用。比較 **defining relative clause** 限制性關係從句。
例如：*That's Mary, who was at university with me.*

non-finite clause 非限定小句：
指 to - 不定式小句、-ed 從句或 -ing 從句。

noun 名詞：
指稱人、物、思想、情感或屬性的詞，如 *woman*、*Harry*、*guilt*。

noun group 名詞詞組：
充當主語、補足語、動詞賓語或介詞賓語的詞組。

object 賓語：
指稱受動詞動作影響的人或物的名詞詞組。介詞也可以以名詞詞組作賓語。比較 **subject** 主語。

object pronoun 賓語人稱代詞：
用作動詞或介詞的賓語的一類代詞，包括 me、him、them。賓語人稱代詞在 be 後面用作補足語。比較 **subject pronoun** 主語人稱代詞。
例如：*I hit him.*
It's me.

opinion adjective 意見性形容詞：
表達對人或物的意見而不是描述他們的形容詞。比較 **descriptive adjective** 描述性形容詞。

ordinal number 序數詞：
用來表示事物的次序或序列的數詞，如 *first*、*fifth*、*tenth*、*hundredth*。比較 **cardinal number** 基數詞。

participle 分詞：
指構成各種時態的動詞形式。動詞有兩種分詞形式，一種是現在分詞，一種是過去分詞。

particle 小品詞：
指與動詞構成短語動詞的副詞或介詞。

passive voice 被動語態：
指 was given、were taken、had been made 等動詞詞組，它們的主語是受該動作影響的人或物。比較 **active voice** 主動語態。

英漢語法術語對照表 Glossary of Grammar Terms

past form 過去式：
常以 -ed 結尾的動詞形式，用於簡單過去時。

past participle 過去分詞：
指用來構成現在完成時和被動語態的動詞形式。有些過去分詞也可用作形容詞，如 *watched*、*broken*、*swum*。

past tense 過去時：
見 **tense** 時態。

perfect tense 完成時：
見 **tense** 時態。

person 人稱：
用於指稱參與對話的三類人。
說話者和作者是第一人稱（I、we）。
受話者和讀者是第二人稱（you）。
被談及的人或物是第三人稱（he、she、it、they）。

personal pronoun 人稱代詞：
包括 I、you、me 的一組詞，可用於指稱自己、受話者和談及的人或物。
另見 **object pronoun** 賓語人稱代詞；**subject pronoun** 主語人稱代詞。

phrasal verb 短語動詞：
由動詞和小品詞連用構成，其含義與構成它的動詞不同，如 *back down*、*hand over*、*look forward to*。

plural 複數：
具數名詞或動詞的一種形式，用來指稱一個以上的人或物。
例如：*Dogs have ears.*
The women were outside.

plural noun 複數名詞：
通常用於複數形式的名詞，如 *trousers*、*scissors*。

positive 肯定：
不含否定詞如 not 的肯定從句、疑問句、句子或陳述句。比較 **negative** 否定。

possessive 領屬格：
限定詞 my、your、his、her、its、our、their 的其中一個，用來表示一人一物屬於另一人或另一物。
例如：*I like your car.*

possessive adjective 物主形容詞：
又稱 **possessive** 領屬格。

possessive pronoun 物主名詞：
代詞 mine、yours、hers、his、ours、theirs 的其中一個。

preposition 介詞：
後面總是跟有名詞詞組的詞，如 *by*、*with*、*from* 等。

prepositional phrase 介詞短語：
由介詞加上作其賓語的名詞詞組所構成。
例如：*I put it on the table.*
They live by the sea.

present participle 現在分詞：
見 **-ing form** -ing 形式。

present tense 現在時：
見 **tense** 時態。

progressive tense 進行時：
即 **continuous tense** 進行時。

pronoun 代詞：
不直接指稱人或物，用來替代名詞的詞，如 *it*、*you*、*none*。

proper noun 專有名詞：
特指的人、地點、機構、建築物的名稱。專有名詞的首字母總是要大寫，如 *Nigel*、*Edinburgh*、*the United Nations*、*Christmas*。

英漢語法術語對照表 Glossary of Grammar Terms

purpose clause 目的從句：
這種從句用來表明某人做某事之目的。
例如：*I came here in order to ask you out to dinner.*

qualifier 後置修飾語：
置於名詞之後，能詳述該名詞的詞或詞組，如形容詞、介詞短語、關係從句等。如 *the person involved*、*a book with a blue cover*、*the shop that I went into*。

quantifier 量詞：
用來指稱某物不確切數量的詞或短語，如 *plenty*、*a lot* 等。量詞後面常跟 of。
例如：*There was still plenty of time.*
He drank lots of milk.

question 疑問句：
在主句前面帶助動詞，常用於向某人詢問某事的句子。
例如：*Do you have any money?*

question tag 附加疑問：
由動詞或情態動詞加上代詞組成的結構，用來把陳述句變為疑問句。
例如：*He's very friendly, isn't he?*
I can come, can't I?

reason clause 原因從句：
由 because、since、as 引導的從句，用來解釋某事為甚麼發生或為甚麼要做某事。
例如：*Since you're here, we'll start.*

reciprocal verb 相互動詞：
描述兩個人互相做同一動作的動詞。
例如：*I met you at the dance.*
We've met one another before.
They met in the street.

reflexive pronoun 反身代詞：
指 myself、themselves 等以 -self、-selves 結尾的代詞，當動詞的主語和賓語同為一人或

一事時，用它們作賓語。
例如：*He hurt himself.*

reflexive verb 反身動詞：
通常指以反身代詞為賓語的動詞。
例如：*He contented himself with the thought that he had the only set of keys.*

regular verb 規則動詞：
指有四種形式，按一般變化規則變化的動詞。
比較 **irregular verb** 不規則動詞。

relative clause 關係從句：
這種從句詳述主句提及的人或物。
另見 **defining relative clause** 限制性從句；**non-defining relative clause** 非限制性從句。

relative pronoun 關係代詞：
that 或 who、which 等 wh- 詞，用於引導關係從句。
例如：*I watched the girl who was carrying the bag.*

reported clause 被轉述從句：
這種從句用於間引結構中表述某人所説的內容。
例如：*She said that I couldn't see her.*

reported question 被轉述疑問句：
這種疑問句用於間引結構轉述，而不是引用説話者的原話。
另見 **indirect question** 間接疑問句。

reported speech 被轉述引語：
這種引語轉述某人的話，而不是引用其原話，又稱 **indirect speech** 間接引語。

reporting clause 轉述從句：
指轉述結構中帶轉述動詞的從句。

reporting verb 轉述動詞：
描述人們所説或所想的動詞，如 *suggest*、*say*、*wonder*。

英漢語法術語對照表 Glossary of Grammar Terms

report structure 間引結構：
這種結構用來轉述某人所説或所想，而不是重複那人的原話。
例如：*She told me she'd be late.*

result clause 結果從句：
由 so、so ... that、such ...(that) 引導，這種從句表述一個行動或一種形勢所產生的結果。
例如：*I don't think there's any more news, so I'll finish.*

second person 第二人稱：
見 **person** 人稱。

semi-modal 半情態動詞：
有些語法學家指稱動詞 dare、need、used to 為 semi-modal，在某些結構中，它們的功能像情態動詞。

sentence 句子：
表示陳述、疑問或命令的一組詞。句子通常含動詞和主語。它可以是簡單句，由一個分句組成；也可以是複合句，由兩個或多個分句組成。書寫句子時，句首要大寫，句末要用句號、問號或感嘆號。

short form 省略形式：
將一個或多個字母省略掉，或將兩個詞合為一體的形式，比如助動詞或情態動詞與 not 合為一體，主語人稱代詞和助動詞或情態動詞合為一體，如 *aren't、couldn't、he'd、I'm、it's、she's*。

simple tense 簡單時態：
指不用助動詞構成的現在時或過去時。
例如：*I wait.*
She sang.
見 **tense** 時態。

singular 單數：
用來指稱或談及一個人或一件事的具數名詞或動詞形式。

例如：*A dog was in the back of the car.*
That woman is my mother.

singular noun 單數名詞：
一般用作單數形式的名詞。如 *the sun、a bath*。

strong verb 強變化動詞：
又稱 **irregular verb** 不規則動詞

subject 主語：
在句子中説明動詞的動作是由誰做的名詞詞組。
例如：*We were going shopping.*

subject pronoun 主語人稱代詞：
用作動詞主語的一系列代詞中的一個，包括 I、she、they 等。

subordinate clause 從句：
由從屬連詞 because、while 等引導的從句，如時間從句、條件從句、關係從句或結果從句。它們必須與主句連用，一般不單獨使用。

subordinating conjunction 從屬連詞：
引導從句的連詞，如 *although、as if、because、while* 等。

superlative 最高級：
指以 -est 結尾或前面加 most 的形容詞或副詞，如 *thinnest、quickest、most beautiful*。

tag question 附加疑問句：
加有附加疑問的陳述句。
例如：*She's quiet, isn't she?*

tense 時態：
表示所指是過去、現在或將來的動詞形式。

future 將來時：
will 或 shall 加動詞原形表示將來事件。
例如：*She will come tomorrow.*

future continuous 將來進行時：
will 或 shall 加上 be 及 現在分詞，表示將來事件。

例如：*She will be going soon.*

future perfect 將來完成時：
will 或 shall 加上 have 及過去分詞，表示將來事件。
例如：*I shall have finished by tomorrow.*

future perfect continuous 將來完成進行時：
will 或 shall 加上 have been 及現在分詞，表示將來事件。
例如：*I will have been walking for three hours by then.*

past simple 簡單過去時：
使用動詞的過去式表示過去事件。
例如：*They waited.*

past continuous 過去進行時：
was 或 were 加上現在分詞，通常表示過去事件。
例如：*They were worrying about it yesterday.*

past perfect 過去完成時：
had 加上過去分詞，表示過去事件。
例如：*She had finished.*

past perfect continuous 過去完成進行時：
had been 加上現在分詞，表示過去事件。
例如：*He had been waiting for hours.*

present simple 簡單現在時：
動詞原形加上動詞第三人稱單數形式，通常表示現在事件。
例如：*I like bananas.*
My sister hates them.

present continuous 現在進行時：
be 的簡單現在式加上現在分詞，表示現在事件。
例如：*Things are improving.*

present perfect 現在完成時：
have 或 has 加上過去分詞，表示過去發生，

直到現在仍存在的事件。
例如：*She has loved him for ten years.*

present perfect continuous 現在完成進行時：
have been 或 has been 加上現在分詞，表示過去發生，直到現在仍在繼續的事件。
例如：*We have been sitting here for hours.*

'that'-clause that- 從句：
以 that 引導的從句，主要用來轉述某人説的話。
例如：*She said that she'd wash up for me.*

third person 第三人稱：
見 **person** 人稱。

time clause 時間從句：
表示事件發生時間的從句。
例如：*I'll phone you when I get back.*

time expression 時間表達式：
用作時間狀語的名詞詞組。如 *last night*、*the day after tomorrow*、*the next time*。

'to'-infinitive to- 不定式：
前面加 to 的動詞原形。如 *to go*、*to have*、*to jump*。

transitive verb 及物動詞：
帶賓語的動詞。比較 **intransitive verb** 不及物動詞。
例如：*She's wasting her money.*

uncountable noun 不可數名詞：
即 **uncount noun** 不具數名詞。

uncount noun 不具數名詞：
只有一個形式，使用動詞單數形式，不與 a 或數字連用的名詞。不具數名詞常用來表述物質、質量、情感、活動和抽象概念，如 *coal*、*courage*、*anger*、*help*、*fun*。比較 **count noun** 具數名詞。

英漢語法術語對照表 Glossary of Grammar Terms

verb 動詞：
與主語連用，説明某人或某事做甚麼或發生了甚麼事，如 *sing*、*spill*、*die*。

verb group 動詞詞組：
指主要動詞帶一個或多個助動詞，或帶一個情態動詞，或帶一個情態動詞和一個助動詞。它們與主語連用，説明某人在做甚麼，或發生了甚麼事。
例如：*I'll show them.*
She's been sick.

vowel 元音：
字母 a、e、i、o、u 所表示的讀音。比較 **consonant** 輔音。

wh- question wh- 疑問句：
這種疑問句預期所得答案會比 yes/no 答案含較多的信息。比較 yes/no- 疑問句。
例如：*What happened next?*
Where did he go?

'wh'-word wh- 詞：
以 wh- 開頭，用於 wh- 疑問句的詞，如 what、when、who 等。How 也被稱為 wh- 詞，因其功能與其他 wh- 詞相同。

'yes/no'- question yes/no- 疑問句：
只用 yes 或 no 回答，不提供更多信息的疑問句。比較 **'wh'-question wh-** 疑問句。
例如：*Would you like some more tea?*

索引 Index

A

a 40-41, 43
able 74-75
about 102
above 100
abstract noun 抽象名詞 90
adverb 副詞 56, 58, 60, 104, 148, 192, 213, 257
adverbial 狀語 56, 58, 60, 104, 148, 192, 257
adverb of manner 方式狀語 104-105, 257
adverbial of degree 程度狀語 58-59, 148, 192, 257
adverbial of duration 持續狀語 60-61, 257
adverbial of frequency 頻度狀語 56-57, 58, 257
adverbial of probability 較大可能性狀語 58-59, 257
adverbial of time 時間狀語 56-57, 257
a few 96-97
a few of 92
after 102
ago 56
all 92, 94
a lot 58
a lot of 92, 94
alphabet 字母 222
although 192
am 4-5
an 40-41, 43
any 38, 96-97
anybody 142
any of 92
anyone 142
anything 142
anywhere 142

are 4-5
around 102
article 冠詞 40-45, 216, 217, 257
as 146-147
at 62-63, 106
auxiliary 助動詞 172, 174, 176

B

bare infinitive 不帶 to 的不定式 126, 257
base form 原形 211-212, 258
be 140
be able to 74-75
because 188
before 102
behind 100
below 100
beside 100
between 100
both 94
both of 92
by 102, 108, 168

C

can 74-75, 76, 120-121
cannot 74-75, 118, 120
can't 74-75, 118-119, 120
cardinal 基數詞 220, 258
capital letter 大寫 213
collective noun 集體名詞 36-37
comparative 比較級 144-145, 192, 213
compound noun 複合名詞 98-99
compound adjective 複合形容詞 220, 221
conditional 條件 186-187
consonant 輔音 214, 222, 258
continuous 進行 6-7, 14, 20-21, 166, 258

could 74-75, 76, 120-121
couldn't 74-75
count noun 具數名詞 34-35, 96, 182, 190, 258
countable noun 具數名詞 34-35, 96, 182, 190, 258

D

definite article 定冠詞 42-45, 216, 259
defining relative clause 限制性關係從句 178, 259
delexical verb 乏詞義動詞 130-131, 259
demonstrative 指示詞 48-49, 259
demonstrative adjective 指示形容詞 48-49, 259
did (not) 18, 80
didn't 18
diphthong 雙元音 215, 222
direct object 直接賓語 86-87, 259
do 10-11, 80, 88-89
does 10-11, 80
doesn't 10-11
don't 10-11
during 102

E

either 176
else 142
enough 182, 190
even though 192
everybody 142
everyone 142
everything 142
everywhere 142

F

(a) few 96-97

索引 Index

for 60
from 60
future 24, 26, 184

G
give 130
go 130
going to 26-27

H
had 22
had better 82
has 8, 10, 12
hasn't 10-11, 14
have 8, 10, 12, 14, 130
have (got) to 80-81
haven't 10-11, 12, 14
help 126-127
herself 138
himself 138
how 32, 172

I
if 184, 186
impersonal it 非人稱 it 84-85,
   260
in front of 100
in order to 188
in spite of 192
in 62-63, 100, 102, 106, 108
indefinite article 不定冠詞
   40-41, 217, 260
indefinite pronoun 不定代詞
   142-143, 260
indirect object 間接賓語 86-87,
   260
infinitive 不定式 122, 124, 126,
   128, 180, 260
into 108

irregular verb 不規則動詞
   211-212, 260
is 4-5
it 84-85, 180
itself 138

L
let 126-127
like 192
lots of 92, 94

M
make 88-89, 126-127
many of 92
may 72-73, 120-121
might 72-73
mightn't 72
modal 情態動詞 72, 74, 76, 78,
   80, 82, 118, 120, 170, 172,
   174, 188, 261
most of 92, 94
much 38, 58, 90
must 80-81, 118-119
mustn't 80-81, 118-119
myself 138

N
near 100
need 120-121
needn't 120
negatives 否定 4-5
negatives 否定句 10-11
neither 176
neither of 92
next to 100
nobody 142
none of 92
no one 142
nothing 142

nowhere 142
numbers 數詞 220-221

O
object 賓語 50, 86, 134, 178,
   261
object pronoun 賓語代詞 50-51,
   261
of 54, 92-93
off 108
on 62-63, 100, 108
one 52-53
ones 52-53
opposite 100
ordinal 序數詞 220, 261
ought (to) 82-83, 118-119
out of 108
over 100

P
participle 分詞 12, 22, 168, 261
-ing and -ed adjectives -ing 和 -ed
   形容詞 140
particle 小品詞 132-133, 134-
   135, 261
passive voice 被動語態 168-169,
   261
past 過去 12-23, 170, 172, 186,
   211-212, 262
past continuous 過去進行時
   20-21
past participle 過去分詞 12, 22,
   168, 211-212
past perfect 過去完成時 22-23
past perfect continuous 過去完
   成進行時 22
past simple 簡單過去時 18-19,
   21, 23, 211-212
personal pronoun 人稱代詞 50-51

phonetic symbols 語音符號 214-219, 222

phrasal verb 短語動詞 132-133, 134-135, 262

plenty of 92, 94

plural 34, 36, 212, 262

plural noun 複數名詞 36-37, 48, 262

possessive 領屬格 46-47, 54-55, 262

possessive adjective 物主形容詞 46-47, 262

possessive pronoun 物主代詞 54-55, 262

preposition 介詞 100-101, 102-103, 106-107, 108-109, 136-137, 262

present 現在 6-9, 24, 170, 184, 211-212, 262

present continuous 現在進行時 6-7, 24-25, 26, 166, 262

present participle 現在分詞 6-7, 24-25, 26, 166, 212, 262

present perfect 現在完成時 12-15

present perfect continuous 現在完成進行時 14

present simple 簡單現在時 8-9, 24-25, 26

pronunciation 讀音 214-219, 222

Q

quantifier 量詞 92-93, 94-95, 96-97, 190, 263

question tag 附加疑問 174, 263

questions 疑問句 10-11, 174, 263

R

reflexive pronoun 反身代詞 138-139, 263

reflexive verb 反身動詞 138-139, 263

regular verb 規則動詞 211-212, 263

relative clause 關係從句 178, 194, 263

relative pronoun 關係代詞 178, 194, 263

report structure 間引結構 170, 264

reported clause 被轉述從句 170, 263

reporting verb 轉述動詞 170, 263

S

same 146

schwa 混元音 215

-self 138

-selves 138

should 82-83, 118-119

shouldn't 82-83

since 60, 84

singular 單數 34, 36, 264

singular noun 單數名詞 36-37, 42, 48, 264

so 148, 176, 188, 190

some 38, 40-41, 90

some of 94

somebody 142

someone 142

something 142

somewhere 142

spelling 拼寫 211-213

stress 重音 217

subject 主語 50, 178

subject pronoun 主語人稱代詞 50-51, 138, 264

such 148, 190

superlative 最高級 44, 144-145, 146-147, 213, 264

T

tag question 附加疑問句 264

take 130

than 146-147

that 48-49, 52-53, 178, 180

the 42-45

themselves 138

there 28-29

these 48-49, 52-53

third person 第三人稱 211, 265

this 48-49, 52-53

those 48-49, 52-53

till 60, 102

to (purpose) 188

to-infinitive 帶 to 的不定式 122, 124, 180, 265

too 176, 182, 190

U

uncount noun 不具數名詞 38-39, 90-91, 94, 96, 182, 190, 265

uncountable noun 不具數名詞 38-39, 90-91, 94, 96, 182, 190, 265

under 100

until 60, 102

V

vowel 元音 214, 222, 266

W

want 78-79

索引 Index

was 16-17
wasn't 16-17
weak forms 弱讀式 218
well 104
were 16-17
weren't 16-17
what 30-31, 32

when 32, 172, 184, 194
where 32, 172, 194
which 172, 194
who 32, 178, 194
wh-question wh- 問句 32-33, 266
why 32, 172

will 26-27, 76-77
wish 186
would 76-77
would like 78-79

Y

yourself 138